The Extremist

ROGER PEARCE

The Extremist

CORONET

First published in Great Britain in 2013 by Coronet
An imprint of Hodder & Stoughton
An Hachette UK company

First published in paperback in 2014

1

A CIP catalogue record for this title is available from the British Library

ISBN 978 1 444 72189 8
Ebook ISBN 978 1 444 72190 4

Typeset by Hewer Text UK Ltd, Edinburgh
Printed and bound by Clays Ltd, St Ives plc

Hodder & Stoughton policy is to use papers that are natural, renewable
and recyclable products and made from wood grown in sustainable
forests. The logging and manufacturing processes are expected to
conform to the environmental regulations of the country of origin.

Hodder & Stoughton Ltd
338 Euston Road
London NW1 3BH

www.hodder.co.uk

For Andrew, Matthew and Laura

acknowledgements

To my agent Sonia Land, publisher Mark Booth, Fiona Rose, Emilie Ferguson and all the team at Coronet.

'There is no occupation that fails a man more than that of a secret agent.'

Joseph Conrad
The Secret Agent

Prologue

The evening sun casts diamonds on the Thames and lights up the terrace of the Houses of Parliament. Fresh from the Whitsun recess, MPs drink with their research assistants and lovers, their laughter floating across the water. Everything is normal.

Detective Chief Inspector John Kerr watches them from the river on a classy boat driven by Justin Hine, his youthful head of technical operations. Both are career Special Branch officers from New Scotland Yard. They have very little time, so Justin is powering fast through the warm evening air as they plane eastwards, leaving an illegal wake that will soon attract the river police.

Kerr is hunting a pair of robbers who intend to transfer stolen gold from a boat launched somewhere on the north bank. This evening, at high tide, they are to make a practice run. That is all he knows.

Kerr deals with extremism and terrorism, not serious crime, so has passed his information to the Yard's Specialist Crime Directorate. The investigators have deployed two pairs of Trojans, the élite tactical firearms officers of CO19, to the south side of the river. Their analysts believe they have figured out where the gangsters intend to hit land, and the Trojans will arrest them there. They have called their operation 'Conjuror', but John Kerr is not expecting any magic. For him, a guess is never good enough. If the Trojans are sitting at the wrong place, the targets will run free.

Kerr wants to intercept the gangsters on the water. Hidden away in its river base in Wapping, the Met has a brand-new reinforced inflatable boat. It is an adapted black Ribcraft 12, jet driven, fantastically fast and menacing, bought for the Olympics to prevent al-Qaeda launching a suicide attack on the Thames. The RIB can hold three pairs of Trojans armed to the teeth, but Kerr's request to use it is turned down flat by the health and safety desk jockeys: his plan evidently hovers at the top of the no-can-do sliding scale that rules their lives. So the Trojans, always up for a piece of hard-core marine action, remain sweating in their windowless vans by Cumberland Wharf in Rotherhithe.

As usual, John Kerr is doing his own thing. His boat is even flashier than the mothballed RIB. It is a Sea Ray 240 Sun Sport, with dark blue hull and white deck, part speedboat, part gin palace. Definitely non-regulation. It belongs to a friend of Justin from his flying academy and is normally berthed in Chelsea Harbour. Justin has come up with a story about taking foreign liaison officers sightseeing, and his pilot friend has bought it.

Under a clear blue sky, with the sun behind them, Kerr and Justin cut in front of a string of barges pulled by a single tug and flash under Southwark Bridge. As they weave between the pleasure craft, Kerr guesses a lot of boat people must be seriously pissed off with them by now. But if Justin has any idea about the rules of the road in this crowded stretch of river, he is totally ignoring them.

The gold belongs to the United States, in transit from Washington to Hong Kong. Stolen fourteen weeks earlier from a secure depository warehouse close to Heathrow, it has disappeared without trace. Until now. Kerr knows about the plan only because a brave Special Branch agent, a Somali Muslim codenamed 'Seagull', went the extra mile. Seagull could not name the bad guys, but whoever they were just incinerated him in his van on wasteground in Stepney.

That afternoon Kerr has visited the murder scene with Dodge, his head of the source unit. Three hours later, despite the wind blasting his face, he can still smell his agent's burnt flesh. Kerr will not wait for the homicide investigation to tell him what he already knows. Those thugs murdered Seagull and, because agents are like family, Kerr wants revenge.

They tear past HMS *Belfast* and beneath Tower Bridge. With the tide on the turn, they are on high alert. Kerr stands beside Justin in the open, hanging on tight, flexing his knees as they crash eastwards. He is finding the race downstream tough because he is still recovering from a bomb blast that fractured his right leg, buried shrapnel in his chest and neck, and left him in a coma for six days. For the past month he has been pretending he is back to full strength. This evening, seventeen minutes from Chelsea Harbour, his whole body is starting to complain, but he urges Justin faster.

The plan is simple. If the gang's inflatable appears, they will watch where it goes in case the analysts have got it wrong, then report back. Eyes and ears only, that's what Kerr has told Justin. But Kerr has brought his Glock 19 semi-automatic 9mm pistol; it sits snugly in his jacket pocket.

He checks out the right bank, looking for the Trojans' covert van. Though they have concealed themselves well, they are in completely the wrong location. The target boat suddenly appears as they emerge from a long right bend bordering Canary Wharf. Even at half a mile Kerr can see it is exactly as Seagull described it: two red inflatable hulls the length of a

Transit van, with a silver outboard engine the size of a giant suitcase.

Kerr is already squinting at the two men on board, both standing forward, like him and Justin, travelling at about five knots. The bad guys have arrived right on time, a few minutes after high tide. As Kerr feared, they are a full half-mile east of the Trojans' position, in midstream and heading to the estuary, not the South Bank.

Kerr overrides Justin's hand on the throttle to drive them even faster. 'I want you to take us right alongside.'

Justin's expression says this is not the plan, but Kerr ignores him. The tide has already turned, and less than three hundred metres of deep water separate them.

The target boat is wallowing in the swell now, which gives Kerr his first good view of the enemy. He sees that both men are wearing bright red T-shirts and wonders if this is a ruse, to make them appear to be on some innocent corporate activity. Perhaps they are, and Kerr has got it wrong. There is one sure way to find out.

The passenger on the right is of regular build, white baseball cap pulled low over his eyes to shield them from the sun. He looks containable, but even from this distance Kerr can tell the man at the wheel will be a challenge. He dwarfs his passenger, massive shoulders flexing, his bulk upsetting the boat's stability.

Justin is closing fast. Any second now the bad guys must spot the Sea Ray hurtling straight for them. Justin turns slightly to port, preparing to sweep past, but Kerr checks his hand on the wheel.

'We're just watching them, aren't we?' shouts Justin. 'Come on, boss, it's not my boat.'

Kerr's face is fixed dead ahead, his hand still clamped over Justin's. 'I'm going to arrest them,' he says.

At less than twenty metres, Justin is preparing to bring them alongside. Then Kerr gets a clear view of both men as their shocked faces turn to stare at the Sea Ray. The big man rockets the boat across the bow of the Sea Ray, its propeller throwing up a giant plume of spray. The prow lifts into the air and, for a second, it seems the inflatable will flip over. This tells Kerr that the driver is inexpert and the propeller as oversized as the engine. He feels the odds sliding in his favour.

Suddenly firearms appear, eliminating the innocent-corporate-jaunt theory. The passenger is holding a pistol, which does not trouble Kerr in such unstable conditions, but then the big man produces a sawn-off shotgun and fires at the Sea Ray. It is little more than a pot shot from a boat practically out of control. But not entirely wild. As Kerr and Justin duck, they hear the *thwack* of heavy-calibre shot against the Sea Ray's perfect blue hull. It also penetrates the windscreen, exactly where their heads had been a split second earlier. Then there is the thump of fibreglass on rubber as Justin T-bones the inflatable's left hull.

Justin and Kerr have had time to brace, but the impact throws the gangsters to the floor. The Sea Ray has actually mounted the target boat at right angles. Trapped high and dry, its prow crushes the inflatable's left hull. For a few seconds the boats remain locked together, slowly rotating in the current, while the gangsters scrabble for their weapons.

As Justin throws the engine into reverse to pull them to safety, Kerr is clambering onto the forward deck. By the time he gets to his feet, legs wide apart for balance, the Glock is in his right hand, and he stands a full metre higher than the enemy, his body a clear profile against the blue sky. The passenger is lying against the right hull, bracing himself as he brings up his handgun to murder Kerr.

But as Kerr lifts the Glock in both hands, the rotation of the boats suddenly floods the inflatable with sunlight. The passenger's baseball cap gives no protection against the glare, and he squints as he fires. His shot misses, but Kerr's, as close as an echo, is true. Kerr is aiming for his assassin's chest, but the boats fall on the swell and his shot strikes the centre of the man's forehead, passing through his skull and skittering along the water. He slumps sideways into the stern, the white baseball cap soaking up his blood like blotting paper.

As Justin guns the engine, the big man braces himself against the wheel to slip another cartridge into the sawn-off. Kerr shouts, 'Police!' a couple of times, but can see this guy is not thinking about surrender. Justin is yelling at him to take cover as the Sea Ray begins to slip back into the water, like a freed whale. But Kerr has unfinished business. At the last moment, just as the boats separate, he manages to launch himself onto the inflatable and lands on the big man just as he pulls the trigger. The shot goes wild as Kerr's shoes sink into the man's bloated belly, propelling him backwards. Then gravity takes over as his animal bulk tips him overboard into the fast-flowing river.

For a second he disappears, then Kerr sees him surface three metres away, floating rapidly downstream. Kerr checks his surroundings. The dead passenger is crumpled in the stern against the deflating left hull. In the front lies a rough platform of timber slats supporting concrete blocks, positioned to replicate the gold bars and offset the weight of the oversized engine, which is still idling.

Justin hovers upstream, waiting for his boss to come to his senses, but Kerr waves him away. The inflatable is seriously unstable now, and steering is difficult as it wallows in the swell. He guns the outboard, then fixes his eyes on the gangster in the water, whose red T-shirt makes a great marker. He is floating on his back facing Kerr, hair streaked across his face, mouth in a giant O, arms flailing uselessly.

Pursuing the gangster downstream, Kerr is dragged left by the deflating hull. Ankle deep in water, he knows he will have to abandon ship very soon. But he carries on, crablike, close enough to hear the gangster's cries over the engine. He is shouting something in a foreign language. Then the man is directly in front of him. Kerr feels a bump against his feet as the giant head slides beneath the sinking boat. The propeller strains in a terrible shredding sound, spewing out a plume of water reflecting bright red in the sunshine, then surges as its bloody wake fans out in the flood. The shredding lasts a couple of seconds longer, then strains and slows before dying completely, the propeller unequal to the task. Adrift on the tide, there is complete silence as Kerr scans the river. The gangster has disintegrated beneath an inflating film of blood, leaving no body parts or flotsam. The engine and Seagull's murderer have killed each other.

By the time Justin reaches Kerr, expertly guiding the Sea Ray to the rescue, he is calmly sitting astride the right hull. He has the presence of mind to reach deep into the water to recover the sawn-off and handgun, tossing them onto the deck. He will need these to justify his actions, to demonstrate that the gangsters posed a clear and present danger. He splashes across to search the smaller man's corpse, retrieves a mobile phone and throws it to Justin. Then he grabs the rail and hauls himself to safety.

'You OK, boss?' says Justin.

'Too heavy. Couldn't lift him on board.'

If Justin is thinking something different, he does not say so. He goes gently astern as they watch the inflatable swept downstream, almost submerged. There is a flash of red shirt as the body of the man Kerr shot dead floats away. Justin throws Kerr a quizzical glance. 'So do we pick that one up?'

'Too risky,' says Kerr, shaking his head. He tests the shattered windscreen. 'And, like you say, this isn't our boat.'

'Don't you think we should try?'

'Those men murdered Seagull,' says Kerr, wringing out his jacket. 'Let's leave it to the professionals.'

One

The alarm was unnecessary for Rob Fleming was already awake. Melanie, his wife, was lying away from him, and he studied her for a moment while 'Skyfall' by Adele washed over him on Heart 106.2. He got out of bed to close the bedroom door, slipped off his boxers and eased back beneath the duvet to savour Melanie's warmth. He snuggled up, his hand sneaking round to find her breast, his hips pressing against her. 'Check this out.' Melanie's hand came to give him a squeeze as he moved closer to kiss the nape of her neck. 'Love you, sexy.'

'No. Totally not. I'm sleeping.' Melanie slipped his hand from her breast and moved beyond reach. 'So put it away.'

But in less than two minutes she was naked, too, and they were having urgent sex, as they always did when Melanie was about to disappear for a few days. Impending separation gave their lovemaking a special intensity, but at this time in the morning they had to work fast and in relative silence, with one eye on the door. There were already stirrings from the other end of the landing. Running feet, the splash of an endless pee, the *thud* of something being thrown, then laughter. Their two sons, aged five and three, would invade at any moment.

Showered and clean-shaven, Rob emerged from their en-suite bathroom to find Melanie decent again in her silk nightdress, relaxing against the pillows. She had the boys in bed with her, Mickey Mouse on one side, Harry Potter on the other, vying for her attention. Dressing quickly in his usual summer work gear of jeans and T-shirt, Rob did a half dive onto the bed. The boys immediately went for him, wrestling him into submission, until Melanie told them they were wearing their daddy out.

Rob checked the clock: ten past seven. He had to be in Pimlico for an eight-thirty start, but always liked to be early. No time for breakfast. He would pick up coffee and a bagel in the Broadway. He climbed off the bed, kissed the boys and leant over Melanie. 'Be careful, darling,' he said softly. 'Keep safe.'

Melanie stroked his neck and kissed him. 'It's an easy one. Promise.'

'See you Friday.' He bent low to whisper in her ear. 'Sex pest.'

The boys scampered to the window to watch their daddy leave. By the time Rob drove off in their black Ford Fiesta, Melanie was already in the shower.

The Flemings lived in the north London suburb of Muswell Hill, one of the highest points in the capital. Home was a large Edwardian semi they had bought as a wreck five years ago and refurbished from top to bottom, restoring the period features and installing a kitchen and two bathrooms. Rob had saved thousands of pounds by hiring a skip and taking on much of the heavy lifting himself, as well as some of the electrical work and plumbing. The house had four bedrooms, sash windows and the original wooden banisters. The back garden was long and green, with fruit trees, a couple of acers and plenty of mature shrubs bordering a healthy lawn. The boys had spent most of the previous summer playing in a dilapidated shed at the bottom of the garden, sheltered by a willow tree. Rob had promised to build them a summer house next year.

The Flemings' home lay in a quiet street between the Broadway and Fortis Green Road. They had chosen well, stretching themselves to buy into an area that was cool and upmarket. The nursery and primary schools were excellent, and the family often enjoyed the green spaces of Highgate and Queen's Woods, and Alexandra Park with its famous palace only a short drive away. Melanie and Rob took huge pride in their house, which they intended would be their home for life. They had done well for a pair of front-line cops in their early thirties. If the professional types buying up the street wondered about the couple who went to work at strange hours in odd clothes, they did not show it.

Melanie was a career Special Branch officer working for John Kerr in the intelligence unit of SO15 Counter Terrorism Command. Highly vetted, she had operated for many years as a specialist in close-quarter, armed surveillance, successfully combining marriage and motherhood with the tracking of terrorists. Less known around the Yard was her work as an undercover officer, the job she was doing now. The woman who loved her family with all her heart was capable of the most convincing deception. John Kerr estimated Melanie to be one of the best operators he had ever known.

Rob was also a surveillance officer, seconded from the Met to the National Crime Agency. His targets were the major criminal gangsters who trafficked in drugs, guns or illegal immigration rackets. Rob's speciality, which he never spoke about, was covert rural operations, known as CROP. Dug into the ground in camouflage clothing, with minimal rations and no creature comforts, he and his partner would maintain static surveillance on a major target for two or three days and nights, themselves immobile, but photographing or filming every movement around them. Invisible in the background, Rob relished his work. Most of the hardened criminals he watched had considered themselves inviolable until the moment the Trojans crashed them to the pavement with Glock 17 semi-automatics to their heads. The astonishment on their faces, the sliding emotional scale of shock, rage and fear, always gave him a serious buzz.

The work of the Flemings required unusual resilience, which was why so few made the grade. Melanie carried a high national-security clearance. 'Need to know' applied at the Yard and at home. She never told Rob about the specifics of her work, and he never asked. Melanie stayed mute because she was professional.

There were personal reasons, too. The dedicated wife and mother did not want her life contaminated by the professional spy. And she wanted Rob never to know about her *alter ego*. She had tried to explain this to Kerr, himself a former under-cover operative and the sole person in whom she would confide. She knew that Kerr had been in far worse scrapes than hers; and as a boss he had the politics to contend with, too.

'You've become a single minded schizophrenic, Melanie,' Kerr had said, with a laugh. 'That's what you're telling me. Like all the best UCs.'

Rob's mother, Brenda, arrived just after tea, around five o'clock, so that Melanie could leave for work. Brenda would put the boys to bed and stay until Rob arrived home, or over-night if he was going to be late. Since her divorce seven years ago, she had downsized to a flat in nearby East Finchley, not far from the tube. She had been a stay-at-home mum, devot-ing her life to bringing up Rob and his younger sister. Rob was a hero in her eyes, doing society's dirty work. But her attitude to Melanie was quite different. A woman's place was in the home, not deserting her family for days and nights without reason, doing God knew what. It was unnatural. So when Melanie left there were no kisses, hugs or warnings to take care. Rob's mother had never faced up to her daughter-in-law's lifestyle, and Melanie had long ago given up making it easy for her.

Two

Hope Farm had started life as a red-brick, rambling Victorian farmhouse in Essex, midway between Ingatestone and the ancient market town of Chipping Ongar to the north-west. Worked by the same family for three generations, it had not been used for its proper purpose since the winter of 1988, when its elderly owner had suffered a massive heart attack while feeding the pigs, his dead body lying unnoticed in the open for three days. It had remained unoccupied for almost a year, steadily deteriorating, until a scrap-metal king from Southend, Terry Bray, had rescued it from complete collapse. In those heady days of self-help, yuppies and dirty money, Terry had sweet-talked the grieving daughter in London and taken it off her manicured hands for hard cash, no questions asked.

Bray had replaced the roof, painted the whole structure white, and reclaimed the outside space. It had taken him less than a year to transform the derelict smallholding into a gold-plated, shag-carpeted citadel of breathtaking vulgarity. Hope Farm was an L-shaped, west-facing building set in three acres. A narrow lane bordered the property to the front, and farm-land to the other three sides. Bray's few visitors approached along a sweeping gravel drive he had laid over the original muddy farm track, protected by wrought-iron gates with an intercom. The house occupied the highest point of the land

and was surrounded by extensive lawns sloping down to woodland and a perimeter fence eight feet high. He had come to regard it as the perfect retreat, meeting the twin business priorities of complete seclusion and fast access to the M25, M11 and Thames Estuary.

'Put the dog out again.' Bray was standing in his state-of-the-art kitchen, a spacious, white-tiled, antiseptic showpiece. Every surface was spotless. Before the night was out, Bray had quipped, the area would be as sterile as his ex-wife. There was an Aga and every conceivable convenience, though the current Mrs Bray, a former topless model thirty years his junior, with silicone in her breasts and a permanent look of surprise, rarely even boiled an egg. The worktops around the walls, and the island in the middle, were covered with roughly cast gold bars laid on sheets of plastic.

Dark hair swept back, in jeans, blue sweater over a cotton shirt and expensive trainers, Terry Bray could have been dressed for a pint at his village local. His two partners worked rapidly alongside him, packing the gold into crates. Sammy was a former weight-lifter in his mid-forties and had been Bray's drinking friend and lieutenant for more than two decades. At just under six feet, he was shorter than his boss but stronger than men half his age. Sammy was a specialist in debt collection and enforcement, and Bray trusted him completely. The junior, Dale, was a muscular, shaven-headed former infantryman in his late twenties, with a couple of tours in Afghanistan and a short fuse. Bray had taken him on the year before as a favour to the young man's father but against the advice of Sammy, who had questioned Dale's stability and had called him a psycho to his face. The three men worked without speaking. Delivery time had just been brought forward forty-eight hours, so they would be packing well into the night.

The dog was a Rottweiler that prowled in the corner, eyes like flint, a thick string of saliva dangling from its jowls. It had no name because it was simply another offensive weapon in Bray's armoury. Enough guns were stashed throughout Hope Farm to start a small war, but Bray favoured the dog. The previous year it had torn into the flesh of a business rival in a way he had never seen before, its killer teeth and vice-like jaws invigorating him far more than any firearm.

'I've already checked down as far as the lane,' said Dale. 'We're clear.'

The boy had a lot to learn, so Bray let his eyes bore into him. 'I wasn't asking,' he said quietly.

Self-discipline had kept Terry Bray free for at least twenty years, always staying a couple of hundred jumps ahead of the cops. For survival in an uncertain world he avoided patterns of activity and clung rigidly to his own mantra, 'DEAF': Documents, Evasion, Alibi and Friends. He had seen too many of his business partners trapped in police stings to fall for one himself. If the deal felt dodgy, he walked away.

Because he knew that the cops followed him, tapped his phone and monitored his bank accounts, Terry Bray had made life difficult for them by diversifying into totally legitimate businesses. His double-glazing, waste-disposal and timeshare interests had led the cops and the well-bred girls from MI5 on muddy trails all over the world, tying up their analysts for months.

Bray gave Dale and the dog a couple of minutes, then grabbed a flashlight and went outside to check for himself. The house was in darkness except for the kitchen: Bray had sent his wife with their infant twin daughters to his villa in Spain for the duration. An executive jet was waiting at Farnborough airfield to whisk him there the moment the deal was done and the farmhouse sanitised. Three local Spanish witnesses would swear he had been there for the past five days, and that the family had travelled out to be with him. Such arrangements were food and drink to Terry Bray.

Between the lawn and the fence was an untended, impenetrable ribbon of woodland, vegetation, brambles and nettles. This was Bray's no-go zone. It was probably six or seven paces wide, but no one had ever tested it. CCTV cameras monitored the gates and various points along the fence, and Bray had even planted sensors at strategic points in the lawn.

Bray kept the flashlight off and stood listening to the dog on patrol. He could see Dale's pencil torch by the gates and heard his footsteps on the gravel as he moved to check the north perimeter.

Bray turned left, away from the light of the kitchen. Here, the night was pitch black, and the stars were bright. An earlier downpour had cleared the air, heightening the scent of his freshly mown lawns. He walked up a short stone footpath leading to an indoor swimming-pool detached from the main house, with a barbecue area beside the entrance. Abutting the pool on the right was another brick structure, about ten feet square. To the casual observer, or from the air, this would pass as housing for the pool's heating and filter plants. In fact, it contained a furnace for the smelting of gold and other precious metals, a new franchise in the business empire of the one-time scrap merchant.

The furnace had been working non-stop for three days and, from halfway down the path, Bray could feel the heat against his face. His latest international client had made a strong impression, agreeing excellent terms with money up front and offering the prospect of new markets in Europe. But the requirements had specified a tight, non-elastic timetable. Having completed the smelting operation on time, Bray was determined not to default on delivery.

He continued walking round to the left, until he reached the north side of the house. In front of him he could see two flashlight beams and hear voices. They came from the old stable block Bray had converted into garages for his Range Rovers, black for him, white for his wife, plus the Bentley. Tonight it also accommodated the reinforced long-wheelbase Transit van he would use to transport the gold bars. He could hear Dale talking to the driver, the third member of his team, confirming the final checks Bray had ordered to prevent any last-minute hitches or breakdowns.

Bray entered the house by the front door, locking and bolting it behind him. He automatically checked a screen displaying CCTV images of the gates and rear of the house. His home was open-plan, designed by Mrs Bray. Confronting him was a sea of white carpet, crystal chandeliers, vast sofas, gold fabric and a giant TV that filled one wall. In one corner of the living room, beside a vase of tulips, stood his personalised Remington 870 Wingmaster pump-action shotgun, both barrels loaded.

Terry Bray paused to admire his life's work, then removed his trainers before stepping onto the white pile. He padded across the room in his stockinged feet, a life study in brutality and bling.

Three

Freewheeling with no lights, the muddy green Land Rover ghosted past the gates to Hope Farm within sixty seconds of Dale and the Rottweiler hurrying for shelter in the kitchen as the rain began to fall again. The vehicle continued south for another thirty metres, then slowed as the rear door swung open to discharge Rob Fleming and his partner. They were dressed entirely in black, masked and utterly silent.

They immediately took cover in a waterlogged ditch bordering Terry Bray's fence, invisible from the lane. As darkness swallowed the Land Rover, they were already checking the fence for gaps, weak places, potential points of access and security cameras. They could see none along the short stretch identified for their incursion. The fence looked strong and well maintained, supported by concrete posts and protected with barbed wire that was probably more dangerous than it looked. Rob had raised the possibility that the perimeter might also be alarmed. But in the rush to deploy, the briefing guys back at the ranch had been unable to help them on that score. Another last-minute bloody panic.

Rob's partner was Jim Marshall, another of the élite band of operatives trained in rural surveillance. Standing in Marshall's interlocked hands, Rob cut the wire anyway, then listened for a couple of seconds, half expecting all hell to break loose. They had been scrambled because 'unusual urgent activity' had been detected inside the house, so he stuck his head above the fence for a first look. But the *leylandii* were so dense that all he could see was a faint light refracted by the drenched, shiny leaves of a laurel bush to their left. Without hesitation he sprang astride the fence, dropped silently onto a soft cushion of leaves inside hostile territory, and gave his partner the all-clear.

They lay on their bellies just forward of the trees, getting their bearings. The rain was falling in a steady stream now. In front of them were several paces of dense undergrowth and vegetation. There was no moon and the environment looked promising, Terry Bray's protective barrier against prying eyes offering the perfect natural cover. The impenetrable shield in which he took such pride would enable them to dig in and hide for ever. They crawled forward into their target's no-go area, Rob in the lead, feeling rather than seeing. He soon found them a depression in the earth beneath a blanket of brambles tangled with ivy. Within the heart of the bush they cut themselves a hidden space, bringing drops of water down on them with every snip. In less than three minutes they had hollowed out a tiny green spiky cocoon that would protect them from their targets and the worst of the elements, night and day if necessary.

They carried minimal equipment: adapted ATN night-vision glasses, energy bars and drinks in sachets, and plastic cuffs. Encrypted radios with throat mikes were supposed to keep them in touch with their makeshift operational base six hundred metres away, though Rob's whispered 'In position' message elicited no response. To communicate with each other the two partners used hand signals. The ground smelt damp, lightened by the scent of the newly mown lawns in front of them. Using their knees and elbows to make body shapes in the softened earth, they settled to keep watch.

The house was about fifty metres away on the highest point of land, with lawns radiating down from each aspect. The whole building was in darkness, apart from the room at the back, nearest to them, which Rob assumed was the kitchen. It had double-aspect windows shielded by Roman blinds, and the door was dead ahead. On the basis that operatives in Rob's line of work were on their own, whatever the bosses might tell them, he always figured out his self-preservation contingencies before anything else, and knew his partner did the same. Because they were unarmed, Rob usually calculated these options in terms of running like hell. He took in the gradient in front of them and the vegetation behind: a twenty-second sprint to the house if he needed to attack, ninety seconds to retreat and escape over the fence if things went belly-up.

Rob and Jim Marshall had been deployed at a rush two hours earlier after a long day on standby in Pimlico, just as they were thinking of home. The intelligence making everyone jump had been 'Most Urgent' and 'Graded A1': the highest quality. It had been the immediacy that had grabbed Rob's attention – it always suggested some red-hot product from a technical intercept. Yet Terry Bray was renowned for his paranoid attention to security. Dozens of analysts who had studied him over the years knew that. He always used code words on his mobile phones, never risked email, and his networking was rarely social. As Rob psyched himself up after a day of inactivity, the rush and buzz around the briefing room had told him that Public Enemy Number One must have screwed up big-time.

The two operatives had briefed themselves as they pulled on their gear, studying aerial surveillance shots of Hope Farm. An album of photographs taken in London and Spain charted the rise of Terence Albert Bray from tattooed street villain to suntanned lord of the manor. It was a life's journey that had taken him from defunct cars, destroyed roofs and stolen railway cabling to precious metals, from crushed steel, ripped lead and stripped copper to pure gold in less than a decade. The photographs had been unnecessary, for everyone in the National knew the face of Terence Albert Bray. They had been told to expect a static long-nighter in the middle of nowhere, cold and wet. Fantastic. Their task: to observe, record and communicate. They should expect two or three other gang members at the farm. The main event: the departure in the early hours of a fully loaded, long-wheelbase Transit van. No one had been able to say if this would contain the whole team. Once they had the go from Rob, assault teams would deploy from a mile away and stop the van in the lane. The interception would be noisy and violent, but the surveillance officers had to stay in place, to see what happened next at the farm. They had told Rob that no one was underestimating the danger. Thanks for nothing.

Through the night-vision glasses Rob saw the door to the kitchen open and a tall, well-built man in his twenties appear. He was shaven-headed, in good shape and standing straight. Rob put him in the ex-military category. Gangster number two, after Terry Bray. He stood framed in the light for a moment and Rob caught a glimpse of another figure inside, shorter and older. Three bad guys, but no sign of the main target. The first man closed the door behind him and stood in the lee of the wall to shelter from the rain. The night flared as he lit a cigarette. Rob watched a red pinprick glow bright as the man inhaled, then fade. There was a shout from the kitchen as the door opened again, then Rob felt a stab of utter shock as a Rottweiler tore from the kitchen across the grass.

'Who said anything about a fucking dog?'

Rob could hear the anxiety flooding his partner's voice. 'Stay low,' he whispered.

'And we're upwind.'

'The rain will cover us.'

Burying themselves deeper in the earth while they had the initiative, they watched the Rottweiler patrol the lawns. Then it must have caught their scent because it started barking, growling and baring its teeth. But it did not make a move towards them. This told Rob the creature was trained, a status dog obeying orders, a fighting machine about to ratchet a crisis into a disaster.

Then there was the pulse of fluorescent light as the man himself appeared, framed in the kitchen doorway.

Terry Bray's voice carried clearly in the night air, evidently aimed at the smoker. 'There's someone out there, you moron.' Bray must have signalled to the dog, for it tore down the sloping lawn straight for Rob and Marshall. It was on them in seconds, baring its teeth, barking and snarling less than a pace away on the other side of the brambles, waiting for its master's command to tear into them.

Rob saw Bray dart back into the house, re-emerge with a shotgun and stride with the smoker towards them. Within seconds the third, shorter man appeared from the kitchen with a flashlight and jogged after them, the swaying beam reflecting off the raindrops and elongating the two silhouettes almost as far as their hiding place.

It was the fight or flight moment, but Rob suppressed the adrenaline surge as he coolly weighed the odds. Combat would be unequal, escape possibly fatal. 'Stay calm,' he said, above the barking. 'Stay with me, Jim. I'll talk us out.'

The two operatives shuffled backwards from the safety of the brambles as the three gangsters advanced on them across the sodden grass. Their retreat seemed to drive the dog crazy. It looked ready to rip a path through the undergrowth to take both men out. Then Jim Marshall was trapped by the flashlight, crouching to the right of their hiding place. He slowly stood straight and then stayed motionless, hands at his sides, paralysed in the powerful beam. To any normal householder, his black, masked figure would have been intimidating, but the man Bray had just called a moron went for him without hesitation. Perhaps he wanted to redeem himself; possibly he was simply too comfortable around violence to experience fear. He kicked Marshall in the crotch and forced his arms behind his back, awaiting orders as Terry Bray quietened the dog.

But it was Rob who spoke, before they even knew he was there. He materialised out of the darkness beyond Marshall's left shoulder, drawing the beam away from his partner. He had his right arm raised in front of him, blocking the light with his palm. 'We're police officers. Let him go. Stand back.'

No one said anything. Then Bray turned his head, gave a slight nod and took the flashlight as the older man slapped Rob on the side of the head and locked his arms behind his back. Bray carefully leant the shotgun against a sapling that had seeded itself. Apparently unfazed by the discovery of two surveillance officers in his grounds, he walked up to Rob, shone the light in his eyes and punched him hard in the stomach. 'You're fucking trespassers.' He expertly located the lead to Rob's bodyset and ripped it out, then paused while the younger man did the same to Marshall.

'Take off your mask.' Rob stood quite still, arms by his sides in a gesture of defiance. Bray lifted Rob's balaclava up to his forehead and shone the flashlight into his face again. Rob turned his head to the right, trying to protect his night vision, and glimpsed the pleading in Marshall's eyes. Then there was a moment's relief as the beam swung away from him. 'And who do we have here?' said Bray, redirecting the flashlight and roughly lifting Marshall's balaclava. The beam hit Marshall's face at an odd angle, illuminating his gaunt, ashen face, the eyes sunk in dark pools. Bray tapped the plastic Speedcuffs on Marshall's belt. 'Tie them. Bring them inside.'

He turned away, patted the dog, picked up his shotgun and started to walk back towards the house.

'Terry Bray, you're under arrest.' Rob's voice stopped Bray in his tracks. He turned slowly, half smiling. He let the Rottweiler lick his hand, walked back to Rob and struck him hard in the face.

Four

Hands cuffed behind their backs, beaten and dishevelled, the surveillance officers stumbled through the kitchen door, shoved by Bray's two accomplices. Their captors pushed them past the island to the opposite wall, the point furthest from the door. They kicked their feet from under them and, once they were on the floor, launched a few well-aimed body kicks in an unnecessary reminder that resistance was futile. At a word from Bray, the youngest of the gang leashed the dog outside the back door. Then Bray put his shotgun on the worktop by the door and disappeared into the house through the internal arch to Rob's left.

Blinking in the harsh white light of the kitchen, Rob took in the scene. Observe and record. At least three targets. He identified Bray's Wingmaster shotgun immediately. The kitchen was large, twelve paces by fifteen, with every surface tiled and, he guessed, as clean as an operating theatre. There were two identical high-chairs in the corner opposite. The nearest had a Smith & Wesson 9mm Sigma handgun on its tray. On the other was a sawn-off shotgun, possibly a Mossberg 500 12 gauge. Lethal. Worktops covered with brown paper surrounded the walls. To the left of the door Rob counted seven crates.

On each surface to his right, including the island, were what appeared to be rough-cast gold bars of irregular size and shape. The worktops to the left were clear except for the brown paper, so Rob assumed the gold from these had already been packed into the crates. By the arch through which Bray had disappeared there was a rocking-horse, with a Browning Hi-Power semi-automatic pistol balanced on the saddle. Without saying a word, Bray's two associates finished packing the crates, apparently oblivious to the intruders at their feet.

Communicate. Squirming sideways, Rob pressed against the Aga, bringing his weight to bear against the secret panic button strapped to his thigh beneath his clothes. The alarm would squirt an encrypted SOS with a precise location. The last resort where life was in the balance, it was known to every surveillance operative as the 'Surveillance Oh Shit!' device. Rob cursed himself for leaving it so late.

Tuesday, 2 July, 23.43;
communications base near Hope Farm

In a spirit of co-operation, partnership and sharing of the glory, the National Crime Agency had entrusted the support of their surveillance officers to officers from Essex Constabulary, which covered Hope Farm. They were a team of three, led by a detective inspector called Simms. Normally based at Chelmsford police headquarters, tonight they were sheltering in a makeshift base the National had acquired for them within an hour of receiving the urgent information against Terry Bray. It was a derelict storage shed less than eight paces square, abutting an ancient dry-stone wall bordering a single-track lane. It lay hidden deep in the Essex countryside, a mile from the village of Wyatt's Green, almost within shouting distance of Hope Farm, and the local farmer had accepted a hundred pounds in cash from the National's sourcing officer, one night only, no questions asked.

The centuries-old stone ruin had no electricity, heat source or furniture, and the night-time rain trickled steadily through dozens of shattered roof tiles. Simms and his team wore extreme-weather lightweight coats, gloves and thick socks, and the communications officer had to work his kit from the ground, an uneven, earthen mass smelling of straw and dung freshened by the rain. He would remain crouched there until the van arrived from Chelmsford with operational essentials, not expected until around half past one.

A seventeen-inch laptop showed a high-definition colour satellite image of Hope Farm and scale relief map of the grounds. While he listened for any routine status transmissions from Rob and Jim Marshall, Simms and his deputy bit into energy bars on a circle of ground at the opposite corner of the shed, the only other relatively dry spot. The communications were poor and the mobile signal weak, but Rob Fleming's emergency signal was unmistakable. It jerked the operator bolt upright. 'Listen up, I'm getting the panic alarm from X-ray Seven,' he said, staring at a red light flashing from the laptop. He looked round, but Simms was already speed-dialling.

'Location?'

The operator was frowning. 'This is weird,' he said. 'Can't be right.'

Simms watched the pulse of red reflecting on the other man's forehead. 'What?'

'The signal has them actually inside the house.'

'Jesus.' Simms was through and spoke without preamble. 'We have a Code Red. Deploy.'

Tuesday, 2 July, 23.46; kitchen, Hope Farm

Terry Bray reappeared in the kitchen at a rush and spoke to the older man. 'Sammy, I want us to be clear in five minutes.'

'No problem,' said Sammy. 'Place is clean.'

'Good man.' Bray nodded, then looked at the moron. 'Dale, get the van brought round.' As Dale disappeared Bray pivoted to the two men on the floor, approached Rob and kicked him hard in the leg. 'And you,' he said, dragging Rob to his feet. 'I need to know if you called the cavalry.'

'Take a jump,' said Rob. As he braced himself for Bray's punch he sensed Marshall also struggling upright. It was his partner's gesture of solidarity, and somehow gave him strength.

Bray looked ice cool, even managing a half-smile. 'Time for a bit of law enforcement,' he said, holding out his palm. Without hesitation Sammy took the Browning from the rocking-horse and handed it to him. It was a practised gesture and left Rob in no doubt that they had done this before. A gun for every occasion. 'I'll ask you nicely again, Superdick,' said Bray. 'What time are they expecting you to check in?'

'Go fuck yourself.'

Without a flicker of emotion Bray shoved Rob aside and expertly shot Marshall in the leg. He recoiled against the Aga, then collapsed to the floor, screaming in pain, his blood bright against the sterile tiles.

Rob immediately knelt beside his partner, but Sammy dragged him upright again. Bray stood so close to Rob that their faces were almost touching. 'I'll ask you one more time.'

Rob looked down at Marshall moaning at their feet. Bray's bullet appeared to have struck his leg above the knee. The black fabric of his boiler suit glistened around the wound, and the trickle of blood was now pooling into a steadily expanding circle. It looked very bad. If his partner was to survive, Rob had very little time. Rob held Bray's gaze and kept his voice low. 'Terry, my partner is married with kids, but he's going to die unless you stop the bleeding. Are you really prepared to go down for murder?'

A vehicle was reversing outside the kitchen, from right to left. Rob could see the glow of the lights through the blinds. This must be the van they had been briefed about. Before

Bray could answer, the kitchen door flew open and Dale hurried inside. But the van was still moving, so there had to be someone else out there. Four gangsters. Terry Bray, Sammy, Dale and one other. Rob heard the engine go silent and the driver's door slam.

Then he made out the shape of a woman framed in the kitchen doorway. It was the last person he'd expected to see: Melanie, his wife.

Tuesday, 2 July, 23.53; kitchen, Hope Farm

Terry Bray swung round, impatient, as his driver and mechanic stood in the doorway, hair unkempt, hands dirty from making her final checks on the van. 'We ready to go, Mel?' He saw her scanning the room, absorbing the man on the floor, the guns and the piano-wire tension. And he spotted her reaction, too. Terry Bray had witnessed shock many times before, mostly on the faces of his victims, and he was seeing it again now, as the blood drained from her face. Something had just sucked the life out of Mel.

'All set.' Mel was scarcely audible. She seemed to swallow the words, as if she could no longer trust her own voice. She quickly turned away to pick up one of the boxes, but was not quick enough.

'Wait.' Bray looked at Rob. The cop was hyperventilating, shaking with fear, his face beaded with sweat, bravado shot through. It was as if *he* had taken the first bullet, not the guy writhing on the ground. He turned to Mel. 'Do you two know each other?'

This time her voice came back ice cold and clear as a bell. 'Do me a favour.' She reached for the crate again. 'We're wasting time.'

'No,' said Bray. 'There's something not right.' He looked to Sammy and Dale, antennae twitching. He knew the dangers of a sting operation. The Yard had tried to entrap him before, but Terry Bray reckoned he could smell an undercover operative the moment he walked through the door. The bastards had used every dirty trick in the book to get him, but his gut had never let him down. Good guys, corruptible cops, traitors and spies. Terry Bray could read them all. And the past thirty seconds had put all his instincts on full alert. He studied Mel shrewdly, staring her down. 'Don't lie to me, Mel.'

'Look, I don't like being in the same room as coppers.' Mel faced him across the island, hands on hips. 'Is that so bad?'

Bray looked between the two of them, deeply suspicious. He didn't like coincidences and was weighing the odds that she was lying.

The psycho was looking anxious now. Perhaps he was thinking Bray might suspect him, too. 'We should get going,' he said, moving to the door.

'Shut it,' growled Bray, not taking his eyes off Mel. 'So you've never seen him before? He means nothing to you?'

'He's a copper, isn't he? What do you think?'

Bray shot Dale another glare. 'Check as far as the gates. Use the dog.'

Wednesday, 3 July, 00.11;
rendezvous point outside Hope Farm

Twenty metres from the gate, concealed by a gentle curve in the lane and untended hedgerows, Detective Inspector Jack Langton, John Kerr's deputy, head of surveillance and motorcycle nut, freewheeled his Suzuki GSX R1000 into the muddy passing place designated as the rendezvous point for the assault teams, within a short sprint of the spot where Rob and Marshall had been dropped from the Land Rover earlier that night. The bike's engine was red hot – Langton had covered the thirty-five miles from his house in Mill Hill, north London, within twenty-three minutes of the snatched emergency call from Melanie to John Kerr reporting a shot fired in the house.

A Loughborough graduate in sports science and former PE teacher, Jack Langton ran Kerr's surveillance teams. He had just reached home after a long day with MI5 following a Chinese espionage target who had led them to a Holiday Inn close to a scientific research centre a few miles east of Winchester. Hungry and thirsty, he had kissed his wife and child, downed a pint glass of water and immediately hit the road again. He was the only man in SO15 capable of getting there in time, often exceeding one hundred and twenty miles per hour on clear stretches of the M25 clockwise to the A12, a lethal stiletto of light piercing the darkness. He parked at right angles to the lane, with the rear tyre sinking into a muddy rut, removed his helmet and waited in the rain.

Lights extinguished, making scarcely any sound apart from the swish of their wiper blades, the two black Range Rovers of the assault teams, also from Essex Constabulary, arrived within three minutes. Langton had left them just enough space to park up, one behind the other. No one would have warned them to expect him, and he guessed this would be a difficult call. He knew they had been held on a concrete patch of wasteground beside the A12 near Mountnessing; his own teams occasionally used the same place as a rendezvous point. Once a garage forecourt, the space had somehow been missed by the county planners. Its fractured canopy, rusting pumps and crumbling office, still with peeling advertisements in the windows, scarred the countryside like remnants from Armageddon. Langton could have made his move there, but had calculated that an earlier approach would allow them time to rebuff him. Here, in the calm before the storm, the ticking clock would overcome dissent.

Langton approached the front passenger in the first vehicle and saw that the team leader was a woman. She looked startled by the man in motorcycle leathers who materialised out of the darkness and pressed a Met ID against her window. As Langton had expected, there were four firearms officers in the vehicle, two pairs, plus a police driver. The second Range Rover would have the same set-up.

'DI Jack Langton,' he said, as the leader wound down her window. 'I'll be coming into the house with you.'

She took his ID for a better look. 'Who says?'

The hostility came as no surprise. Langton glanced at the three men cramped into the rear seat, then back to their leader. 'We have an interest in one of the people inside.'

A man in the back started to say something, but the team leader held up her hand. 'Shut it, Pete,' she said calmly, without taking her eyes off Langton. 'What do you mean, "an interest"? Do you know how many are in there? Even we don't have that, not for certain.'

Another voice came out of the darkness, laced with the toxic anger of the front-line officer left out of the loop. 'So, on your bloody bike and wait till we bring them out.'

Jack Langton sympathised with that, too. It was predictable, understandable.

In their place, any of his surveillance operatives would have reacted in exactly the same way. He knew all about pre-match nerves, the high-octane, gum-chewing silence and recurring clicks from unnecessary weapons checks.

In the inevitable wash-up there would be a row about another Met departure from protocol, with stiff emails about memoranda of understanding and codes of practice flashing their way into New Scotland Yard. The official apology would amount to sod-all. The bosses would spend weeks point-scoring and arse-covering as they toured the bloated chief officers' conference circuit. And while the brass went head to head over the finger buffet, it would be business as usual for the guys on the ground.

Langton held out his mobile to the team leader. 'Sorry, but I have to come with you. Number's on the speed dial. Check it out if you think we've got time to kill.'

Langton was from the north-east, a fanatical Newcastle supporter. Perhaps his soft, deep Geordie accent eased the pain of interference from the Met. More probably, the team leader was a seasoned player. He could sense her weighing power games against the threat to hostages in clear and present danger. Politics versus rescue. Her door opened silently as she prepared to do her duty. Then there were eight of them in the lane, dressed in fire-retardant coveralls and ballistic vests, armed with Heckler & Koch MP5 semi-automatic carbines, Glock 17 pistols, Tasers, CS spray, batons and Speedcuffs. They stood in the rain fixing their ballistic helmets and studying their unexpected guest.

'I won't get in your way,' murmured Langton, putting on his motorcycle helmet.

'He's OK,' whispered the team leader, still taking messages from Simms as she led them to the ditch alongside the fence. 'Heads up, everybody.' She spoke in a whisper, but every word was audible. 'We're assuming three or four targets, probably armed, plus the two hostages.' She nodded at the fence. 'Good cover from the greenery on the other side, then it's a twenty-, thirty-second sprint across grass. Rear door to the right into the kitchen, that's where they're doing the job.'

'Are we still sure they're all working in one room?'

'I'm not certain about anything. The info's limited.'

'This job's a right crock of shit,' murmured another voice from the back.

'We do the best with what we've got. Silent approach, guys, but no pissing about when we get there. Everyone ready?' The team leader took a couple of seconds to look into each face. 'So, let's do it.' On her signal, without hesitation or sound, the eight heavily armed firearms officers, plus Jack Langton, scaled the fence, disappeared into the undergrowth and reassembled. From now on, as trained, they would operate by hand signals.

Hunched in the bushes, the team leader made a final check through binoculars to identify any watchers outside and signs of life beyond the pool of light in the kitchen. She immediately spotted a man chaining the dog outside the door. She exhaled silently. A minute earlier and he might have heard or seen them, but the danger from the dog trumped her relief. 'There's a dog, guys,' she whispered, breaking her own rules. 'Rottweiler.'

'What do we do about that?'

'Run faster and quieter. I'll take care of it.'

Wednesday, 3 July, 00.17, kitchen, Hope Farm

Bray heard Dale returning with the dog. 'Well?' he said, the moment the door opened.

'We're clear,' he said.

The Browning was lying on the worktop beside him, but Bray was holding out his palm again. Sammy went over to the high-chairs, picked up the sawn-off shotgun and 9mm Sigma handgun. He handed the Sigma to Bray and stood guard by the door with the sawn-off. Covering her, Bray tossed Mel the Browning. 'So he's yours. Make it a head shot.'

She held the gun loosely at her side. 'Just leave them here. It's not as if they're going anywhere.'

Bray raised the Sigma against her head. It was as if she had finally convinced him about something he had suspected all along. He pressed so hard that the barrel made an indentation in her temple. 'You were last in, Mel. You gonna be first out?'

She kept the Browning by her side. 'You really want me to waste a cop? Are you crazy, or what?' She tried to turn her head to Bray's accomplice in chief. 'Sammy, are you ready to do life? Talk to him.'

But Sammy moved even closer beside Bray. 'Do what the man says.'

Mel swayed her head sideways, away from the Sigma, but Bray just kept on pressing. With his free hand Bray clenched her neck, forcing her head against the Sigma. He studied the cop's eyes as he stared at Mel. It was a look of pleading, and he seemed to be mouthing something. Yes, they knew each other.

Then he saw Mel raise the Browning in both hands and swing it through an arc to fire a single round into the cop's right knee. And he clocked the astonishment in the man's eyes as he screamed and collapsed to the floor in agony. Mel dropped the gun and knelt to staunch the wound, his blood flowing down her hands and arms.

'I said do him in the head,' said Bray, giving her thigh a gentle kick. 'Leave him there. Get the van ready . . . What the fuck?'

Outside, the Rottweiler was suddenly going crazy again. Then there was a *pop*, followed by silence. In the same instant the kitchen door crashed in and an army of ninjas steamed into the kitchen, Heckler & Kochs identifying their targets. One of them hit Bray as he was about to shout something. It was a woman, which angered him even more. He caught up with his jaw as she dropped him to the floor.

Bray watched them overpower Mel, Sammy and Dale, then attend to the two injured cops. They seemed to work as a single unit, which impressed him. Everyone was shouting at them and screaming for paramedics. One of them charged into the hall, presumably to open the gates.

Flat on the floor on his belly, hands high behind his back, Bray forced his head sideways to see a tall man in black motorcycle leathers, shiny from the rain, standing by the door. He was wearing his helmet, with the tinted visor lowered to hide his face. Bray could tell that this man was different, set apart from the other raiders by his demeanour as much as his clothing, and the separateness intrigued him. Bray watched him cross the room, murmur something to the armed cop holding Mel, then drag her away. By the door she struggled, but it was half-hearted resistance against someone she knew, not that of a prisoner fighting a cop. Bray watched her glance back at the man she had just shot, then the cop bleeding on the floor, who was staring at her. He saw the connection in their eyes. And then, most remarkably of all, he witnessed the injured cop draw his lips back in a snarl as he mouthed a single, unmistakable word: '*Bitch.*'

Humiliated on his own kitchen floor, a woman's knee on his neck, a female hand pulling his hair, Terry Bray made space for grim satisfaction. Mel's face had left him in no doubt that the two knew each other; and the cop's word had told him his instincts had been right all along.

Five

John Kerr's home was a refurbished apartment in Islington, north London, on the top floor of a Victorian mansion block overlooking Upper Street. It was light and airy, with high ceilings and the original cornices. There were two bedrooms, a large living room and a custom-built kitchen installed by the previous owners. Kerr's favourite place was the balcony where, in the summer, he would often spend the last moments before bed, enjoying the city's tranquillity over a nightcap of Irish whiskey.

In light blue cotton T-shirt, dark trackies and scuffed white trainers, he sat there now, waiting for an update on Melanie from Jack Langton as Sky News drifted out from the living room. He had just returned from a late-night run with his daughter, Gabriella, who was already asleep in the spare bedroom. Gabi was a Royal College of Music violin postgraduate. She shared a flat close to the Royal Albert Hall with two other music students but also stayed the occasional night with Kerr or her mother, Robyn, in Rome.

Robyn had been one of Kerr's unwitting security targets during a long-term undercover assignment more than two decades before. Against all the rules, and without Robyn knowing his true identity, Kerr had suggested sex one drunken night in the back of his van. Gabi, the outcome, had brought pleasure to Robyn, a confession from Kerr and a surprisingly workable relationship as they raised their child in separate countries. Seven years of estrangement between father and daughter had come to a shattering end the previous winter, when Gabi had witnessed Kerr come within a heartbeat of losing his life in a terrorist attack. Since that catastrophic moment they had worked hard at reconciliation and Kerr loved his daughter more than anyone else in the world.

This should have been a late-night celebration, for Gabi had just won an audition with the Royal Philharmonic Orchestra. She had been rehearsing until nine, reaching Kerr's apartment an hour later. The late evening run had been her idea, to be followed by pasta at their favourite haunt off Upper Street, then back to the apartment for Dad's champagne on ice.

Long experience had taught Kerr to respect the unexpected, so he always carried his BlackBerry, just in case. It had rung deep in his pocket as he and Gabi jogged the residential streets bordering Highbury Fields. The screen showed 23:47. Melanie's voice had been measured, the crisis understated, but it had stopped Kerr in his tracks. 'I just heard a shot fired inside the house. I think you need to get me out of here.' In Kerr's world, such calls were coded 'Detox': an operative on a covert mission in clear and present danger, in need of immediate extraction. From the street, struggling to control his breathing, Kerr had immediately deployed Langton, the only man on his team capable of challenging the sound barrier.

When Jack Langton's call came through, it had Kerr on the run again. Langton had flattened his bass Geordie voice to the monotone cops keep in reserve to admit the wheel has well and truly come off. Kerr grabbed a sweatshirt and was out of the door in twenty seconds, racing down the steps to the underground garage and blue-lighting his white Alfa Romeo 156T Spark as soon as he had cleared the ramp. Kerr and Melanie

Fleming went back a long way. A little more than a year earlier she had been one of his closest allies in ripping the lid from a political conspiracy reaching the highest levels of government. As he tore up Highbury Park towards Seven Sisters Road, he wondered if she would ever agree to work for him again.

Kerr was heading for a decaying Victorian police station at Enfield, a suburb ten miles away in the far reaches of north London. In the late eighties the Flying Squad had adapted part of the building to house their highest-value supergrasses until they could find something more permanent. Tonight it was serving as a temporary place of safety for Melanie, whom Langton had spirited there on the back of his bike after extracting her from the disaster at Hope Farm.

Kerr raced north through Stoke Newington, Tottenham and Edmonton, accelerating to almost ninety along a clear stretch beside King George's Reservoir near Ponders End. His mind sprinted ahead of the car. If half of what Langton had just told him was true, he was heading into another tornado that could finally destroy his career. For now, though, his thoughts lasered on Melanie and her family as he sliced a path between drunk drivers, taxis and night buses, reaching the safe house at twelve thirty-eight. The Alfa had flashed him there in just seventeen minutes.

Still in his motorcycle leathers shining wet from the rain, the unzipped top half spilling over his trousers, Langton was waiting for him in what the facilities manager had referred to as the 'relaxation area', a converted interview room about twelve paces square with one of the two fluorescent strip-lights on the blink. The room was windowless and still had its original reinforced door. A couple of worn black-leather armchairs, hollowed out by a generation of heavy-duty guests, were separated by a battered Mexican coffee-table. On opposite walls frameless prints of *The Haywain* and *The Fighting Temeraire* hung lopsided, and a twenty-seven-inch plasma TV was fixed to the wall opposite the door above a sagging red sofa-bed. Since the conversion three decades ago, the walls and carpet had remained lime-coloured, or 'supergrass green', as the Flying Squad had regularly joked to their tabloid drinking buddies.

Langton was perched on one of the armchairs, with his crash helmet, draining coffee from a paper cup. He pulled a face and tossed it into a bin. 'Machine's by the bog, but don't bother.'

'Where is she?'

Langton nodded over his shoulder. There was the sound of water running from the bathroom next door. 'Taking a shower.'

'Is someone with her?'

Langton shook his head. 'She's pretty bad. Didn't want to leave Rob. Fought me all the way from the plot. I had to chuck her over the fence, practically strap her to the pillion. This is not good, John.'

'What do you have?'

'Only part of the story. Rob was on standby, almost at the end of his shift, around nine. The National scrambled him and his mate the moment they heard Bray was bringing the exportation forward forty-eight hours.'

'Melanie's call at eight forty-five.'

'If you say so.' Langton shrugged. 'I've been on the road.'

'They're both at Tommy's, right?'

'Rob, yes. Since twenty minutes ago. But they took Jim Marshall to North Middlesex.'

'Which means Rob is more serious.'

'He's going to need surgery, apparently.'

'What a fuck-up.' Kerr exhaled. 'All right, Jack. I'll take it from here.'

'You sure?'

Kerr knew that Jack Langton, recently remarried, had a young child, with another on the way. 'Hey, I know you've had a hell of a long day . . .'

'It's no problem.' Langton was already zipping up his leathers. He grabbed his helmet. 'I'll go back to the farm. Find the moron who—'

They both turned as the door crashed open. Melanie was standing before them. Her soaking hair, normally shoulder length but cropped for the operation, was slicked back. She looked shorter than usual, until Kerr realised she had nothing on her feet. She was wearing baggy tracksuit bottoms the same colour as Kerr's and a light grey short-sleeved vest, also several sizes too large.

Langton took a step back in mock surprise. 'Which joker gave you those?' It was the kind of quip that, as a former sports teacher, he might have used on the sports field. Or he might have meant it as an ice-breaker, a stab at levity after Melanie's brush with death and race to safety. Whichever, it was the wrong thing to say.

'Jack, why don't you piss off?' she snapped, pushing past Langton into the room. Kerr saw that the right side of her face and both arms were covered with scratches and glanced at Langton. He hoped they were from the brambles, not their struggle at Hope Farm.

When Langton had closed the door behind him, Kerr stood facing her. Despite the shower, Melanie's fingers were heavily oil-stained from working on Terry Bray's van, and the blotchiness covering her face was from tears, not hot water. Kerr's heart went out to her as she stood weeping before him. They were a decade and two ranks apart, but when Kerr took a step forward and held her tight, he was comforting her as a father would his daughter.

'Christ, what have I done?' sobbed Melanie. 'I had to shoot him. Bray was going to kill both of us.'

Kerr felt her relax into him, hair wet against his cheek. 'Whatever went wrong, we're all going to have to deal with it.'

Melanie pulled away and looked up at him. 'But you understand, don't you? That I had no choice?'

Kerr took off his sweatshirt and helped her on with it.

'Please tell me Rob's not going to die,' said Melanie, as her head reappeared.

'Rob's at St Tommy's. They're going to operate.'

'You have to take me to him right now.'

'Where are your clothes?'

'Covered with my husband's blood,' said Melanie, flatly.

In the Alfa, Melanie slumped in the front passenger seat as they raced south through the deserted streets to Westminster. To Kerr, she seemed weighed down by the guilt of what she had done. Near St John's Wood, without asking, Kerr stopped at a petrol station to buy her a Mars bar for energy. She stared through him, motionless, as he returned from the pay kiosk, then took the chocolate and devoured it in three bites, without a word.

Only when Kerr accelerated through a red light on the approach to Westminster Bridge, with St Thomas's Hospital in view across the river, did she seem to revive. 'I might have killed him, for God's sake,' she said, above the noise of the racing engine, as if the thought had just occurred to her. 'Left our children without a father. And all because of that stupid, sodding need-to-know crap.'

'No. The Detox call saved his life.'

'You know I don't mean that one. I'm talking about my earlier message to Dodge. About the forty-eight-hour delay. They deployed Rob and the other bloke because of that, didn't they?'

'It's still confused. Jack will find out.'

'You can drop the bullshit. If it hadn't been for my information Rob would be home with the family by now. Instead he's probably going to lose his leg. I lured him to that farm, to Terry Bray and those evil bastards. Then I kneecapped him. This is down to me.'

'That's ridiculous.'

'End of. I'm no better than the bloody IRA.' Melanie glared back at Kerr, eyes full of reproach. 'John, how could you let this happen?'

'Rob's going to be OK.'

'You think so?' She gave a harsh laugh. 'You weren't in that kitchen.'

'Trust me.'

'You don't know what he said to me.' Kerr sensed Melanie's eyes drop to her lap. Her voice fell, too, and sounded choked, full of despair. 'And don't make me go there. But Rob is going to hate me for destroying his career.'

There had always been a special relationship between New Scotland Yard and St Thomas's Hospital, just across the Thames. Flashing his ID at Reception, Kerr led Melanie through automatic double doors into Accident and Emergency. 'Situation normal,' he whispered, as they made their way through Westminster's shadowy underclass of drunks, homeless and the fallen.

The night-duty sister was from the Seychelles, immaculate, no-nonsense and kind. Kerr recognised her from a previous visit with one of Langton's surveillance officers injured in a car smash. He shook hands and asked after her husband, a sergeant from Fulham she had met when testing him for hepatitis B from the blood of a stabbed drug-dealer.

She led them to a cubicle at the side of the plaster room, tiny but private, and pulled the curtain across. Before speaking she glanced at Melanie, taking in the dishevelled appearance and signs of violence. 'I'm sorry. You are . . .?'

'The bitch that shot him.'

'Next of kin,' said Kerr.

The sister looked unsure for a moment, then told them everything about Rob. Evidently the paramedics had wheeled him from the ambulance direct to triage. Within thirty minutes of his arrival the doctor had sterilised the wound, taken X-rays and rung the orthopaedic surgeon on call. With another glance at Melanie, she said the wound inflicted by her single shot to Rob's right leg was 'serious', the depth of the bone and ligament damage so traumatic that the specialist had decided to operate that night.

'When can I see him?' said Melanie.

The sister hesitated. 'Is that a good idea?' she said tentatively. She focused on Kerr, as if hoping he would decline.

'It's all right,' said Kerr. 'Please.'

She took them to a room in the far corner of the unit. Rob was tubed up and scarcely conscious, and Kerr could tell he was pumped full of pre-med. A nurse was prepping him for theatre, but the sister gestured her outside. 'Two minutes,' she said to Kerr, closing the door on them.

Kerr took a quick look at Rob, then stepped back to give Melanie space. She took Rob's free hand and spoke urgently into his ear, repeating over and over that she was so sorry. Rob was trying to say something back. She put her ear right against his mouth, but Kerr could hear every word.

'The kids,' he murmured. 'And Mum. Don't tell.'

'Tell them what, darling? That you've been hurt?' Melanie glanced round at Kerr. 'But they'll want to come and visit you in the morning.'

'No, not that,' he said, trying to pull his hand away from hers. 'What you fucking did to me.'

He seemed to fall unconscious then, as Melanie dropped her head on his chest and sobbed as if her heart would break.

Kerr led her outside gently and told her he would speak with Rob's mother. This was for reasons that were both professional and personal. Kerr's instincts were already telling him he needed to control the information flow – and he was beginning to find Melanie's guilt contagious. 'You need to rest,' he said. 'Come and get your head down at my place. Gabi can shift up, no problem.'

In the corridor outside A and E, as they watched the porters wheel Rob down to theatre, Melanie seemed to read Kerr's mind. 'I'll talk to Brenda myself,' she said, 'seeing as it's all my fault.'

'All you have to say is that Rob's been injured at work and they're checking him out. Keep it simple,' said Kerr. As the gurney taking Rob disappeared into the lift he grasped Melanie's shoulders and turned her to face him. 'Melanie, it's the middle of the night. No need to upset her now.'

'I almost killed her son, John,' said Melanie. She looked up from dialling, flushed with anger. 'Do you think it's going to sound any better in the morning?'

Six

Big Ben was striking the quarter-hour through his open window as Kerr drove across Westminster Bridge back to the Yard. The air was cool through his T-shirt but he would need to be wide awake to deal with the troubles that lay ahead. He was alone. Melanie had insisted on staying the night at the hospital, close to Rob, so one of the nurses had let her use a couch in their rest station next door to the recovery room.

He parked the Alfa in the underground car park, took the lift to the high-security area on the eighteenth floor and headed for his tiny room. Kerr's workplace was little more than a glass-partitioned rectangle five paces by three. It was tucked away in a corner of an open-plan office that covered a quarter of the floor space, with an ill-fitting door he rarely bothered to force shut. There was scarcely room for the desk and a couple of hard chairs, so additional visitors generally leant against the glass or sat on the carpet tiles. In a small floor safe he kept a kettle and his Glock 19 semi-automatic pistol, both strictly against regulations.

The workplace looked temporary and did not appear in any floor plan, yet Kerr had been there for more than three years. Officers who worked around him referred to his room as the 'Fishbowl' because Kerr was always visible from any part of the office, except on rare occasions when he shut himself off behind dusty, lopsided Venetian blinds. On the plus side it also meant he could watch what was going on around him, which was the way he liked things.

The deserted main office was in darkness. Kerr flicked on his desk lamp, making a solitary pool of light in the vastness of the eighteenth floor. He unlocked the safe and connected his laptop. *John, how could you let this happen?* Melanie's plea still rang in his ears. His priority was to discover the facts. He needed to assess just how bad things would get before the morning, when the bosses would start covering their arses. Kerr had been around long enough to know that, whatever the operational outcome, the political fallout was going to be nuclear.

While the laptop fired up he filled the kettle in the men's washroom, plugged it into the socket by his feet and called Dodge, head of his source unit. Dodge had recruited and handled Seagull, the murdered Somali agent. He had also held responsibility for the day-to-day management of Melanie's undercover operation. Dodge's voicemail kicked in, the accent suggesting he had never left Belfast. Kerr was not surprised: he expected Dodge to be working the phones through the night to get to the bottom of the disaster around Hope Farm.

Most of the Yard's creaking infrastructure was asleep but the air-con, so often cranky during the high days of summer, was cooling the empty building at full power. Kerr reached for the emergency sweater he kept in his bottom drawer, Googled North Middlesex Hospital and called A and E to check on Rob's partner. The receptionist immediately rang him back through the Yard's switchboard, to be sure of his identity. Jim Marshall's condition was evidently much less serious than Rob's, for the bullet had made a clean wound through the leg above the knee joint. He would undergo minor surgery later that morning but was expected to make a full recovery. The realisation that Melanie had inflicted more damage to Rob than Terry Bray had to Marshall made Kerr wince.

Waiting for Dodge to return his call, he poured black coffee into a red mug Gabi had brought him from Rome, now chipped in two places, and checked his email. Jack Langton had forwarded the current batch of surveillance taskings. On the screen were operations against four home-grown jihadis conducted jointly with MI5, an anti-globalisation protester suspected of a firebombing, and a terrorist financier from south London. As usual, Langton's teams were overstretched and Kerr estimated they could only maintain coverage at this level for another seventy-two hours, tops. Later that morning he would work with Langton through the intelligence product, then make fingers-crossed decisions about which targets to drop from the radar.

Kerr missed the figure emerging from the darkness in the main office.

'How is she?'

Kerr recognised the voice, but not the scuffed loafers and muddy, thick green corduroys that appeared in the overspill from his lamp. He pushed back in the chair. 'She just shot her husband. Shattered his leg and almost got herself killed. How do you think?'

Kerr felt a storm building as Detective Chief Superintendent Bill Ritchie squeezed into the chair opposite his desk. Ritchie was a career Special Branch officer, like Kerr, and head of SO15 intelligence operations. He would carry ultimate responsibility for the night's disaster. 'And I should put one between your eyes right now.'

'Bill, can't this wait till the morning?'

'How the hell could you let this happen?' said Ritchie, driving Melanie's words even deeper into Kerr's brain.

'Who told you?'

'Does it matter?'

Kerr regarded Ritchie's angry face. He bent down and flicked the kettle on again. 'Want some coffee?'

'Don't change the subject.'

When they were in private, the two men often spoke candidly, free of deference and bullshit. Ritchie had been Kerr's off-and-on boss for nearly twenty years, working on more risky operations than either could remember. 'Separated by rank but joined at the hip,' was how Jack Langton described them.

'I was just about to call you,' lied Kerr.

Unshaven, greying hair flat from the pillow on one side, Ritchie had thrown on a shabby sweatshirt to go with the corduroys, as if he had come straight from the garden. 'When I last checked, Terry Bray was a serious organised criminal. National Crime Agency territory. Bugger all to do with us. What suddenly elevated him into a national-security target?'

'A phone call.'

Ritchie looked thunderous. 'We almost lost two officers tonight, so I expect a lot better than that.'

'One of the thugs who murdered Seagull last month had rung Terry Bray on the mobile I grabbed from their boat. The log shows Monday, June the tenth, at fourteen oh seven. That's the day I intercepted them. Terry Bray was involved in the smuggling of the stolen US gold from the outset.'

'Which still sounds like crime to me.'

'Political crime,' said Kerr, as the kettle clicked off. He bent down to make Ritchie's coffee, black, no sugar. 'Bill, I'm saying this was a plan to damage the US. Forget gold as a precious metal. They were using it as a political weapon. And we have to think that way, too.'

Ritchie rotated the coffee mug, checking the rim for chips. 'Meaning?'

'The gold was in transit from the US to Hong Kong, transported in a special US flight overnight on Saturday, March the second, and stored in a Bank of England vault less than a mile from Heathrow for twenty-four hours max. No one knew it was coming here. The consignment was ultra-secret. Tight enough to make terrorist rendition look like a budget flight to Barcelona.'

Ritchie reached up to scratch the back of his neck, revealing a flash of pyjama under his sweatshirt. 'Who knew on our side?'

'Only a handful in government were briefed on it, starting with the minister. The theft was overnight Sunday, quietest time of the week. No violence, no forced entry. They knew everything. So you have someone at the top of the pile tipping off an enemy of the US intending to remove the gold from London. Inside betrayal facilitating external attack, with America the victim. Not great for the special relationship.'

'And the investigation got nowhere.'

'Not a thing leaked out. Until Seagull came along. The gangsters hired him because of his politics. That's my point.'

'What the hell does that mean?'

There was a crash from far down inside the main office, followed by a couple of oaths. Ritchie swung round to peer into the darkness. 'Dodge?'

Kerr was searching his drawer for the sweeteners he kept for Ritchie. He slid them across the desk with a coffee-stained spoon. 'I'll let the man tell you himself.'

Seven

Wednesday, 3 July, 01.41; the Fishbowl

Dodge appeared from the gloom, squeezed past Ritchie into the remaining chair and vigorously rubbed his right knee. He was more dishevelled than usual, still in his baggy, ill-fitting suit. 'Morning,' he said, hunching forward over the desk to remove his jacket in the confined space. The smell of cigarettes wafted through the tiny office. He looked at Kerr. 'Sorry I missed your call. Been kicking arses.'

'I guessed,' said Kerr.

Dodge wheezed. 'And Jack's on his way in.'

'You OK, Dodge?' said Ritchie.

'Good.'

'He always looks like that,' said Kerr. The man clearly needed a caffeine boost so Kerr reached for the coffee jar again. 'Dodge, I'm trying to explain to the boss that this job was always political. Down to us. I was just going to tell him about Seagull. Perhaps he'll take it from you.'

Kerr was not joking. The veteran who managed his source unit was a former RUC Special Branch officer who had spent years in west Belfast running agents. He was in his mid-fifties, a couple of years older than Ritchie, and everyone called him Dodge, though no one knew why any more. He had received multiple threats to his life. On two occasions his RUC bosses had lifted him with his wife and daughter overnight from their home into secure temporary accommodation.

In 2002, four years after the Good Friday Agreement, the Real IRA had attempted to assassinate him as he drove across the border. 'I felt the hand of history all right,' he had once told Kerr, 'against the back of my fucking head.' It had been time to get out of Northern Ireland. Dodge had moved his family to Edinburgh, then in 2009 to Ruislip, a quiet suburb of north-west London.

He took a sip of instant coffee and winced. 'Yeah, I suppose I knew that kid better than anyone. Except his poor wee wife. Seagull had been putting it about that he hated America. For Iraq, Guantánamo and all the rest. That was the pitch I gave him, to reel in the bad guys. They would use him, and we would get to them. It worked for a while. But then it cost him his life.' Dodge paused and Kerr threw Ritchie a warning glance. Kerr knew that Seagull was the only agent Dodge had lost in his entire career, and that the scars ran deep. Dodge had admitted that every visit to Seagull's widow and children made him sick with guilt.

Dodge took a deep breath and swirled his coffee. 'Anyway, these boys must have believed him, the same as everyone else. He had a small car-repair business in Rotherhithe. One-man band doing OK with a bit of extra cash from us to keep him afloat. Some welding on the side and other bits and pieces. Mostly legit. The two boys John saw off approached him in his workshop. They knew about his politics. They shut the doors and asked him if he wanted to help them damage America. "How far do you want to see America fall?" That's what they said to him. Exact words. Then they contracted him to adapt the boat. Special floor to support the weight of the gold. Strengthen the transom to take the oversized engine. Fit ballast for the test run, same weight as the gold. But they chose him for his extreme political beliefs, not his engineering ability. That's the point of it. They were testing our man on how deeply he hated, not how much he could earn. John's right. This was ideological. About sabotage, not greed.'

'And who were they,' said Ritchie, 'the two hoods?'

'Well, he didn't get the chance to find out, did he?' said Dodge. Everyone listened to the droning air-con for a minute.

'Is it possible they found out he was speaking to us? Could he have been betrayed?'

'No. Dispensable is what our boy was. Used up and then murdered.' Dodge's head went down again, sinking under the awful possibility that Seagull had been blown. 'If I'm honest, it's something I'd rather not think about.'

'So where did they come from?' said Ritchie.

'Seagull always insisted they were foreign intelligence agents. He knew enough criminals to be sure these were not your average south London scrotes. Seagull overheard them taking a call in his workshop, arguing about the number of bars for each load.'

'That's what robbers do,' said Ritchie.

'No, this was different. They used a special mobile Seagull hadn't seen before. He drew me a sketch and it was obviously a satellite phone. I sent it down to Camberwell for Justin to take a look.' Dodge reached into his jacket for a tiny hardback notebook. The cover was pink, at odds with everything about him, and Kerr wondered where he had found it. 'A Thuraya or an Inmarsat, according to Justin. These are phones you use in, I dunno, Kabul, not Rotherhithe. Very unusual in towns and cities, unless you have to avoid cell-site interception. And Seagull said it was weird to see such aggressive guys intimidated by a phone call. They called the man at the other end Peter.'

'Go on,' said Ritchie.

'That was the last I heard from Seagull. Next thing I knew he was dead.' Suddenly Dodge looked away, covered his mouth and coughed, an echoing, smoker's rattle that masked his emotion. 'Game over for a brave little guy.'

Ritchie rubbed his chin and turned to Kerr. 'So, are you trying to persuade me they also used Bray for his politics, not his greed?'

'Who knows?' said Kerr. 'I'm saying that phone call on June the tenth gives us the direct link between a hostile intelligence agency and Bray. When the waterborne plan went wrong, they used Bray as a fall-back. Which makes this case national security as well as criminal. Special Branch territory, Bill. We should have handled the whole job from start to finish. It should never have gone to the National Crime Agency.'

A deep voice came from the darkness in the doorway. 'And not Essex, either.' Unlike Dodge, Jack Langton had made his way through the darkness in complete silence and Kerr wondered how long he had been hiding there, absorbing Ritchie's scepticism. Langton grabbed a chair from the main office, sat in the doorway and nodded to Ritchie. 'Morning, boss.' His leathers were shiny from the rain, the front spattered with mud, and water dripped to the floor as he laid the helmet at his feet and swept his hair back.

Kerr estimated Langton had been on duty non-stop for nineteen hours, though his face was ruddy and fresh from the race between the Yard and Hope Farm. Catching his reflection in the glass partition, Ritchie ran a hand through his hair but most of it sprang back to where it had been. 'So why did the National take it?'

'Because Specialist Crime downstairs insisted,' said Kerr. 'Basically they were pissed off with the way I handled the business on the Thames. But they were working with a large-scale map of the Thames and a finger in the air. Put the Trojans in the wrong places. Their cock-up embarrassed them, so they wanted us out of the game. That's my take on it, anyway. Commander was in the US and you weren't around to fly the flag, so I negotiated with the National direct.'

'John's right, boss,' said Langton. 'Everyone wanted a piece of the action. It was bound to go tits up sooner or later. This should have been kept in-house. Dodge to manage Melanie's undercover deployment, me to run the surveillance at the farm and bring in our own Trojans for the assault. That way Melanie would never have come face to face with her husband and there would have been no blue on blue.'

'So whose brilliant idea was it to lend Melanie?' said Ritchie, looking hard at Kerr. 'Yours, I suppose?'

'Theirs,' said Kerr. 'The National Crime Agency don't know who they can trust any more within their own organisation, so they came to ours. They're paranoid about Bray's ability to corrupt police. It goes back decades and they have a name for it, the "legacy of contagion". How do you think Bray has managed to stay out of prison all these years? Isn't it obvious? He always knew when he was being watched because he had people telling him. Gold-plated insider information.'

'Speculation.'

'Fact, according to the National. But we're the outsiders, Bill, highly vetted and clean, with no debts owing to scum like Terry Bray. I contracted Melanie out to Ray Gatting at the National on the condition that the secret stayed with him alone and that Dodge managed her. No one else within the National was to know.'

Ritchie was slowly shaking his head. 'What a cock-up.'

'Is that why you dragged yourself out of bed,' said Kerr, 'to give me a bollocking?'

'What time was Melanie's Detox call?'

'About three hours later, shortly before midnight,' said Kerr. 'Shots fired inside the farm. She called me because Dodge's phone was engaged.'

Dodge shifted in the chair, his bulky frame jogging Kerr's desk. 'Still dealing with the original info.'

'And I was on a late-night run,' said Kerr, indicating his clothes.

'So how did they brief the assault team?'

'That's where I came in, boss,' said Langton. 'I watched out for her.'

'You dragged her out of the house and threw her over the fence,' said Ritchie, without taking his eyes off Kerr. 'If you'd bothered to run the job past me I'd never have allowed it. Who signed off on Melanie's deployment?'

'You,' said Kerr, surprised, then concerned by his forgetfulness. Ritchie had recently suffered a recurrence of the prostate cancer he had had two years ago. He evidently believed he had kept his treatment secret, but Kerr knew about it because Ritchie's wife, Lynn, had confided in him. It had accounted for his frequent absences from the office. Kerr located a folder on his laptop and swivelled the screen to face Ritchie. 'The green light came from you, Bill.'

Ritchie stayed silent for a few moments, remembering. He reached awkwardly to scratch his back; for a split second Dodge seemed about to do the job for him.

'For Terry Bray there are two types of cop,' said Kerr. 'The straight guys in his rear-view mirror following him and the crooked bastards keeping warm in his pocket. Yet Melanie spent weeks right in his face. She schmoozed his wife, played with his twins, patted his dog. And Bray never saw a thing.'

Eight

With her face to the sun, Anna Rashid stood leaning against her dark red Vauxhall Corsa and bit into a cheese roll. She was illegally parked in a quiet residential street within easy walking distance of Wormwood Scrubs prison. The car was twelve years old, though she had only acquired it the previous week in preparation for today. It had two doors and was covered with dents and scrapes; there was a faded 'England – World Cup 2006' sticker on the rear windscreen.

Rashid had her eyes on a round, tiled pedestrian tunnel cut through the tube-line embankment from Du Cane Road, which ran alongside the main gate with its 'Family and Visitors' Centre'. A yellow sign said the tunnel was monitored by CCTV so she had found a space about thirty paces away beside a Catholic church, half hidden between a black taxi and a florist's van. The air was warm, yet she was in the jeans, Doc Martens, shirt and mid-length coat she wore every day of the year. These were her anarchist clothes, everything black, and she had dressed like this ever since she'd become radicalised at Brighton University a decade ago.

She was waiting for Danny Brennan, who was about to be released after serving nine months for his part in the London riots of summer 2012. Brennan had been convicted of ransacking three shops in Tottenham. The cops alleged he had also intended to destroy a men's outfitters using a home-made firebomb, but had been unable to prove it.

At Rashid's feet a couple of pigeons were squabbling over crumbs from her breakfast. Distracted, she failed to spot Brennan emerge from the tunnel. The two had never met but she immediately recognised him from his description: five feet ten, slim build, with shoulder-length hair and straggly beard, red shirt and black jeans. She felt a spark of irritation that he must have clocked her first from the wrong side of the street, while her eyes were on the gutter. He was carrying his possessions in a blue and green Tesco 'bag for life' and she wondered whether he had looted that, too.

She watched him cross the street and amble towards her, wondering how he would make himself known. Because she had been ordered to assert control from the outset, she decided to say nothing. She leant against the driver's door, legs loosely crossed at the ankles and completely still as he drew level. 'Hi,' he said. She gave a slight nod but kept her face expressionless. On the church wall a giant banner read, 'Alive and Kicking! God Sees Hope in You!' She could have broken the ice with a joke, but instead got back behind the wheel.

Brennan climbed in beside her and tossed the bag into the back as the engine refused to start. At the third attempt, with the starter motor running down, Rashid swore under her breath. Caught out twice in less than three minutes, she hoped Brennan would stay silent. It was hot in the car so Brennan tried to wind down the passenger window, but the handle was jammed. She leant across, twisted it in a certain way, shoved her palm against the glass and lowered it for him. He gave a short cough or laugh, his breath striking her cheek, but still no words. She caught a wave of fresh sweat as she leant over him. His smell instantly revived the memory of her Muslim lover Parvez Rashid, murdered by the state, whose name she still bore. For a second Parvez's body was on hers again, and she felt a spasm of pain.

The car started at the next attempt. She revved the engine, made a three-point turn and swung left into the busy Westway. At the first roundabout she turned right into Wood Lane, heading towards Shepherd's Bush. Traffic was heavy as they entered Shepherds Bush Green, with roadworks on the inside lane and a broken-down lorry stranded in front of the war memorial, and Rashid rarely changed above second gear. Something was wrong with the accelerator: the engine kept surging without warning, propelling them towards the tail-lights in front and forcing her to brake hard. The pads must have worn down because she sometimes had to compensate with the handbrake, and there was a strong smell of rubber.

'They never told me you had such a shit car,' said Brennan.

'So fix it,' said Rashid, sliding him a glance. 'Isn't that what you're supposed to be good at?'

At the western border of the green, Rashid stopped in a bus lane outside the Australian Walkabout pub, just short of the post office. She scraped up five one-pound coins from the driver's door compartment, dropped them into his cupped hands and gestured to the north side. 'I'll wait for you up there.'

Brennan got out of the car and loped to the post office as Rashid leant forward over the wheel, watching until he disappeared. A bus pulled up behind her, headlights flashing in her mirror. She revved the engine, cut across three lanes of traffic without indicating and veered right, tracing the perimeter back towards Wood Lane. Halfway up the main drag she took a left, turned and squeezed into a space between a pound shop and a tanning salon, nudging the bumper of the car behind as she reversed. She felt the stare of a girl having her nails treated as she got out of the car and took up watch on the post office, just visible three hundred metres away through the trees.

A busker was in full flow on the concourse outside the tube station, within shouting distance of where Rashid was standing. He had an over-amplified guitar and a giant plastic water bottle for a bass drum, and was working through a Johnny Cash repertoire. She had to wait fifteen minutes before Brennan reappeared and threaded his way back to her through the shoppers. When they were in the car again he produced a strip of four passport photographs from the booth inside the post office. He waved it, as if it was still damp from the processor, then handed it over. To Rashid, carefully studying each image, he seemed like a child expecting praise. She let him wait, dropping the strip into the driver's door compartment.

This time the engine started at the first turn. Rashid regained Wood Lane and swung right at the Westway, heading for central London. It took nearly an hour to reach Marble Arch, then another ten minutes stop-starting through Hyde Park Corner. At Victoria she carried on south-east, crossing the river at Vauxhall Bridge. With the green and glass structure of the MI6 headquarters filling her mirror, she swung away towards Nine Elms, then turned right towards the river, coming to a halt on a piece of raised ground.

The scene Rashid had visited several times on foot now induced a stab of anxiety, so she left the engine running. Directly in front of them was a massive building site with three giant cranes, four concrete mixers and a row of tipper trucks. They sat in silence, the air through Brennan's open window alive with reversing beeps, men's shouts and the clanging of automated labour.

Brennan looked sideways and raised his eyebrows.

'The new American embassy,' said Rashid.

'So?'

'Remember this day and this place.' She pushed the Corsa into first. 'You and I are going to return here soon.'

Nine

They retraced their way past Vauxhall Cross and continued along Albert Embankment. Dead ahead they saw a skip lorry collide with a dark blue motor scooter careering onto the roundabout from Lambeth Bridge. The rider was a young girl with fine, shoulder-length brown hair spilling beneath her helmet and she had fixed a giant plastic red nose for Comic Relief above the headlamp. The lorry catapulted her into the air, right in front of their eyes, as the scooter hurtled into a tree on the other side of the road, engine still racing. The girl struck the iron railings bordering Lambeth Palace, then bounced back onto the road like a doll, motionless, helmet and limbs askew. Rashid and Brennan were the nearest witnesses, but neither spoke a word nor took a second glance. The lorry driver sat stunned in his cab as Rashid swerved round the body, then fiddled with the radio and switched on LBC as if nothing had happened.

Soon she became aware of Brennan easing back in his seat as they surged and braked their way along the riverbank. She felt more comfortable now with the space between them: Brennan's completion of the first task had smoothed the edginess. That and the recce, with the realisation of what they might be capable of together. They crossed the river again at Waterloo Bridge, then drove through Aldwych into Fleet

Street. By the Law Courts Rashid slowed, peering across at the layout of the narrow streets leading down to the sets of barristers' chambers, then continued east towards the Tower of London.

Rashid half hoped Brennan would ask her where they were headed so that she could blank him. Beyond Whitechapel she turned right into Bethnal Green Road and cruised past a long row of shops. There was an Indian takeaway, a pawnbroker and a clutch of pound and charity shops before they drove through the market and turned left by the Mason's Arms pub, its side wall held upright by giant timber supports, a huge England flag hanging limply from the upper windows.

Two daytime drinkers loitered on the pavement outside the pub. A young man in baggy tracksuit bottoms and trainers, white football shirt stretched taut over his belly, clutched a pint of lager. He was sharing a cigarette with an emaciated woman in her fifties, opposites attracted by tobacco and boredom. Rashid felt their eyes vaguely track the Corsa, then drift back to the middle distance. She had switched to a higher level of alertness now, on the lookout for threats.

This street was much wider than other turnings off the main road, with cars parked at each kerb and easily enough space for passing traffic. To the left, beyond the pub, were industrial premises, SeeJay Autos – MOTs, Servicing, Body Repairs, a tyre and exhaust workshop ('New and Part Used from £12'), and Sonny's Print and Reprographic Studio. The other side was given over to residential properties, mostly two-storey maisonette cubes built during the eighties.

Beyond the print shop, out of tune with the rest of the street, there was a row of nine Victorian terraced houses, with small front gardens, mostly concreted over, and waist-high brick walls bordering the pavement. Their condition varied greatly, some freshly painted and others left to decay, dirty curtains and rubbish left at the front. Opposite the terrace there was an open area about a third the size of a football pitch bordered by a low brick wall. Interrupting the row of maisonettes, it was little more than scrubland connecting the adjacent street, with red dog-waste bins, diseased-looking trees and patchy grass, shredded by dogs and scorched by the sun.

Rashid parked and led Brennan to the end house at the left of the terrace. The front door was protected by an ugly brick porch with a flat roof and approached through a black wrought-iron gate. The house seemed derelict and she could hear Brennan mumbling in complaint. Taking a ring of three keys from her coat, she ignored the front path and approached the back of the house along the left wall, between the house and the printer's. At the back she unlocked a strong wooden garden gate built into a high fence. The length of the garden was impossible to determine because it was overgrown with shrubs, weeds, thistles and wild saplings, completely screening the house from view.

The kitchen door was secured by a Banham deadlock and heavy-duty padlock. Rashid quickly opened them and led Brennan inside. The kitchen had been stripped bare and smelt strongly of damp, with lumpy flooring and the walls shiny with condensation. The smell followed them into the hallway, made dark and almost inaccessible by a mass of junk and old timber piled high by the front door, preventing entry from that point. To the left the living-room door was blocked, too.

'Watch your step,' said Rashid, as she squeezed past an old washing-machine and twisted right to climb the stairs. The banister and several steps had collapsed long ago but she was sure-footed, avoiding the gaps, keeping to one side or the other and finding the few safe ones. Conditions were no better on the upper floor, with two tiny bedrooms, both derelict, and a bathroom where only the blackened toilet bowl remained. With no electricity or water the house would rate no points even on a squatter's wish list.

At the end of the landing, on the side facing the back of the house, a cupboard had been built into the wall from floor to ceiling, large enough to hide two adults. Rashid opened the right-hand door, which was designed to swing shut behind her. She gestured Brennan forward and pointed to what looked like the fourth in a line of screws securing the cupboard to the wall. 'Press it,' she said, making room for him. As he did so the top of the cupboard slid back, revealing an aperture a metre square and the bottom rung of a loft ladder. Rashid pulled the ladder down and climbed into the attic. She flicked a switch by the gap, filling the space with light from six bulbs built into the roof.

The attic was in total contrast to the rest of the house. Carpeted and painted white, with everything brand new, it filled the roof space, about ten paces by thirteen. A king-size bed, with new duvet and pillows, faced the street. A toilet and power shower had been built into one corner, and in the other, the fitters had found room for a modest kitchen area with sink, microwave, fridge and small stove. The only window was a skylight in the sloping roof above the bed, but it had been blacked out.

At the foot of the bed there was a twenty-seven-inch flat-screen plasma TV with DVD recorder. A brightly lit work-bench filled the space opposite, with two drawers to one side, a cupboard at the other, and a bar stool. Neatly piled on the floor were a used pair of walking boots, a hoodie, a wet-weather coat, a couple of waterproof beanie hats and a ruck-sack. Everything was in black, just like Rashid's clothes. A second set of house keys lay on the coat, with a couple of chocolate bars and energy drinks.

Rashid opened the deep lower drawer and beckoned Brennan over. It held a bundle of Oyster cards, six pay-as-you-go mobile phones and a page torn from a large-scale Ordnance Survey map. Beside the map were a hammer, a collection of screwdrivers, a small power drill, a soldering iron, a stop watch, a torch, two chisels, three vicious-looking knives, a holdall and a packet of latex gloves. The drawer smelt of resin from a neatly coiled length of rope beneath the tools. With the exception of the boots, everything was brand new. A white blanket was pinned to the wall on the left.

She watched Brennan carefully as he checked the drawer. He looked back at her. 'Can't see a laptop.'

'No Internet. Everything you need is in this room.'

'You sure about that?' he said. His face cracked into a half-smile, yet his eyes never altered. He opened the fridge and bent down to check the contents: milk, eggs, tomatoes, bread, margarine and cheese. Rashid saw him peering at two identical unmarked bottles containing a colourless liquid in a corner of the bottom shelf. Each was about the size permissible to carry onto an aircraft. 'What are these?'

'Not yet.' Rashid checked him before he could reach inside. 'Either will kill you.' She closed the fridge, took a sheet of A4 paper from the upper drawer beneath the worktop and laid it on the surface. 'Our first communiqué. Study it tonight until you know every word by heart.'

Brennan nodded, but Rashid was already spreading a sheet of plastic over the floor. She placed the stool in the centre of the plastic, rotating it left to face the wall. When he was seated she took a pair of scissors and some electric clippers hidden among the tools and began cropping his hair, the plastic crackling underfoot as she moved around him. The air was warm in the unventilated attic. The shirt around his armpits was a darker red, and there were more damp streaks on his chest and upper shoulders. Rashid immediately found herself inhaling the scent of his body again. His sweat and the texture of his hair between her fingers were bringing Parvez back to her. She had been without sex for a long time and could feel this young stranger reviving her. His body was a distraction she had not foreseen, and it made her wary.

She reached across to the wall and pulled away the blanket to reveal three enlarged photographs of an attractive woman in her thirties, evidently taken secretly. Her long blonde hair was in a ponytail and she wore slacks with a tight sweater. In one photo she was holding a child, in another patting a dog. In the third she was swinging the dog's leash, happy and laughing.

'That's her?' said Brennan. He tried to turn to Rashid, but she held his head still and bent down to plug in the clippers. She left her free hand on his shoulder for balance, and felt the muscle tense through his shirt.

'Her name is Diane Tennant. American. Study her.'

She worked methodically in direct lines over the top of his head, leaving pale furrows. His scalp felt soft through the cropped hair.

Brennan stayed silent beneath the buzz of the clippers. 'The dog is going to complicate things,' he said, when she had finished.

'It's a golden retriever. Deal with it.' She bent down to collect the hair into the plastic sheet.

Brennan was tugging his beard. 'What about this?'

'Do it yourself.' Rashid hid the folded sheet in her coat pocket and nodded to the bathroom. 'Razor's in there.' She took out a seventh phone and placed it on the work surface. 'I'll call you on this when you're cleared to go. But you don't leave the safe house. Is that clear, Danny?' It was the first time she had spoken his name and she groaned inwardly for sounding like his mother.

Without answering, Brennan slid off the stool and stretched, then vigorously rubbed his head. Rashid felt another stab of desire. Shorn of hair, his body seemed to have tightened, as if the act of cutting had given him new strength. 'You could do with a shower,' she said, but did not mean it.

Brennan moved to the bed, flopped down and took off his trainers. 'So why don't you stay with me . . . Anna?'

She caught his look and felt control slipping away again. He had been reading her thoughts and was letting her know. Mocking her, and making it obvious. She felt a flush wash over her throat and face and suddenly needed to get away. 'You know I have things to do,' she said, moving to the ladder.

'So where's the anarchist stuff they promised me?'

'Just read the communiqué. Study the map. Memorise them. Practise using the ladder. Wait for my call.'

The lopsided smile came at her again as he lay back on the bed. 'And how else am I supposed to amuse myself?'

Rashid reached into her coat and tossed him a plastic bag containing a couple of joints. 'Have these for now,' she said, then lowered her head as she started down the ladder, silently cursing herself for making it sound all wrong, like she was holding out some kind of promise.

Ten

John Kerr pushed aside a pile of pink and white files marked 'Secret' and 'Top Secret' and poured five glasses of Australian Merlot and a can of Coke. He was sitting in Room 1830, a square corner office diagonally opposite the Fishbowl. For years the intelligence hub of Special Branch, Room 1830 was still the most sensitive room in SO15. Its double aspect, five windows long on each side, overlooked St James's Park and Horse Guards Parade through dusty grey Venetian blinds. A glass-partitioned reading room, just large enough to take a desk and two chairs, occupied one and a half windows to the left.

Perched on the vacant desks beside Kerr were Jack Langton and Justin Hine. Langton had found an overnight spot for his bike in the underground car park and changed for the tube into pale chinos and a navy polo shirt. Justin wore his usual jeans and a white T-shirt and had caught a 185 bus from Camberwell, where he spent much of his professional life in a workshop beneath a row of railway arches.

Justin's south London hideaway was disguised as a computer-repair shop: dark, shabby and deliberately unwelcoming to potential customers who made it as far as the reception desk, brightly lit, spacious and hi-tech for the privileged few who worked behind the locked door. A brilliant engineering-science graduate from Durham University, Justin had been recruited by Kerr the moment he had finished his uniform probationer training. He was still only twenty-six but led a team of engineers making housings for microphones, cameras and any other intrusive devices necessary to defeat terrorists. He often co-ordinated with Jack Langton's surveillance officers and always said no job was too difficult.

Kerr had saved a sixth glass for Dodge, who had rung to say he was delayed in Lewisham, debriefing one of his sources, but hoped to be there within the hour. 'Either that or I'll take them for a pint.' Dodge actually preferred the pub because he could indulge his ten-a-day habit outside, but his agents always came first, so no one really expected him to appear. Kerr handed the first glass to Alan Fargo, who managed the office. 'Have a good one.'

Fargo was still at his workstation, the cluttered desk nearest the door where he often spent twelve hours each day, plus weekends if required. Forty-four years old today, he adjusted his glasses and rolled up his shirtsleeves, leaving bits of cuff and the buttons showing. 'Cheers.' He tucked his shirt into his trousers and smiled across at his sister.

Pauline Fargo was in her mid-thirties and had Down's syndrome. A laminated Metropolitan Police 'Visitor' badge clipped to her blouse, she sat opposite Fargo and beamed at Kerr as he handed her a tumbler of Coke. After the death of his father, Fargo had moved his ageing mother and Pauline from Falmouth, and they now shared a former police flat off Caledonian Road. Since the move, it had become a tradition for him to bring Pauline to 1830 to celebrate his birthday. Their mother would drop her at the Yard on the way to spend a couple of hours shopping in Oxford Street. Later, the three would go for a meal together in Victoria before catching the train home.

The Merlot and Pauline were strictly illegal in 1830, but Kerr was applying his usual flexible interpretation to the letter of the law. He and Fargo went back many years, having joined Special Branch in the same intake, and the two remained close friends. Alan Fargo was occasionally overweight, usually single and always uncool, but his record as an intelligence officer was brilliant. He seemed to have a sixth sense that took him into the mind of the terrorist, Irish or jihadi. Time and again he had predicted the unexpected, named the unidenti-fied and tracked the untraceable. But with every discovery he said it had been simply a question of joining the dots.

To assist him, he relied on a powerful ultra-classified computer linking SO15 to MI5, MI6 and GCHQ. Excalibur was a featureless grey rectangle as tall as Fargo and twice as wide, secured in a padlocked steel cage. Situated against the wall furthest from the windows, and beyond the bank of desks, it was accessible to no one but Fargo and a GCHQ engineer, who regularly drove up from Cheltenham to maintain it. Excalibur emitted a constant hum of which Fargo, its protec-tor, seemed unaware, and a heat that neutralised the air-con and kept the temperature just below sauna level.

An additional desk had recently been installed in isolation just inside the door, but its occupant perched on the main bank with the others. Melanie Fleming had ensured her work-station was so inconveniently placed that no one could doubt this was a strictly temporary measure. Bill Ritchie had wanted her to take a month's compassionate leave to be with her husband, but here she was, laughing with the others for the first time in three weeks, hair conditioned, nails varnished, everything growing back to normal. She was wearing the navy suit she used for white-collar surveillance operations in the City, with a crisp white blouse and shoes she could run in. She had also found her jewellery: a charm bracelet, stud earrings and a silver pendant that had belonged to her grandmother. This was her third working day in 1830, and Melanie was counting every hour. Kerr had sold her premature return to

Ritchie as 'recuperative duty', flexi-hours built around child care and Rob's home recovery, nine to five max, but Melanie was already talking up her husband's rapid progress and lobbying Jack Langton for a return to the chaos of the surveillance operations she thrived on.

Wednesday, 24 July, 18.43; counterfeiter's flat, Brick Lane

After the death of her lover, Anna Rashid had been forced to move from their rented flat in Battersea to a modest, roughly furnished bedsit five minutes from Rectory Road mainline station in Clapton. Waiting for her next assignment, she returned home for a couple of hours, cooked some pasta and immersed herself in a biography of the nineteenth-century nihilist Sergey Nechayev. She needed to continue her research for an article she was preparing, but never risked going online from home. Instead, in the late afternoon she walked to an Internet café in Stamford Hill, spent an hour there, burying her work within a stream of trivial searches, then walked back to collect her car.

She headed south through the rush-hour, the engine as erratic as ever, almost cutting out, then surging towards the car in front. A collision was on the cards. It happened crawling down Kingsland Road towards Shoreditch, where she bumped into a silver Audi with a child seat in the back and a rear-windscreen sticker saying 'Angel on Board'.

He was out of the car before she had even reversed, a stubbled thirty-something with gelled hair, big shades and white suit, Coldplay spilling out of the sound system behind him as he started shouting and playing up. Rashid was taller by at least a fist and stood over him, black on white, as the traffic streamed past. She had bumped him beside a bus stop, and a clutch of waiting passengers watched as she gave his car a quick check. 'There's no damage,' she said flatly, as he jumped about demanding her details.

'Your car is unmarked,' she said again. 'Go home to your yummy fucking mummy.' But he seemed not to hear, yelling that she was a stupid bitch who shouldn't be allowed on the road. Then he jabbed a finger in her chest, so Rashid head-butted him and left him in the gutter, where oil from a thousand buses ruined his white trousers. The bus queue gave her a ragged cheer, so she keyed his precious Audi before climbing back into the Corsa. The engine started first time.

Her meeting was with a counterfeiter, who lived in a rundown tenement block off Brick Lane in Whitechapel, just south of Fashion Street. There was a small parking place for her, as promised, and he buzzed her in without speaking. The lift was out of order so she had to walk up six flights of stairs. When she pressed the doorbell there was no audible ring, but a figure appeared in the frosted glass almost immediately, moving slowly towards her.

The door opened to reveal a pale figure in his mid-seventies with a straggly grey beard and lopsided glasses magnifying sad eyes. In his baggy grey cardigan and stained, shapeless trousers, he peered unsmiling through the gloom to study her. Rashid had been instructed that this man was one of the best forgers in Europe, but she was already wondering whether such a husk of humanity could be equal to the task.

'Maxim?' she said. Even his name seemed wrong. She handed over her half of a torn picture of a little girl. Without a word he matched it against his own segment, lying ready beneath a lamp on the hall table. He beckoned her inside, closed the door and shuffled in threadbare slippers back down the hall. He turned to face her, reaching out for Danny Brennan's passport photographs. His hands were delicate, like a pianist's, and she noticed signs of arthritis as his papery skin brushed against hers. He ushered her into the kitchen and flicked the switch on the kettle. A plain black suitcase on wheels, with a Bangkok Airways label, waited in a corner. 'Sit here,' he said, with an accent she could not pin down. 'Refresh yourself while I work.'

Rashid was suddenly anxious. 'Will the pictures be good enough?'

The old man glanced at the photographs for the first time and looked at her as if the question was irrelevant. 'Did they tell you to ask these things of me?'

She shrugged.

'Not your concern.' He waved vaguely at the suitcase. 'Everything is arranged.'

Rashid stayed by the door, hoping he might invite her to watch him work, but he seemed to read her thoughts. 'You will be comfortable here in the kitchen,' he said, as the kettle clicked off. He shuffled away. After a few moments, classical music drifted into the kitchen. She imagined him in the adjacent room, absorbed in counterfeiting Danny Brennan's passport, and wondered what secret things he had done in his long life to earn such high regard.

The kitchen had one chair, and a single cup, saucer and teaspoon lay on the draining-board. There was no freezer and the small fridge held only a carton of milk and some cheese. She found a brown loaf in the cupboard, with coffee and a handful of teabags. She wondered if she was in some kind of safe house, though the musky smell suggested this dark flat really was the old man's home. She drank her coffee black, leaving the milk for Maxim.

Wednesday, 24 July, 18.48; Room 1830

Kerr was busy replenishing the glasses as he heard the door click open and saw the commander's PA enter, security pass in one hand, a bowl of crisps and cashews from her boss's official entertainment stash in the other. Donna was a Jamaican in her fifties. Cool as a cucumber, she had been at work for ten hours but looked as if she was just starting the day. She was on her way to a dinner date but had promised Kerr she would drop by. With a birthday kiss for Fargo and Pauline, she perched beside Melanie.

'Ajay finally let you go?' said Langton, with a grin.

'Commander's gone to Prague. Europol convention,' said Donna, as Kerr took the glass he had kept back for Dodge and poured her a drink.

'So, what's the latest?'

'Need to know,' she said deadpan, clinking glasses all round. Her nails were deep purple, matching her skirt, and glittery. She held out the bowl to Fargo. 'Happy birthday, Alan.'

Over two decades Donna had worked for legions of senior officers, from the commissioner down, supporting them through a seam of racism, corruption, incompetence, political naïveté and enforced resignations. Few at the Yard had endured the centre of so many storms as Donna, yet she always emerged on the other side serene and stoical, picking up the pieces for the next in line.

Kerr knew how highly Donna rated their new commander because she had told him. Donna liked Ajay because he asked her view and sought her advice. He had also paid the airfare for her recent Caribbean vacation.

Kerr sat quietly, watching his team enjoy their downtime. It was good to see Melanie relaxed again, pink-cheeked and laughing, almost back to her old self. He knew she desperately wanted to return to the front line and he would have a word with Ritchie about her soon. Kerr noticed another piece of jewellery, too: her wedding ring. Kerr had once asked her what she found most difficult about undercover operations as opposed to surveillance work. He had expected her to say something about risk and stress, or the sheer exhaustion of living the double life. Her answer had surprised him. It was being unable to wear her ring at home with her family, she had said, for fear it would leave a white mark.

After a few minutes he caught her eye and nodded at the clock: just after seven. He saw Fargo's sister gently nudge Melanie's arm: 'John says you have to go home now.' It was supposed to be a whisper, but everyone heard.

'Whoops.' Melanie checked her watch, made a face and slid from the desk. 'You're right, Pauline. And I'm not here.' She emptied her glass, grabbed the tan designer handbag she had just bought as a morale booster, and headed for the door. Smiling, she rotated her free arm in a big wave. 'See you, guys.'

As the door clicked shut, Donna turned to Kerr. 'Actually, there is something to tell you. The commander wanted me to wish you luck tomorrow. He says to be careful.'

'That's nice.' Kerr had been summoned to appear before the Ethics and Professional Standards Committee the following morning, where he was to be 'examined' regarding Melanie's undercover deployment at Hope Farm. Everyone knew about it except Melanie, and everyone sensed trouble except Kerr. He reached over to pour Donna more wine. 'It'll be fine.'

'Come and see us the moment you get back.'

'I'm going to tell it like it is.'

'You sure that's a good idea, boss?' said Justin, holding his glass under the outstretched bottle. 'I heard those guys like to lynch before lunch.'

Eleven

It was raining when Melanie left the Yard and she had forgotten her umbrella. She hurried across Broadway to St James's Park station and, taking the steps two at a time, just caught the eastbound train, holding her bag clear as the doors screeched shut. Leaning against the handrail she checked her watch – ten past seven – and immediately felt a flood of anxiety and guilt.

The doors had closed on her cheerfulness, too. Her mood in the office, surrounded by her friends, had been completely genuine; she was having to bury the sadness within herself. Three weeks after the disaster at Hope Farm, her life felt quite different, and she was beginning to think that the change was irrevocable. Or, rather, the altered state in Rob.

His treatment had been complicated. Melanie's shot had entered his right leg, fracturing the kneecap in two places and tracking downwards through the surrounding soft tissue, damaging the tendons, ligaments and muscle. The surgeons at St Thomas's had repaired the patella with pins and wire and kept him in hospital for twelve days after the operation. Halfway through the first week they had eased him into physiotherapy with encouraging sounds about a complete recovery, provided he worked hard.

Melanie had been constantly at his side, only returning home to look after the children and, on alternate days, bring them to visit him. But from the moment he had regained consciousness Rob had been terse and uptight, turning his face away from her.

Specifically, he had refused to discuss the shooting. Melanie desperately needed to talk about the night at the farm. To melt Rob's anger and ease her conscience, she knew they had to bring it into the open, to confront their living nightmare so they could defeat it, but by the evening of Rob's discharge the crisis still festered.

Since Monday, 15 July, the day of his return home, Rob's mood had descended from unresponsive to outright hostile. Melanie found herself longing for a shouting match to clear the air but he spent most of the time reading the newspaper or drinking, his leg elevated in its knee brace, fast becoming an overweight shell of the attractive man she had married. Though he could walk only with crutches he took the bus to visit his pistol club in Hornsey, at the bottom of Muswell Hill, almost every day, sometimes returning for a second stint at the range in the evening. He regularly helped the club secretary update the membership list and had recently become a key holder. The children had seen the change, too. After school he would snap at them and pretend he had more important things to do than play or read with them.

'Look, Terry Bray did this to you,' Melanie had blurted in exasperation on the third night. 'Why are you treating us like we're the bloody enemy?' It had been her first explicit reference to the shooting, but Rob had simply turned away again.

The northbound train to East Finchley came to a halt in the tunnel at Warren Street. Melanie checked her watch for the umpteenth time, the knot in her stomach tightening. With every day that Rob's injury healed, Melanie's psychological wounds deepened. She had come to fear their relationship would never be the same.

Evidently Rob's mother sensed it, too, for she had become a more or less permanent fixture in their lives. What had started with an overnight bag had become a large suitcase installed in the small front bedroom. She cooked for them, helped Rob with his crutches and showered him with maternal sympathy. Melanie felt abandoned on the sideline, watching her man become a boy again.

One morning, when Melanie returned from the school run, Brenda had stood with her by the french windows, sipping tea and watching Rob limp down the garden. 'What a shame,' she had said, for the hundredth time. 'And all so unnecessary.' It had been meant to hurt, but she need not have bothered. For Melanie, each of Rob's lurching steps between the apple trees had been like watching her own walk of shame.

On the Friday, the fifth day of Rob's home recuperation, Melanie had asked to meet Kerr at a coffee shop in Strutton Ground, opposite the Yard, and told him a pack of lies. Rob's recovery was progressing better than either had dared hope, she had assured him. It would be even easier to manage the children, with Rob home on sick leave and his mother helping out. She needed to get back on Langton's Red surveillance team 'as soon as' to avoid becoming de-skilled.

Kerr had got back to her that evening with a compromise wrung from Bill Ritchie: a month in Room 1830.

She reached East Finchley station just before eight in pouring rain. The 102 bus was about to pull away but she sprinted after it and caught the driver's attention. It was early, and dawdled along Fortis Green, tyres hissing in the rain. By the time she had walked the quarter of a mile from Muswell Hill Broadway she was soaked.

For the past two days she had been home before six, so the children had shouted her name as soon as they heard her key in the lock, but this evening there was only the sound of the TV from the living room. When she called, Rob appeared immediately on his crutches, wearing the tracksuit bottoms he always hung around in these days. It struck her that he must already have been on his feet waiting for her.

'Hi,' she said, taking off her jacket and shaking the rain from her head. On her way to the kitchen she kissed him. Rob rarely bothered to shave these days, so the softness of his cheek surprised her. His breathing was rapid, exhaling beer and anger, and he looked more paunchy than usual. He also looked belligerent, leaning forward on his crutches, and Melanie felt her stomach churning again. 'Sorry, Rob. I'm a bit late. Boys all right?'

'Well, they'll be in bed, won't they?'

'Where's Brenda?'

'Evening class.'

Melanie half filled the kettle and flicked it on. 'What's up?' she said, spreading her wet coat on the back of a kitchen chair. Then the realisation hit her like a train. 'Oh, shit. The twenty-fourth. Your medical. It was today, wasn't it?' She banged her forehead in frustration but Rob was already picking his jacket off the hook. 'Rob, I'm so sorry. How did it go?'

'MO's entering me for the London Marathon,' he said, leaning the crutch against the wall while he struggled into his jacket. 'How do you think it bloody went?' He frowned a bit, hummed a bit. 'He said it doesn't look good. Shoved the X-rays back in the envelope, then asked after you. How's that for fucking victim support?'

'It's ridiculous.' Melanie came back out to the hall.

'Yeah,' he said, tapping the crutch against his left foot. 'I'd say that covers it perfectly.'

Melanie found a place between him and the door. 'Please, Rob. Stay and talk to me.' She took hold of his arm as he tried to push past. 'We have to get through this, for the sake of the children.'

'Get over it, you mean? Pretend my wife never shot my knee to shreds?'

Melanie was stunned. This was the first time he had volunteered anything about the incident since his operation. It was as if today's bad news from the medical officer had released something in him. 'I had no choice,' she choked. 'You know that.'

Something seemed to snap in Rob and everything came out in a torrent. 'You could have waited for the firearms guys. They were seconds away. Right outside.'

'I didn't know that.'

'You didn't have to screw up my life, Melanie.'

'I saved your life.'

'You should have fucking waited,' he yelled.

Then Melanie was shouting, too, fired up by wine and days of frustration. She leaned right into his face. 'How long do I have to spend on the guilt trip, Rob? Another month? A year? For ever? Are you going to throw the vicious-heartless-bitch thing at me every time I come through the bloody door?' She kicked off her shoes, sending them flying down the hall, then turned her back to him, holding onto the banister. When she faced him again her voice was calm. 'Look, I'm sorry I forgot about your medical. But it's not just the injury, Rob. You have to find a way to get over yourself.'

'It's always about me, isn't it?' said Rob, with a harsh laugh. He kept his bloodshot eyes on her as he limped down the hallway. 'I'm going to the range.'

'You've been drinking,' she shouted, as the door slammed. 'They won't let you on.'

The kettle clicked off as Melanie went upstairs to check on the boys. She could hear them whispering and realised they must have been hiding on the landing, peering through the banisters, listening to everything. They slept in bunk beds in the back room overlooking the garden, and she read to them until they were settled. 'Will you make breakfast for us tomorrow, Mummy?' said the younger child, as she stroked his head.

'Of course. Why? What's wrong?'

'Daddy gets so cross with us.'

'Daddy loves you very much. We both do. Go to sleep now.'

Then the voice of her elder son floated to her from the top bunk. 'So why doesn't he love you any more, Mummy?'

'Don't be silly,' she whispered, turning out the light to hide her tears. 'Of course he does.'

Melanie hurried downstairs in bare feet. The child was right, of course. How could she inflict such violence on Rob and then expect him to love her? Cold-hearted and callous, obsessed with her precious job, she had almost killed him. She returned to the kitchen, ignored the kettle and poured the last glass of red from the bottle Rob had started. Then she flung herself on the sofa, stared at the TV and wept loudly.

**Wednesday, 24 July, 20.38;
counterfeiter's flat, Brick Lane**

The old man was gone for nearly two hours, and Anna Rashid was on her third cup of coffee. He appeared without warning, catching her with her thoughts. 'It is completed. You can drink your coffee and go,' he said. 'I need nothing more from you.'

'Can I see it?'

He produced the counterfeit passport from his cardigan pocket, a rabbit out of the hat. 'You must not touch. No fingerprints.' The cover looked slightly worn and he had done something to age Brennan's photograph. The date of issue was 2007 and there was a smattering of entry stamps on the inside pages.

'Maxim, it looks perfect,' said Rashid, as the passport disappeared into the cardigan.

'It will get the young man to Bangkok,' he said.

Rashid looked at him for some sign of pride in his work, a twinkle of appreciation for her praise, but he sounded matter-of-fact, as if he performed such miracles every day. 'Now you can begin your own work and make that perfect, too,' he said, already shuffling back down the hallway as she drained her coffee and followed him.

Outside, she turned to say something else, but he was already closing the door on her, slowly, as if to avoid causing offence.

She could hear footsteps echoing on the staircase below her. As she reached the fifth flight a young man came into view. He wore jeans and a red shirt, with a beard and shoulder-length brown hair. He speeded up when he saw her, taking the steps two at a time and passing without a glance.

Sitting in the car peering up to the flat, Rashid took out her phone and called Danny Brennan. He picked up at the second ring. All she could hear was his breathing, slow and steady. 'You're clear. Go for it,' she said, then cut the call.

Twelve

Danny Brennan prepared for his first action as if it were a military operation. After Rashid had left he had spent the afternoon familiarising himself with the safe house. He checked and rechecked the equipment in the drawers and selected his weapon, the more vicious of the two chisels Rashid had provided. It was five inches long, made of steel with a bevelled edge one eighth of an inch wide, with a beech handle. He passed an hour practising the climb from the back of the house to the attic. After five attempts he could navigate the hallway, locate the few safe steps on the dilapidated staircase, press the secret button, climb into the roof, retrieve the ladder and seal the hatch behind him in less than two minutes. When he had absorbed every detail of the map and photographs, he destroyed them in the flame of the gas hob. He familiarised himself with the communiqué until he knew every word, tested that the boots fitted and packed the rucksack.

Satisfied with every detail, he became himself again. Stretched on the bed with the phone beside him, flicking through the TV, he lit one of Anna Rashid's joints and inhaled deeply, the soldier's discipline trumped by the activist's free will.

But at dusk, when Rashid's call came, he was ready. Wearing the waterproof coat and the beanie pulled low against the heavy rain, rucksack slung over his shoulder, he turned the corner by the Mason's Arms within seven minutes, walking casually through the glistening streets to the tube station. He used the first Oyster card to take a tube from Bethnal Green, changing at Tottenham Court Road for the Northern Line.

Brennan was headed for High Barnet, a north London suburb at the very end of the line, and arrived just after ten o'clock. The rain had turned into a fine, penetrating drizzle as he climbed the slope from the station and walked into the town, past a girls' school, a barber's and an ancient pub with its original black timbers. By the church he took the right fork, the route from Rashid's map seared into his memory. A group emerged from the higher-education college to his left carrying portfolios from an art class, so he tagged along in their wake until they peeled off into the nearest pub.

The town was almost deserted now and he kept his face low, on the lookout for CCTV cameras. Outside Iceland a bus swished through a dark patch of road water and drenched his jeans, but he scarcely noticed as he made his way past the shops, banks, estate agents and a modest shopping mall. At the end of the town he emerged from a row of solicitors' offices and car showrooms onto a pleasant green running along each side of the main road. He recognised this area from the map as Hadley and veered right into a minor road, tracing the edge of the green past a duck pond and a clutch of mock period houses with a distant view of the London basin and the lights of Canary Wharf. He passed other grand houses set back from the lane behind walls, hedges and high metal gates as he continued past an old brewery pond. Through one lighted window he glimpsed the flicker of a TV and a couple in their fifties relaxing in armchairs. They were twenty paces away, across a curving gravelled drive, but he stood in the rain to watch for a moment as they drank wine and laughed with each other, people he would never meet, living in a house he could only imagine. He reached Monken Hadley Church, smaller than the first, and stood by the wooden gate while his eyes adjusted to the darkness stretching out in front of him.

The clock in the bell tower was chiming the half-hour as he crossed the road and headed down a slight decline towards the common, where the road narrowed to little more than a lane. He paused again to collect his bearings. Ahead of him lay the dark mass of Hadley Wood, its tree tops a black smudge against the grey cloud backdrop. He spotted the target house less than a three-minute walk down the lane to his right, facing the woods. The high brick wall, security lights and ornate black iron gates to the left of the front door gave it away; those, and the cop he could see just beyond them cradling a Heckler & Koch semi-automatic. Rashid had told him it was a Georgian red-brick mansion and it was certainly the grandest house he had seen on his walk across the green. A couple of lights showed on the ground floor and in the porch, and a drenched windsock sagged from a white pole deep inside the grounds.

Brennan veered onto the rough ground to the left of the lane and found a path through the darkness into the woods, his feet making no sound on the damp earth and leaves as he carefully moved forward through the dripping foliage. As he drew roughly level with the house he entered a clearing, hidden from the lane by a dense barrier of trees, saplings and vegetation. He tentatively eased his way into the foliage until he had sight of the house. He could see the police post now, a converted garden shed to the left of the gates at the furthest point from the front door.

Even in the dark Brennan could tell this terrain offered many possibilities for the killing site. He took a pair of water-proof trousers from the rucksack, slid them over his boots and jeans, then began to explore. He chose a hollowed patch of ground in a dense clump of bushes beneath an oak tree slightly to the left of the house and about thirty metres away. Burrowing inside on hands and knees, pushing the rucksack in front of him, he found this spot offered reasonable protection from the elements and a half-view of the house frontage.

He still had to check his escape route. He shuffled back out of the hollow, retreated into the clearing and descended through the woods until he reached the main railway cutting he remembered from Rashid's map. He turned right, tracing the line until he came to a railway bridge closed off to vehicles leading to a made-up path. This would be his route tomorrow morning when it was done. In daylight, he calculated, he could reach the bridge and safety within four minutes.

Crawling back into his hiding place he pulled a clump of brambles behind him to conceal the aperture. Taking an energy bar and drink from the rucksack, he began his watch. The rain was still falling, dripping loudly from the oak tree onto his tangled green cocoon, yet Brennan felt perfectly dry in the clothes Rashid had given him. Traffic in the lane was quiet: in fifteen minutes he counted only three cars and an Ocado delivery van. No more lights came on in the house, but in an upstairs room to the left Brennan could see a bluish glow, presumably a child's nightlight, and some kind of toy dangling from the ceiling.

Just after eleven o'clock the gates silently opened as a black Jaguar swept down the lane and into the gravelled drive, then closed again. There were two male passengers, and Brennan's senses were instantly on high alert. A man in his mid-thirties immediately got out of the front passenger seat. He was tall and well built, wearing a dark suit. The jacket was unbuttoned and Brennan thought he saw a flash of holster. He was sharp and heavy-duty, just as a bodyguard should be. He opened the rear door with his back to the gates, using his body to obscure the passenger from view. Covering his right flank from the lane, he escorted him to the front door, denying Brennan a clear look.

There was a rectangle of light when the front door opened, then darkness again as the bodyguard walked over to the police hut and said something to the cop while the driver turned the Jag around. Brennan was close enough to hear their voices carrying before they were smothered by the tyres crunching on the gravel. The bodyguard got back into the Jaguar. The gate opened, the car turned left up the lane and the night-duty cop with the machine-gun made another patrol of the drive. The house fell into darkness, apart from the child's blue nightlight. The cop looked bored. The end of another day, start of a new shift. Everything normal, nothing to report.

Fifty paces away, Danny Brennan rested his head on his rucksack and waited for the dawn. The rain stopped at around three o'clock, with the sky clearing from the east. He saw it turn from black to grey, then a wave of red. With daybreak, clean white clouds drifted across the sun, separating it into shards of light. Billions of droplets still pattered in a gentle shower all around him, refreshing the scent of the trees. High in the canopy a magpie took off, its flapping wings shattering the stillness, and somewhere to his left he heard a cock crow. Brennan began methodically stretching his legs, arms and neck, preparing his body.

At a quarter to six a police van drew up and he watched the cop hand over to the day shift. Forty minutes later the gates opened again to admit the Jaguar. He watched the same bodyguard go through an identical routine in reverse, escorting his boss from the house to the car, but this time Brennan caught a glimpse of the man in the rear seat as they swept back up the lane. He was in his forties, jacketless in a white shirt, with a thick head of dark hair swept back, already engrossed in paperwork.

Time to get ready. To avoid the risk of forensic traces, Rashid had provided a clear plastic suit and overshoes. He removed these from the rucksack, turned onto his back and put them on. Then he slowly ate his last energy bar and took out the chisel.

Thursday, 25 July, 07.15;
home of Marcus and Diane Tennant

In her Smallbone kitchen at the rear of the house, Diane Tennant sat at the pine table and played a computer game with her four-year-old daughter. It was an educational app, designed to encourage reading. Diane was a woman of routine and regarded every moment with her child as precious. She had been up for more than an hour, in good time to see her husband leave for the department, and was already showered and dressed in a tight sweater, blue jeans and the Ugg boots she used for walking in the woods. Yvette, the au pair, stood by the Aga preparing the little girl's breakfast of porridge, boiled egg and toast with fresh orange juice. Diane would make her own once she returned.

Her golden retriever was a creature of habit, too. It scratched at the kitchen door, eager for its walk. 'Henry, don't be so impatient,' said Diane, peering into the garden to check the weather. The windsock was already drying in the light breeze and it was going to be a beautiful day. She picked up the leash, opened the back door to release the dog and kissed her daughter. 'See you in a few minutes, honey. Eat all your breakfast.'

She went out and round to the left, waving to her daughter through the window and blowing a kiss. The retriever was tearing round the garden, as it did every morning. Diane waited for it to come to heel, leashed it and walked round the side of the house.

Danny Brennan was draining the last drink when he saw her approaching the gate with the dog. She was animated, brushing her long hair back over her face as she spoke with the armed cop just out of view by the police post. Then the gate opened and he had Diane Tennant in his sights. He estimated her height and weight, five feet five or six, under sixty kilos. Controllable. He checked out her clothing, the thin sweater, no coat. No resistance. He pulled on a pair of blue rubber gloves as he tracked her across the lane, the dog pulling her forward. The cop appeared behind the gate, machine-gun cradled in his arms, watching her progress. Brennan closed his hand around the chisel.

When Diane released the dog it raced downwind into the bushes about fifteen paces to Brennan's right, then careered into a crop of trees. 'Henry! Henry! Wait for me,' she called playfully, swinging the leash in a wide arc. Her American accent carried easily on the still morning air. Brennan checked the gates, but the cop had gone back to his hut. Start of another day, the same nothingness as the last. Everything normal.

Brennan peered at her as she walked past him, still calling to the dog. He waited thirty seconds before crawling backwards out of the bushes on his stomach, leaving the rucksack in his hiding place and covering his exit with brambles. The ground behind him sloped downwards towards the heart of the woods. She had disappeared by the time he started walking after her, but he could hear her voice echoing off the trees, still calling for Henry. The night's rain had drenched everything, deepening the green of the leaves and polishing the trunks of the oak trees. The leaves underfoot were turned to mulch, deadening his pursuit. She was still calling for Henry, luring Brennan to her. He jogged after her, easily jumping a small stream, his feet making scarcely a sound.

When he came upon her she was standing perfectly still in a small clearing, beside the blackened circle of an old bonfire. She was listening for the dog in silence, probably playing a daily game of hide and seek. Her stillness took him by surprise and he darted behind a tree, turning the chisel in his hand. She must have heard something for she began to turn. Brennan could see that she was smiling again, probably imagining it was Henry, missing her only chance to save her life.

Brennan left the cover of the tree as she swung round and was almost on her by the time she realised her mistake. He saw her mouth open in surprise as she took in his transparent suit and blue gloves, and the steel of the chisel glistening.

Brennan spoke her name as a statement. 'Diane Tennant.' He walked towards her, but she made no attempt to run. Perhaps she was worrying about the dog. She seemed only to register fear as he stabbed her hard in the stomach. Placing his free hand behind her back, he drove the chisel deep inside her until he felt the point come up against her spine, then pulled her body to his so tightly that only the beech handle separated them. He twisted the blade then tilted the whole chisel upwards, practically lifting her off the ground, until their faces were almost touching. He glanced down to check the blood seeping into her sweater, then stared into her eyes, relishing the dying light. As she died she gave a violent cough, spurting blood into his face.

He dragged her to the area of burnt ground, stretched her on her back and pulled out the chisel. She was still gripping the leash so he gently opened her fist, looped it around her throat and trailed it on the ground above her head. This was on impulse, not part of the plan. Then he trotted back to the stream, kneeling to wash Diane Tennant's blood from the murder weapon, his face and the front of his plastic smock.

The retriever raced out from the bushes, shaking itself, spraying water in all directions. Brennan patted the dog as if it belonged to him. 'Good boy, Henry,' he said, as it wagged its tail and licked its mistress's blood from his hand.

When Brennan was clean he gently pushed the dog away in the direction of the warm corpse, retraced his steps and burrowed back into his hiding place. The armed cop was hanging around by the gates so he waited for him to return to the hut, then replaced the chisel, plastic smock and overshoes in the rucksack and slipped on his watch: 07.27. For two minutes he listened for any sign of life deeper in the woods then backed away and skirted the trees until he was clear of the house.

Remembering his recce from the night before, he walked quickly down to the railway line, crossed the bridge and climbed a slope to take cover behind an oak tree. He reached into the rucksack for Rashid's first mobile and the communiqué. Another time check: 07.36. He waited for the second hand to reach twelve and pressed speed dial. A woman answered on the second ring.

'Samaritans, how can I help you?'

He knew the words by heart, but read anyway. 'Get this down, 'cos there'll be no second chance. "Today we executed the defence minister's wife. Diane Tennant was taken out by People's Resistance . . ."'

'I'm sorry, who is this?' The voice sounded plump and kind. A do-gooder's voice, used to talking people down.

Brennan checked the time. Twelve seconds. 'Shut up and listen. "We put her to the noose to show the power of the ordinary people her bastard of a husband sends to war and destroys with his weapons of mass destruction. We have only one aim, one science, and that is destruction . . ."'

'I'm sorry, I can't write that fast.'

Brennan could hear the woman's rapid breathing as she jammed the receiver closer to her face, suddenly conscious of the urgency. Twenty-three seconds. He wondered if she had just come on duty or had been there all night. He could hear her pen frantically scraping the paper as she tried to get the ink to flow. A quiet night or a slow start to the day. She was asking someone for a pencil, but still found time to say 'please'. Thirty-three seconds.

' "We believe that no great change or revolution was ever accomplished without force. Everyone admits that society is on the verge of another great revolution and that soft words are not going to accomplish it. We have shown you the secret state is vulnerable. This is just the trailer. Soon you will see the complete film." '

'Please. Will you just repeat that last—'

Brennan cut the call and checked his watch: fifty-five seconds. Replacing the phone and communiqué in the rucksack, coat slung over his shoulder, he wandered down the track to the cover of early-morning traffic, the rush-hour tube and safety.

Thirteen

The Metropolitan Police Ethics and Professional Standards (Best Practice) Committee had been set up in the wake of disasters about phone hacking, racism, manipulation of crime figures and corrupt relationships between reporters and police. Recently it had also begun to examine the mismanagement of undercover officers. Each scandal had generated tough speeches from the top brass about deep regret, speedy reform and Action This Day. The eighth floor grew red hot with declarations, undertakings, threats and promises. 'Integrity First and Last' was about driving out, clamping down and getting a grip. The bosses talked the talk but nothing ever happened. 'Affirmative Inaction' was how John Kerr's guys described it.

This morning the committee had been convened to dissect the circumstances around Kerr's deployment of Melanie Fleming and identify 'improvement measures'. It sounded benign, but Kerr could smell a kangaroo court a mile off. He calculated that they were cobbling together a defence for the day Melanie or Rob decided to sue. When that happened they would plead that the defect lay in Kerr's maverick judgement, not their fabulous policy. Kerr had seen it before. It happened all the time.

Kerr's inquisition was scheduled for nine thirty sharp in the Peel suite on the fifth floor, a room twelve feet square with a view of the tube station and the revolving triangle with its 'Working for a Safer London' logo. The room had evidently been designed to soothe, with beige carpet, hotel-room abstract prints, a round table and impractical designer chairs inches from the floor.

Kerr made a bad entrance. Delayed in the Fishbowl by a call from Jack Langton about a surveillance operative injured in a car crash, he waited ages for a lift and had trouble locating the room. By the time he arrived the panel was already assembled, empty china cups on the table. No one stood up to welcome him. Looking down on them, Kerr could see the effort would be too great.

The head honcho was the youngish red-haired boss of the professional standards unit, the corruption busters. He was tieless in a short-sleeved white shirt with commander's epaulettes. His pale arms were hairless and mottled and he appeared to be growing a moustache, a work in progress that twitched when he spoke. His name was Gill but he was known as 'Mr Lessons Learnt' in recognition of his former role as the Met's apologiser-in-chief. Gill invited Kerr to join them in the remaining easy chair, strategically placed between the jaws of the horseshoe. He tried to make it sound like an informal social gathering, but Kerr had already clocked the note-taker in the corner and assumed the worst. He slid the chair back and to the right, destroying the symmetry.

The committee opened its business with a lie. In his introductions Gill announced that the lawyer sitting to his right was from the Home Office, invited simply to observe the process. He omitted to attach a name, but Kerr immediately recognised him from way back as an officer of MI6. And he knew MI6 would have zero interest in observing how brilliantly the Met cleaned up its mess. He was a lanky, desiccated-looking figure in his late fifties (Julian? Julius?), with wavy grey hair and a strong upper body but spindly legs. Kerr remembered him from his trademark red socks and would have expected him to be pensioned off by now. The deception intrigued him. Why was Vauxhall Cross poking its nose into the Met's internal affairs?

To Gill's left was a superintendent from Safer Neighbourhoods, who looked surprised to be there, and beyond him, Stella Ward, the most dynamic figure in the Mayor's Office for Policing and Crime. Ward was in her thirties, well groomed in white blouse, red skirt above the knee, high-heeled patent shoes and fingernails that outglittered Donna's. A London gang member until her late teens, she had matured into a red-hot political activist with a high public profile. She was known as a thorn in the Met's side, though Kerr and Dodge had secretly worked with her while investigating a Newham councillor with jihadi links. Kerr liked her a lot. This morning he could not take his eyes off her legs.

Gill and Safer Neighbourhoods each nursed a blue ring binder holding no more than two or three sheets of paper, the cover stencilled with name, rank and number. Kerr could see that Stella had one, too, but it lay unopened on the floor. Possibly she had read the file earlier; perhaps she reckoned she already knew enough about the exploits of John Kerr. The nameless non-lawyer from Vauxhall Cross sat paperless, the observer observing. He crossed his arms and dangled one weedy leg over the other, darting a flash of red sock straight at Kerr.

Gill produced tortoiseshell half-rimmed glasses and referred to the top page in his binder. In the monotone of a custody sergeant reading the charges, he asked why Kerr had deployed Melanie to infiltrate Terry Bray's gang at Hope Farm rather than an operative from the list of undercover officers maintained by the National Crime Agency. Kerr fired straight back that the undercover operation could have been leaked to Bray.

'Are you suggesting the National is corrupt?'

'No more so than the Met.'

Silence. Kerr had calculated this would seriously piss Gill off, because he was supposed to be the great corruption eradicator. Kerr had done his homework and knew that Gill had spent his career hopping from one policy unit to another, insulated from the front-line dilemmas he and his team faced every day. Gill's was laptop-led policing, where crisis was an exclamation mark, stress an emoticon and risk the header on a PowerPoint. Kerr watched him play with his pass, pretending to study the charge sheet. Everyone else folded their ID over the breast pocket, but Gill's was looped round his neck on a pale blue ribbon. As the ribbon tautened Kerr made out the words '*fidelité*' and '*honneur*'. Probably something he had lifted on one of his EU freebies.

'Do you have evidence of corruption in the Met?' said Gill at last. He had opted for the peering-over-the-top-of-the-glasses routine. It was designed to impress, but Kerr knew Gill had dipped his finals at Leeds.

'Shouldn't you be telling us that?' Kerr felt Stella's eyes on him and shrugged. 'Look, all I'm saying is that Melanie Fleming works within a trustworthy, highly vetted circle in the intelligence unit of SO15. A career Special Branch officer with no previous links to Terry Bray or his gang. Or the police officers who have investigated him over the years. She was my best option by a mile. Bray's gang are also highly professional. Check out their "no comment" interviews.'

'If that's the case,' said Gill, 'how did Detective Sergeant Fleming infiltrate them so quickly?'

'The panel does not need to know that.'

Kerr was stonewalling because he knew that, ethics wise, the truth would really freak them out. The reality was that Jack Langton's surveillance officers had taken Terry Bray's first choice of driver out of the game in a traffic accident. Two days later, Dodge had arranged for the understudy to be arrested for possession of cocaine, then introduced Melanie through an informant. Bray, in a hurry by now, had settled for third time lucky.

Gill murmured something to himself, then whispered to Safer Neighbourhoods. When he looked at Kerr again he had obviously decided to go for the jugular, the shooting of Rob Fleming. Checking his sheet, he described Melanie's wounding of her husband as a 'friendly fire incident'. Kerr felt a pulse of anger. It was a phrase Gill had hijacked from a war report. The jumped-up prick was pretending he knew what the hell he was talking about, and Kerr was having none of it.

'We're talking about a place called Hope Farm, in Essex, not Afghanistan. A woman acting under duress against the man she loves, not some Top Gun firing a rocket at complete strangers. These officers are married to each other, in case you hadn't realised. Friendly fire doesn't get close to what happened that night.' Kerr paused, struggling to keep the lid on his emotions. 'Your choice of words is offensive. Melanie and Rob Fleming deserve better.'

'Really?' Gill's eyes were peering over the glasses again. 'So how would you describe your fiasco?'

Kerr fired straight back: 'A tragedy waiting to happen. Too many action men in search of glory, everyone wanting the lead. Something as terrible as this was inevitable, sooner or later.'

Fourteen

Alan Fargo appeared to be crying, constantly sniffing and wiping his eyes with a giant maroon handkerchief. For the umpteenth time Melanie Fleming looked across at him and winced. Fargo's mother and sister had treated him to contact lenses for his birthday and this morning was the first trial. Fargo had worn them on the tube that morning and was obviously finding it tough. Melanie, who had shed many tears since her fight with Rob the night before, laid a hand on his arm. 'Is it worth the hassle, Al?'

Fargo blew his nose. They were sitting in the tiny reading room of 1830, squashed side by side at the desk facing the window to study the latest readout of the People's Resistance communiqué. Three other officers worked in the main office. The wall-mounted TV was showing a rolling report on Sky about the discovery of Diane Tennant's body by a dog walker two hours earlier.

The murder of the wife of Her Majesty's secretary of state for defence elevated this case into the national-security league, at least until the cops arrested the local nutter or regional sex maniac. Since the initial alert from local police just before eight, the SO15 Communications Room on the sixteenth floor, known simply as 'Reserve', had been forwarding 1830 any information from the public that could be relevant, along with all the hoaxes, crank calls, vile emails, gloating tweets and other perverse rubbish.

Fargo had also been working Excalibur hard, download-ing every scrap of classified source intelligence used to draft the most recent government threat assessments. He was data-mining anything that could be remotely relevant to the career of Marcus Theodore Tennant, MP. Public records showed Diane to have been his second wife, whom he had met in the nineties while working in the US before returning to the UK to seek election to Parliament. A search of the organisation People's Resistance was 'No Trace'. 'That should come as no surprise,' said Fargo. The geeks in Data Protection had ordered 1830 to cull its subversion records. 'Anything not reeking of al-Qaeda went into the shredder.'

'When was that?' said Melanie.

Fargo turned away to blow his nose again. 'The day Islamic Fascism displaced domestic leftism as the great Satan.'

There was a tap on the glass door as the senior communi-cations officer arrived from Reserve. Gemma Riley had spoken with the woman who had actually scribbled down the communiqué. Fargo had asked Gemma to drop by 1830 so that he could 'squeeze every detail' from her. Gemma was forty-three but always dressed like a stylish thirty-year-old about to hit the Mayfair clubs. Her roots were in deepest east London, but during the past decade her voice had defected to Kensington. As a member of the civilian staff she had been around Special Branch for a long time, dumping a couple of husbands and several lovers on the way. Renowned for filter-ing out the cranks, conspiracy geeks and time-wasters from the real thing, Gemma could sniff out a religious fantasist before he could say, 'Jesus Christ.' MI5 had tried to poach her for a similar comms job at Thames House but she had told them to get lost. 'What can Toad Hall give me that I can't get right here?' she had confided to Fargo, with a wink. Everyone thought she was brilliant.

Gemma perched on the desk beside Fargo and crossed her legs, a knee nudging his left arm. To Melanie it looked accidental on purpose, and Fargo immediately broke the contact by sliding his coffee mug away from her bottom. She smiled at Fargo but said nothing about his new look, which made Melanie think she already knew. Then she saw Fargo turn bright red and smiled to herself. Fargo needed information, all right, but he wanted to squeeze Gemma, too.

Gemma spoke confidently from memory. She explained that the communiqué had been phoned in to a Samaritans duty counsellor in her fifties, who obviously listened to distressed people on the phone the whole time. The ideal witness. She had described the caller to Gemma as a man in his twenties with a London accent. He had sounded sure of himself, displaying no obvious stress signs, which the counsellor had found surprising for someone claiming a murder.

The guy had spoken slowly, suggesting he was reading from a script, and refused to repeat anything. Eager to get off the line. The counsellor had taken the message down in longhand and handed the original to police.

'So how did we get this?' said Melanie.

'I rang her as soon as we got her contact numbers. She agreed to scan us a blind copy from home without telling the locals. And she believes she captured every word, which is very good going.' Gemma picked up Fargo's copy and waved it around. 'I just made a Word document from her scrawl and hey presto.'

'Thanks, Gemma,' said Fargo, blinking up at her. 'Great work.'

'Any time,' said Gemma, unfolding her legs and easing off the desk. 'And I'll keep the rubbish messages coming, too.'

When she had gone Fargo studied the text again. 'This language is very heavy,' he said. 'Some of it looks sort of nineteenth century. You know, anarchist tracts. Remember the dynamitists?'

'No.'

'That's why we were formed. To combat them. It's weird. Like some old leftie just burst out of a time bubble and started hacking away.' He scanned Gemma's note again. 'And there's another phrase here that's interesting,' he said. 'Something bang up to date.'

'What's that?' said Melanie, but Fargo was already heading out to Excalibur.

She reached for her mobile and called through the open door. 'I think we should get John out of there.' She texted: 'Claim on DT 1830 now.'

Thursday, 25 July, 10.08; safe house, Bethnal Green

Anna Rashid was waiting in the safe house at Bethnal Green when Brennan returned. She had been there since eight o'clock, pulling the ladder up behind her and closing the hatch. She told herself this was to test how rapidly Brennan could access the attic, to assert her control. But it was also to welcome him back to safety, to feel part of what he had done. She had brought with her bread, cheese and fruit, and a paperback commentary on the nineteenth-century anarchists Mikhail Bakunin and Sergey Nechayev, with copies of the anarchist journal for which she regularly wrote articles.

There was an indentation on the bed where Brennan had been resting before his mission the previous evening, so she took off her coat and lay on the side next to his with the TV on Sky, waiting for the breaking news. By the time she heard Brennan enter the kitchen, the drama of Diane Tennant's murder under the noses of the police had displaced every other story to the bottom of the screen. He was moving quickly through the house and was sure-footed on the stairs, which impressed her: it showed he had followed her instruction to practise. By the time the aperture slid open and the ladder disappeared, she was standing by the workbench, looking busy.

If Brennan was surprised to find her there, he hid it well. 'Hi,' was all he said, then dumped the rucksack at her feet and went to stand by the TV in his beanie and waterproof coat, pulling off his boots and wet socks, watching his actions do the speaking for him. Rashid searched his rucksack for the chisel and plastic suit, transferring them to her own bag. She found the communiqué in the side pocket, damp and torn, and burnt it on the gas ring, pouring the ashes down the sink.

'They're not saying much about People's Resistance,' she said. 'Did you tell them?'

Brennan flicked away the hat and vigorously rubbed his head. 'See for yourself,' he said, nodding at the screen. He shook his coat off and let it drop to the floor. A piece of twig followed it. 'She's dead. It's over.'

'It's only beginning, Danny,' said Rashid, pointing at the wall to the left of the worktop. There was no covering blanket this time. The space from which the face of Diane Tennant had smiled at them was now occupied by three enlarged photographs of an old man walking down a central London street. Lying on the worktop, a folder contained a map and instructions she had brought for the second attack. She held it out to him. 'Danny, do you want to see?' she said. Brennan shrugged, his eyes still on the TV, and she could tell he was wet through from the woods. 'And you need to get out of those clothes.'

This was the first time Rashid had seen him shorn of the straggly beard. He seemed younger, quite different from the man she had collected from prison, and the change startled her. He was good-looking, boyish even, cheeks fresh from his night in the open, and she had a sudden urge to feel his skin beneath her fingers again. She started towards him, folder outstretched, but he seemed to ignore her, pulling the red shirt over his head. He unbuckled his jeans as she took another step to him, then his pants disappeared too and he stood naked by the bed, unselfconscious, as she cursed herself for letting him outmanoeuvre her.

She tried to keep moving past him to the other side of the bed but missed her footing on his clothes. They touched, grappled, kissed and fell to the bed, equal combatants. Then Rashid was naked, too, her black clothes mingling on the floor with his red.

Their sex was quick, no names, no words, no affection, just mutual need. Rashid liked her body. Her clothes made her look shapeless but she had good breasts and legs, and her belly was OK. No one had seen her naked since Parvez, so she was disappointed that this man seemed hardly to notice her.

She could smell the dankness of the woods as he shifted on top of her and noticed he still had a smear of Diane Tennant's blood on his forehead. She wet her thumb with his saliva and wiped it away. When he came his body arched and his face contorted, but the eyes never altered. They seemed to reflect something else going on in his head. It was unfathomable, beyond lust or desire, and she wondered whether he had looked at Diane Tennant in the same way: two female bodies possessed for a different purpose, one for killing, the other for sex.

Afterwards she shared a joint with him, watching the rolling news in bed, then took the folder and talked him through the next action. Rashid didn't care that he spoke scarcely a word back. She knew their time would be short, so it suited her. At least it would never become the sapping, toxic silence of couples living with familiarity or contempt.

After a few minutes she washed, dressed and picked up her bag from the worktop. She produced a syringe with a plastic cap over the tip and a pair of strong gloves. Then she took out one of the phials of poison from the top shelf of the fridge and held it up to him. 'Want me to do it for you, Danny?'

'No. It's my action.' Still naked, Brennan padded over to join her. He put on the gloves, skilfully drew poison into the syringe, replaced the cap and stored it in the fridge.

'Good,' said Rashid, picking up her bag and moving to the ladder. 'Rest. Wait for my call.'

Fifteen

The Ethics Committee was unravelling fast. After several minutes of listening to Kerr outline the risks of joint operations with no clear ownership, Commander Gill, a matrix, audit and template man, appeared close to meltdown. 'Let's move on,' he said abruptly, turning to the second sheet in his binder. It floated ten inches to the floor and Kerr noticed a different typeface and a format of bullet points.

Gill quickly recovered the note and read from it. 'I also want the panel to review your handling of the incident on the Thames.'

Kerr frowned. 'I thought we were here to examine the decisions around Melanie Fleming's deployment.'

'Including the surrounding circumstances,' said Gill.

'Such as?'

'The phone call.' The enigma sitting to Gill's left uncrossed and crossed his legs, directing the other red sock at Kerr. 'One of the gangsters who died that day had made a call to Terry Bray,' read Gill. He sounded unsure. 'That's right, isn't it?'

'Yes, using the mobile phone I grabbed as the inflatable was sinking. So what?'

'It proves that both operations were linked.' Gill was following the text word for word now, like a man who had been primed.

'And what has that got to do with Melanie Fleming?'

'Do you accept any responsibility for the deaths of those two men?'

'They both tried to shoot me,' said Kerr levelly. 'I shot one of them back in self-defence. The other died in the river while I was trying to rescue him.'

'You killed them both, didn't you? Out of revenge for the murder of your agent, codenamed Seagull.'

'Who told you there was an agent?'

Suddenly Gill seemed to go off piste. He looked directly at Kerr, the note lying abandoned in his lap. 'Two lives for the sake of one,' he said, in case anyone was taking a body count.

'The investigators have already looked at this,' said Kerr. 'Are you formally accusing me of a crime?'

'Are you admitting to one?'

'The second guy tried to shoot me and ended up in the water. I tried to pull him out but he drowned. End of. And this is way beyond your brief.'

The nameless non-lawyer-observer cleared his throat and looked accusingly at Gill, like he was a man who had failed to deliver. He was trying to sit up, but his knees were practically level with his chest.

Then Kerr's BlackBerry vibrated, ruining his intervention. Kerr made them wait while he checked Melanie's message, feeling the waves of their irritation wash over him. 'Apologies. Urgent operational matter.' He looked at Red Socks. 'I think you were building up to say something.'

'Mr Kerr,' he drawled, 'do you know who had been tasking these two men before their unfortunate demise?'

'Do *you*?' Kerr snapped back. He nodded at the sheet of paper in Gill's lap. 'Is that your script he's reading from?'

'I think you should answer,' he said, suddenly lawyer-like. 'The panel has an interest in understanding all the circumstances of the undercover deployment, including the totality of the events that led up to it.'

'Where are you from again?' Kerr looked straight at the MI6 man. 'Which part of the Home Office, exactly?'

'We all know how it ended under your mismanagement. We need to explore how it began. Simple cause and effect.'

'I think you should go back to observing.'

The MI6 man suddenly seemed aggressive, squirming in his seat, frustrated again by the non-confrontation furniture. Kerr slowly shook his head. The guy did not know when to abandon his charade.

Then Stella Ward silenced them. 'You two need to back off,' she said quietly, looking hard at Gill and the spook. 'Your attack on Mr Kerr is unseemly. I consider it inappropriate. Show some respect for the man who deals with risks in the field, not in some cosy office. We should be concentrating on process here, not victimisation.'

It shut them up. Red-faced, the spook receded into himself, arms folded. Safer Neighbourhoods looked like he had never been there and Gill stared down at his papers. Kerr glanced at the empty china cups and wondered what they had been saying before he arrived. Perhaps that was when Red Socks had handed Gill his script and tried to hijack Stella with their clumsy subterfuge.

Kerr was curious to know why MI6 would use deception to discover how much he knew about the US gold heist. If they believed the robbers on the Thames had been foreign intelligence agents, why not declare it? If there were sensitivities around Britain's relationship with America, the most natural reaction would be to say so. Why the lie, unless MI6 had something to hide?

The inquisition left Kerr intrigued rather than angry. But until he had answers to those questions he would protect Seagull's intelligence with his life. No one else had a need to know, especially these people.

Above all else, he was grateful for Stella's final lacerating intervention. In the chill atmosphere her faint smile was telling Kerr she knew what made him tick. No one understood revenge better than Stella Ward.

Thursday, 25 July, 10.36; Room 1830

Kerr was already escaping to the fifth-floor lifts when he received a second text from Melanie. The panel had broken up after Stella's intervention, adjourned by Gill '*sine die*'. With a secret wink of gratitude Kerr had left them struggling out of their low chairs without handshakes or farewells. Justin's feared lynchers before lunch had not even made it to the coffee break.

The possibility that MI6 might be culpable in some way tugged at Kerr as he hurried down the corridor. His working assumption, that a foreign intelligence agency had carried out the robbery, had been skewed by the MI6 man's hostility. Why would Julius (Julian?) react so aggressively unless he believed Kerr had compromised his own agency? And if this were true, Kerr was left with the suspicion that MI6 was involved in some way, perhaps by sponsoring the heist or even contracting the robbers. It was a chilling prospect.

Kerr dropped by the Fishbowl to make himself some coffee, then walked round the corridor with Gabi's Italian mug to join Fargo and Melanie in the reading room. He looked cheerful, so neither of them wasted time asking about his encounter on the fifth floor. A low ball from Commander Lessons Learnt and an ageing spook did not even register against the savage murder of Diane Tennant.

Fargo and Melanie sat in silence with an eye on the TV in the main office while Kerr sipped his coffee and absorbed the communiqué line by line, then the initial police report from the scene. He had been aware of the attack on Diane Tennant since the news had first broken. The claim could be a

game-changer, for it upgraded murder into political execution
with national-security fallout. No one knew where it might
lead them. Alan Fargo's judgement about the unusual language
had been sound, too. Even before Kerr had stepped out of the
lift Fargo had identified two sections of the text as extracts
from the early anarchist newspaper the *Herald of Revolt.*

'And this group, People's Resistance?' said Kerr.

'No trace,' said Melanie.

'Sounds retro, like those anarchist collectives from the
seventies and eighties.'

'Not completely,' said Fargo. 'Look at the last phrase: "This
is just the trailer. Soon you will see the complete film."
Remember the jihadi attacks in Mumbai 2008?'

'That was Lashkar-e-Taiba?'

'Army of the Good. Yup.'

Kerr frowned. 'Shootings in the railway station and the
Jewish Centre. Invaded the Taj Mahal hotel?'

'With guests giving media interviews on BlackBerrys from
their rooms, before the jihadis scorched it,' said Fargo.
'Telephone intercepts recorded those exact words just before
the final attack.'

'So is this bravado bullshit or the start of a campaign?' said
Kerr.

'And if it's the real deal is it anarchist or jihadi? Home-
grown or international? We have to decide which way to jump.'

Kerr held up the communiqué as Jack Langton clicked
himself into 1830 and walked to the reading room. 'Has Bill
Ritchie seen this yet?'

'I asked Gemma to copy him in. He wants to see you as
soon as,' said Melanie.

Kerr exhaled. 'Do I have anything to give him?'

'Let's start with some decent surveillance targets,' said
Langton, sliding his helmet down the desk, leathers squeaking
as he eased into the remaining chair beside Kerr.

'Reds on standby?' said Kerr.

Langton exchanged a smile with Melanie. 'Waiting for the off.' He looked up at the TV in the main office. 'And heads up for the grieving husband.'

They turned to see Marcus Tennant arriving home. The gate was thronged with hi-vis uniforms and reporters who scattered as the Jaguar swept down the lane and into the gravelled drive. The cameraman had a view of the front door to the right and captured the minister as he climbed out of the back seat and hurried to the house, escorted by his protection officer. Someone opened the door from the inside, so Tennant was only visible for a few seconds. He was pale and distraught, and no one called out to him.

Kerr was concentrating on the man who walked with him. 'And I need to speak with Karl.'

'He already called in from the car,' said Melanie.

This was Karl Sergeyev, who had been Marcus Tennant's close-protection officer since Christmas. A Russian, he had joined Special Branch seventeen years ago. For most of his career he had cultivated Russian dissidents and former Soviet Bloc *émigrés* in London. An experienced operator, strongly built, always impeccably dressed and stylish, he was liked by men but admired by women.

He was married to Nancy, a former analyst in Special Branch Registry. They had two young children but had been separated for more than a year. But it was Sergeyev's extra-marital life that served as an ever-rolling source of entertainment, speculation and wonder among his colleagues. Karl Sergeyev fell in love completely and often; in fact, he appeared almost permanently lovestruck. His most recent dalliance had been with a beautiful Romanian escort called Olga, who had almost cost him his job.

John Kerr rated him highly, as a brave, effective operator and friend. Provided the rules were a little pliable, Sergeyev could just about live within them. He always spiced initiative with imagination, sometimes spectacularly. No one ever described Karl Sergeyev as a safe pair of hands, but when he fell short Kerr was always ready to intercede with the top brass on his behalf. However deep the scrapes, no one ever questioned his integrity.

'Get him to drop by the Fishbowl, will you, Melanie? I think we'll start with Marcus Tennant.'

Sixteen

Kerr knew he had to act quickly. With nothing in the intelligence pool he could not wait days for the usual source stream of hoaxers, reward-seekers and the deluded to drip in. The execution by British extremists of Diane Tennant, beautiful American wife of a senior government minister, would rapidly escalate into a major crisis. Kerr was already anticipating an intense period of verbal briefings, rolling updates and relentless interference from politicians and Whitehall officials fearful of attacks against other ministers.

His team had worked on similar plots before and always disrupted them in time. But this attack had been different. The killers had found a new way to cause maximum damage, using a soft target to score a hard political goal. Over the body of Diane Tennant hung the real prospect of a prolonged campaign with dual benefits: execution plus propaganda victory. Unless he rapidly closed down People's Resistance, Kerr predicted future attacks and government demands spiralling out of control.

An idea had come to him with his first careful read of the communiqué. 'People's Resistance' and the anarchist language in the text resonated with Kerr's early days in Special Branch. Each carried echoes of an era of extremism dormant for two decades, and both led him to the same radical plan with a very tough sell.

Bill Ritchie was standing by his desk, locking the secure briefcase he used for carrying classified papers around Whitehall. He glanced at the clock as Kerr entered. 'Better make it quick. They just called a COBRA for eleven thirty.'

It stood for 'Cabinet Office Briefing Room A', the place to which a senior official, minister or even the prime minister would summon the government's advisers to work out the national response to a major crisis. From volcanoes to foot-and-mouth, treachery to terrorism, every cock-up, conspiracy, natural disaster and national threat beat a path to number seventy Whitehall. Many of these emergency meetings were announced to the media, some shrouded in secrecy and a few deliberately leaked. If the threat was sky high or his popularity ratings were scraping the floor, the prime minister might stride through a phalanx of cameras to take personal charge. COBRA was the government's favourite platform for executive muscle-flexing, political cover-up and operational blame-gaming.

Kerr groaned. The pantomime was starting early. Ritchie shot him a bleak look. 'Thought you were being interrogated.'

'I came back for this.' Kerr took a seat by his desk. 'Five minutes, Bill. You saw the communiqué?'

Ritchie tapped his briefcase. Kerr imagined it contained little other than the latest threat assessments from Room 1830. 'Is it genuine?' said Ritchie.

'I think so, yes. The caller says, "We put her to the noose." Diane Tennant was stabbed in the stomach, then stretched out in the middle of the clearing with her dog's lead encircling her neck and the strap trailing above her head. The media haven't reported that. Only the murderer could have known.'

Ritchie looked bad-tempered and worried. 'Well, they're going to be hungry over there and I've got nothing to throw them.' Kerr stayed silent as his boss dumped the case on the desk and used his fingers as a check list. 'Wife of the secretary of state for defence slaughtered in retaliation for her husband's policies. Armed officer picking his nose within shouting distance. Perfect wife and mother. Photogenic. Blameless. The press are going to love it. Oh, and she also happened to be an American citizen under our protection. Have I missed anything?' Ritchie slumped into his chair. 'This is going to cause a shit storm on both sides of the Atlantic.'

'I agree. Let's see what the investigators come up with this morning.'

'Bollocks. Forensics will take ages. I'm going to need a plan by the time I get back, so tell Fargo to throw some red meat into Excalibur.'

'I don't think Excalibur will tell us much,' said Kerr. 'This is looking like it's UK-based. The caller, the content, the name of the group. It's like some weirdo walked out of the eighties and said, "Hey, I'm back." '

'But the message is contemporary. WMD, Afghanistan, Lashkar-e-Taiba. The politics are bang up to date.'

'My gut says we're talking Peckham not Pakistan,' said Kerr. 'Unless MI6 have something they're not sharing.'

'I'll be checking that out at COBRA.'

'So I'm looking for domestic extremist targets and it's a blank page. Nothing on Excalibur because everyone's been majoring on Islamic terrorism. Anything non-al-Qaeda doesn't count, apparently. Apart from anti-globalisation stuff whenever the City gets paint-bombed.'

Ritchie swore under his breath.

'Anarchists are shiftless, secretive and totally paranoid,' said Kerr. 'Very limited scope for a technical operation. I think we have to get someone into them.'

'An agent penetration?' said Ritchie, exactly as Kerr had predicted. 'No time to recruit.'

'I'm thinking of something more immediate, if you really want to move quickly on this.' He looked at Ritchie, who glanced at the clock, nodded and beckoned with his hands. 'We force the pace through one of our own. An undercover deployment.'

'Who?' Ritchie propelled his chair sideways to the safe and spun the combination lock. 'No time to move an existing operative across. It'll show out.'

'I'm not suggesting that.'

'And a new deployment will take weeks to set up.'

'Exactly.'

Ritchie stared at Kerr for a moment, grabbed his case and stood up. 'Are you out of your mind? Didn't those ethical tossers teach you anything this morning? Forget it.' He headed for the door, conversation over.

Kerr followed him into the corridor. Ritchie was moving fast, already halfway to the lift lobby. 'Look, she's bored stiff in 1830. Desperate to get back to the front line. Bray's gang are in prison, no access, so her cover's secure.' Ritchie barged through the double doors and punched the call button. He looked like he wanted to hit Kerr, too. 'We can use the same legend Dodge prepared for her. She's ready to go, Bill.'

'She's still recovering from the last fiasco.' Ritchie had his eyes on the floor indicator. 'You're crazy even to suggest it.'

'I'll keep it tight between me and Dodge. Take personal responsibility. Cover every move.'

'Keep her safe, you mean?' They stepped into the lift side by side and Ritchie pressed the button without taking his eyes off Kerr. 'Same as you did at Hope Farm?'

'No. Like you did for me.'

The lift stopped on the tenth floor to admit a group of civilian workers from the adjacent Victoria block, squeezing Ritchie and Kerr to the back of the lift. Everyone faced the doors in silence and Kerr guessed that Ritchie was remembering again. Two decades ago he had been John Kerr's mentor during a high-risk undercover operation. For nearly half a decade Ritchie had watched over Kerr, making himself available every minute of every day. Ritchie had always seemed calm about the whole thing but, years later, Lynn Ritchie had told Kerr about the hours of sleep he had lost, worrying about his protégé. Those years had forged the powerful bond that transcended rank.

The doors opened and everyone spilt out. 'That was different,' said Ritchie, as they headed for the crowded Back Hall.

'It's the same,' said Kerr, then lost Ritchie again as he stepped into the revolving door. On the other side, officers entering the Yard acknowledged them. Kerr looked for a car but Ritchie kept walking. Soon they were in Tothill Street, heading towards Parliament Square, and Kerr remembered that Ritchie walked everywhere these days, as if someone had told him he could defeat his cancer with exercise and fresh air.

'We're about to get kicked for failing Diane Tennant. You need ideas, Bill. I'm running one past you.'

'And I'm shoving it back in its box.' Ritchie forgot to look and almost stepped into the path of a black taxi. 'You haven't said anything to her, I hope?'

'This is the only sure way to generate intelligence fast.'

'So think of something else.'

They walked on in silence, Kerr at his boss's shoulder. When they reached Victoria Street Ritchie pulled up sharp and faced him. 'Are you going to bug me all the way to Whitehall?'

'Will you run it past Ajay?'

'Forget it. Commander's in Czech Republic till tomorrow. He'll think you're insane, too.'

A number eleven bus swept past in the opposite direction, drowning Kerr's voice. 'At least Ajay's got bottle.'

'What did you say?'

'Just tell me, Bill. When did it all go wrong?' They had reached a triangle of cobbles in front of the Queen Elizabeth

II Conference Centre, directly opposite Westminster Abbey. The stop light leading to Parliament Square turned green, so Kerr had to shout to make himself heard above the revving traffic. 'You were always a top operator. No one had more bottle than you. But these days you don't seem to give a toss.' Kerr put a hand on his arm. 'What the fuck's happened to you?'

This was calculated to bruise and Kerr immediately regretted it. At Eastbourne the previous winter Ritchie had failed the extended interview for the strategic command course at Bramshill police college, the essential qualification for chief-officer rank. This setback had destroyed his ambition to succeed the disastrous Paula Weatherall as commander. It had been the greatest disappointment in Ritchie's career and Kerr had just compounded the pain.

The traffic had come to a halt again at the red light. 'Cancer,' said Ritchie, quietly. 'What's your excuse?' He turned and walked away, leaving Kerr by the roadside.

Seventeen

Moments later someone touched Kerr's arm. 'John, have you got a minute?'

Kerr was back at the Yard, about to swipe into the revolving door, when he heard Melanie's voice. She must have been loitering in Back Hall waiting for him to return, which meant she had tracked him in pursuit of Bill Ritchie.

'You want to go for coffee again?'

'Anywhere outside will be fine.'

Kerr led the way back into the street and crossed to the post office, putting distance between them and prying eyes. It was warm so Melanie had left her jacket in the office and carried her pass in her hand. 'It's about the Reds,' she said, as they strolled up Caxton Street. 'You've put them on standby and I should be with them. You know how short Jack is of trained people.'

Kerr had his hands in his pockets. 'Surveillance is not the deal. You know that.'

'John, I'm fine. Everyone knows what a great job Alan and the guys do in 1830 but Excalibur is so not my scene. I'm dying of boredom.'

'Don't tell Fargo that.'

'It was Al who told me to speak with you,' said Melanie. They had reached the old Bluecoat School at the junction with Petty France and loitered in the cobbled courtyard beneath a clump of trees. 'This Diane Tennant thing is going to run and run. We're about to be stretched to the limit on targets we haven't even identified yet. I want you to send me back. Let me work the plot. It's what I'm good at. Jack needs me.'

'So does your family.'

'Not like this. Rob is getting stronger every day. No one wants Mum coming home bored out of her mind.'

Kerr laughed. 'You've only done four days.'

'I need to be tested, John. I can do better than this.'

'It's Bill Ritchie's call and I'm sorry. You know how I feel about it.'

Gemma walked by and waved.

Melanie sighed, then gave a rueful smile. 'OK. It was worth a try. Thanks, anyway. I need to speak with her,' she said, and turned after Gemma.

While he was still organising his thoughts, Kerr called, 'Hold on.'

Melanie walked slowly back, quizzical.

'You want a challenge?' said Kerr. 'I can offer you a bigger test than 1830 or the Reds.' In the shade of a plane tree on the right side of the ancient school, a stone staircase led to a disused side door. Beneath the steps was the cellar, blocked off. There was just room for them to sit side by side and Kerr laid his jacket on the top step. 'Provided you really mean what you say.'

Behind them a queue of black taxis waited with their engines running, but the plane tree was alive with birdsong. Melanie crossed her legs and Kerr realised he had not seen her in a skirt for as long as he could remember. The shoes were different, too, black patent with a high heel.

'I'm intrigued,' said Melanie. 'Doing what?'

'Identifying those new targets you're so anxious about.'

She frowned. 'Surveillance, you mean? With Jack?'

'Not that.' Kerr glanced at her, suppressing a pulse of doubt. 'I want you to find these people for me. Get alongside them.'

'Alongside?' Kerr saw Melanie's eyes widen with understanding, then her back went bolt upright. 'Get inside, you mean, don't you? You want me to go undercover again, to infiltrate them. Am I right?'

Kerr nodded.

'I don't believe I'm hearing this.' Melanie was half frowning, half smiling. Then a squirt of bird's mess landed an inch from her left foot, making her laugh. 'Are you serious? You spin me all that welfare crap, then come out with the pitch from Hell?'

'It's not like before. You know what we're talking here. Anarchists, nothing fancy. Follow up on the targets 1830 and Jack throw up. A few weeks, Mel. As much overtime as you need. Not too many nights away from home. Look out, listen in, report back.'

'Simple as that.'

'Dodge and I will manage this completely in house. I'll be your cover officer.' She turned away, but Kerr had already noted the spark of interest. 'Like Bill Ritchie was for me.'

She swung back to him. 'Did he put you up to this? Is Mr Ritchie that desperate after all I've been through?'

'You just told me you were fine.'

Melanie fell silent again, and Kerr guessed she was rewinding the morning's events, trying to freeze-frame the moment they had come up with his plan: in the street, after Ritchie had already left for the Cabinet Office.

Kerr shrugged. 'You're good to go, Mel. New address, different car, same legend.'

This time Melanie stayed quiet for a full minute, listening to the song in the tree above. She craned her neck, trying to locate the bird, while Kerr checked his BlackBerry. Seven emails and texts had arrived since he had bumped into Melanie, all about Diane Tennant.

'I could do it,' she said eventually. 'But I have to put my family first this time.'

'Of course. And Rob has to be absolutely OK with it. Would that be an issue?'

'You didn't answer *my* question. Did Ritchie approve this?'

'Talked it through with him just now. How about Rob?'

'Rob would not be a problem.'

The answer came back too quickly, the voice too sharp and abrupt. Kerr suspected she was being as disingenuous as he was. He felt another pang of doubt. He could have drawn a halt right there but let the moment pass. Instead he allowed the lies to flow easily between them as they sat together enjoying the warmth, two professional deceivers practising on each other.

Melanie was twisting her wedding ring, and Kerr could see the temptation in her face. 'We're supposed to be having a day out on Monday, as a matter of fact. Me, Rob and the kids. No Brenda.'

'Sounds perfect. Have a great time.' The seed planted, Kerr got to his feet and stretched. 'No pressure. Don't rush. It's a lovely day. Listen to the birds while you think about it.' He gave a cheery wave and turned away, feeling her eyes on his back. That was something else about them. In any agent recruitment, they both knew a timely retreat was as important as the pitch itself.

Thursday, 25 July, 12.23; the Fishbowl

Karl Sergeyev rang from 1830 while Kerr was on his way back to the Yard and caught up with him in the Fishbowl. He looked cool in his navy suit as he wove through the main office, throwing around high-fives, thumbs-ups and banter. They shook hands and Kerr asked after Nancy and his family.

'Everyone is fine, John,' he said. 'Thank you for asking.' Sergeyev regularly travelled the world protecting Marcus Tennant and Kerr wondered when he had last visited his two children. He noticed Sergeyev was not wearing his wedding ring. Perhaps the split from Nancy was permanent this time.

Kerr squeezed back behind his desk. 'So what was she like?' They had not spoken for several weeks but knew each other well enough to keep small-talk to a minimum.

'I did not have many dealings with Mrs Tennant, to be truthful, John. But she was always very civil to the protection team. Kind of old-style American, you know? Very gracious. And adored her daughter, of course.'

Sergeyev was over six foot three, dark and powerfully built, but his deep voice and sheer energy filled the room as much as his physical presence.

'Who is looking after her?'

'The boss's parents will take her back to Wiltshire.'

'Is that safe?'

'We're having the security layout checked.' While he was speaking Sergeyev removed his jacket and carefully hung it on the back of the chair. His crisp white shirt had a lot of pleats and deep double cuffs held by gold links. 'Tennant is keeping his head down at Hadley until we can get some sense from this.'

Kerr caught a whiff of new leather as Sergeyev removed the tan shoulder holster and hooked it over the other chair, like a gunslinger. He assumed the Glock 17 was loaded. 'How's he taking it?'

'Very badly. It's wiped him out.'

'Is he speaking to anybody?'

'Just the police. And only because he has to.'

'Is there anything about him I should be looking at?'

Sergeyev gave a short laugh and leant back. 'Apart from ego, vanity, ambition and self-obsession, you mean? John, he's a politician.'

'Any specifics?'

'His diary secretary whispered to me he's about to be shifted.'

'Which direction?'

'Downwards. Out of the cabinet.'

'Why?'

'PM's decision.'

'Can you find out for me?'

'Depends. This is strictly top secret, John. He's been looking pretty pissed off all week. Acting like a jerk.'

'So could this demotion be relevant? Do I need to explore it?'

'It's not just that, actually. Tennant will also be feeling a lot of serious guilt.'

'He feels he could have prevented his wife's murder, you mean? Thinks she was attacked because she was married to him?'

Sergeyev crossed his legs, sliding his left ankle up to his right thigh and revealing a well-polished tasselled loafer. Probably purchased on one of his visits to America, thought Kerr, before Sergeyev brought him up with a jolt.

'No, a bad conscience because he was shagging the au pair.'

'Jesus. How do you know?'

'I just do. The girl's name is Yvette.'

'Karl, please don't tell me you heard this from her?' Something about Sergeyev's reaction was already making Kerr fear the worst: that his friend had been sharing the girl with his principal. 'Is there anything else?'

Sergeyev shrugged. 'She certainly wasn't teaching him French.'

'You know I don't mean that.'

Sergeyev tried to look aggrieved.

'Is that why he's being demoted? Did Number Ten find out?'

A shrug.

'I need to speak to her.'

'The uniforms on the gate told me Yvette left the house this morning a few minutes after Mrs Tennant. Probably while she was still alive. In a hurry, on foot with a wheelie case. Like it was goodbye.'

'Where to?'

'No one knows. Yvette has disappeared.'

Eighteen

For nearly half an hour Danny Brennan loitered at the exact spot where the Strand merged into Fleet Street, eyes fixed on the High Court slightly to his left on the other side of the road, its Gothic turrets and ornate clock dominating the scene. He had taken the tube to Bank, changing to the westbound District Line as far as Temple station, then taken the short walk up Arundel Street. Rashid's second beanie protected his shaven head and the hoodie concealed his face. Unobtrusive, rucksack on his back, Brennan slouched against a delivery entrance on the right side of a law firm sandwiched between a shop selling hot pasties and a heel bar. This was where she had instructed him to wait. Strewn with litter blown in from the Strand, the recess between the rusting iron gate and the pavement was the perfect vantage-point to absorb the comings and goings around the courts and wait for the arrival of his victim.

The Strand was thick with buses and taxis plying between the West End, Fleet Street and the City. Pedestrian traffic was two-speed, with groups of leisurely foreign tourists obstructing the path of dark-suited lawyer types strictly on the clock. From the left a group of robed barristers in well-travelled wigs hurried towards him, haughty and bad-tempered, like geese around a duck pond. Everywhere he looked people were clutching paper bundles secured with pink ribbon.

Brennan's target was Hugh Selwyn. He appeared several minutes later than Rashid had predicted but was instantly recognisable from the enlarged photographs she had pinned to the wall in the safe house. Brennan spotted him as soon as he emerged from Bell Yard, a lane running adjacent to the High Court, and turned left. His face was parchment white and he wore a black homburg, charcoal grey suit and barrister's tabs, with a rolled umbrella hooked over his forearm. He moved like a man running late, with short, rapid paces. Even among the other lawyers crowding the Strand, he looked out of place, a figure from a bygone age.

Without warning Selwyn wheeled right onto the pedestrian crossing even though the light was flashing, angling the umbrella in front of him like a white stick. He did not acknowledge the van driver who stopped for him, or the abuse shouted at him through the open window. At the other side he hurried right and came within a single pace of Brennan, who weighed the old man's strength, just as he had with Diane Tennant the previous morning. Selwyn looked slightly heavier than in the photographs but still agile, which might complicate things if he tried to fight back.

As Brennan stepped clear of the pile of rubbish it started to rain. Selwyn paused to unfurl his umbrella, waving it from side to side like a water-diviner as he felt for the release button. He turned through the giant black studded gates guarding Middle Temple Lane, just as Rashid had said he would, continuing at the same pace, protected by his umbrella.

A tour guide appeared, leading a group of cagoule-wearing students, went through the gates just as Brennan was pulling on another pair of blue rubber gloves. Brennan knew Selwyn's chambers were in the last building on the right, first floor, so he fell in behind, keeping the noisy kids between him and his quarry. He dropped back as they abruptly followed their guide left through an arch, heading for Temple Church, leaving him exposed. A few paces further down he took cover by Middle Temple dining hall, roughly the midway point between the Strand and the Thames. He sheltered in the doorway, scanning for CCTV and other potential witnesses, taking in his surroundings.

There were few passers-by and they were all making their way up to the Strand, safely in the opposite direction. Brennan receded further into his hoodie and pulled the beanie low over his eyes. The worn cobbles and slabs, polished from centuries of wear, were now shiny with rain as he peered round the wall to check Selwyn's progress. The target was drawing close to his destination and safety. A woman barrister was making her way up the slope, head bent beneath a golf umbrella. He waited for her to pass, then sprinted down the lane after Selwyn.

He knew timing was critical: there would be only seconds between Selwyn entering his chambers and the door closing on him. A moment too late, and the lawyer would be lost in the safety of his room.

Brennan thought he had timed his move to perfection but Selwyn did not behave as he was supposed to. Before opening the door he stopped to shake the umbrella, so abruptly that Brennan almost collided with him. Skidding to a halt, he found himself trapped in the old man's glare. "Scuse me,' he mumbled, as he eased round Selwyn and pretended to continue down the lane.

The building was accessed through double oak doors. Brennan lingered by the board listing the barristers' names as Selwyn reached the entrance and let himself in, then turned and caught the door before it closed in his face. With his shoe in the gap he peered through the frosted-glass door pane in time to see Selwyn start up the stairs, then let himself in and clicked the door shut.

The stone-floored lobby was deserted, with a closed office door both right and left of the entrance, each made of oak with an old-fashioned brass handle. The staircase opposite the entrance was also made of stone with a wrought-iron banister. As Rashid had warned him, the staircase also led down one floor to a basement. Selwyn's steps echoed against the bare walls as he climbed to the first floor but there was no other sign of life. Brennan darted across the lobby and sprinted up the stairs two at a time, making scarcely a sound. He found Selwyn on the landing, sorting through keys on a fob. There were two doors, replicating those in the lobby, and Selwyn was standing by the one on the left. The staircase led up to one more floor but there was silence apart from the click of Selwyn's keys.

In his left pocket Brennan's gloved thumb flicked away the cover to the syringe. 'Judge,' was all he said. It was almost inaudible, like the apology moments earlier, but Selwyn's head shot up, the old man surprising Brennan with the speed of his reaction. His look was of recognition, not fear, which disappointed Brennan.

'You shouldn't be in here,' Selwyn growled, his voice resonating off the stone walls. He looked bad-tempered and mean as he took in Brennan's appearance. 'You're trespassing. Who are you looking for?'

'I want you, you old bastard,' said Brennan, quietly.

The building was still silent, above and below. 'Get away.' The order was strong for such an old man but now his eyes showed a glimmer of fear. 'Do you hear me? Or I'll have you thrown out.'

Brennan whipped out the syringe and stabbed Selwyn in the neck. It happened so quickly that he did not even register the glint of the needle, his eyes still fixed on Brennan's face. The cocktail of drugs acted immediately and Brennan caught him as his legs gave way, lowering him to the floor so carefully that the only sound came from the clatter of the umbrella and the soft thud of the homburg as it came to rest against the wall.

Rashid had warned Brennan that the cocktail would be fast acting, but its immediacy took Brennan by surprise. It fascinated him, paralysing the old man's body but leaving him conscious. Brennan needed to be sure the poison had worked as effectively as she had promised. He lifted Selwyn's arm and let it drop limply to the floor. He did the same to his leg, holding it beneath the knee, then slapped his face. Nothing in the frail body worked except the eyes, glinting as they flickered frantically from side to side.

He bent down until their faces were almost touching. 'You're totally fucked, aren't you?' whispered Brennan. 'Can't fight, can't even speak. This is what it's like to be powerless.' He injected the rest of the poison into Selwyn's neck, then carefully replaced the cap and returned it to his pocket. From that moment Brennan was entering uncharted territory. The next part of the plan, Rashid had said, lay at his discretion, but he should do nothing to compromise the mission. His sole priority was to escape.

Brennan acted quickly and without hesitation. Slipping the rucksack off his shoulders, he moved to the rectangular stairwell and looked above and below, checking for signs of life. There was still silence in the vast echo chamber, the front door locked. He took a coil of rope from the rucksack. Each metre was marked with blue tape, one end tied expertly into a hangman's noose. Brennan leant over the banister, calculating the drop to the floor of the basement, and found the marker for six metres. He looped the noose around Selwyn's neck. Saliva dribbled down the old man's chin as he tried to say something, but Brennan just smiled as he tied the rope to the banister. 'The sentence is death and I've been playing the hangman, working out the drop.' He slapped Selwyn's face again, hard this time. 'You're a bit fatter than I thought, so this is going to do some serious damage,' he said, checking the knot.

Selwyn's eyes were working frantically. A groan came from deep in his chest as Brennan hauled him up by the scruff of the neck. He bent him over the banister, lifted his legs and tossed him into the void. He had estimated well, allowing enough rope for Selwyn's body to hang between the ground floor and the basement. A dull thud made him think he had miscalculated, but then he realised that the drop had ripped off Selwyn's head. It had rolled a full metre away, bumping against the opposite stair. Selwyn's crumpled corpse lay in the centre of the basement floor, legs and arms at unnatural angles, back broken, the rope swinging like the snapped string of a puppet. Brennan watched as the pools of blood from the neck and head slowly expanded towards each other.

Less than three minutes had passed since he had entered the building.

Suddenly a door opened on the floor above and he heard voices, a man's and a woman's. Brennan saw a pair of ankles appear on the staircase, black tights and sensible patent shoes. He dropped Selwyn's hat after him, grabbed the rucksack and pattered down the stairs. As he opened the door and turned right, towards the Thames, he heard a woman scream. It seemed to go on for ever, echoing through the building.

Brennan took his time. He lifted his face to the sky. The rain was cool on his skin but he scarcely noticed, the exhilaration of the kill wiping out everything else.

There were no more cagoules to hide him but he felt relaxed as he covered the final stretch of pathway leading to the Embankment and safety. An old-timer in uniform at the lower gate was speaking urgently into his phone as Brennan strolled past. He heard another scream for help but then the rush of the real world obliterated her voice as he dodged the traffic to the riverbank and swung right towards Westminster.

To deliver the communiqué, Rashid had directed him to a telephone box near Victoria Gardens. Carefully flattening the sheet of A4, he reached into the rucksack for the second mobile she had given him and dialled the Law Society. He checked his watch as a girl answered. Another woman's voice, younger than yesterday's. 'Law Society, good morning.'

'Grab a pen and make sure you get down every word.'

'I'm sorry?' Just two words, enough to sound officious, up herself, disinterested. Until he started reading.

' "This is People's Resistance. Today we executed a judge, a lackey of the British state and America . . ." '

'You what?'

No, not a proper receptionist. A girl, ill-educated like him, probably covering for someone.

'Don't interrupt me again. "This was done for all the innocent victims of state repression and your so-called anti-terrorism laws. For all the people you turn away and lock up and kidnap and torture on fabricated evidence. For the conspiracy with America." '

'You'll have to speak slower.'

'Shut up and write . . . "Your occupations are acts of terrorism, of new imperialism. This is our act of terrorism in reply, our good war against your campaign of evil." '

There were sirens now and Brennan had to raise his voice. At least two vehicles, probably in the Strand, then a police car flashing past him along the Embankment. He found himself imagining the panic in Middle Temple Lane, its tranquillity shattered. The thought made his face burn with pleasure. ' "Further actions will follow until you withdraw the imperialist forces from oppressed nations. This is People's Resistance." '

Check. Fifty-seven seconds.

Nineteen

'One five. You need to work out more, Dad.'

Hands planted on his knees, Commander Ajay Khan leant against the rear glass wall of the squash court and fought for breath. While forensics teams examined the corpse of Hugh Selwyn at Middle Temple, Khan, forty-two, was being thrashed at squash by a sixteen-year-old. Introduced to the sport three decades ago by his father, a one-time regional champion in India, Ajay had brought his own son to the game as soon as he could hold a racquet.

As head of the intelligence unit in SO15 Counter Terrorism Command, Ajay was boss to Bill Ritchie and John Kerr, but this morning he was spending precious family time at Bushey, one of four Metropolitan Police sports clubs dotted around London. He had taken an early flight from Prague, reaching his office before nine, then grabbed his kit and driven straight to the club, leaving his driver at the Yard. Ajay had upgraded the dull Toyota Prius used by his predecessor to a silver Audi A6 with black-leather upholstery, siren, blue lights embedded in the radiator and special anti-bomb coating on the underside. He enjoyed driving it. Everyone knew the man and the car meant business.

'You want to concede, Dad?' Sweat dripped from Ajay's chin to form a pool on the floor but the boy was bouncing from one foot to the other, dry as a bone.

Ajay stayed low and shook his head. 'No way.'

The commander's real name was Ashok Jamal Khan, but everyone knew him as 'Ajay'. He was not your average nine-to-five overseer with every weekend off. From his first day on the eighteenth floor ten months earlier he had insisted on being informed about every significant event. He worked solidly, with his phone and mind permanently switched on and Saturdays spent at the office. With a master's in business administration from University College of Los Angeles, Ajay Khan had an insatiable appetite for absorbing raw source material before it was cooked, boiled or watered down. He visited 1830 most mornings for a personal update from Alan Fargo and would often intercept officers in the corridor or the lift to ask what they were working on that day.

Ajay's energy was boundless, his questions penetrating and his rationale simple. 'How can I command this unit,' he had said to Bill Ritchie, at the end of his first week, 'unless I understand how difficult their lives are?' Word had soon got round that Ajay Khan was unusual: somehow they had acquired a commander who cared.

Because he worked quickly and needed telling only once, Ajay managed to escape the grind by sneaking to the squash court for a couple of hours once a week, either for a match with his son if he was on study leave or to lob practice shots alone. Donna happily covered for him because she knew it was good for his family life and sanity, though she was shrewd enough to let Kerr in on their secret.

'Somebody wants you,' said the boy, in a tone that told Ajay he was letting him off the hook. Ajay looked through the glass wall and spotted the BlackBerry's winking red light beside the towels, water bottles and his son's designer iPhone case. He opened the door, left the court and slumped on the spectators' bench, scrolling through the messages as he towelled his glistening neck. Since his last check five minutes earlier, with the score at one–two, three texts and a couple of missed calls from his PA had appeared.

Donna picked up on the first ring.

'Ajay,' he said, still short of breath.

He encouraged Donna to call him Ajay in private, though first-name terms with the boss seemed to elude her. Trapped between her natural deference and his familiarity, Donna tended not to call him anything. 'You sound like a stretcher case,' she said.

'I'm dead. What have we got?' Through the glass Ajay watched his son aim a series of perfect backhands along the side wall.

'You need to come back now. There's been a second attack, like the Diane Tennant thing. Same people, says Mr Ritchie. Commissioner's already been on.'

'Where am I?'

'Foreign Office about the Pakistan visit.'

'Very good.' Khan checked his watch and tapped on the glass to his son. 'OK, back by half twelve.'

Friday, 26 July, 12.36; Ajay's office

Kerr had warned Donna he would be a few minutes late while he waited in 1830 for the checks on Hugh Selwyn and the readout of the second communiqué, so Ajay was already catching up with Bill Ritchie when he arrived. Ajay's office was as large as Room 1830 at the opposite corner of the eight-eenth floor. It had a double aspect with panoramic views of Buckingham Palace and St James's Park, though Kerr sensed Ajay would be happier at a regular workstation among the troops.

Ritchie was sitting at the conference table with his trade-mark yellow legal pad. He had his back to the window and scarcely acknowledged Kerr. He looked tired, in a purple shirt that seemed to match his mood. Ajay was at his desk sipping tea and talking about his Europol meeting in Prague while he scanned Donna's filtered emails. He even found time to glance at the rolling news on Sky. All hell might be breaking loose in the world around them but the atmosphere in this office was always calm, its multi-tasking occupant unperturbed.

Ajay had showered and looked refreshed in a crisp white shirt but Kerr spotted the racquet handle hidden beneath the desk. He took the chair opposite Ritchie, facing the window within line of sight of the TV screen. As Ajay stood up with his tea, a coaster and a tablet PC, Kerr noticed him give the sports bag a gentle kick deeper beneath the desk. Ajay sat at the head of the table to Kerr's right and squared his tablet with the edge of the table. 'Well, I already have most of the gory details.' On the table he delicately laid one hand over the other, like a cat resting its paws. 'Who wants to bring me up to speed?'

Ritchie tapped his pen on the table. 'The first murder scene is looking pretty unproductive, Ajay. They're working on the assumption the killer hid in the woods facing the house and watched Diane Tennant come to him.'

'Brilliant.'

'They've found several possible sites, you know, hollows in the bushes. But a lot of rough sleepers hang out in those woods.'

'With plenty of rain to wash away the evidence. And I see the tabloids are already entering "frenzied attack" territory.'

'Yeah, which is wrong. This was actually pretty calculated in my view.'

'And a stabbing should produce DNA, yes? Frenzied or not?'

'No forensics yet.' Ritchie shrugged. 'No weapon, not even a footprint they can be sure about. Zero witnesses. They're still collecting CCTV from the high street. That's about it on Diane Tennant so far.'

'There was the emergency Cabinet Office meeting,' said Kerr, looking at Ritchie.

'Sure,' said Ajay. 'Bill and I already covered that offline.'

Kerr was surprised that Ritchie had excluded him, then realised he must have raised it while they waited for him to arrive. He glanced at Ritchie, but his head was down. He wondered if his boss had also briefed Ajay on his proposal about Melanie.

'They're more hopeful about the Middle Temple scene,' said Ritchie. 'Indoor attack, everything sealed within minutes. Pathologist thinks the victim may have been drugged. She'll be checking for puncture marks.'

'Bit difficult with the head ripped off, I imagine,' said Ajay.

'And there are more potential witnesses, too.'

'Except from the Law Society,' said Kerr. 'The woman covering the phones was an agency temp, first day on the job. Calls are automatically recorded, but this morning there was an equipment defect so we're relying on her memory.'

'Which is?'

'Patchy. She thought it was a hoax, then didn't have a pen to hand. Only used a keyboard since leaving school but managed to scrawl a few notes.' Kerr unfolded a sheet of A4. 'Gemma managed to get us a printout of her statement. She says the claim was from People's Resistance.'

'Unprompted, presumably?'

'Let's hope so. Says the caller was male with a London accent.'

'Where is she from?'

'Ilford. Said he spoke like her. The rest is proving hard work.' Kerr smoothed the paper on the table. 'She remembers him saying they had killed "a lackey of the British and Americans". And something about "revenge for people turned away, kidnapped and tortured". She's certain about those words because she managed to get them down.'

'Any descriptions from the scene?'

Kerr glanced at the television and nudged Ajay's forearm. 'Perhaps the man himself will tell us.'

Ajay swung round to see Derek Finch, overall head of SO15 Counter Terrorism Command, investigator in chief and Ajay's boss, taking questions at a press conference in the briefing room thirteen floors beneath them. He reached for the remote and cancelled the mute as Ritchie came round the table for a better view. Finch was known as the Bull and TV always bulked him up by at least thirty pounds.

He had obviously arranged the conference to cover the Diane Tennant murder. The second added a serious complication: the prospect of serial killings within a politically motivated campaign was more difficult to explain away than a lone-wolf assault. Hugh Selwyn's execution added a layer of planning, organisation and structure for which the Bull was unprepared. It also opened a rich seam of questions, to which the reporters wanted answers now. No one cultivated crime reporters more assiduously than Derek Finch, but today he looked rattled as the pack closed in. His lunch hosts, drinking buddies and ticket procurers were letting him know that nothing in life was free. Today was payback time.

Kerr's focus was on Ajay: Donna had told him there was bad blood between him and Finch. Evidently the Bull had crudely tried to block Ajay's appointment by parachuting in his senior investigator to run the intelligence side for him. The plot had failed because Ajay had neatly outmanoeuvred him with the commissioner, resulting in a humiliating retreat. As soon as his position had been secured, one of Ajay's first acts had been to invite MI5 to embed a liaison officer within his unit at the Yard. Kerr could see that Ajay was thinking long term, more interested in moving closer to MI5 and MI6 than appeasing Derek Finch. Real strength lay in strategic alignment, not tactical power grabs.

The Bull's resentment ran deep: almost a year later he had yet to shake Ajay's hand in welcome. So Kerr watched Ajay watching Finch. But Ajay remained the cool cat, his face unreadable.

The reporters' questions came in a torrent. What do you know about People's Resistance? How many members does it have? What level of organisation and sophistication? Was any warning given? How many attackers? Do you have any descriptions? Will we be getting photofits?

The Bull floundered, dissembled and pontificated.

Why had People's Resistance selected these victims? Had there been any indication that they were under threat? Had they interviewed Marcus Tennant? Any connection between Diane Tennant and Hugh Selwyn? Was it true the lawyer had been drugged?

The less Finch knew, the more he blustered. Twice he accidentally knocked one of the microphones. Only his body language was unambiguous, and the camera magnified his irritation as much as his weight.

Why would People's Resistance risk telephoning the claims? Why not use the Internet? What kind of voice? Any accent? Would they be releasing the text of the communiqués in full? Were they looking for home-grown extremists or Islamic terrorists? Was the public at risk? Would MI5 upgrade the terror threat level? Had the police asked for their help?

The Bull kept saying he was keeping an open mind but Kerr knew the journalists' were already made up. The media would be sending out a single message: People's Resistance, whoever they might be, had caught police asleep at the wheel.

Ajay pressed mute and turned round. 'I think you tell it better, Bill,' he said drily, then smiled and finished his tea. 'So let's circle back to what we know.'

Twenty

Brennan's orders had been to escape the scene the moment he had delivered the communiqué. Instead he crossed to the riverbank, adjusted the beanie, took off his rucksack and sat on a bench a few paces east of the entrance to Middle Temple Lane, head and face almost completely concealed. The converging blue lights held him back, drawing him to the scene, like an arsonist seduced by his own fire. A couple of sirens were still active inside the lane, their shrieks echoing off the ancient walls. For a few seconds it sounded as if a dozen vehicles were crammed in there, a whole riot squad mobilised because of one man.

A third car raced up the Embankment from the direction of New Scotland Yard. This was an unmarked Ford Mondeo with three plain-clothes cops inside. It overshot the entrance, skidding to a halt on the wet surface, then reversing and wheel-spinning into the lane. Not much business around the Inns of Court, Brennan thought, except to get people banged up to the max. No one was looking in his direction. He tracked the blue lights of an ambulance racing across Westminster Bridge from the South Bank. Turning into the Embankment it seemed to charge straight for him before swaying left through the narrow gates.

Brennan was transfixed. Single-handedly he had reduced this whole area to a war zone and it gave him a powerful buzz. The cops had been sent there because of him, just as they had chased him with their shields and batons during the riots two years earlier. For a few moments this oasis of privilege and injustice was no better than Tottenham, and it was all his doing. As the sirens fell quiet, shouts and radio static carried to him across the street while a couple of medics in green loitered by their ambulance. Brennan guessed a decapitation made them redundant.

He stood to take a last look up the lane. As he had followed Selwyn he had been struck by the trees, grass patches and centuries-old buildings, conscious that he had trespassed into another world. Brennan had never been near a university but imagined Oxford or Cambridge would be just like this, an oasis of privilege beyond the city's bustle.

Now the cops were rolling out their tape, cordoning off the area from which he, the outsider, had just walked. Men and women in black suits and white shirts with tabs instead of a tie swarmed down the slope to rubberneck, powerless as penguins waddling to the scene of a cull. People who spent their days judging the lives of others could only crowd behind the cordon to watch the scene he had created. Today Brennan was the one in control and the realisation transformed him.

Until the conflagration in Tottenham he had always thought of himself as a man with limitations. In prison he had been told it was more inventive to instil collective fear than torch a single furniture store, and today he was beginning to understand, to believe in his creative potential. Adrenaline surged through him, expelling any self-doubt, and he found himself thinking of his father. Face uplifted to the rain, he pulled the beanie over his forehead and prepared to get away to the safe house and Anna Rashid. He needed her to tell him he was capable of even greater things than this.

A number 388 bus came hissing along the Embankment from Westminster. He grabbed the rucksack, yanked the hoodie over his head and sprinted for the stop.

Friday, 26 July, 12.47; safe house, Bethnal Green

The bus journey gave Brennan time to decompress. It took fifty minutes to reach Bethnal Green, his face lowered on the top deck away from the CCTV camera, and another three to access the house.

Sweet cannabis smoke hit him as soon as he reached the top of the ladder. Rashid was waiting for him, naked on the bed, smoking a joint as she watched breaking news of their action, clothes abandoned on the floor. He immediately felt a stab of resentment. In less than three days he had come to regard the safe house as his home, his private space, and Rashid was an intruder. Beside the bed was a plate with ash from an earlier smoke. 'Welcome back,' said Rashid, but this disappointed him, too, because her voice was slurred and he wanted to talk with her about Selwyn and their future work.

He took the syringe from his pocket and returned the gloves to the drawer, then stayed glued to the TV as he undressed. News crews had approached the murder scene from the top of the lane, tracing Brennan's pursuit. The reporter was sheltering beneath an umbrella twice as large as Selwyn's, and it fascinated him to see her standing on the glistening cobbles along which he had sprinted just two hours earlier.

Standing beside the bed he found himself reliving the attack through Sky News and wanted Rashid to share it. He told her about the students who had covered his approach and pointed to the spot by the dining hall where he had taken refuge before the final chase. He described how he had almost crashed into the old man just before hanging him, even tried to make a joke of it. He had never spoken so much to Rashid and tried to restrain her as she reached out and pulled him down beside her. He wanted to talk some more. 'Don't you want to see how I did the old bastard?'

'It's mood music,' she said, climbing on top of him.

Brennan was quick because the TV had pumped him up again and Rashid sent them both spinning out of control. As they rolled apart, the camera closed in on Derek Finch taking his seat for the press conference. They watched in silence as Rashid lit her third joint, enjoying Finch's discomfort. 'What a moron. The cops are nowhere,' she said. It was the first time they had laughed together.

She pointed to the book she had brought him, lying open on the worktop. 'Is that to impress me or have you actually been reading it?'

'Nechayev.' He felt embarrassed. 'Took a look last night.'

'Don't waste your energy, Danny.'

He turned to her, provoked by the mockery in her voice. 'You study it, don't you?'

She laughed again, but it was different this time, almost like a cough, with no warmth in the eyes. She reminded him of the teacher he had hated most at school. 'That's different,' she said.

'Why?' He felt a flash of anger. 'Because I'm stupid?'

'No. I'm just saying the nineteenth-century language doesn't translate well.' She looked awkward. 'Not if you haven't tried this stuff before. That's all I meant.'

'But is that what you think? That I'm just here to do the action in the street, then run back here and do you? Is that what this is about?'

'Doesn't matter what either of us *thinks*,' said Rashid, leaning over to flick ash onto the plate. 'We're both here to make this work.' Now she reminded Brennan of the woman from Jobcentre Plus, making violent direct action sound like overnight shelf-stacking at Tesco.

'Well, I did read a bit of it and it made a light come on in my brain. Suddenly I know why everything has pissed me off for my entire fucking life. What they did to my dad. How they treated him, how they didn't care.'

'What do you mean?'

'My dad was electrocuted. Burnt alive. They said it was his own fault.'

'How?'

'Doesn't matter.' He nodded across the room. 'Those words can be two hundred years old for all I care. But they're showing me what it means to get back at them. And that old guy has taken me there.' He padded across to the worktop, flicked on the desk lamp and picked up the open book. 'Listen. "He should not hesitate to destroy any position, any place or any man in this world." It's about fighting injustice. Like I just did to that bastard lawyer.'

They sat for a while, watching TV, then Rashid turned to him. 'What do you mean, "get back at them"?'

'It's obvious, isn't it?'

'Don't get any ideas. We have a long way to go.'

'I'm an anarchist, aren't I? Isn't that why I'm here? Anna, you have to make sense of this stuff for me. You and your friends, when you're not stoned. I want you to take me to them.'

'That's not possible.' The words came at him like darts. Suddenly she even sounded like his teacher. Rashid swung her legs off the bed and made for the bathroom, conversation over. He called out but all he got was the sound of running water as she washed his body from hers. White noise, screaming inside his head.

When she reappeared she was using his towel and immediately searched his clothes for the communiqué. Suddenly she seemed in a hurry.

'I said why not?' he said.

Rashid lit the gas hob and held the communiqué over it. The paper was still damp and hissed in the flame. A fragment floated onto her breast and she leapt back and swore.

'Why not?' he repeated.

'Because secrecy is paramount.' Spoken like a professional. He stared at her as she rubbed herself dry and threw the towel onto the bed. 'You turning out to be some radical-chic street-fighter is not part of the plan.'

He noticed she was no longer slurring. It was the voice she had used when they had first met, distant and unfriendly. But there was another layer now. Was it anger or fear? 'You what?' he said, confused. 'You don't own me, you know.'

She dropped her voice, as if someone might be eavesdropping. 'How much do you think it cost to build this place for you, Danny? Do you think they're going to let you charge off on some private rampage of your own? This is about resistance, not revenge.' Now he knew. It was fear. He watched her grab her clothes from the floor and hurriedly get dressed. 'Your job is to carry out the mission, read the message, get back here and hide until I send you out again. What part of that don't you understand?'

'What about after that? My life when this is over?'

'Your life is People's Resistance.' She already had a foot on the ladder. 'You want to do something useful? Fix my car, like I keep telling you.'

Twenty-One

'So, to paraphrase. Diane Tennant blameless, husband a bit of a shit. Right?' said Ajay, sitting back in his chair. He looked from Ritchie to Kerr. 'All perfectly understandable. But why hit a geriatric barrister?'

'Senior judge, actually,' said Kerr. 'High Court. And Hugh Selwyn hasn't been winning popularity contests either. A lot of people hated him with a vengeance. This is not your benign old granddad with short-term memory loss and a dodgy prostate.' He frowned at his clumsiness, throwing an apologetic look at Ritchie. 'He advised government on the 2000 Terrorism Act. Very right-wing, in bed with MI5. No real public profile but active behind the scenes, security-vetted with all the right clearances.'

'Tame, you mean,' said Ajay. 'Sold out to the spooks.'

'A lot of seriously pissed-off people were saying exactly that. But what really sets him apart is his involvement with SIAC.'

Ajay frowned. 'He worked on immigration cases?'

'Special Immigration Appeals Commission. Yup.'

'What – presenting the appeal?'

'No, providing the grounds to reject it. When an appeal fails the panel can deport on national-security grounds. And they don't have to give detail because everything is secret. They don't tell the appellant why he is being kicked out. It looks like they were using Selwyn to channel the damaging intelligence. His official role was adviser to the panel. Which means he could be trusted to do the right thing.'

'To betray Muslims, you mean,' said Ajay. 'But the panel would already have access to MI5 and MI6, surely? Why would they need him?'

'The allegation is that he was helping them invent grounds for rejecting dodgy appellants,' said Kerr. 'For example, let's say MI5 believes a guy is a jihadi but they have no actual proof. How do they get round it? Easy. Sex up the intelligence, stamp it Top Secret and feed it in through Selwyn. Next stop Heathrow and out. That's the story bouncing around the blogosphere. No one would ever find out it was a lie.'

'The perfect cut-out,' said Ajay.

'That's the word on the street. They were already rejecting appeals on a rock-bottom burden of proof. Judge Hugh Selwyn pulled it down into the sewer.'

'The girl at the Law Society also mentioned the Americans,' said Ajay.

'Two Muslim activist groups were claiming that Selwyn had been helping the Americans draft their extradition requests for the British courts, then lobbying to get them through.'

'How do they know that?'

'It's what they're blogging, Ajay. A lot of people are going to think it's true.'

'So the state deports innocent Muslims on the basis of secret lies provided by our esteemed judge,' said Ajay. 'Yes, that would make people pretty sore.'

'Or worse. Check out the communiqué.'

Ajay sat quietly for a moment, eyes still flicking between them as he computed the information. He opened his tablet. 'So how do we take this forward? We have a number of emerging features common to both attacks, yes?' He started tapping. 'The unusual nature and level of violence, the communiqués, the claim by People's Resistance?'

'Plus the thing with the noose,' said Kerr. 'Symbolic in Diane Tennant's case, then actually stringing Selwyn up. Both made to look like an execution.'

'Agreed.' Kerr could see three bullet points on the screen. 'So, I need a decent intelligence strategy I can take to the commissioner.'

'John and I are already working on that,' said Ritchie, with a warning look at Kerr.

'Is MI5 assisting?'

'Too busy learning Arabic,' said Kerr.

'So what's the value added from the Branch?'

Kerr and Ritchie exchanged a glance. Ajay had recently begun to refer to his unit by its original title again, reviving a sense of history and restoring morale overnight. He regularly used the title 'Special Branch' at meetings and had spoken about establishing an entry examination separate from that used by the rest of the Met. Since the débâcle over phone hacking and corruption it had become essential, he argued to anyone who would listen, inflaming the Bull even more.

Kerr knew from personal experience that Ajay was also fiercely protective of his officers. That June, his gunfight on the Thames had triggered intense media speculation until its referral to the Independent Police Complaints Commission. Ajay had not only shielded Kerr from the press by issuing his own statement, but had also refused Finch's demand that Kerr be suspended from duty until the IPCC investigation was concluded. 'I'm supporting you, John, naturally,' Ajay had said, when Kerr thanked him, 'because I can't afford to lose a man of such integrity. Not for a single day.' Later, Donna confided that Ajay had even been prepared to support Kerr before the Ethics Committee.

One evening, only a week after his appointment, Ajay had invited Ritchie and Kerr to his office for a glass of whisky. Talking about his plans, he had told them his father had been a senior Special Branch officer in Delhi. 'Many years ago Britain was kind enough to give the Special Branch to India, guys,' he had said. 'It worked so well that Dad and I want to return it to you.' For this, everyone forgave Ajay his use of American management-speak. Bill Ritchie had even joked that Ajay was so brilliant he bore him no hard feelings for having stolen his job.

'I think the anti-US rhetoric is a major factor, Ajay,' said Ritchie. 'If this continues we can anticipate more American targets. And let's not dismiss potential jihadi involvement. Or hostile state activity, for that matter.'

'You really believe that, Bill?'

'It's a possibility. I certainly think we should be involving the US embassy right away.'

'OK. Sure. I'll raise that with the commissioner,' said Ajay. He worked the tablet again. 'But what actual leads can we develop right now?'

'Start with the ambiguity,' said Kerr. 'The assaults are obviously well planned and the claims suggest an organised group, plus the threat of further actions. But the actual attacks don't fit the profile. They seem utterly reckless. Diane Tennant practically disembowelled, the judge decapitated. Both in broad daylight. The murderers could have been disturbed at any moment.'

'So at one end of the pipeline we find an organised dissident campaign they claim can run and run,' said Ajay, 'and at the other a series of savage, high-risk murders.'

'Exactly.'

'Collective anti-state rhetoric versus deep, personal hatred.'

'Extremist and psychopathic, or made to appear that way,' said Kerr. 'We have to ask ourselves why they would do that.'

Ritchie gave a short laugh. 'To force us into a conversation like this. Muddy the water.'

Ajay smiled. 'And the two claims mirror that contrast,' he said, 'connecting condemnation of a foreign war with a grievance against injustice.'

'It's crude, but so what?' Ritchie was sounding impatient. 'Two high-profile butchered corpses guarantee we take them seriously.'

'So where do we start to drill down?' said Ajay, steepling his fingers.

'With this much violence they're bound to have left forensic traces,' said Ritchie. 'Let's see what Derek Finch comes up with.'

'But if the attackers have been clever, or lucky, and we get no evidential leads, we're going to have to make sense of this ourselves,' said Kerr, nodding at the TV. 'We can't waste a moment. You just saw what they're going to throw at us unless we crack this quickly. It'll only get worse with each attack. We have to squeeze the most from what we know right now. Today.'

Ajay was looking at him intently. 'Which is?'

Kerr threw a glance at Ritchie. 'The first claim is drenched in anarchist terminology. Today's may have been, too, but the girl didn't manage to scribble it down. We can't be sure about external involvement at this stage. I say we run a domestic-extremism intelligence op until we find something better.'

'Specifics?'

'Something Bill and I discussed yesterday.' Ritchie was shaking his head so vigorously that Kerr had to look away. 'I propose we return Melanie Fleming to the field to generate human intelligence and search for leads. If she comes up with something, great. If not, we can move on and turn over another stone. At least we'll know.'

Ritchie punched straight back: 'John ran this past me and I already rejected it. We can't allow a fishing expedition using a damaged officer.' He glared at Kerr. 'Find another way.'

But Kerr had already caught the lift in Ajay's shoulders and drove deeper. He had also heard about Ajay's plan to create a dedicated undercover unit. 'It's classic Special Branch territory,' he said, 'and low risk.'

Ajay raised his hands in conciliation but looked to Ritchie. 'Point taken, Bill. Absolutely. This officer has endured enough. Quite beyond the call of duty, in fact.' Then he turned to Kerr. 'Out of interest, is there any low-hanging fruit for her out there that she could pluck without putting herself in jeopardy?'

'Our surveillance has covered a lot of domestic groups, usually before anti-capitalist demos. You know, Occupy London, Anonymous, et cetera. Jack Langton tells me none would be capable of carrying out these attacks.'

Ritchie opened his hands. 'Which says it all.'

'Since yesterday afternoon Derek Finch's teams have been busy carrying out raids on anything remotely alternative. Knee-jerking all over London, with more to come.'

'Did we help them with addresses?'

'I think they searched "anarchist" on the Internet. One of the first to get hammered was the *Flag of Liberty* in Shoreditch. This is one of the few anarchist ideological centres still in existence. They didn't find a thing because everyone was at a conference in Manchester. It all checked out. Point is, the *Flag* is a propaganda journal with wide access.'

'And completely non-violent,' said Ritchie.

'But its people are in the know. I heard their printing press is out of action and they urgently need volunteers to help get the journal out. They won't be expecting another visit from police. If we want a quick result, this is the perfect infiltration opportunity, boss.'

Ajay looked from one to the other. He seemed to be absorbing the tension. 'I take it you haven't raised this with Melanie yet.'

'Melanie is a fish out of water in 1830,' said Kerr, who always interpreted 'yet' as a sign of encouragement. 'She's desperate to go operational again, to get back to surveillance. Pesters me every day. She's practically stalking me.'

There was a knock on the door and Donna put her head round. Ajay gave her the thumbs-up and checked his watch. 'Commissioner.' He looked to his right again, pointedly addressing his deputy: 'All right, Bill. Let's park this for now and loop back later when we've all had a chance to think.'

For now. Kerr was impressed. Ajay was reassuring Ritchie with words meant for Kerr. The perfect manager.

Ajay wheeled round to his desk for his jacket and another nudge of the sports bag. 'Stay close to Mr Finch's investigators, yes? Let me know if you run into a headwind.'

Kerr looked at Ritchie, but he was not smiling.

Ajay squeezed them both on the arm as he headed out. He turned back by the open door. 'Oh, and if Marcus Tennant's au pair with benefits turns up let me know, won't you?' He gave another thumbs-up and nodded at Kerr. In Ajay's eyes Kerr saw a green light. He got out before Ritchie could berate him, speed-dialling Jack Langton as he hurried round to the Fishbowl.

Saturday, 27 July, 02.40;
Flag of Liberty, Shoreditch

Justin eased his shoulders under the weight of the rucksack on his back. It was unusually heavy: it contained a crowbar and hammer as well as his usual lock-picking equipment. Tonight's mission would not be about technical finesse. He was waiting for Jack Langton in a service alley twenty metres from his flat near Putney Bridge, and the motorcycle emerged from a bend in the road fifteen seconds after he heard it. Another ten to climb aboard, fit his helmet and tap Langton on the shoulder, and they were on the move again. Without a word they rode south of the river through the quiet streets of Battersea and Lambeth, crossing the Thames over a deserted Waterloo Bridge and continuing to Clerkenwell. The journey deep into east London took just sixteen minutes.

They were headed for the *Flag of Liberty* press, bookshop and office in Shoreditch, just north of Liverpool Street station. John Kerr's briefing that evening had left little time for a proper recce. All they had to work from were two external photographs Justin had snatched of the main door late on Friday afternoon, while the building was still occupied, plus a few internal shots taken by Finch's officers during their visit following Diane Tennant's murder.

The *Flag* was located two hundred paces from Shoreditch High Street, at the dead end of an unlit Victorian alleyway separating two rows of shops. It was on two levels, with the only entrance at the rear of the building, completely hidden from view by a brick wall and high, windowless buildings on three sides of the alley. Langton parked the bike in Bateman's Row, close to the town hall and a short sprint from the deserted alleyway. Both men wore gloves. Justin defeated the giant padlock almost before Langton could aim his pencil torch and they were inside within fifteen seconds.

They moved quickly: their task was limited and specific. On the ground floor Justin used Langton's torch to examine a heavy, ancient printing press. His brief from Kerr was to determine whether the press was still operational. Justin could not be sure, but found new grease and oil on the floor, signs of recent use. They turned right and climbed the rickety staircase to the first floor. Up here was the shop and, straight ahead, a glass-partitioned office.

The flimsy door was secured with a Yale but this time Justin used the crowbar. Langton had already shone his torch inside and seen what they were looking for. Taking the hammer from Justin's rucksack, he smashed the Goss computerised printing press and collating machine, putting them beyond use.

As they retraced their steps Justin carefully took video of every area. At the main door he secured the padlock again then stepped back for Langton to rip away the hasp with the crowbar, making it appear they had entered that way. Their visit that night would appear a clumsy break-in, the sabotage an act of wanton vandalism.

Back in the main street Justin photographed an ancient maroon VW caravanette parked outside the entrance to the alleyway.

Three minutes later they were on the road again, mission accomplished.

Twenty-two

Anna Rashid knew her controller only as Peter. He maintained contact through an electronic dead-letterbox built into a slab of reinforced concrete at the junction of Highgate and Fortess Roads, close to Kentish Town Underground station. Cracked, discoloured and lopsided, half covered with empty beer cans and takeaway cartons, the concrete appeared to have been dumped long ago in a triangle of dead ground between a mobile-phone shop and a computer repair shop. A stretch of rusting iron railings that had somehow escaped the attention of Camden's metal thieves separated it from the pavement.

In fact, this innocuous rectangular block housed technology more advanced and engineering sharper than any of the products in the specialist outlets each side. A short-wave device the size of a postage stamp, powerful enough to communicate with a strolling pedestrian or crawling car ten metres away, was concealed in a rod of reinforcing iron. Rashid had to drive here twice a week to receive orders and communicate information, and at any time in cases of urgency. To service the device Peter had issued her with an innocuous rectangle of black plastic the size of a matchbox and just as light, small enough to be sewn into the lining of her coat. It had a receiver for capturing instructions and a transmit button for squirting her own signals via the keypad of her mobile phone.

The device was used principally to set up their meetings at one of three safe locations within a mile of Highgate. The sites were coded 'Topaz', 'Coral' and 'Jade'. Topaz was in Parliament Hill Fields. Rashid would park her temperamental Corsa at a meter in Gordon House Road and walk through the lower field as far as the running track four hundred metres away, then sit by the adjacent pavilion with a book and wait. Peter always watched her from the top of Parliament Hill, more than three hundred feet high with panoramic views of London. Disobeying his order never to look, Rashid had occasionally spotted him sitting on a bench between the trees, tracking her, ensuring she was being observed by no one but him. He told her the bench had an italicised plate of dedication 'To Larry, a resident of Highgate for sixty years, who found tranquillity in this beautiful spot. "The peace of the Lord which passeth all understanding ..."' Every time they used Topaz he repeated it. The irony seemed to amuse him – he considered that he and Anna Rashid were joined in war.

If Peter needed to see her in the evening he would direct her to Coral, a dark wood Victorian pub in Belsize Park, just off Haverstock Hill and a stone's throw from the Royal Free Hospital. It sold overcooked food, real ale and badly poured Guinness, and had a 'No Working Clothes' sign outside. The Churchill Arms claimed to be a gastro pub but Peter seemed to hate it as much as Rashid did. He had once found something crawling in his limp lettuce leaf and told her it captured England perfectly.

This morning he had directed Rashid to Jade, a pretentious coffee and cake shop called Day Break in Swains Lane, just south of Highgate Cemetery. It lay in the middle of a short parade of shops between a hairdresser and the local post office, with a couple of outside tables spattered with bird shit and an old-fashioned delivery bicycle chained to the wall. The French proprietor and his wife wore matching striped aprons and made their own croissants in the kitchen to the rear of the premises. The shop was long and narrow, with pine furniture and the aroma of fresh coffee and baking. To the left, running down one wall, the counter was stacked with French bread, open sandwiches and patisserie, in addition to the croissants. A pile of CDs recorded by their son, a classical guitarist living in Marseille, was for sale beside the till.

For security, Peter always required Rashid to arrive first. She took the table in the far-left corner beyond the counter and ordered a cafetière for two. Peter arrived three minutes later. He was in his sixties, lean-faced and dapper in a double-breasted navy suit and grey trilby. The weather was mild but, as always, he carried a neatly folded black raincoat on his arm. In his other hand he held two identical carrier bags.

It was the interval between elevenses and lunch, so the shop was fairly quiet. Three elderly ladies sat alongside the wall opposite the counter, and a couple of Muslim boys lingered by the bar stools in the window with cans of Coke. Rashid watched Peter beam at the proprietor and clock the other customers all in one sweep. He placed the carrier bags on the floor, laid his hat and coat on the chair beside him and carefully flattened his thinning hair. A few strays escaped but Rashid decided not to tell him, relishing the moment.

As Peter took his seat classical-guitar music began flowing from a speaker above the toilet sign. Every time they came here Rashid realised how incongruous they must look: she unconventional, dressed in black, her controller at least three decades older, the archetypal English gent. Only his shoes gave Peter away. They were of black, matt leather with thick rubber soles and metal eyelets for the laces. On the night she agreed to work for him she had called them his 'secret-agent giveaways'. She caught the proprietor's wife studying them as she laid their crockery on a tray, relationship spotting. Father and daughter? Uncle and niece? Weirdo lovers?

'Shall I be mother?' said Peter, as the coffee arrived. This was another part of the ritual, like his repetition of the story about the bench of tranquillity.

Rashid shrugged, as always. Peter spoke fluently but with the indeterminate accent of a man who had lived in many countries. He had never told her his surname or, she suspected, his true first name; in fact, he had yet to volunteer a single detail about himself, except that the coffee here reminded him of his favourite place in Paris.

Peter had been wearing the same suit when he had pitched to her on a Saturday evening three months ago as she was heading home after a 'Stop the Torture Coalition' demonstration in Trafalgar Square. Intercepting her as she walked up Charing Cross Road to the tube, he had quietly called her by name, tipped his hat and told her he wanted to talk about Parvez Rashid. His style had been disconcerting, but the substance had grabbed her. When she wavered he had held out his card and invited her to call him. Rashid had been overcome by curiosity – no one had mentioned her lover's name in a long time. This old man, non-threatening and courteous, had intrigued her; something about him had made her feel strong again. 'Let's do the talking now,' she had said, slipping the card into her pocket.

Peter had taken her to the Eagle, a quiet pub off the tourist trail just behind Old Compton Street. Without asking he had bought them both a double whisky, her favourite drink, and she had guessed this was to show how much he already knew about her, and that they were similar. His plastic seat cover was ripped but he had seemed not to notice. Even in his suit on a Saturday evening Peter had not looked out of place.

For twenty minutes Rashid had listened in astonishment as Peter recounted the circumstances leading to Parvez Rashid's death. Then he had told her about the deep hatred he knew she bore against those who had killed him. It was all true. In the weeks following her lover's cremation she had become politically active again, fired by resentment, his death radicalising her far more than any zealot from her student days in Brighton. She had looked up a few of her most trusted anarchist comrades only to find they had sold out and mortgaged up. Latching onto the ragbag detritus of London's radical left, Rashid had always returned home feeling isolated and marginalised.

Peter had expressed this as 'ideological disappointment'. 'So many causes, so little anger among the British,' he had said, sipping his whisky. 'But I know what motivates you.'

'Oh, really?' Rashid had taken her cue. 'And what's that?'

'In my business I deal only in revenge, money or betrayal. They are my stock in trade.'

Rashid had smiled. Over the years she had read many stories of hostile foreign states seeking to stoke the dying embers of the British hard left. 'You're a foreign fucking spy, you mean?'

'Point one. The British and American governments are joined in an evil conspiracy that effectively murdered Parvez Rashid. Two. The British legal system is slavishly subservient to America. These are the things you believe. Am I right?'

Peter had been spot on. 'So I want revenge, do I?'

'I simply observe that these two governments have created a ferocious enemy in you.'

'And you want to recruit me.'

'Not exactly.'

'Who do you work for?'

Peter had smiled. 'The pitch is we want to work for you.'

'Believe every statement is a deceit,' she had said. 'Isn't that the first rule of spying? To assume everyone is a liar?'

'Very good.' Peter had laughed and produced far more money than was necessary to buy her another drink. 'But I think I can persuade you our ends are exactly the same.'

*   *   *

Peter sipped his coffee, black and unsweetened, held up his palm sideways and moved it an inch to the right. Rashid immediately slid her chair to the left, giving him a clearer view of the window into the street. He nodded a thank-you and scanned the café again. 'You have something for me?'

Rashid reached down to the bag by her feet, pulled out a Jiffy-bag and slid it across the table. It contained the chisel Brennan had used to murder Diane Tennant. He moved his head again.

'Have this, too,' she said, handing him a parking ticket in its plastic envelope. 'I copped it last time we met.'

Peter glanced at the ticket, took a wad of cash from his inside pocket and peeled off three new twenties. It was Rashid's turn to smile, though money had never been a problem with Peter. From the start he had offered her a monthly salary, payable in cash. Though chronically short of funds, she had angrily turned him down on ideological grounds. Instead, Peter had funded the purchase of the Corsa, the congestion-charge fee for driving across London and all associated running costs.

'So how is our young man?' said Peter. 'Will he do?'

'Isn't it a bit late for that?'

'I only watch TV. The cutting edge is you, Anna. The boy is controllable, yes?'

Rashid shrugged. 'He's done what I've told him so far.'

'Messages delivered within the timescale?'

'So he tells me. He's using the Oyster cards and the phones.'

'So your young man is cutting the mustard, yes?'

Rashid felt a spark of irritation. 'Fuck it, Peter. Speak English.'

'You know much greater things lie ahead.' Her controller was unfazed. 'Is he competent for the main film or do I replace him?'

'Replace? You want to get rid of him now, after he's come so far?' Rashid felt Peter's eyes bore into her and silently cursed herself for sounding protective. 'I'm telling you, he's all right.'

'I need to be sure, naturally.' Peter gazed at her silently for a few moments. 'Is he remaining in the house at all times?'

'Far as I know.' Rashid shrugged. 'I'm not with him constantly.'

'Aren't you?'

'No.' She glared across the table. 'What's the problem?'

'He has everything he needs there, of course.' Peter suddenly looked shrewd. 'Constantly or not. Including you.'

Rashid felt herself reddening. 'You didn't tell me you had eyes everywhere.'

'No, Anna.' Peter leant towards her as if this, not Danny Brennan's tradecraft, was the most secret part of their conversation. 'It is *your* eyes that give you away. Remember. Discipline is everything.'

The group of ladies had left the café, though the two boys still lingered by the window. She saw Peter scan the space again, then felt his carrier bag against her ankle. 'Three devices. You know he has to handle them with extreme caution.'

'When does he do it?'

'For now I want you to pick up your regular life. The heat is on and everything must look normal.' He drained his coffee and slipped the Jiffy-bag into the second carrier. 'Exploit the mundane to cover the spectacular.'

'You what?'

'Socialise with your friends. Continue your radical academic work.' He slipped a ten-pound note under the cafetière and reached for his hat. 'Sleep in your own bed.'

Twenty-three

The discipline between Anna Rashid and Peter required her to wait at least five minutes in the café after he had left. As she drank the rest of the coffee, picked up the carrier bag and drifted to the counter to pay the bill with his money, Melanie Fleming was about to hear from her controller.

When the first call came through, Melanie was with Rob and their sons nearing the top of the London Eye. She was relieved to have made it this far: the family day out she had wanted for so long had come close to imploding. The original plan had been to drive the hundred and fifty miles up the M1 to Alton Towers theme park. On Friday evening Melanie had arrived home from her talk with Kerr beneath the plane tree to find Rob sitting behind the wheel of their Ford Fiesta. He had been parked in the street, revving the engine with his injured leg.

'Don't panic,' he had said, as she bent down to kiss him through the open window. 'I'm not bloody going anywhere.'

Entering the house Melanie had heard the car door slam, the sure sign of another brewing storm. She had guessed the cause the moment he had followed her into the kitchen: sitting in their car Rob had finally conceded that, despite regular physiotherapy to strengthen the muscles around the patella and all the exercise he could tolerate, his injured right leg was still refusing to obey orders. Melanie had tried to make light of it before he escaped to the shooting range again. 'They told you a year, Rob. Slow down. I'll do it. It's no problem.'

'No way. If I can't drive my family, we don't go.'

'Because you're not a proper man, you mean?' Hot from the tube and bus, still intrigued by John Kerr's offer to rehabilitate her, she had laughed in his face. 'Is that what you think I think? Really?' She had thrown her bag on the kitchen table and made straight for the fridge. 'Well, it's 2013 and I'm actually quite capable of driving a Ford bloody Fiesta up the motorway. It's fixed. We're going. So park your pride with the crutch and enjoy the ride.'

Melanie had known straight away that this was more than the usual guy thing. In Rob's case, inability to drive had done more than anything else to batter his self-esteem. At work, extreme driving in the most difficult urban conditions had been part of a normal day for them both. But on family trips, especially their holidays in Cornwall, Rob had always taken the wheel. His head-of-the-family display had become a given in their marriage, an old-fashioned quirk that Melanie found endearing.

But once Rob had disappeared to the range, leaving her alone with her glass of chilled wine, she had remembered Brenda's note of caution years ago. Her mother-in-law had been preparing tea for Melanie and the boys after school in her flat. Rob's insistence in the driving department was a remnant of his father's chauvinism, she had said, as the children watched TV in the living room, her left hand a blur as she whisked the eggs. 'I always gave in, too, and look where it led.' Melanie had tried to steer Brenda to calmer waters, but she had check-listed her husband's decline and fall in the time it took for the toast to pop up: adultery, divorce, young wife, sports car, new baby and cardiac arrest.

They did not go to Alton Towers. The London Eye was Rob's non-negotiable no-one-drives-anywhere concession, reached late on Sunday night after a weekend of searing arguments and aggressive target practice. They took the Northern Line south to Waterloo, Melanie on one side of the carriage with the boys, Rob glowering on the other. The walk from the station took twice as long as normal and the overtaking flood of able-bodied tourists squeezed them to the side of the path. The boys kept urging their dad to hurry up, and when they finally reached the Eye, Melanie could tell the long wait in line was troubling him as much as his temper.

There were eleven others in their pod, mostly foreign tourists, including two families of four. Melanie identified French, German, Scandinavian and American voices. Rob was the only person sitting on the bench but it was his expression, not his disability, that set him apart. The sky was deep blue with perfect visibility and everyone crowded him as they took in the spectacle of Parliament and Buckingham Palace. Standing with the boys less than a metre away Melanie saw him wrinkle his nose at the scent of yesterday's sweat.

She had the phone on vibrate but Rob must have heard it straight away above the shutters of a dozen cameras. Melanie saw Kerr's number on the screen and pressed ignore. Rob called to her through a screen of multi-tasking trousers, rucksacks and anoraks. 'Why didn't you pick up?' He spoke loudly and a couple of ruddy-faced beards looked down, as if noticing him for the first time. 'It's your friend, isn't it?'

She shook her head, leant down to him and whispered, 'Alan Fargo. Probably about Selwyn.'

Rob's outburst was another new development. Sunday's rows had brought a new dimension to his self-hate and resent-everyone campaign. By now Melanie had accepted that her culpability would always hang over them as Rob's domestic-argument clincher. But this weekend he had begun accusing those above her, specifically her immediate boss. Perhaps Brenda had planted the thought, possibly the guys in his team.

Whatever the source, Detective Chief Inspector John Kerr now lay clearly within Rob's line of fire.

Melanie spent the time on the opposite side from Rob where the pod was less cramped, leaning against the safety bar. As they neared the ground he eased through the crowd and limped over to join her. 'That was him, wasn't it? Kerr?' The children drifted over, looking quizzically from one to the other. Since reaching the zenith they had started squabbling, bored with their confinement, their stomachs telling them it was lunchtime.

'No, 1830, like I said. Alan probably wants me to research something tomorrow.' She touched his arm, as if she needed him to support her. 'Rob, this is difficult for me, too. I hate it in there. I'm trapped.'

'*You*'re trapped,' he shouted. 'How the fuck do you think I feel?'

Everyone had heard his outburst and it needed no translation. It took nearly thirty minutes of extreme awkwardness for the pod to reach the ground. The children had stopped fighting and burst into tears. Everyone stayed silent in their groups as far from Rob as possible, each face signalling the same message: great ride, wrong pod, crazy British.

The aroma from a fast-food kiosk wafted over them as they disembarked. As they reached a clear part of the square around the Eye the boys started pulling at Melanie to buy them burgers and fries. 'In a minute. Calm down,' she said.

Rob immediately hooked the stick over his forearm and beckoned the boys to him. He stood square to Melanie, holding their hands. 'Stop being such a killjoy.' It could have been hurtful but Melanie detected an inflection of lightness in his voice and it gave her a pulse of hope. Without the stick he looked taller and sure of himself again, a man standing on his own two feet. He was half smiling and, for a second, Melanie believed she was looking at the old Rob. He could have followed up with a joke to make up for his exhibition in the pod and rescue their day, but instead he completely destroyed it. The smile had flown away. 'No way am I going to let you spoil their day.'

Rob let the boys go and they scampered away to the kiosk. Melanie stared after them, close to tears. Her phone vibrated again as Rob called to the children and turned to follow them. This time he gave a dismissive wave. 'Go off and do your bloody desk job. I'll stay and be a father.'

The screen showed a number Melanie did not recognise. 'Don't hang up again,' said the voice. It was Kerr. 'Where are you?'

'The Eye. I'm supposed to be having a day off, remember?'

'Can you talk?' Melanie knew this was the make-or-break moment. He might as well have said, 'Will you do it?'

Melanie looked at Rob limping after her children. 'No' was what it needed. 'Two minutes,' she said.

'Ritchie and Ajay are both on board. We're cleared to go, Mel.'

Melanie pictured him in the Fishbowl with the door shut and someone else's mobile clamped to his ear to trick her. 'I haven't decided yet.'

'No pressure. I know how much you want this.'

'I'm still thinking about it.'

'You're the only officer capable of doing it.'

'That's emotional blackmail.'

'It's fact. But I understand if you don't feel ready yet. Say the word and I'll look for someone else.'

Melanie watched her family again. The boys were jumping up and down with excitement as Rob paid for the burgers and Coke. 'No. It has to be a no. I'm sorry.' She cut the call and watched them walk slowly back to her. She could see only three fast-food cartons and tried a smile. 'Where's Mum's?'

Rob stared at her. 'We thought you were going back to the office.'

'You told them that?'

'Why else would they keep calling on your day off?'

'Why do you use the children as a weapon against me?'

Rob took a mouthful of burger. 'I don't need to. It's me who's always there for them because you're never home.' He had moved in close and a fragment of beef flew past her shoulder. 'You have the front to complain you're trapped in an office when I may never work again. What are you trying to do to me?'

The boys had run off towards the river, looking for a place to sit on the grass. Rob shouted to them and they waved back. 'Hurry up, Dad. There's a ship coming.'

He shrugged at her. 'You see?' He turned and walked off.

Melanie perched on the back of a bench, watching Rob catch up with the boys and ease himself down beside them. They were only thirty paces from her but it might have been a mile. Melanie saw him throw the stick aside and collapse on his back. He was making his disability look like fun, wearing a face he had not shown her in a long time.

She saw them eating their burgers in a neat circle of three, the boys cross-legged, Rob with his damaged leg stretched out. She could just hear their voices, excited again. Rob was making them laugh and no one was looking back at her. Perhaps he had told them Mum was busy with work. They were a self-contained family. They didn't need her.

The French couple from the pod strolled by, beard, frizzy hair, anoraks and walking boots, calculating the distance between her and Rob. Was their glance one of sympathy or contempt? Had they concluded Melanie was an abused wife? The woman was staring at her. Or was she guilty of something so bad she deserved to be excluded? God, perhaps they were right.

Melanie stood up, took out her phone and dialled. Kerr picked up on the second ring. She turned her back on everyone. 'I'll do it.'

'You sure?'

'Changed my mind. When do I start?'

A pulse. 'First things first. I'm going to be your controller, Mel. Personally. With Alan Fargo. Dodge handling logistics. You call in to Alan every day and he briefs me. We keep it tight within 1830. That sound OK?'

'How much time do I have for the legend?'

'None. We use the same identity and life history as before.'

'That's risky.'

'Your background's cast iron.'

'You sure about that?'

'I'm talking different targets here, Mel. Trust me, you're covered. Dodge and I have been working over the weekend.'

'You what?'

'He's arranging the cover address and car.'

'Assuming I would say yes?'

'We're getting everything in place. But if you're not absolutely sure . . .'

'I already told you.'

A pause. 'How's Rob doing?'

'Good. Getting through it.' Melanie swung round to check everyone out. Rob was still playing with the kids but she guessed his real game was to demonstrate how much fun they were having without her. 'He's absolutely fine. What's the target?'

'Drop by the Fishbowl tomorrow. Is Rob there with you now?'

'I already talked about it with him.'

'What did he say?'

'That it's my decision.'

'Is that Rob speaking or you?'

'I've said I'll do it.'

Kerr was silent for a moment. 'Well, I want to see you both tomorrow evening.'

Melanie gave a short laugh. 'You're not exactly man of the moment in our house.'

'Look, you two have already been through a lot. I have to be sure Rob really is comfortable with this.'

'John, forget it.' She looked at her family again. 'You meeting Rob is never going to happen.'

Twenty-four

Justin Hine had won a place in Special Branch with a view to spending his whole career beneath the radar. He loved his job as Kerr's technical specialist but had also been successful in his previous role as an intelligence officer cultivating sources, with Dodge often telling him he would make a great agent runner.

That had been before the absorption of Special Branch into SO15 and the economic recession. A perfect storm of reduced career opportunities, government cuts, deteriorating conditions of employment and front-line service into their late fifties was provoking the best of the Met's young specialist talent into a rethink.

Justin was hoping for the best but planning for the worst, with a back-up scheme to train as an airline pilot. He loved the job he could never talk about but if it became non-viable to work with John Kerr he would fly the flag for British Airways. And because Kerr, ever the loyal boss, had backed him all the way, Justin had been snatching hours and saving money to study for a commercial pilot's licence.

This evening Justin was having a drink with Tom, his best friend from flying school. Tom's father owned the Sea Ray powerboat he had borrowed for his pursuit down the Thames with Kerr exactly seven weeks earlier. Tom had rung him with the news that the boat was back in the water at Chelsea

Harbour, repairs completed. 'A few scratches, some dents here and there. Good as new.' He said his father was relaxed about bullet holes in the deck and windshield ('For my dad that shit is nothing') and had insisted on meeting Justin for a drink.

Tom described his father as a patriot who admired specialist cops like Justin working behind the scenes. Evidently he had been an RAF hotshot selected for special duties, embedded in secret missions no one talked about in trouble spots never disclosed. There had been no mention of actual flying experience, though Tom had spoken of ambushes and shootouts being a regular feature of his father's adventures at the sharp end. Justin wondered what line his old man had spun the boat repairers. Tom had been reassuring: 'I'm telling you, mate, Dad will make sure he gets the first round in.'

Justin anticipated a difficult evening followed by a lawsuit.

They met at the Prince of Wales, a smart tavern in a mews between Belgrave Square and Sloane Street, with well-stocked hanging baskets and a roped-off pavement terrace with oak tables and chairs (no benches) beneath a maroon retractable awning. Justin arrived to see a couple of plummy-voiced men enjoying red wine and fat cigars in the evening sun, mirroring each other in loose-fitting shirts, designer jeans and blue suede loafers. Talk of Porsches and looks of disparagement trailed him into the pub.

To prepare for Belgravia Justin had stopped by his flat in Putney to change. Order of the evening was navy pinstripe with polished black lace-ups, ironed white shirt, crumpled Special Branch tie recovered from the bottom of the wardrobe and a plate of scrambled eggs to line the stomach.

He knew exactly where he would find his hosts. Though it was Monday evening the saloon was well populated by young professionals and relaxed men in their fifties. A handful of couples sat at tables but the men lined the long polished oak bar to the right. The glasses held either cocktails or spirits and nobody appeared to have been anywhere near an office all day.

Justin headed straight for the dark area at the rear of the saloon beyond the bar. Beside the door leading to the toilets there was a second, unmarked entrance leading to a narrow staircase. At the top he found a room about fifteen paces square with heavy net curtains over the windows, probably blast-proof remnants from IRA days. The area was officially open to the public but served almost exclusively as a hangout for ex-forces types, the walls covered with service portraits and photographs representing the two world wars, the Falklands and Iraq.

Up here the bar was to the left of the entrance. It looked prefabricated, with metal beer kegs on show, plywood surfaces, skewed beer taps and shaky wooden stools on a threadbare carpet. There were six folding tables with chairs for preheated snacks 'when available – ask at the bar' but no tablecloths or cutlery. Justin had been here on a handful of occasions and always by invitation. The room had the Spartan feel of a military base, the exclusivity of a gentlemen's club and a silent barman who knew his place. Justin disliked all private clubs, and this one smelt of damp.

Justin spotted Tom's father immediately at the very end of the bar, with Tom beyond him. He looked perfectly at home, on first-name terms with the barman, Mustafa. There were only two other men in the room, both in their seventies perched precariously on wobbly bar stools, walking sticks close by, and Tom's father was joking with the old-timer nearest him.

He spotted Justin without any prompting from his son, loped over to greet him and clamped Justin's hand in his. 'I'm Alec. And you're most welcome, my friend.' With his other hand Alec gripped Justin's forearm, simultaneously nodding at Mustafa. 'Only club gins here, I'm afraid. Doubles or trebles.' He gave a stage wink. 'You ready for that, young man?'

With a glance at Mustafa's overwashed white shirt and stained bow-tie, Justin made a face to match Alec's bonhomie. 'Sounds good. Brilliant.'

Without releasing Justin's forearm Alec led him along the bar, inserting him between his stool and the man he had been entertaining seconds earlier, now forgotten. Justin waved a hi to Tom, who was suddenly squashed even harder against the far wall. Father and son had the breath and eyes of men whose drinking had started early.

Justin tried to talk about the Sea Ray but Alec had batted away his thanks and apologies even before the drinks arrived. 'It's only a bloody boat. Sun, sea, sangria and a bit of sex. If I'm lucky.' The face creased again and Justin saw Tom look away. 'You used it for something special, knocking off those bastards. Happy to serve Queen and country again. Be sure to tell your boss.'

Alec was dressed in his summer kit: crumpled fawn linen suit with pale green shirt, faded Hush Puppies and a tie with an unidentifiable logo. He was well over six feet tall, narrow-shouldered but with a paunch overhanging a heavy brown belt. Justin could plot his increase in girth from well-worn holes and ridges in the leather.

Despite Alan Fargo's quick-fire research that afternoon, he immediately had misgivings about Alec. In addition to genuine veterans, the upstairs room was notorious for attracting Walter Mitty interlopers and charlatans wearing regimental ties, telling paper-thin tales of heroism. On record, Alec appeared to be the genuine article. Fargo had confirmed his service in the RAF with postings in Northern Ireland, Bahrain and Sierra Leone, followed by secondments as military attaché to several unspecified embassies. He had left the RAF early for unknown reasons and invested family money in property development, becoming seriously wealthy through a dodgy venture in the Caribbean.

By the second round Alec was emerging as a serious bulls-hitter and champion name-dropper, majoring in one subject: himself. He showed no interest in Justin, belittled his son and denigrated his diplomatic service overseas as 'sweating it out in the bloody sandpit'. By the time Mustafa slid the third glass across the bar Tom had slipped twice from his stool and Justin was planning his escape.

Then the name of Marcus Tennant dropped from Alec's lips and everything changed in a flash.

'So tell me, young man, how are you guys getting on with the Diane Tennant murder?'

Justin's glass was midway to his mouth. 'I'm sorry?'

'It's all right. Need-to-know and all that. Just that Marcus was a mate of mine. In another life, if you get my meaning.'

'Really?' Justin switched his brain to high alert. Was this why Alec had made his son introduce them, so that he could brag about his friendship with Marcus Tennant? 'That's interesting.'

'Well, associate, really.' Seriously drunk now, Alec leant in and changed to loud-whisper mode. Justin had a close-up of his snaggle teeth and felt ice-cold splashes of spittle against his right cheek. 'You never get really close to those chaps, do you? For all their hail-fellow-well-met bollocks.'

Tom slipped from the stool again and Justin seized the moment. 'Shan't be a tick.' He scraped his friend from the floor and helped him to the Gents at the top of the staircase. He waited outside the cubicle while Tom noisily threw up, then escorted him back as far as the bar entrance, raced downstairs and eased his way through the saloon into the mews. He walked clear of the upstairs bar windows, speed-dialling and shaking his head to clear his thoughts.

'You sound pissed,' said Kerr.

'John, this boat guy knows Marcus Tennant from the past. He's dancing round some kind of secret stuff but I think I can get him to open up. Is that OK with you?'

'What's he like?'

'A tosser.'

'Whet his appetite. Feed him, bleed him and get back to me.'

Justin dashed upstairs, took a leak and rejoined Alec. He was talking to Mustafa and ignoring his son, who was propped against the wall, face white as a sheet. 'Chin chin.' Justin clinked Alec's glass, which was already half empty, then spent five minutes talking about the Diane Tennant case. Most of the details had already been reported but Justin dressed them up and delivered them as privileged information.

'So, are you thinking lone-wolf sex psycho or organised political group?' slurred Alec. 'Who's masquerading as what?' He was having serious difficulty now. 'Masquerading' almost eluded him completely.

'The judge murder makes us think it's political. We need all the help we can get, Alec.'

'Such a tragedy for Marcus.' Alec was staring at a giant portrait of Wellington directly above Mustafa's head. He took another slug of gin. 'Poor sod must be jinxed.'

Justin frowned. 'He's got Defence. I mean, come on, Alec. I can think of worse breaks in life.'

'You're making my point for me.' A hint of aggression had slithered into Alec's voice, as if Justin had spoken out of turn. Then he stopped and Justin feared he might have lost him. He was staring at Wellington again. 'Sorry, train of thought leaving the station. What I mean is this. Every time poor old Marcus gets a bit of good luck, something drags him down. Or someone. Understand what I'm getting at? This time it's his lovely wife getting butchered. Like being back in bloody Kosovo. Like fucking Washington, more like. And those bastards who screwed his career.' Alec drained his glass. 'You know about that?'

'Of course.' Justin had not the faintest idea. He gripped the man's arm, leant in close and spoke urgently in his ear: 'But that's secret, Alec.'

'Sorry. Shouldn't be saying all this.'

'It's not that. I just had no idea you were involved.' Justin rapidly downed his drink and threw a glance at Tom. His friend was swaying behind Alec's shoulder but still upright. It was time to wind Alec up and set him loose. He gestured to Mustafa for two refills and brought Alec back to his favourite subject. 'How close were you to it?'

Alec held up his left hand, forefinger and thumb a millimetre apart. He watched Mustafa pouring the gin and licked his lips. 'Air attaché at the embassy same time as Marcus was posted to Washington.'

Insufficient information. 'Do you know where in the pecking order?'

'Number three, I think. Head of station was a wanker. Perhaps four. Something like that. And still married to his first missus, but I expect you boys know about that.'

Justin's head was awash with questions but he simply nodded and looked down.

'Actually, not the same time as Marcus,' Alec continued. 'I think we just overlapped by a few months. Not close, but the Beltway is full of bars. I occasionally bumped into him on the circuit. You know how it is.'

'Of course.'

'Right until the enemy tried to pitch the poor bastard.'

Stunned, Justin covered himself with a murmur of encouragement. 'Now that's where you can help us, Alec. As one professional to another.'

Alec gave another exaggerated wink. 'Just between us and our vetting officers, yes?'

Justin reciprocated. 'Who do you think did it?'

'Who knows?' said Alec. 'Russia? Far East? China? Take your pick, dear boy. And don't forget those bloody treacherous EU bastards. Or your fucking Americans, for that matter. Don't ever get taken in by our so-called bloody allies.'

'Yes. We're having a lot of difficulty resolving this.'

Alec was on a roll. 'Course you are. Everything was hushed up. But I'll tell you this for what it's worth.' He leant in again and Justin braced himself for another dousing. 'Marcus was tapped up at the French embassy. Some piss-up late in the evening when every bugger was plastered. Somebody definitely tried to recruit him to their side.'

'What happened?'

'Who knows? Word on the cocktail circuit was that Marcus never actually got around to reporting it. Next thing you knew the poor sod was on a plane to London, career in MI6 totally kyboshed.'

Bingo. Justin clinked glasses with Alec again, shaking his head in sadness and suppressing the thumping in his chest. He wanted to punch the air. Instead, he led Tom to the toilet once more, sprinted downstairs and pressed redial.

Twenty-five

John Kerr drove out to interview Marcus Tennant at his home in Hadley the following afternoon. Justin had generated a series of tantalising questions. Now Kerr wanted answers from the main man, and quickly. Given the significance of Alec's information, Kerr's instinct had been to see Tennant immediately after hearing from Justin. Only professional caution had restrained him. That, and strong advice down the phone from Alan Fargo.

On his second call from the mews Justin had told Kerr to grab a pen. He had poured out the story in a torrent of key words, as if coherent sentences eluded him or had suddenly become superfluous. This was the drink-and-dial phenomenon, to which Kerr and Dodge had become accustomed from years of managing stressed agents in the field. Justin had sounded like a man fighting against the clock, with only seconds to go before the alcohol slammed his brain shut. Without discernible pauses for breath, the information had seemed to hurtle down the line in one giant exhalation.

Grabbing the Alfa keys, a loaf of bread and a bottle of water as he raced from his apartment, Kerr had told Justin to lose Alec, find his way to Harrods and wait for him on the street. He had covered the seven miles from Islington to Knightsbridge in eighteen minutes to find Justin slouched against the far wall, the pale blue of the illuminated window display reflected in his face. Kerr had poured him into the passenger seat, driven round the corner into Hans Road and parked. While Justin drank and chewed, Kerr had spent twenty minutes working through his notes, peppering him with questions, checking every detail before taking him back to rehearse the whole evening again.

After an emergency stop in Brompton Cemetery for Justin to relieve himself, they had reached his home in Parsons Green, near Putney Bridge, at just after eleven thirty. Justin shared a flat on the first floor of a converted Edwardian house with his girlfriend, a physiotherapist at the local hospital. Because he had forgotten his key she had padded downstairs in her pyjamas and furry slippers to let him in. As Justin tripped on the step Kerr had tried to lighten things by telling her it had all been in the line of duty. She had stared at Justin in disbelief. 'You're kidding me.' Even Justin had laughed at that.

Kerr had gone to bed around one, knowing Fargo had been right. He would need to drag Justin's account from him again when he was office-bound and sober. And Fargo had to search Excalibur for anything to corroborate Justin's story and construct some kind of timeline.

Kerr also knew that, however searching the questions he needed to ask Marcus Tennant about his past, he had to avoid appearing confrontational with a bereaved husband in the depth of his grief. He was relying on protection-officer Karl Sergeyev for a pretext and to set up the meeting without going through the private office.

Evidently Marcus Tennant had remained more or less incommunicado since the murder, cancelling a visit to his Cheshire constituency. Brilliantly, Karl had managed to fix a meeting within an hour of being asked on the basis that Kerr had important information for Tennant's ears only. Karl had told Kerr he would be escorting Tennant to Downing Street the following morning for a private meeting with the prime minister. 'To be comforted or sacked?' Kerr had asked. 'Are we talking condolence or demotion?' They had been speaking on the phone, but Kerr sensed Karl's shrug. The girls in the private office had suddenly gone quiet, Karl told him. No one seemed to know anything.

Kerr's meeting was scheduled for three o'clock and Karl had briefed the armed cops manning the police post. The gate swung open as soon as Kerr drove up, three minutes early. Karl was waiting for him by the front door, immaculate in a charcoal suit and maroon tie. They shook hands in the lobby and Karl invited him to take a seat in the hall, an area of deep white carpet five paces square beneath a sparkling crystal chandelier. Kerr stayed on his feet, indicating that he wanted a look around, so Karl gave his signature thumbs-up as he went to tell the minister that Kerr had arrived.

Kerr checked out the open doors to each side of the main entrance. The dining room to the right contained a long pale wood Scandinavian table, with eight leather-upholstered chairs, silver-framed mirrors and tasteful curtains. With the police post just visible through the side window, the drawing room opposite had three comfortable sofas with giant cushions, original watercolours from around the world and a baby grand piano, with a cluster of family photographs displayed on the lid. Kerr only had time for a glance. There was a wedding portrait with the happy couple squinting into the sun, one of Marcus and Diane holding their infant daughter and another with an elderly couple, presumably grandparents. In both rooms the wallpaper and furnishings were light and contemporary, perfectly suited to a politician of the modern world.

Straight ahead, a broad staircase separated in elegant curves as it reached the first-floor landing. Karl had disappeared down the hallway to the right of the stairs and returned as

Kerr completed his recce. 'Bad day, John,' he whispered. 'Be careful.' He led Kerr down the hallway towards the airy kitchen, then veered right along an uncarpeted narrow corridor leading to an oak door protected by two heavy-duty locks. Karl knocked and simultaneously opened the door, standing aside for Kerr to enter.

Marcus Tennant was sitting at his desk against the far wall. Two plain wooden chairs faced the occupant's, which was leather-upholstered with brass studs. The leather-inlaid desktop was clear, apart from the ministerial red box, and Tennant appeared so absorbed in his papers that he did not even look up. Unfazed, Kerr used the space to nose around.

The ticking from an ancient grandfather clock in the corner to Kerr's right dominated everything. In most houses it would have occupied the main hallway, but the décor in here was the opposite of that in the other rooms he had checked out. Kerr suspected it had descended through generations of Tennants, but the rest of this beautiful house had clearly belonged to Diane.

To the left a high window looked out past the kitchen to the rear garden and the helicopter pad, half hidden behind a row of *leylandii*. The curtains and pelmet were heavy and dark. A worn Afghan rug covered the polished parquet floor and in front of Kerr were two deep brown-leather armchairs. Set into the external wall to the right, the original fireplace had stained-glass peep windows to either side. Bereavement cards crowded the mantelpiece.

A rectangular oak table beneath the window held a whisky decanter and several photographs of a beaming Tennant shaking hands. Kerr did a rapid name check. In addition to the prime minister there was a US congressman Kerr recognised from televised defence hearings, plus various foreign dignitaries, including the French president. At the edge of the group Tennant was pictured with the UK ambassador to the

United Nations, and in an action shot he was addressing an emergency session of the UN Security Council.

The smell of cigar smoke sealed the atmosphere of this men-only retreat. Perhaps Marcus Tennant was not such a modern politician after all. His study did not belong in the house, and Kerr wondered whether Diane and their daughter had ever been allowed in here. Hands in pockets, he was standing by the window gazing at the garden when he sensed Tennant finally look up. The voice was deep and unfriendly. 'What can I do for you?'

Kerr walked over, hand outstretched. Tennant's face was grey with exhaustion. Grief or anxiety? 'Good afternoon, sir. Thanks for seeing me.' Tennant half stood, the backs of his knees pushing against the chair. He was wearing heavy green corduroys with a checked shirt and appeared slighter than his TV image. He seemed irritable as he took in Kerr's summer jacket and white trousers. Perhaps he had been expecting the stand-to-attention, jacket-buttoned-up routine. The handshake was brief and half-hearted. He waved Kerr to the nearest high-backed chair by the desk. He made a show of replacing the papers in his red box and closing the lid. 'As you can see . . .'

Kerr nodded. 'I appreciate how busy you are and how difficult this must be.'

'As everyone from your lot keeps saying,' said Tennant, immediately aggressive. 'They must have interviewed me a hundred times.'

Kerr aborted his short speech of condolence. 'The homicide investigators. Yes.'

'Karl tells me you have something for me.'

'This is unconnected to the main enquiry,' said Kerr, crossing his legs and stretching his arm across the adjacent chair. 'A possible motive. Something that has just come to light.'

'So, let's have it.' Tennant was beckoning with both hands impatiently.

'It concerns your career with MI6. I'd like to hear your—'

Tennant jerked forward with his palm outstretched. 'Stop right there.'

'I think it could be relevant.'

'Listen. Everything you need to know about me is in my bio.' Suddenly Tennant's right forefinger was jabbing at Kerr across the desk, punctuating every word. 'Ask my private office. Or search Wikipedia if you're that desperate.'

Kerr met hostility with a smile, the look that said he had heard it all before. He had a flashback to the Ethics Committee and Red Socks, the unnamed non-lawyer. 'When did you serve with the MI6 station in Washington?'

Tennant stared back in silence, allowing the ticking clock to take over. Kerr gave it five ticks, then pressed on. 'I understand there was an attempt by a hostile intelligence agency to recruit you. Is that true, Mr Tennant?'

'No comment.'

'Which country was it? Did you report the pitch to your MI6 head of station?'

'No.'

'Why not?' said Kerr, evenly.

'I mean no to everything.' Tennant looked angry, like a man who had been expecting sympathy, not an interrogation. 'Nothing in my past life has any bearing on the investigation.'

'Let me be the judge of that.'

'Enough.' Abruptly Tennant stood up, interview over, and this time the chair crashed back against the wall.

Kerr stayed seated, looking up at him. 'Tell me about Yvette.'

'What?' Kerr saw fear spark in his eyes.

'Your au pair. The investigators obviously want to interview her but she's vanished. Do you know where she is now?' Tennant sat down so heavily that the cushion exhaled. 'Where we can find her?'

Tennant's forehead was glistening now. 'I expect you people to be hunting my wife's killer,' he blustered, 'not wasting my time with irrelevant detail.'

'Yvette appears to have packed her bags and left without warning around the time Mrs Tennant was attacked. Why would she disappear from the scene of the crime?'

'Haven't the faintest. You're the bloody expert. You tell me.' Tennant still sounded angry but his face showed relief. Kerr knew the reason. Disappearance was fine. The arrogant bastard believed his secret was safe.

'Doesn't that seem odd to you?' said Kerr.

'You think I concerned myself with the comings and goings of our au pair?'

'Didn't you?' Tennant shifted in his chair and Kerr paused, leaving space for the implication to sink in alongside his discomfort. 'Do you know anything about her at all? A surname, for example?'

The retort came a second too quick. 'How would I know that?'

'Who hired her? Was it you or your wife?'

'Diane hired this au pair directly, so far as I know.' Tennant took a deep breath. 'Not that it's any of your damn business.'

'We can find no record of Yvette, surname unknown, being security-vetted. And your private office knows nothing about her. So where did your wife find her?'

'No idea.'

'Did Diane and Yvette get along?'

Tennant sat like a statue, his eyes hard with realisation that Kerr knew. 'I want you to leave now.'

Kerr tracked a bead of sweat sliding down the minister's forehead. 'Did Diane know you and Yvette were having sex in this house?'

Tennant slumped back in his chair. 'Get out,' he said, but the anger had left his voice.

'Where did you have her? In her room? In your bedroom? Did your little affair go terribly wrong, Mr Tennant? Have you considered Yvette might be connected to Diane's murder in some way?' The ticking of the clock filled the room again and this time it was Kerr who stood. 'I need to speak with this young woman urgently. If you know where she is you must tell me. If you don't, we'll find her anyway. And then I'll come for you.'

This time neither man held out his hand. At the door Kerr turned, hoping Tennant might invite him back or say something. But the minister was slumped in his chair, staring into the garden at the windsock. He looked like a man whose career had just hit the buffers.

Twenty-six

On the first night of her undercover mission Melanie Fleming drove slowly down Shoreditch High Street from Dalston, heading for the *Flag of Liberty* office. She found the alleyway entrance at the first attempt, a black rectangle in a row of shops between a halal takeaway and Shaba Food and Drink, two doors up from the Seven Stars pub. An old Volkswagen caravanette was parked on a single yellow line to the left of the entrance, just as Jack Langton had confirmed for her an hour earlier. This vehicle would be her first target. There were a couple of other parking spaces but Melanie drove slowly past and continued through the traffic lights at Commercial Street, her stomach tied in the double knot of fear and excitement she experienced before every undercover operation. She carried on towards Old Spitalfields Market, mentally replaying the slideshow of video images Justin had captured from inside the premises during his search with Langton.

Though tonight would be her first contact with the targets, she had disappeared the day before, Wednesday morning. Carrying a holdall with a few personal possessions and a change of clothes, she had met Dodge at Wandsworth in the underground car park beneath a row of shops where Jack Langton kept his eclectic fleet of surveillance vehicles under wraps.

The vehicle Dodge had acquired for her was a battered, dark grey Renault 19, fourteen years old with at least a hundred and forty thousand miles on the clock, an interior Dodge euphemised as 'shabby' ('Back seat knackered, dried sick on the carpets and a smell like something died') and an engine he described as 'reconditioned' ('Take you anywhere and bring you back'). Dodge had assured her the brakes were relined and the tyres good as new. He had sounded pleased with himself when he tossed her the keys, as if he had just been made salesman of the month. 'Have to hand it to you, Dodge,' Melanie had said, prodding him in the stomach, 'you find me the ugliest, dirtiest, rubbishest car in London and make it sound like I won first prize.'

Dodge had also given her a new mobile phone and a residents' parking permit, totally legitimate and correctly made out. This was for the cover address he had found for her in Dalston, and Melanie had driven straight there from the garage. From now on home was to be a rundown upstairs bedsit in Collis Street, at the poorest end of a long stretch of Victorian houses running west to east between Hackney's London Fields and Kingsland Road, less than a ten-minute drive from the *Flag of Liberty*. Of the five flats in the house, two were on the upper floor and Melanie's faced out to the rear yard, ensuring any light through the thin curtains would not be visible from the street.

In addition to the driving licence in her cover name and address, Dodge had obtained local documents, some to be kept in her wallet, others to be left in the car. They included Internet café receipts, a Blockbuster membership card, expired local parking tickets, final gas and electricity demands and a personalised letter from the local council about her tax-band status. She had spent Tuesday afternoon settling in at the address, airing the sheets and duvet by the popping gas fire and cleaning the fridge, stove and tiny bathroom. Dodge had already given her a head start with the previous weekend's *Independent on Sunday* and *Sunday Times* and three second-hand paperbacks from an obscure anarchist book-shop in a back-street near Highbury. Late afternoon she had passed an hour wandering around the local shops buying milk, fresh food and the ingredients for a high-octane curry.

She had spent the evening making her presence felt. TV loud, she had left her door open for the curry to permeate the house and lain in wait for her top-floor neighbour. She had heard the stairs creaking at just after ten. He looked a local-government type in his forties, inoffensive, with round glasses, V-necked pullover and receding hair. Melanie had appeared as he reached the top of the stairs, leaving her door ajar on the catch in case he wanted to sneak a look inside. Door key at the ready, breath smelling of booze, the man had smiled a friendly hello. Mobile clamped to her ear, Melanie had given him a quick nod as she had brushed past and hurried down to the lobby.

After her first night in the lumpy queen-sized bed Melanie had driven home to check on Rob and the children, only to find the house empty. Apart from her mother-in-law. She had opened the door to the sound of the Hoover, the smell of frying bacon and the sight of Brenda bustling around in her apron. As she took her peck on the cheek and refused the offer of coffee, Melanie had felt like a visitor in her own house. Rob had taken the boys out for a proper treat, Brenda had said, as if their ride on the London Eye had been a total flop. 'But they knew I was coming back to see them this morning.'

'No need to worry about us,' Brenda had said, looking Melanie up and down. 'You do what you have to do. I'll let them know you dropped by.'

Melanie had not strayed beyond the hall and had felt Brenda's eyes on her as she retreated to her Renault. By the time she turned to wave, the front door had closed on her.

Dusk had fallen while she was driving around so she switched on her side lights before making a U-turn in

Commercial Street and driving back the way she had come, stomach churning. Then she turned again. One more time, she told herself. On the third slow pass she saw that the parking spaces were taken and breathed a deep sigh of relief: she had an excuse for another drive-by. Then in her mirror she saw a woman walk to a Vauxhall Corsa parked four vehicles in front of the old VW. As the woman unlocked the car, Melanie reversed a few metres and waited in gear, double-parked in the light evening traffic. She saw the Corsa lights fade with each turn of the ignition, then finally glow bright as the engine fired. Melanie threw the driver a wave of thanks as she accelerated past, engine surging, but she did not respond. The rear window sticker said 'England – World Cup 2006', but the woman drove as if she couldn't get out of first gear.

Melanie reversed neatly into the parking space and cut the engine. From the glove compartment she took a pencil torch, a small screwdriver and a pair of pliers. She got out of her car, walked unhesitatingly to the rear of the VW, which was parked close to the front of a high white delivery van, and took a look around. A couple of young men were chatting in the halal shop and three women in hospital scrubs waited at the bus stop ten paces away. There was a steady flow of traffic, mostly buses, all moving, and across the road a line of parked cars offered a protective shield. With darkness falling around her she checked the entrance to the alleyway. Clear. She crouched down in the gutter, rolled onto her back and crawled beneath the VW engine compartment. She shone the torch at the engine, loosened a retaining screw on the alternator box and used the pliers gently to pull away one of the wires. She wriggled out and walked unhurriedly back to the Renault. Sitting in the driving seat, she replaced the tools, brushed herself down and checked out the environment, tracking from the alleyway entrance up the street, then in her rear-view mirror. Clear.

The operation had taken less than two minutes because Melanie had known exactly where to shine the torch and work the screwdriver. Late Sunday evening, after a weekend of searching, Dodge had finally identified an identical van through a local paper in Bedford and purchased it for cash, no questions asked. Langton had arranged for it to be collected first thing Monday morning on a nondescript low-loader and transported to Wandsworth. By early afternoon on Tuesday, after seeing Kerr, Melanie had been lying underneath the vehicle in the gloom of Langton's underground garage wearing overalls three sizes too large for her. Crouching by her side, Dodge had made her sabotage the engine again and again until she could do it without a torch, eyes shut, fingers gloved.

It was just after nine, time to make her next move. Melanie locked the car and walked into the alleyway. It was gloomy in here and the Victorian bricks of the buildings each side of her were blackened with age and grime, close enough to touch. The walls towered above her to a rectangle of sky turning grey with the dusk, and the only working light came from the upper windows of the *Flag of Liberty* building, shrouding the walls in an orange glow, luring her in. The deeper Melanie penetrated, the more apprehensive she became. She knew exactly what was required of her. 'Look out, listen in, report back, no big deal,' John Kerr had told her, true to his word. But Melanie knew it could never be that simple. Among those nervous of being watched, suspicion would always fall upon the quiet newcomer. To get through this she would have to be up-front. Whatever Kerr might say now, she also recalled him talking about his own experience: 'When paranoia takes them over it's better to be holding the spotlight than caught in its glare.'

Melanie braced herself, growing more nervous with each step.

Twenty-seven

The reserve printing press at the *Flag* sounded as old as the brickwork. The racket it made hit her before she was halfway down the alley, bouncing off the walls in a rhythmic, pre-laser clacking, slapping and sifting. The heavy black wooden door was hidden behind the left end wall, where the alleyway expanded each side. Melanie recognised it immediately from Justin's photograph and spotted a new steel clasp screwed to the leading edge, just above the section of splintered wood from Jack Langton's crowbar attack. The padlock hung unsecured from the hasp, yet the door appeared locked.

Melanie knocked, tentatively pushed, then gave a hard shove. It scraped open against the concrete floor, sucking her inside the print shop. The noise obliterated her senses as she stumbled over the threshold, squinting against the sudden light. Justin's slideshow was playing in her head again as she breathed in a heavy mixture of grease, old paper, damp and stale sweat. The windowless space was about fifteen paces square and the press stood in the left corner, a cross between a spinning wheel and a threshing machine, tended by a heavily bearded man, his face half covered with a shroud of tangled, greasy hair. He wore steel-capped boots, shapeless jeans and an oil-stained denim waistcoat over a grey T-shirt, with a red scarf knotted around his throat. Stooped over the machine, he checked the copy and loaded more paper into the feeder. Beside him on a bench running the length of the far wall lay a tin of tobacco, cigarette papers and a pile of ash and fag-ends.

Melanie recovered to shout, 'Hi,' but the man was working without ear protectors and appeared oblivious to everything except the press. She got right alongside him and shouted into his ear, pointing at the lopsided staircase to the right of the door that she knew was the only access to the bookshop. 'Shall I go up?' The head stayed immobile but one oily hand flicked in suit-yourself dismissal, so she crossed the workshop and began to climb.

'Hold on!'

She turned to see him waving her back.

He walked to a trestle table and picked up a pile of printed A3 sheets. Clutching them tight against his scrawny smoker's chest he ambled back to her, sucking in air. 'Take these up,' he shouted, exhaling a stale mix of tobacco and whisky into her face. 'Save me a trip.'

The rickety staircase made two turns before reaching the bookshop above. Jack Langton had warned her some of the steps were missing or broken so Melanie climbed cautiously, peering over the pile of paper. The upper room was directly above the press and the same size, lined with bookshelves and with two sash windows overlooking the alleyway. Even up here the thump of the press dominated.

In the centre of the room four more trestle tables, pushed together into a square, held three piles of A3 sheets. Three women and a couple of men in their twenties, dressed in combat pants and radical-chic T-shirts, were collating sheets from each pile into completed copies of the journal. They worked methodically, heads down without saying a word. Melanie found the right pile and dumped her copies on top. She had her story ready but no one acknowledged her, so she presumed these must be the volunteers, outsiders who perhaps thought she already belonged there. Melanie inserted herself between the two men, worked out their system and slowly began to relax, folding to the rhythm of the press below and wondering if anyone would speak to her.

At the far end, opposite the staircase, she recognised the office with the Goss press and the damaged door. To the left there was a kitchen area with a cracked butler sink, a dirty electric cooker and a worktop to prepare food. The smell of stale urine wafted into the shop from the adjacent toilet, its door hanging open. The office was separated from the main area by a wooden partition a metre high, topped with Perspex to the ceiling. A TV flickered in the corner and Melanie saw a young man and woman in their twenties sitting close together at a desk, peering at the single laptop. They worked as if they were an item and were arguing with a third man who suddenly appeared in Melanie's line of sight, pacing round them and gesticulating. He was older than them, tall and well built, with a dark beard and long, curly hair. Hard-looking.

Even above the noise from the press Melanie could hear snatches of raised voices. The young woman was called Becky. Tough guy's name was Jez, unmistakable as Becky yelled it at him. There was a pause, as if they had run out of things to shout, and all three gave a cursory glance into the shop. Then Jez threw a second look at Melanie, which might have been a flicker of interest or suspicion.

Melanie read the front page of the journal while she folded. There was an account of Derek Finch's search entitled 'Another Turn of the Screw', spiced with condemnation of the violence in the People's Resistance actions:

In another lurch to the police state . . . six sweaty bastards in suits smelling of stale beer and cheap aftershave lumbered up the stairs of the *Flag* to check whether we were sheltering the latest bunch of urban guerrillas under our printing press ... Old Bill were as ridiculous as ever. Can you guess the first words they said when they reached the top step? 'Who's in charge?' Yes, comrades, to an anarchist collective. We swear they actually said it! Hysterical! ... We gave the cops a lesson in anarchism ... the fight for liberty for all ... not about violence to do the state's work for it ... not ripping the head off a decrepit old judge, and certainly not stabbing a woman just because she was stupid enough to marry a corrupt bastard like Marcus Tennant ... Put it this way, Mr Plod, if People's Resistance comes through our door we'll deal with them ourselves.

Before long the office door opened and the three insiders filed out, the young man at the rear carrying his laptop. They did not bother to lock up, presumably because there was nothing left to damage or steal. Jez threw Melanie another glance. She gave them five minutes and followed, leaving without a word to the other workers. She made her way down the rickety stairs, hurrying past the thumping press and its morose keeper into the cool evening air.

Halfway to the main road, where the alleyway was darkest, she found her path blocked by a couple having stand-up sex, the woman's skirt waist high, the man's trousers around his ankles, their thighs white as torch beams. 'What are you staring at, bitch?' said the woman to Melanie, as the man grunted into her chest. Melanie pushed past them and hurried for the square of light at the end of the alleyway. The situation in the street was exactly what she had planned. In her peripheral vision to the right the three from the office were trying to start the VW, with Jez at the wheel and the battery running low, which pleased her even more. Melanie turned left, walking slowly to her Renault, keys in her hand. The shout came as she was unlocking the door. 'Hey, wait up.' The voice Melanie had heard yelling at Jez now focused on her. She turned as Becky ran up, jabbing her thumb back at the VW. 'We need a lift.'

Melanie looked at the VW. 'What's the trouble?'

'Isn't it obvious?'

Melanie shrugged and checked her watch, like she had somewhere else to go. 'I can fix engines. Want me to have a look?' She walked back with Becky and nodded at Jez through the windscreen as she made for the engine compartment. The young man stood back holding his laptop, hands clean and useless. 'Turn it over again . . . Hold it,' Melanie called to Jez, as she fiddled with the spark plugs. She shouted the same thing several times, until the battery died. She looked at Becky, wiping her hands on her jeans.

'It's flat.'

Becky snorted. 'So you'll take us in your car, yeah?'

Melanie sensed Jez walking round the side of the vehicle. 'Sure.'

Then Jez was facing her. 'Except we're definitely going to the *Star* first.'

Melanie shook her head. 'Stuff to do.' She had her own rules about undercover work. Number one was never to go for the quick win or ask questions. Further down the line they would remember her eagerness.

'Just one.' Jez smiled and knocked her shoulder.

Melanie puffed her cheeks out and looked away for a rethink. She doubted their worth as a security target and Kerr had said he wanted a quick look, nothing more. A couple more visits to the *Flag*, three at most. 'Why not?' she said, to herself as much as them. She glanced at Laptop Boy. 'Someone better put a note on the windscreen.'

'Didn't get your name back there,' said Jez, loping beside her.

Melanie looked behind her. Becky had stayed with her partner by the VW, searching for pen and paper. The couple she had disturbed having sex emerged from the alleyway and immediately separated. 'You haven't told me yours.'

'Jez.'

In less than an hour Melanie had manufactured her first step to indispensability. She felt her anxiety evaporate, replaced by the high of raw deception. 'To succeed under-cover you have to live over the top,' Kerr had told her, the night before she had started driving for Terry Bray.

They had reached the pub door and she gave him the flicker of a smile. 'It's Mel.'

Twenty-eight

'Cheers. Absolutely fantastic.' Kerr tapped his bottle of Corona against his daughter's wine glass, pushed the wedge of lime through the neck and drank. They were sitting on a dark velvet sofa in the Concerto, a flashy wine bar near the Royal College of Music in the shadow of the Royal Albert Hall. It was newly remodelled and everyone behind the bar was a classical musician, either on sabbatical or waiting for the next break. Holograms of Chopin, Mozart, Brahms, Mendelssohn, Strauss, Elgar and Britten peered eerily from wall cavities, and spotlights had been cleverly suspended from cables to look like stage lighting. The bar itself was a circle of smoked glass and steel with every spirit bottle on the planet and three resting blonde violinists mixing cocktails.

Kerr and Gabi were there to celebrate her offer of a six-month trial as a violinist with the Royal Philharmonic Orchestra, starting in September. She was on her third large glass of Sancerre but Kerr was sticking to a couple of lagers because he had the car. He felt comfortable in this place for young people because Gabi had wanted him to share her success. They were getting on well, these days, after their long alienation, and Kerr had been trying hard to become the father she wanted. He was in more regular contact with Robyn, Gabi's mother, because he knew Gabi longed for a normal family life. Gabi had just ordered him to visit Robyn in Rome soon, perhaps before she started at the RPO while she was staying with her. 'No ifs or buts or too busy.' She wanted to take them out for red wine and spaghetti, to enjoy Mum and Dad spending quality time together. 'Then you can have a proper grown-up conversation that's not all about me.' Gabi knew about her parents' complicated relationship because Robyn had told her as soon as she could think for herself. 'Just because I'm finding my own way at last doesn't mean you guys can lose touch, Dad. Who knows? You might even find you fancy each other again after all these years,' she had said, then flushed with embarrassment.

Kerr had noticed a good-looking young man enter the bar shortly after they had sat down. Now he wove across to them and kissed Gabi on both cheeks, congratulating her on the RPO trial. Kerr picked up her glass and made for the bar before Gabi could introduce him. People were sitting on stools but he found a space in the circle. The barmaid who had served him before was a friend of Gabi and came over to him. She smiled. 'Same again?'

Kerr placed a tenner on the bar. 'Cheers.'

Then there was another voice to Kerr's left. 'And I'll have what he's having, young lady.' A twenty-pound note slapped down on the frosted glass and displaced Kerr's, as if its owner was making a bet. The girl was already on the turn and her face clouded as she looked back at him. Kerr recognised the drawl of entitlement as he turned to face the MI6 infiltrator from the Ethics Committee. The girl glanced at Kerr. 'Corona?'

'Lager will do fine,' came the voice again, as if tonight he was making an exception. The hand that had held the note now thrust at Kerr like a blade and the face wore a phoney look of surprise at running into him again. 'Small world.' It was warm in the bar but he was dressed in Home Counties retiree's uniform of brown corduroys, unbuttoned waxed jacket and dull brown lace-ups spattered with dried mud. He looked as if he had just come off the farm, as much an imposter there as at the Yard, and this time his name came to Kerr in a flash. Julius. No surname.

'Is it?' Ignoring the outstretched hand, Kerr scanned the bar. 'Always drink alone, do you?'

'Nice girl.' Julius nodded back to Gabi. 'I'm impressed. What does she see in you, I wonder?'

The server knew that Kerr was Gabi's father. Pouring the wine within earshot, she shot Kerr a little lift of her eyebrows.

Julius dropped his voice a couple of decibels. 'I heard you paid a visit to Marcus Tennant.' Kerr leant on one elbow but stayed silent, leaving Julius in the void, forcing him to continue. 'Asking inappropriate questions about his past, compounding his grief. All completely irrelevant to the terrible tragedy he's just been through.' He looked at Gabi. 'Sounds like harassment to me.'

Kerr glanced at her, too. Her friend had moved on. Another man was talking to her now but she was peering at the bar, anxious. 'Who told you?'

'Marcus Tennant is a good man. Served Queen and country in a way you could never understand.'

'Try me.'

'I'm just advising you to back off. A friendly warning,' he said nastily.

'A threat.'

'A word to the wise. Take it from me, he doesn't deserve this.'

The drinks arrived, and the server took the MI6 man's twenty, sliding Kerr's money back to him. 'One for yourself,' said Julius, without looking at her. By the till she was mouthing something and Kerr made out the word 'prick'.

'This case requires sensitivity. Discretion.' Julius removed the lime wedge and laid it on the bar. 'A step back to appreciate the wider picture.'

'Which is?'

'Co-operation. Mutual benefit . . . Cheers.' He paused to drink from the bottle but Kerr left his untouched. 'You've been in a few scrapes lately. Bluntly, I can help give your career a much-needed lift.'

'Fuck off,' said Kerr.

'Let me keep this simple for you. Digging up Marcus Tennant's past is irrelevant to his wife's murder.'

'Why are you so desperate to protect him?'

'His loyalty is not open to question.'

'That's not what I asked.'

'What you are doing is completely out of order.'

Kerr laughed. 'Like your pathetic masquerade on the Ethics Committee, you mean?'

'Take it from me and try not to be such a fucking pleb.' The spook's voice had suddenly risen with his temper, attracting attention. A couple of drinkers at the bar were giving the corduroys the once-over.

'Here's the situation,' said Kerr, quietly. 'I always go wherever the intelligence leads me, and your desperation to warn me off just made Marcus Tennant a lot more interesting. For example, why is your man about to be sacked? If he's such a good sport.'

'Rubbish. Who told you that?' said Julius, sharply, but he appeared momentarily deflated, perhaps disconcerted by the extent of Kerr's knowledge. Kerr considered raising the stakes by disclosing Tennant's affair with the au pair but held back. When he glanced at Gabi again the second man was still with her and he felt a pulse of anxiety that he and Julius might be connected. 'And I know exactly where you're from,' he said. 'Agent-handling course seven, eight years ago. I remember your name. Why is MI6 getting so worked up over this man?'

'You don't need to know.'

Kerr looked Julius up and down. 'Did they scramble you from home so you could catch me at the bar? How did you know I'd be here?' Julius seemed lost for words as Kerr picked up Gabi's wine and nodded across the bar. The man had disappeared and she was laughing again now, surrounded by a group of young women. Kerr moved away with the drinks, then turned. 'She's my daughter, by the way. And you always did have shit on your shoes.'

Friday, 2 August, 20.37; Kerr's Alfa Romeo

'Who was that ghastly bloke at the bar, Dad?'

'No one. Just a man I know through work.'

'He looked weird. My God, what was he wearing? Creepy. Seriously pissed off, too. What were you saying to him?'

They were in the Alfa, cruising down Exhibition Road to Gabi's flat in Battersea, and this had been their first chance to talk privately. Gabi was leaning forward, scanning Kerr's CD changer as she interrogated him, using her free hand to keep her hair out of her eyes.

'This and that. He just bumped into me.'

Since witnessing his near-death experience, Gabi had grown wary of people just bumping into her father. 'No way would he be in Concerto by accident. Kaiser Chiefs OK?' She pressed play. 'He was looking for you, Dad.'

'Nah. Just waiting for someone.'

'You.' She paused to catch the first bars of 'I Predict A Riot'. 'And he cleared off as soon as you brought the drinks over.'

Gabi was right. By the time Kerr had reached the table and squeezed in among Gabi's friends Julius had made his escape. 'I think he was expecting a call as well,' said Kerr, checking his mirror. 'Who was the guy with you?'

'Which one? A lot of men talk to me, Dad.'

'But you knew him, yeah?'

She gave his arm a playful punch. 'I know everybody,' she said, cranking up the sound.

Kerr's mobile rang. It was on hands-free and the screen showed Karl Sergeyev. 'Karl, what's up?'

A woman's voice came out of the speaker. 'John, it's Nancy. How are you?'

'Good, thanks. How about you?'

'And you've still got me under Karl's name.'

'I keep thinking you guys might get back together,' he said, with a wink at Gabi to turn the volume down.

Nancy giggled. 'Is this a bad time?' The laugh sounded carefree, the voice young.

Kerr had no idea why Nancy should be calling him on a Friday evening. He knew he should tell her his daughter was in the car and she was on the speaker. 'No, it's fine.' He asked about Nancy's children and spent a couple of minutes bantering with her about life in general. Gabi's eyes were on him the whole time, making him feel awkward.

Nancy did not mention Karl, which meant the call must be social. 'I was wondering. Are you free for lunch any time soon? It's been ages. One day next week, perhaps? It would be lovely to see you again.'

'Tell you what, Nancy. I'm in the car. Let me check the diary and I'll get back to you.' Caught in Gabi's stare as he rang off, Kerr felt himself flush. Awkward plus furtive. They were crossing Albert Bridge and he looked out at the river, waiting for Gabi to say something. He reached to turn the volume up but Gabi's hand restrained him.

'You're not going to, Dad.' She glared at him. 'Are you?'

'It's no problem.'

'She's a married woman with two children. What's she doing asking you on a date?'

'It's not a date. Not really. She probably wants to tell me something about Karl.'

'Your colleague, you mean? No, the close bloody *friend* who risked his life to save yours, remember?'

'It's not like that.'

'Ah, so you'll be telling Karl you're going out with his missus, will you?' Gabi was suddenly sounding slurred, as if the alcohol had been biding its time. 'You can't do this, Dad. It's impossible. God, we've just spent a nice evening talking about you and Mum. Why don't you fly out and see *her* once in a while? Take *her* out for a nice spot of bloody lunch?'

They had reached Gabi's street and the passenger door was open before they had come to a halt. 'Anyway,' said Kerr, 'I'm delighted for you.'

'Don't change the subject.' Gabi was already out of the car. 'Just try to think of other people for a change,' she said, leaning back in. Then the door slammed and she was gone.

Kerr watched Gabi until she was safely through the front door, then drove back slowly over the river. He parked in Cheyne Walk and checked the time: just after nine thirty. Not too late. He took the phone off hands-free, as if Gabi's spirit might still hear him, and pressed last-number redial.

Twenty-nine

It was hot in the safe house. Despite the screen over the skylight, warm air from outside permeated the roof tiles and hung over the room in a heavy cloud, sapping Danny Brennan's energy. Stripped to his shorts he sat at the workbench, shaven head bent in concentration. Had he been simply reading or watching TV he would have left the stairway open for ventilation, but his task was too secret to allow the slightest risk. The soldering iron he was using to construct the incendiary bomb added to the heat and his face shone with sweat as smoke swirled in the light from the desk lamp.

This was the second of two devices, both to be deployed in his own special mission. In Wormwood Scrubs he had spent many months dreaming of their effect but here, in his hiding place, he had worked out the physical details in the space of a weekend. The shape and size were identical, small enough to be concealed in an A4 sized Jiffy-bag, sufficiently powerful to be lethal.

Sky News rolled in the background. Eleven days after Brennan had disembowelled Diane Tennant, ten since his decapitation of Judge Hugh Selwyn, media interest in People's Resistance was as strong as ever. Holed up in this roof space in Bethnal Green, he revelled in more attention than he had received in his whole life. When not glued to the TV, he had spent his time absorbing the anarchist literature Rashid had brought him, struggling to make sense of some of the original tracts but understanding every word of the revisionist literature. Everything he read had inspired him for the action he was preparing now. This attack would be private as well as political, a personal act of vengeance for his father, plus a strike against the state, to be kept secret even from Rashid.

To construct the bombs he was using regular household materials stretched in a neat row along the back of the workbench. No single item in the line-up was in the least threatening, let alone deadly. On Saturday, when Brennan had embarked on his shopping spree, it had been raining heavily. Disobeying Rashid's instruction never to leave the safe house, he had spent the afternoon, protected by his hoodie and beanie, walking around the food shops, chemists, hardware stores and garden centres of Bethnal Green, Spitalfields and Stepney. Shaba Food and Drink, Pound Crazy, Zara Pharmacy and Rachel's Secret Garden had supplied all the necessary soft ingredients and chemicals. Metal and electrical components for the detonators he had acquired in Mile End Road, courtesy of Cobb's Ironmongers, Established 1894, run by a couple of brilliantined Cockneys in brown work coats, smelling of talcum powder. Brooms, plastic bowls, waste bins, padlocked ladders and a wheelbarrow had crowded the pavement, with every other conceivable item stacked inside on three sets of high metal shelves running the length of the shop. 'Everything you need to make a comfortable home,' the hand-painted sign, with its outdated 0171 telephone number, had said. Or a bomb, Brennan had thought, as he filled his pockets. Nothing had cost him a penny, for he had been an accomplished thief long before he had matured as a London rioter.

The lack of Internet access in the safe house for technical research had not been a setback: the design of the bombs and method of initiation were his own. Danny Brennan had no use for the blogs of laptop anarchists and urban guerrilla fantasists because his own knowledge was greater than theirs, reaching back to his boyhood. Halfway through his first year at secondary school, Brennan had begun smuggling chemicals out of the laboratory to work on his own experiments. He had soon acquired the nickname 'Dynamite Danny' on account of his obsession with chemistry and its power to harm, and would spend hours designing fireworks with time delays.

Brennan had grown up in a council house on the roughest estate in Dagenham. Twenty paces away at the bottom of the narrow garden there was a small shed that he had helped his father build. As a boy he had done everything with his dad, whether it was riding their bikes in the park, tending the neat garden or going to watch West Ham on a Saturday afternoon and stopping for a burger on the way home. Within a few weeks the shed had become Danny's private domain and he had nailed an old sheet to the window frame to prevent his mum watching him from the kitchen. He had used it to hide the smuggled chemicals and acids in small, unlabelled bottles behind his dad's seed boxes and cans of paint. As soon as he arrived home from school he would disappear into the makeshift laboratory, losing himself in his experiments. With the onset of winter he had stolen a rubber waterproof torch with its own stand and several filters over the beam. The light in the shed would be green when he was feeling happy, red when he was angry or upset, and the shadows always fired his imagination.

Just before his thirteenth birthday the prettiest girl from his class had asked to observe an experiment close up. Her name was Mary and she lived in a private house in Hornchurch, arriving at school with clean hair and shiny shoes in her mother's BMW. She had been younger than Brennan but cleverer in every subject except chemistry, often glancing at him across the classroom with a smile he had believed was love. Then she had destroyed everything. In the shed's dull green light Mary had told him his laboratory looked as weird as he did and that she had only asked to see it for a dare. By the time she had flashed her mocking smile again the torch had already been switched to red.

Brennan had mixed chemicals with acid in a cereal bowl and promised her they would light up with all the colours of the rainbow. Pressing her close to the makeshift bench he had allowed her to light the fuse. The explosion had blinded Mary and left her face and throat irreparably scarred. Whatever the official suspicions of the authorities, none had disproved Brennan's claim that Mary had been helping him to make fireworks. He had been questioned by police, counselled by Social Services, chastised by his mother and even fought over by the two fathers. Through it all, no one had heard the boy express a word of remorse. 'Classic callous unemotional,' was how one of the doctors had described Danny's condition, but his father had never given up on him.

The boy's second major experiment had come a year later, soon after his next-door neighbours had acquired a pit bull for security and fighting. The animal had powerful shoulders and mad eyes, and they would regularly deploy it around the estate as an offensive weapon. It had roamed next door's back yard on a chain, lying in its own filth, looking murderous and barking all day while the neighbours were out drinking, going crazy whenever Brennan stood by the fence to stare it down.

At that time his dad had been working permanent nights on the Underground and, because the dog prevented him sleeping, he would be yelling at Danny's mother as soon as he awoke. Danny loved both his parents and their misery had provoked him almost as powerfully as the pit bull, which he had come to hate more than anything in the world. Returning early from school one day, he had laced a piece of steak with poison from his own special recipe, tossed it over the fence and retreated to his laboratory. Peering through the window, he had watched the dog tear at the meat, then writhe in agony until it was dead, timing the incident from first bite to final twitch.

The son had killed the dog to save his parents, but it had not been enough. The anger had continued right up until the day his dad had punched his mother in the face, crammed a few things into the sports bag they had given Danny for Christmas and slammed the door behind him. But Danny had never given up on him, knowing that one day he would return. The hero worship he had felt as a boy never left him: ultimately, he realised he had never been closer to another human being, even after his dad was killed.

It took Anna Rashid three minutes and fifteen seconds to enter the kitchen door, negotiate the staircase and climb the ladder to the roof space; Brennan knew, because he had timed her on many occasions. Nearly a fortnight into his mission he knew every sound and movement Rashid made as she moved through the house. He disconnected the soldering iron and slid the first incendiary beneath the bed when she unlocked the kitchen door and, by the time she reached the foot of the staircase, had followed it with the second. As she climbed the stairs he collected the materials into a cardboard box and hid it in the bottom drawer. By the time the hatch opened and the ladder slid downwards he had lit a joint to mask the smell of the soldering.

A black holdall appeared through the aperture before Rashid. Brennan reached for it but she brushed him away. Breathless, she placed the bag on the floor beside the work-bench, threw off her coat and tossed a copy of *Flag of Liberty* on the workbench. Brennan saw a fragment of solder roll onto the floor and covered it with his foot. 'Read the latest,' she said, taking Brennan's joint and crashing onto the bed immediately above Brennan's inert bombs. He sat at the bench, aware of her eyes flickering between him and the TV, and read the headline: 'Another Turn of the Screw'. He scanned the piece, then read it again in silence, scowling at the page. '. . . anarchism is the fight for liberty for all, not about violent, arrogant élites claiming to act in our name.' He felt his anger growing with each word. 'When did they put this crap out?'

'Thursday.'

'Today's Monday.'

'Been busy.'

He read the final sentence out loud. ' "If People's Resistance comes through our door we'll deal with them ourselves." Is that right? That's what they think, is it?'

'No. It's Becky. Or Sacha, her boyfriend. It's just her having a vent. She does it to impress.'

'Street-fighter, is she?' said Brennan, drily.

Rashid inhaled deeply and laughed. 'Philosophy grad from Sussex. Daddy pays their rent and Becky behaves like an extra in *Les Misérables*. The *Flag* is their ego trip. They're nothing.'

Brennan looked at her in disbelief. 'So why didn't you block it?'

She propped herself on one elbow. 'You what?'

'You work there, don't you? Write for them?'

Rashid shook her head. 'Not a single word in months. You know why I hang out with them.'

Brennan held the paper up. 'This is a complete fucking betrayal.'

'It's cover for me.'

'So why are you not as totally pissed off by this as me?'

'I'm not the unofficial censor to the alternative press, Danny. Becky's ignorance keeps the *Flag* and me off the cops' radar so I really don't give a toss what she writes. Our actions speak for themselves.' She nodded at his books piled at the end of the worktop. 'Or haven't you found that bit yet?'

Rashid's voice had acquired the sarcastic edge she had used when she first referred to his anarchist reading and he felt a pulse of anger. The buzz outside Middle Temple, the affirmation from the mainstream media, all of it was being drained out of him by anarchist writers who should have been their strongest supporters. 'So I'll ask them myself. When do I get to meet your friends, so they can educate me?' He stabbed at the journal, screwed it up and tossed it at her. 'You know. *Deal with me.*'

'Not possible. I already told you. No way are you guys ever going to get together, so forget it.' Rashid finished the joint and climbed off the bed. 'I've got the go-ahead for the next action.'

'When?'

'Soon.'

Brennan lifted the bag onto the worktop. 'Show me.'

Rashid carefully pulled back the zip. She took out a white chef's tunic, unfolded it and held it against him, checking it for size. 'Try it on.' She helped him with the buttons, then stood back and made a face. 'You'll do.' Brennan had a flashback of his mother dressing him for school. Before his dad had left she had always kissed him on the forehead, using those exact words, and it made him glance towards the incendiaries beneath the bed. He tugged at the tunic and threw her a half-smile. 'I was just about to make pasta, actually.'

'Later.' Rashid reached into the bag for the three devices Peter had given her in the coffee shop and lined them up on the workbench. Each was numbered and sealed in a black plastic case the size of an old-fashioned video cassette, with none of the contents visible. Brennan picked up the middle device, marked '2', and weighed it in his hand. 'Very neat. Very clean,' he murmured, secretly comparing these state-of-the-art devices with his own crude incendiaries.

'Each has a different make-up.' Rashid pointed to a plastic sliding switch on the side of each. 'You arm them here. Thirty minutes tops to plant them and escape.'

'Burn or blast?' he said.

'Both. Plus poison, so you can forget *clean*, Danny. These are the dirtiest bombs you'll see in your entire fucking life.'

'Where?'

Rashid reached into the side pocket of the bag, took out a folded sheet of A3 paper and pinned it to the wall. It appeared to be a simple architect's drawing of a public space such as a restaurant or large conference room with a main door to the street, kitchen at the back and toilets to the right, but with nothing to identify the location. Rashid pointed to three red spots, marked with the numerals one, two and three. 'You plant them *exactly* where it says. This is the big one, Danny. High-value targets. High risk. The attack to really wind them up.' Rashid's eyes were shining as she stared at the drawing. 'It's going to be amazing.'

'Where?' said Brennan, again.

Rashid produced the communiqué from the bag and held it out to him. 'Read it.'

'And what shite will the *Flag* write when this is done?'

Rashid looked hard at him. 'Are you sure you're ready for this?'

'I'm telling you to get a grip of your friends, Anna. Or I will.'

'Forget about the *Flag*. The shock waves from this will reverberate around the world.' Rashid unbuttoned his tunic, gently pulled him close and kissed him. 'Just let the action speak for itself.'

Thirty

'HOLMES tells me Derek Finch is getting nowhere,' said Alan Fargo. 'Not a shred of hard evidence on who killed Diane Tennant and the judge, whatever he's telling the media. Zeros all round. No confirmed sightings around either murder scene, no useful forensics at this stage. Zilch CCTV footage. Only one of the four cameras in Middle Temple Lane was working.'

Tieless, in a maroon shirt that was too big for him, Fargo kept dabbing at his eyes, still sore from his new contact lenses and weary from a Sunday checking out Finch's murder investigations. John Kerr was squeezed beside him in the tiny 1830 reading room, facing the window, opposite Jack Langton and Justin Hine. Langton sat in his motorcycle leathers nearest the door, ready to check out the five surveillance plots he would be running this week. After a long morning trapped in the Fishbowl by the hated weekly admin, Kerr wanted ideas to crack People's Resistance and prevent the next attack.

HOLMES was the Home Office Large Major Enquiry System, the standardised confidential database for storing all investigative information. Finch guarded it jealously from officers outside his immediate circle, especially if they belonged to Ajay's intelligence unit. Knowledge was power, and the Bull's ambition was boundless. 'Finch treats HOLMES like it's the Crown Jewels,' said Kerr. 'So how did you get into it?'

'I didn't actually access it myself,' said Fargo, suddenly embarrassed. 'Someone in Reserve got it for me.' His phone started ringing in the deserted main office. 'Better take that,' he said, easily extricating himself from the cramped space, as if he had just lost a few pounds.

Kerr knew his friend had worked a tough weekend protecting 1830 while engineers made emergency repairs to an overhead leak. Above them a long stretch of ceiling was a scarred maze of exposed pipes, cables and air-conditioning vents covered with silver foil. Langton's helmet was balanced on a stack of ceiling tiles that should have been in the main office. 'No asbestos, I hope,' said Justin, waving his hand through the cloud of dust particles floating in the sunshine. Beyond Fargo's desk in the deserted main office, Excalibur was concealed under dust sheets. The engineers had abandoned their stepladders and planks in the far corner, giving SO15's intelligence hub the look of a storeroom. When he returned Fargo was carrying a small bottle of saline.

'You all right?' said Kerr, as Fargo blew his nose.

'Two days of dust and chaos,' said Fargo, jabbing a thumb at the ceiling as he slithered into his chair. At least a stone lighter, thought Kerr. 'That was Donna. Ajay's coming to join us.'

'So which comms operator gave you HOLMES?' said Justin, with a knowing look at Langton. 'Or shall we guess?'

Fargo flushed again. 'Gemma's got a friend in Finch's admin unit,' he mumbled, blinking at Justin. 'What of it?'

'Nice work,' said Kerr. 'Last time we needed HOLMES I had to steal it, remember?' He frowned across the desk. 'OK. So, until Finch gets a lucky break everything depends on intelligence. Down to us, and we don't have much to offer.'

He told them about his hijack by Julius on Friday evening. 'I want us to follow up on this jerk as a possible lead, starting with the reason MI6 were so desperate to get him inside the Ethics Committee.'

'And who they leant on to infiltrate him,' said Langton.

'I already tried the committee secretary,' said Fargo. 'Sorry. Have to do this.' As he stretched his head back to drop saline into his eyes, Kerr spotted the unmistakable imprint of a love bite on the right side of his throat. Perhaps Fargo's weekend had not been so tough after all. Fargo blinked rapidly and screwed the lid back onto the bottle. 'She ignored me but I tracked down the official attendance record. No mention of Julius in any capacity.'

'Falsified by the Ethics Committee,' said Justin. 'What a joke.'

'There's another channel I can try,' said Kerr, then paused. 'But why should MI6 be so pissed off about me door-stepping Marcus Tennant?'

'Because he worked for them,' said Justin. 'And they're protecting their own.'

'From what?'

Langton leant forward. 'And there's still the question hanging over your inquisition at the Star bloody Chamber. What makes MI6 so interested in the deaths of a couple of gold smugglers on the Thames? Unless there's a connection somewhere down the line.'

'Given up the ghost, has she?' The voice came from the main office, soft and clear. 'Or just shrouded in mystery?' Immaculate in crisp white shirt with the cuffs rolled back, razor-creased navy trousers and brightly polished slip-ons, Commander Ajay Khan had stopped to pat Excalibur through the dust sheet before joining them. Fargo stood to offer his seat but Ajay was carrying a chair through from the main office. He put it down and sat astride it, with its back pressed against the desk. He looked rested, his moustache perfectly trimmed, and Kerr wondered how much squash he had played over the weekend. 'Which of you gentlemen has been annoying Mr Finch?'

He broke into a smile as everyone exchanged glances. 'Mr Finch has just requested, correction, *demanded* a meeting with me tomorrow morning at eleven to discuss what he tells me are serious deficiencies in process. Translated, I think he wants to give me a rollocking.' He looked at Kerr. 'Care to join me, if you're free? Man on the ground, et cetera.'

That was the time Kerr was due to meet Melanie. 'I know he would much rather deal with Mr Ritchie.'

'Unavailable. A more pressing commitment,' said Ajay.

That was code for the chemotherapy Bill Ritchie was undergoing to fight his prostate cancer. Ritchie had shoved his health strictly off limits, though everyone knew he was increasingly working from home, these days, and Kerr kept himself updated through regular conversations with Lynn. Evidently she had been receiving calls from Ajay, too, and was full of admiration because she knew he was quietly taking on her husband's workload without making him feel sidelined or undervalued. 'I'll be there.' He glanced at the others. 'Are you going to show him our work from the other day? Tomorrow might be a good opportunity.'

'Depends. Perhaps. The Bull seems provoked. Which of you has been waving the proverbial red flag?'

'He probably heard I went to see Marcus Tennant at home,' said Kerr.

'As grieving victim, presumably?' said Ajay, encouragingly. 'To offer condolences?'

'And to tell him his intelligence background could be relevant to the attack.'

'Ah,' sighed Ajay.

'There's also a business profile I've been researching over the weekend,' said Fargo, shuffling through his notepad. Ajay was so close that the pages brushed against his hand. 'Before entering politics Tennant was an officer in MI6, posted to Washington in 1994 and recalled to London after the hostile recruitment pitch in 1996, well before completing his full term.'

Ajay looked at Justin. 'Which confirms your excellent information from the other night, yes? Risking life and liver. Thank you.' He gave Fargo a little nod to continue.

'In 1998 Tennant had resigned from Vauxhall Cross and moved back to the US to take up the position of marketing director for Aircore Inc.'

'Defence?' said Ajay.

Fargo nodded and flicked a couple of pages. 'A major American company trading in fast British and American jets, helicopter gunships, missiles and other lethal military equipment.' Reading verbatim from his notes seemed to accentuate Fargo's Cornish accent. 'Which would have left him extremely well placed for a political role here in defence.'

'And exposed him to a possible conflict of interest, perhaps, or some other threat arising from his background as a spy,' said Ajay. 'So, the murder of Diane was actually an attack against Marcus. Is that what we're working up to?'

'It's possible.' Kerr shrugged. 'Look at his reaction to me. People who spray that much poison often have a lot to hide.'

'And who would bear him ill will?' said Ajay. 'Apart from his poor wife, of course, for having it off with the au pair.'

'I was thinking of the French, as a matter of fact,' said Kerr.

Everyone stared in silence except Fargo, who had already spoken with Kerr from 1830 the night before.

'Really?' Ajay shifted in his chair. 'Based on real-time fact or centuries-old prejudice?' No one laughed except Ajay, who reached over to touch Kerr's arm. 'Pulling your leg. Go on.'

As Ajay withdrew his hand a lump of cladding crashed from the ceiling onto the desk, sending dust and fragments in all directions. 'Christ!' shouted Langton, as Justin recoiled violently against the wall.

'OK,' said Kerr, reaching for Justin. 'It's nothing.' Less than a year earlier Justin had been injured rescuing a mother and child from a bombed building, and Kerr knew that the mark on his forehead was not Justin's only scar.

Fargo looked resigned, as if he had been dodging ceiling bombs all weekend, and Ajay seemed unperturbed. 'You see what happens, John,' he said, calmly picking fragments of debris from his shirt, 'when you defame one of our closest allies.'

Thirty-one

They reconvened in Ajay's office. 'Never realised working in 1830 could be so dangerous,' he told a surprised Donna, as he led the way through her outer office and flicked the kettle on.

They sat round the conference table looking out to St James's Park and Buckingham Palace. 'The French,' said Ajay, as if they had never been interrupted. 'As a nation, or do you have someone particular in mind?'

'Their external intelligence service, specifically,' said Kerr. 'The DGSE.'

'Direction Générale de la Sécurité Extérieur,' said Ajay in rapid French. 'Behind People's Resistance? You're serious?' Ajay looked at Fargo. 'And how many dots did you join to reach those bastards?'

'We just followed the trail,' said Kerr.

Fargo shook a fragment of plaster from the coiled spine of his notebook. 'This is something John and I talked through last night. But it's not speculation, sir. There's a link to the French in everything we've come up against since the gold theft in March. DGSE are notorious for industrial-espionage operations.'

'Against Aircore?'

'Yes. Tried to bribe one of their vice-presidents in 1997, which was when the Americans started taking a serious look at them worldwide. The French are probably more aggressive in Europe than the US, Russia or China.'

'Which would take some doing.'

'And they have previous in London,' said Kerr. 'Five years ago we believe they carried out an eavesdropping operation in the Ministry of Defence against a Labour defence minister. Inside his own office.'

'Bad form when we're supposed to be friends,' said Ajay, raising his hand for a pause. 'Let's circle back for a moment. What makes such disgraceful conduct relevant to the grieving Marcus?'

Fargo glanced at Justin. 'We go back to his MI6 days for that. Justin's drinking pal claims Tennant was pitched at the French embassy in Washington.'

Justin leaned forward. 'And Tennant was sent back to London because he failed to report the approach. That's how Alec understood it. Tail between legs, definitely.'

'The official unofficial version of a drinking partner,' said Ajay.

'Or perhaps the pitch was successful,' said Fargo. 'Tennant succumbed, his head of station found out about it and MI6 covered the whole thing up.'

'Let's assume for now that he rejected the approach and stayed loyal to Queen and country,' said Kerr. 'Now fast forward to 2013 and look at Marcus Tennant through the eyes of the same hostile intelligence agency. The DGSE, say. This guy has a lot to offer from his time with MI6 and as a businessman in the US winning top-secret defence contracts. Unparalleled access to the American and UK military defence network.'

'Which would account for his meteoric rise to defence secretary with a seat in cabinet,' said Ajay.

'Probably. Intelligence, business and politics. A triple whammy that makes Marcus Tennant an extremely high-value target and prime material for another attempt to turn him.'

'So, patriot or traitor?' said Ajay, looking between Kerr and Fargo. 'Where does your trail lead us?'

'Into his au pair's bed,' said Kerr. 'Regular sex with a young woman called Yvette, who disappeared moments before the attack on Diane Tennant. No surname, no vetting history, *nada.*'

Ajay was steepling his fingers, the sun lighting the hairs on his forearms. The little finger of his left hand bore a gold signet ring that Donna said was engraved with his father's initials. 'A honey trap by an agent of the DGSE?'

'Chapter two of the attempt in Washington sixteen years ago. But more aggressive this time, using blackmail in place of enticement.'

Donna brought Ajay's tea in a giant blue cup and saucer. 'I wouldn't put it past them,' said Ajay, with a smile at Donna. 'Can't wait to hear what happened next.'

'Tennant rejected them again and they murdered Diane to get back at him,' said Kerr. 'A revenge attack. A drastic attempt to force his co-operation.'

'Or warn him against reporting their approach, perhaps,' said Ajay. 'Would they risk such a vicious murder on British soil?'

Langton and Justin had been sitting quietly, hearing the analysis worked up by Kerr and Fargo the previous night for the first time. Suddenly Langton leant forward, his leather jacket squeaking on Ajay's table as he folded his arms. 'You already said it, boss. The French are very bad bastards. Dirty tricks against Algerian dissidents living here, kidnappings, you name it. Nothing's off limits. And remember all that stuff about Londonistan in the late nineties? DGSE were seriously active here against Islamic extremists, everything secret and undeclared. Some ally. Am I right, Al?'

'Yes, and still making themselves busy after a recruitment drive in 2010,' said Fargo. 'Last year five of their agents got caught in Bulgaria on what they claimed was a training mission.'

'No way would I put the murder of Diane Tennant past them,' said Langton. 'And they have cover through People's Resistance to make everything look UK-inspired.'

Like a boy in class, Justin raised a hand and looked at Kerr. 'Didn't one of the gangsters we were chasing down the Thames shout in French?'

Kerr nodded. 'Possibly. The mobile I recovered definitely had French numbers in the log as well as the call to Terry Bray. It gives us the common thread, the connection between the gold heist and the People's Resistance attacks.'

'Which is?' said Ajay, eyebrows raised.

'A resounding hatred of America.'

Ajay sipped his tea. 'You're saying the ultimate DGSE mission is to damage the United States?'

'And our so-called special relationship. The gold was American-owned, stolen in transit through London. The communiqués from the attacks on Diane Tennant and Judge Hugh Selwyn are toxic against America. History is littered with French hostility towards the US and battles to win commercial contracts, especially in aircraft and warships. The French plant agents in US companies and spy on American businessmen working in France. In return America insults the French by accusing them of double-dealing through kickbacks.'

' "The French know how to bribe," ' said Ajay. 'If memory serves.'

'It does. And remember all that ridiculing years ago of Sarkozy as an emperor without clothes, touchy, unpredictable, that sort of thing? I think everything's linked. The gold, Diane Tennant, Hugh Selwyn. The single thread is hatred of America.'

'And MI6 appear to believe it, too,' said Justin. 'How else do we explain Julius's interest in both the Thames attacks and Marcus Tennant?'

'Hmm.' Ajay looked at each of them. 'Anything else to chuck into the mix?'

'Yes.' Fargo had brought his saline and was applying more drops. 'With MI6 we have to consider another possibility. Are they already investigating DGSE? Are they pissed off with John because we're treading on their toes?'

Ajay drained his tea, stood up and went to the window. Hands in pockets, he gazed at the park and the big sky for a few moments. The breeze had strengthened during the day, stiffening the flag over the palace, and thick black clouds blowing in from the west threatened rain. He turned and perched on the air-conditioning vent, silhouetted against the window. 'Fine. A good first stab but here comes the devil's advocate. Guard against becoming *distracted*. We have to channel all our energies into preventing the next attack. That's our clear public duty. The encounter between Marcus Tennant and the girl may have been no more than sex.' He smiled. 'Hardly unusual for a politician to behave in such a way. The fact that young Yvette found her way from Toulouse to the London suburbs does not make her a French spy. Our Mata Hari may be no more than an impressionable young woman seduced by a powerful man. It's happened before, so let's not get ahead of ourselves. Until Derek Finch's investigation gathers traction, if it ever does, we drive forward a domestic intelligence operation to identify People's Resistance. Everyone OK with that? Good.' Ajay returned behind his desk. 'Let's have another chat tomorrow.' He called softly to Kerr as they filed out. 'Another minute, John?'

Kerr murmured at Justin and Langton to wait for him in the Fishbowl and closed the door. He took the seat Ajay offered him beside his desk, an elegant upholstered chair he had brought from home.

Ajay stroked his moustache. 'How's Melanie?' He made it sound as if he was asking after a relative.

'Fine, thanks.' Kerr blew out his cheeks. 'It's only her fourth day out but she calls Alan Fargo every day and has my number twenty-four/seven. She spent the weekend in the cover address making herself known, wandering round the shops, that sort of thing.'

'Assimilating.'

'Exactly.' Kerr knew Ajay was not trying to be clever. He sensed his commander mentally ticking the box marked 'operational security'. 'Dodge has done a great job around the logistics, so I would say her cover's strong.'

'But a weak intelligence flow?' said Ajay.

Kerr shrugged. 'It's very early days. She's identified a few regulars, drop-ins, volunteers, vehicles and so on.'

'Nothing we can't identify from other sources, presumably. Any chatter about People's Resistance?'

'No one seems to mention it. Hot words in the journal condemning the attacks but no signs of secret knowledge, basically.'

'What about the personal aspects?'

'One of the guys at the *Flag* is coming on strong to her, apparently.'

'She told you that?'

'Last night.'

Ajay looked anxious. 'Welfare has to be paramount, John, especially after all we've put this officer through. If there's the slightest doubt . . .'

'Harassment comes with the job and Melanie will deal with it in her own way,' said Kerr, shortly. 'I really believe we should continue. You want us to pursue a domestic intelligence operation and we're all determined to close this down. The *Flag of Liberty* is the most prominent anarchist journal in the country and its editors have wide access.'

'Logically, if the perpetrators are British extremists, Melanie is the best chance we have. Is that it?' said Ajay. 'So let's keep digging away in the British back yard. Bill Ritchie has over-sight but I'll support the guys in every way. This is a difficult time for Bill and we have to make things as stress-free for him as possible. Keep a close eye on everyone and brief me personally.'

Kerr nodded. 'No problem.'

'And a word of caution. If you acquire firm intelligence of activity by the French or any other malign foreign power, you notify me immediately. We're talking counter-espionage here.'

'MI5's remit,' said Kerr.

'You know I'm working my nuts off to re-establish a toler-able working relationship.'

'Absolutely,' said Kerr, palms open.

'Our principal partners must be allowed first bite at the obnoxious Mr Tennant, if necessary,' said Ajay. 'Brothers and sisters at arms and all that.'

'And they can slug it out with his protectors in MI6.'

Ajay gave a rueful smile. 'Precisely.'

Langton and Justin were waiting for Kerr in the Fishbowl and both looked eager to get on the road. Kerr closed the door, pulled the blinds and moved behind his desk. 'What are you doing tonight, guys?'

Thirty-two

In the upstairs bookshop at the *Flag*, Melanie worked at the clutch of trestle tables helping to collate the next issue of the journal. It was her third evening there and she stood in the same place, mechanically reaching, folding and inserting from the piles of A3 paper by her left elbow. In the office at the far end Becky, Sacha and Jez were arguing again. Melanie could hear Becky's voice dominating the other two and it was obvious they were disagreeing about the lead story, which had to be printed the following evening and collated into the journal on Wednesday night.

The ink smelt heavy and acrid, competing with the toilet stench and staining her fingers black. Only one of the volunteers, a woman with cropped red hair and a dove tattoo on her forearm, had attended on the same nights as she had. This evening there were three newcomers, a young man with a teachers'-union bag and a paunch from a diet of school dinners, a spiky punk, who kept getting her pages in the wrong order, and a skinny woman in her forties with a vegan's pallor and the cold, chapped hands of a rough sleeper. They worked in silence, their heads bowed over the papers. The only sign of life came from Jez, who suddenly stormed out of the office and slammed the door behind him with a force that made the plastic partition shudder. Melanie watched him grab a pile of

A3 and push himself between the teacher and the punk, positioning himself directly opposite her. Beer breath washed across the tables. He was angry.

'What's up?' said Melanie.

'I need a drink,' said Jez, tossing the papers across the tables. He went back to the office and flung the door open. 'We're going to the pub.'

After engineering the breakdown of their vehicle Melanie had joined Jez in the Old Star with the two editors on the Friday. That evening, impatient in the bookshop, he had come alive the moment he had led them into the crowded bar, easing through the crush and joking with the bar staff as he bought the first round. It had been standing room only and everyone had seemed to know him. In that crowded place, Jez had become larger than life, towering over Becky and Sacha, making them look insignificant beside him. Whenever Jez said something amusing his laugh had filled the bar, and even Sacha had smiled as Jez recounted his battle to keep the old printing press alive. At each quip he had closed his big hand around Melanie's arm, as if he had been telling his story to her alone, wanting to make her laugh.

Of the three, Melanie knew most about Jez because that Friday evening he had asked a couple to make room for the two of them, leaving Becky and Sacha standing by the toilets. Jez had been brought up on a farm in Dorset, one of four children who had deserted the countryside for London in his early twenties, drifting through a sea of short-term manual jobs until he had washed up at the *Flag*, where he had offered to do some maintenance work. He had volunteered this over his first pint without a single question from Melanie.

She had discovered something else that evening. Jez wanted sex with her. She knew this because he had told her so there and then in the pub, his strong, weathered face creasing into a knowing smile, teeth bright white against his beard. This had increased Melanie's anxiety and actually heightened her sense of isolation. It had also created guilt because she had found herself attracted by his strong physicality and zest for life, just as she had been by Rob's in their early years.

Tonight the Old Star was full of police officers. Cordoned off from the few other drinkers, the cops stood in their suits and half blues around a huge oval dining table, red-faced and boisterous. The pub had evidently laid on one of its multipurpose spreads, pork pies and tandoori chicken for a one-size-fits-all celebration: marriage, divorce, promotion or cremation, everything at £9.95 a head. The cops stood with pints of lager and their plates piled high, chewing and drinking, clocking everything that moved. Melanie felt their eyes track her as she followed Jez to a table in the far corner. She ran the gauntlet, her heart in her mouth, dreading the call of recognition yet half wanting to join them.

'Fucking cops,' said Jez, quietly, returning with the drinks.

'Yeah?' said Melanie. She made a show of shifting on the bench to conceal herself. 'Best we talk about something else, then.'

She knew Becky was writing a second scathing leader about People's Resistance because Jez had been ranting about it right to the door of the pub. 'She can't keep judging what's right and wrong, sitting on her bourgeois anarchist arse up there,' Jez had shouted in the alleyway. 'Not when real fighters are taking direct action to the street. We've got the *Daily* fucking *Mail* for that.'

By the time Becky and Sacha joined them Jez was downing his third pint. Becky glared at him, as if she was geared up for round two, until Jez nudged her and nodded across the bar. 'I'm not going to let those bastards stop me,' said Becky, in her freedom-fighter's voice, finding a tissue to wipe circles of stale beer from the table. She fired up her laptop and spread out a few papers while Sacha bought two halves of lager shandy. They worked as a couple, ignoring Melanie while she drank her Coke and watched Jez grow drunker.

She was despondent: Kerr had texted her to change their meeting the following day to the afternoon, which she had set aside for Rob and the children. If he wanted her on the inside track of People's Resistance it was time to try elsewhere. The situation was clear. The *Flag*'s core was a pair of middle-class *faux* intellectuals shouting from the sideline and a man with strong appetites but no political credibility; if Jez had ever been radicalised since his exile from Dorset he had learnt to conceal it. The rest were a transient, irrelevant mix of inadequates, retro punks, delinquent Goths and wannabe radicals as counterfeit as their designer labels. She had wasted five days catching people in the act of being themselves.

For the third time Melanie took the three of them home to Stoke Newington in her Renault, Jez in the front passenger seat again. It was raining heavily, the black roads glistening, and she drove cautiously north up Kingsland Road, distracted by the incessant bickering from the back. Becky and Sacha rented a classy one-bedroom refurb just off Church Street but Jez lived with three others in a barely habitable house on the border with Stamford Hill, a stone's throw from the Guinness Trust estate. Their homes reflected the hierarchy of the *Flag*, with Becky and Sacha at the top and Jez floating somewhere between the demented guy in the print room and the screwballs who folded the paper. Becky always acted as if she was in charge of everything.

Jez made sure Melanie dropped him last. He was drunk and playful, mocking Becky and Sacha the moment they slid across the back seat and slammed the door without a word of thanks. 'Remember when "Occupy London" camped outside St Paul's, everyone freezing their bollocks off? Well, they spent every night back here, tucked up in their warm, cosy bed. Office-hours revolutionaries, those two.' He leant right up close to Melanie and tapped his watch, almost collapsing in her lap. 'Man the barricades nine to fucking five.' He stayed in the car when she parked in an unlit side-street off Dunsmure

Road, alongside the railway line. They sat with the wipers on and Jez mumbled something as a train shot by.

'What?'

Jez leant across her again and tried to switch off the engine. She batted his hand away and they both laughed.

'I said why don't you come up for a drink? Everyone's out.'

'You're pissed.' She realised she had to be as playful as Jez now as she stretched across to open his door.

He twisted to get out, then pulled his legs back out of the rain, throwing her a big, lopsided smile. 'Can I kiss you here, then?'

Melanie looked at him but did not speak. The wipers scythed once across the windscreen, then again. Three seconds. She might have said no, put the car in gear, threatened to drive off, feigned anger or amusement. She could have done a bunch of things but instead she surrendered to a moment of inertia, watching to find out what he would do next, waiting for him to kiss her cheek. Drifting past the point of no return, she moved to meet his lips, surprisingly soft and gentle beneath the beard, and found herself responding, opening her mouth to meet his, reaching through the thick curly hair for the nape of his neck. His hand had already found her breast and moved between her legs before she pushed him gently away. 'Not here.' She sat back, blew her cheeks out and shook her head. 'Gotta go.'

'Suit yourself,' he said, but in a nice way, stroking the side of her face. 'Soon, yeah?'

She could have let Jez down in a hundred ways. *Not here, not now. Never in a million years because sex with you will screw my job and my marriage.* But she let in the silence again as he crouched in the rain telling her to sleep well. Then they smiled at each other while another train rattled by from Stoke Newington and she felt a pulse of excitement. 'Thanks,' was all she could trust herself to say. 'See you later.'

Thirty-three

Tuesday, 6 August, 02.38; Marcus Tennant's house

Lights extinguished, with Justin riding pillion, Jack Langton freewheeled the last three hundred metres down the lane to the walled perimeter of Marcus Tennant's house in Hadley, north London. The rain had stopped, though the clouds were still heavy and threatening, and the bike's tyres hissed on the lane's wet surface. Dressed in black, they were taking no chances, even though they knew Marcus Tennant had finally left that evening for his constituency in Cheshire and Karl Sergeyev had assured them the house would be empty.

It had been a long day for both men. Following John Kerr's briefing late that afternoon, Langton had left the Yard to check out each of his surveillance plots, arriving home at Mill Hill around seven to babysit while his wife attended her weekly yoga class. Starting at eleven o'clock that night, Justin had completed two hours of flight-simulator training. He had driven direct to Langton's home from the facility just outside Heathrow and was still buzzing.

Langton hid the motorcycle in a dense clump of bushes away from the lane. Before travelling home he had dropped by Camberwell to collect Justin's black bag containing forensics kit, skeleton keys and other tools necessary to defeat alarms and safe combinations. Justin grabbed it from the pannier, and they scouted the golf course to the south of the garden, hoisting themselves up to peer over the crumbling red-brick wall. A couple of spotlights lit the main lawns and the sagging windsock like a film set, but the house beyond the screen of *leylandii* lay in complete darkness. They clambered over the wall, circled the windsock and sprinted across the helicopter pad to the rear of the house, crouching by the kitchen door to brush brick dust from their clothes. The premises were classified by police as 'lock and leave' when unoccupied, and earlier that evening Sergeyev had provided Justin with a back-door key and the code to the alarm system.

To reassure himself they would not be disturbed, Langton signalled Justin to run round the side of the house and double-check that no one was covering the police post.

He watched the other man make a final scan of the grounds and wheel back, nodding that all was clear. They pulled on rubber gloves, then Justin unlocked the door. He stepped inside without hesitation as the alarm beeped, swung left and entered the code into the alarm pad as Langton followed. He locked them inside, leaving the key in the door in case they had to make a quick exit, then took two pairs of plastic over-shoes from his pocket, which they put on by the doormat.

They were to search the house on the direct, personal instructions of John Kerr. Langton had interpreted Kerr's proposal in the Fishbowl that afternoon as a request rather than an order or authorisation, for it was unofficial, unsigned and unprotected by the Regulation of Investigatory Powers Act, the legislation that governed all covert entries of private property by government agencies. And they were pretty certain their escapade had not been discussed with Commander Ajay Khan.

'MI6 are either protecting Tennant or covering for him and I want to know why,' Kerr had said. 'Just the upstairs for now. First stop, check out the au pair's room. I'm not going to wait for another attack while everyone blows smoke in our faces. What do you think?'

Langton had looked at Justin and shrugged. Their law-breaking, truth-seeking, deceiving boss of utter integrity had invited them to put their careers on the line for the greater good. He had done it before and it would happen again. 'Worth a shot,' Langton had said.

Justin's thumb had already been hovering over his BlackBerry. 'Do I ring Karl Sergeyev, boss, or will you?'

Working by Maglite torches, they padded down the hallway to the front of the house, making no sound on the thick white carpet. Ignoring the ground-floor rooms, Langton wheeled right at the staircase and took the steps two at a time. Where the stairs divided at the top they each took a fork and rapidly checked the bedrooms. Karl had told them where to find Yvette's room, tucked away on a half-landing three steps higher on the east side of the house. It was small, no more than four paces by five, possibly the original servant's room, with a window overlooking the front of the house to the woods and, at a stretch, the police post.

It had a single bed, a wooden vanity unit, with drawers each side, and a bare wooden chair. Justin lowered the uneven roller blind to hide their torchlight from the lane. On the floor there was a threadbare rug, and a narrow entrance to the right led to a tiny windowless bathroom just large enough to accommodate a toilet and shower compartment. The bed had been stripped to its frame, with the mattress and pillows removed, and the drawers in the unit were empty. There was nothing to show that Yvette or anyone else had lived there and the space smelt fresh, the sign of a methodical clean rather than a rushed, panicky exit.

On hands and knees they spent twenty minutes checking for fingerprints or DNA traces and discovered the cleaner had been less thorough than it first appeared. Though all the surfaces had been carefully wiped, Justin recovered a couple of blonde hairs caught beneath the mat and a smudged print on the side of the toilet cistern nearest the wall.

Staying upstairs they stole along the landing to Diane Tennant's sitting room on the western corner, looking up the lane. At eye level against the inner wall, neatly concealed behind an original watercolour of a South African winery, Justin found a domestic safe with a combination lock that Justin defeated in less than two minutes. Inside, a large white envelope contained a series of A4 colour photographs showing Diane's naked husband having sex with their au pair. This was Marcus Tennant MP seriously at play, as seen by his wife but never his constituents. Justin photographed all ten prints. The couple were shown having sex in bed, spread-eagled on the carpeted floor and on a sofa. The girl had worked hard to expose the nation's defence secretary in all his red-faced, bug-eyed, lily-white glory, penetrating, giving and receiving, with an open bottle of champagne and secret camera within touching distance. Justin replaced the photographs, locked the safe and made a quick search of the room. 'Time to leave?'

Langton checked his watch: 03.17. He peered through the blind up the deserted lane and thought for a moment. 'Karl said they slept in separate rooms. Let's see if Diane's been hiding anything else.'

The room next door was large enough to be a master bedroom, though the furnishings immediately showed this to have been Diane's private territory. Opposite the door a king-size bed was made up for one, with a lilac sheet and white duvet. Fitted wardrobes extended the full length of the wall to the right, with a dressing room to the left next to the en-suite bathroom. A few soft toys scattered at random probably belonged to her daughter. In the corner diagonally opposite the door, to the left of the window, there was an old oak dresser with two top drawers and three of full width beneath. A quick search showed the unit to be full of American picture books, puzzles, old pairs of shoes, drawings, diaries, notebooks and other personal items of no material value, the kind of treasures people keep as childhood mementoes.

In the top right-hand drawer, an album crammed with photographs recorded Diane's family life in the United States. Towards the back Langton found more recent pictures, many with Marcus, some with their daughter. Then he struck gold. Tucked into the back cover, still awaiting proper attachment, probably forgotten, an old wallet of photographs was waiting to be catalogued. Some showed the couple at constituency events, others at private family get-togethers. There was one of the family by the seaside. It was a bright, sunny day and everyone was smiling into the sun. But they were four, not three. An attractive blonde woman was holding the child so that Marcus and Diane could stand arm in arm.

'Didn't recognise her with her clothes on,' said Justin.

Yvette was in her late twenties, tall, shapely and toned. She wore a white T-shirt with a black silhouette of a woman holding a child's hand and, above it, 'IAAS' in large red letters.

Langton stabbed the shirt with his finger. 'Bingo.'

Tuesday, 6 August, 08.17;
Melanie's cover address, Dalston

To be seen and heard, Melanie timed the departure from her bedsit so she would bump into other residents leaving for work and be noticed in the street. The crawl along the Balls Pond Road to within half a mile of Kerr's apartment in Islington, then the slog north-west through Holloway and Highgate, took over an hour. To hide the Renault, Dodge had rented her a lock-up in a dead-end street behind Cherry Tree Wood, so it took her another twelve minutes to park and hurry through the recreation ground leading to her road.

She was not surprised to find the house empty because she had told Rob to expect her around lunchtime, after her meeting with Kerr. Brenda spent Tuesdays cleaning her own flat and Melanie presumed Rob had taken the boys out on their bikes. She ran a bath and put in the expensive crystals he had bought her a lifetime ago, emptied her pockets and stripped naked to begin the ritual she always followed when working undercover. Her tatty knickers and sweaty red socks went into the laundry basket, but the rest of her clothes, sweatshirt, Doc Martens and dirty handkerchief included, she stuffed into an unused black bin liner.

She dropped her keys, local business cards, a cheap diary with contacts corroborating her legend, official letters from the council, driving licence in her false name, scratched watch, about three pounds in change and a wallet containing a couple of crumpled tenners into a canvas bag she kept beside the bed. She placed this with the clothes, concealing her life of deceit in a single bin liner. Tying the bag tightly at the neck to contain the used smell, she pushed it to the back of the wardrobe, then cranked Aerosmith to volume seven on the old CD player she and Rob kept in the bedroom. The ritual complete, Melanie padded through to the bathroom, checked her weight, stepped into the bath and slipped underwater.

By the time she heard Rob's key in the lock she was dressed in jeans, low-cut white top and flip-flops. She had the coffee on, two sugars in each mug, and two beakers ready for whatever the boys wanted. She ran into the hall to hug him, then saw he was alone.

Rob had abandoned the crutch since she had last been home and looked surprised to see her. 'I just dropped them at Linda's,' he said. 'You're not due till this afternoon.'

'Sorry. Change of plan.'

'You didn't tell me.'

'I'm making coffee.'

'Already had one at Linda's.'

She bounded in front of him as he limped down the hall, arms round his neck. 'Let's go upstairs and have sex, then. Unless Linda gave you a shag, too.'

'Due at the range,' he said, sour as ever. He reached for his shooting bag from the under-stairs cupboard and turned back to the front door. 'Back about two.'

She intercepted him again. 'No, Rob. I have to go to the office this afternoon.'

'To see bloody Kerr, you mean?' he said, leaning back against the banisters. 'You turn up without calling, then just bugger off again. Is that all you think of us?'

'Rob, I'm asking you to make love to me.'

'What's the rush?'

Melanie laughed. 'Do you have any idea how ridiculous that sounds?'

He pushed past her. 'Give us a warning next time.'

The front door was already open when something clicked inside Melanie. The old lady from two doors up was walking past, the wheels on her shopping basket squeaking as they had for the past year. She called out a neighbourly greeting and Melanie managed to wave and say something nice back. Then she slammed the door, blocking Rob's path. She smelt last night's beer on his breath and had a flashback of Jez kissing her. 'Just fuck me, then, you bastard,' she said, into his face, 'if you really can't love me any more.'

Rob looked at her in silence, his face unreadable, then gently removed her arm and opened the door again. Tears streaming down her face, Melanie watched him walk down the path without looking back. It was not his rejection that upset her. At that moment she hated him for pushing her towards the only man who truly enjoyed being around her.

She closed the door quietly, stumbled into the kitchen and collapsed, sobbing, at the table. In all her life Melanie had never felt so vulnerable and lonely.

Thirty-four

Derek Finch, counter-terrorism national co-ordinator, was almost ten minutes late for his meeting with Ajay and Kerr, who waited for him at Ajay's conference table. Neither was surprised. They knew it was almost an article of faith for the Bull to keep subordinates waiting, a performance of bad manners to show who was boss. Suddenly the door was flung open and they saw him pause to address Donna in the outer office. 'Black, two sugars.'

'Without milk, you mean?' replied Donna, effortlessly putting him on the back foot.

Ostentatious and egotistical, the Bull rarely wasted time on handshakes or good mornings. He glared at Kerr as he took his usual chair at the foot of the table facing Ajay. 'What is this man doing here?' The Bull's dealings with Kerr had never been happy, even before the incident on the Thames. He stared at Ajay while vaguely pointing a stubby finger at Kerr, like a bad actor aiming a gun. 'You got any idea of the grief he's caused me?' Kerr assumed Finch was referring to the chase and shooting on the Thames, about which he had evidently already spoken to Ajay, and probably a whole lot more. 'I want to speak *about* him, not to him. I said I wanted Ritchie.'

'Good morning, Derek,' said Ajay, calmly slowing the pace. 'Bill Ritchie is unavailable. Donna called your office yesterday.'

'What is it? Playing golf? Fun in the sun?'

'Chemotherapy.'

The finger was stabbing at Kerr again, without a moment's hesitation. 'Well, this loose cannon is no substitute.' Ajay might as well have told him Bill Ritchie was having a haircut. He and Kerr were unfazed. There was nothing unusual about the verbal combat that constituted the Bull's version of an opening exchange. Each time Kerr saw Finch on TV, or in the corridor before he took action to avoid him, his hair seemed blacker, his teeth whiter, and somewhere between the Yard and his mock-Georgian semi-detached in Bromley, with its orangery extension, he had acquired a perma-tan. The previous year he had narrowly escaped censure over the long-running scandal engulfing police relationships with the press but had angrily batted away every allegation of dirty dealings and kick-backs. He always signed himself 'Derek V. Finch'. No one had bothered to find out what the V stood for, but Justin said it was Venal. The Bull's belief in his own invincibility never wavered.

'How can I help you, Derek?'

Finch opened a thin brown file. The cover and the three or four pages inside, so far as Kerr could tell, were stamped 'Secret' in bold red. He made a show of scanning each page as Kerr studied him.

Finch's dress sense was a cross between City banker and rogue trader. This morning he had gone for a crumpled dark grey chalk-stripe suit with polished tasselled shoes, evidently acquired on his most recent visit to the FBI at Quantico. His trademark crimson power braces, tie and handkerchief shouted louder than blood on a gunshot victim, and his watch seemed to cover every time zone on the planet. On the little finger of his right hand he wore a huge gold ring that might have come straight from the props store of *Dallas*.

Finch looked up from his file. 'I understand your Mr Kerr has been door-stepping the secretary of state. Unauthorised by me, outside my evidential chain and completely inappropriate. My senior investigator has already interviewed Marcus Tennant three times and he doesn't deserve this kind of senseless harassment. The minister's loyalty is not open to question.' He glared at Kerr. 'All you've done is compound his grief.'

Kerr was already rewinding to his hijack in the bar by Julius. 'Loyalty not open to question', 'compound his grief': the MI6 man had used those exact words. Kerr cast another interested glance at the Bull's file.

'And?'

'What do you mean, "*and*"? I want to know who the hell is responsible. Who gave John Kerr permission to interview a government minister without reference to me?'

Kerr looked at Ajay but his boss, poker-faced, was holding Finch's stare. 'I did, of course,' he lied, without missing a beat. 'As John's commander.'

Brilliant. Kerr breathed a secret sigh of relief.

'Who told you?' asked Ajay, mildly.

Finch glanced in irritation at the door, probably wondering what had delayed his coffee. 'You what?'

Ajay spoke slowly, as if addressing a backward pupil. 'How did you find out that John Kerr went to interview Marcus Tennant?'

'What the hell has that got to do with you?'

Ajay checked a fingernail. 'The approach to Marcus Tennant was highly confidential, shared with no one outside my team.'

'Bollocks.' It was probably the best he could come up with. Finch dominated Ajay in height, bulk and sheer naked aggression, the personification of shock and awe, but intellectually they swam in different gene pools.

'A parallel strand to your investigation, following a sensitive intelligence lead,' continued Ajay.

'Well, we don't do parallel any more so you can put your bloody intelligence escapades back in their box,' he sneered, flooding the table with resentment. 'And I'm getting seriously pissed off with your constant references to "Special Branch".'

Ajay raised his eyebrows.

The Bull's nostrils flared. 'Yes. I've got my spies too, you know.' He snorted angrily. 'And I know what your game is. The title is banned, so you can forget any idea of re-forming any special unit outside SO15.'

'Really?' said Ajay. 'Is that what I was thinking?'

'There's no room for élites in my command.'

'Clearly,' muttered Kerr.

Finch snatched a sideways glance, unsure what he had heard. A lock of his gelled hair shook loose. 'I know you've got some kind of operation going on outside my investigation.'

Silence hung between them as Ajay sat back in his chair and looked levelly across the table, dapper and cool. Kerr knew what was to come, that Ajay was choosing his moment. He could hear the Bull's shoes raking the carpet and silently counted down from ten.

On the fifth beat the Bull's slim hold on self-control snapped. 'Just who the fuck do you think you are,' he yelled, 'running things in secret outside my command?' Kerr knew that Ajay's refusal to be intimidated had detonated the explosion.

Ajay looked through the window. Rain was forecast from the east by lunchtime but the sky was still a beautiful electric blue and he seemed content to leave Finch seething at the opposite end of the table. Then he calmly stood, went round to his desk and unlocked the bottom right-hand drawer. Kerr realised he had been making his decision.

Ajay returned with a slim pink file, removed a sheaf of photographs, silently handed them to Finch and took his seat again. The change in Finch was cataclysmic, the blood drain-ing from his face as he instinctively shielded the images from

Kerr. 'No need for that,' said Ajay, quietly. 'It was John who acquired them. That was on my authority, too, just in case you're wondering.'

Kerr could have told the Bull exactly what the photographs showed. This batch featured six images taken between 07.36 and 07.41 on Thursday, 11 July, eight days after the arrest of Terry Bray's gang, and only forty-eight hours after his televised display of injured pride and blustering denial of misconduct in public office. Taken by Justin, supported by Jack Langton's surveillance team, they showed the Bull outside one of west London's most discreet boutique hotels. In each he was lingering up close and personal with the British tabloid world's most powerful crime reporter. In three of them they were kissing.

Stunned, Finch stared blankly at the images, the raging Bull display replaced by shrunken disbelief.

'Those copies are for you. We have many more where they came from. Restaurants and rooms in different locations, but always champagne,' said Ajay, quietly, flicking through the thick batch of photographs in the file.

Donna entered with tea for Ajay in his giant cup and saucer. No sign of coffee, with milk or otherwise. Ajay smiled as Finch immediately slapped the photographs face down on the table. 'Don't bother,' he said, as Donna turned to leave. 'Who do you think prepares my most sensitive files for me?'

As soon as the door had closed, Finch sent the photographs skittering across the table. 'Why would I want the bloody things?'

'You see why I need a firewall to protect our sensitive intelligence,' said Ajay, carefully sorting the photographs and returning them to the file. He looked the Bull straight in the eye. 'After all, what man of integrity would breathe anything valuable to you?'

The Bull stormed out, slamming the door behind him, and Kerr remained silent in his chair. In the past Ajay had been jocular about his rocky dealings with Derek Finch. 'The Cowboy versus the Indian' was how he had apparently described their bouts to Bill Ritchie. 'Thank you again for your support, John,' was all he said now. He seemed unperturbed as he went to the safe to lock away the file but Kerr sensed danger. He knew the past seven or eight minutes had changed everything. This was open warfare.

Thirty-five

Danny Brennan had completed his second incendiary the previous evening, after Rashid had left. Then he had made a meticulous check of both devices, tracing the circuit from the timer to the detonator to the personalised explosive mix he had learnt to make at school, and placed them neatly beside the devices Rashid had brought him. The whole project had taken him nearly five hours but he had worked steadily, refreshed by sex and fired up by revenge.

Anger had returned in the darkest hours of the night, stoked by thoughts of the woman who had condemned him in the journal. Shortly before dawn he had switched on the light and read Becky's leader over and over. He had determined that one day they would meet, whatever Anna Rashid said. At breakfast, over peanut-butter toast and three mugs of tea, he had studied each word again and begun to write his reply. He would use ideas to crush Becky and her clever boyfriend, deploy their own weapons to subjugate them. But words had failed him. After nearly an hour the page had been filled with obscenities, phrases that made no sense and crossings-out that confronted him with his ignorance. As the language had refused to come, he found himself venting his feelings through boyhood images of screaming mouths and gaping wounds scrawled so violently across the journal that he had ripped the pages to shreds.

Soon he had become calm again and accepted the truth: only face to face could he confront his accusers. Resolved, he had taken an ice-cold shower, dressed, pocketed another of Anna Rashid's Oyster cards, collected the torch and holdall from the cupboard beneath the workbench and sneaked out of the safe house. The threatened rain had arrived in a thin, penetrating drizzle but Danny Brennan was going home. Loping into the high street with beanie pulled low over his face, he attracted no attention from a row of blank-faced smokers sheltering against the wall of the Mason's Arms and soon lost himself among mid-morning shoppers. The wind was at his back, catching the holdall as it funnelled down the high street, and a flank of three mothers behind a phalanx of umbrellas forced him into the gutter. Head lowered beneath the CCTV cameras at the entrance to Bethnal Green Underground station, he took the Central Line one stop to Mile End, then hurried across the platform to catch a waiting District Line train to Dagenham East.

Brennan's family home lay in a treeless loop of identical dark brick semis between Rainham Road and Heathway, just north of Old Dagenham Park. He had lived there all his life, right up until his imprisonment. In its heyday most of the men had been employed at the giant Ford car factory but these days money was short, the houses neglected and the jobless young men and women as angry as Brennan.

His mother's name was Sylvia but everyone called her Sal. She was one of the lucky ones who still had a job, as a receptionist in the Trauma and Orthopaedics Department at Barking Hospital. After her husband had deserted her, Sal had heard nothing from him except via an appointments clerk in the hospital's blood-testing unit, a gossipy divorcee with a vodka problem. Then, on a winter's evening eight months

later, in the middle of *Coronation Street*, Sal had heard his key
in the lock. Cold and defeated, he had come home, as if nothing had happened, and Sal had taken him back into their lives
without a word. No one could have been happier than Danny
Brennan and, as far as he could tell, there had been no more
cruelty or violence between them, right up until the day his
dad was killed at work. His mum and dad had been good
together and their happiness fired his thirst for revenge.

Brennan had not come to see his mother, who would be at
work. This was through secrecy, not choice, for he loved her,
too, and knew she had never recovered from losing her
husband in such terrible circumstances. Walking down the
side entrance, he found the spare back-door key where it had
always been since his first day at secondary school, beneath a
brick in the flowerbed. His shed at the bottom of the garden
was derelict now, with the roof felt coming loose, the door
lopsided and the window cracked, though the sheet he had
used for privacy still hung from a nail and he could see the
shelves inside, empty now of chemicals and anything else that
might cause harm.

Inside the kitchen he called out to check he was alone,
removed his boots and drank water from the tap to avoid leaving any sign that he had been there. He took the stairs two at
a time, entered his mother's bedroom and faced himself in the
full-length mirror on the wardrobe door. He slid open the
door and pushed her dresses to the right of the hanging rail.
At the opposite end, zipped into a plastic suit holder after his
death, as a kind of memorial, were his father's Transport for
London overalls and hi-visibility jacket with the TfL logo.
Brennan folded them into the holdall, recovered his dad's red
safety helmet from the corner and placed it with the clothes.
Then he knelt down and reached along the wardrobe floor.
He was searching for a folder and found it exactly where his
mother had placed it years before, hidden beneath a strip of

carpet. The blue plastic cover contained a single document, a detailed scale map of the tunnel layout and signalling system on the approaches to Camden Town Underground station, the stretch of track on the Northern Line where the Edgware, High Barnet, City and Charing Cross branches intersected.

The configuration here was so complicated that the platforms carried a drivers' red warning notice that they were entering a 'Signal Passed at Danger' area, or SPAD. It was also the place where his father had lost his life. The map had been a vital source document for the investigation into his death and pinpointed the exact location of the accident. Sal had kept it after the company agreed compensation because, as she had told Danny while rolling back the carpet, she distrusted the 'pen-pusher with the rat face and weasel words' who had signed the settlement.

Back on the landing Brennan pulled down the loft ladder, climbed through the narrow aperture into the roof space and delved into his holdall for the torch. To the right was a makeshift chipboard floor covered with suitcases, discarded ornaments and other redundant items Sal thought might come in handy one day. But Brennan shone his torch in the other direction, towards the iron water tank by the adjoining wall. There was no flooring on this section and he had to balance on the joists as he edged through a mass of ancient cobwebs, stringy with dust and weighed down by insects' corpses suspended eerily in the torchlight. The sticky tangle pleased him, for it showed that this section of the roof had lain undisturbed for many years.

Between the water tank and the wall dividing the two houses there was a gap of less than nine inches, invisible from the hatch. Brennan's father had laid his own floor here from three crudely cut planks running the length of the tank. As a teenager Danny Brennan had secretly used this space to make poisons and devise other experiments after his parents had banned him from the shed. Standing against the tank, almost buried in dust and debris, he spotted a solitary marmalade jar with a screw top and carefully brushed away the dust to reveal the clear liquid inside. This was one of many similar jars he had stored here, long forgotten, and on impulse he stood it carefully in the holdall.

The object of his search lay beneath his father's makeshift floor. Two of the floorboards were screwed to the joists but the third, nearest the wall, was fixed with nails. It lifted easily to reveal a blanket containing a sawn-off double-barrelled shotgun lying between the final joist and the bricks, its mechanism covered with an oil cloth. Beside the stock was a box of ammunition. Brennan knew his father had been hiding the weapon on behalf of a drinking partner, an armed robber and killer sentenced to life for murder, then death from cancer. Sal had never known about the arrangement and fifteen-year-old Danny had only discovered the hoard by chance, while stashing chemicals behind the tank. When challenged, his father had told him everything and sworn him to silence; six years after his dad's horrific death, it fell to Danny Brennan to exploit the secret that had brought them close.

Brennan carefully buried the shotgun and ammunition beneath the clothing in the holdall, climbed with it down to the landing and pushed back the ladder. Closing the aperture he retraced his steps to the kitchen, replaced the key beneath the brick and walked slowly through the drizzle along the northern edge of the park. He caught the 145 bus from Church Elm Lane to Barking garage, changing to the number five for Canning Town, then waited twenty minutes for the 309 that would take him the final leg to Bethnal Green.

Just after four he was back in the safe house, unpacking his possessions and cleaning the weapon.

Around him, within touching distance, were a loaded shotgun, a bottle of acid and five bombs. Completely calm at last, he screwed together the shredded remains of his words and pictures from the morning, the reminders of his insecurity, and destroyed them on the gas hob. All-powerful again, he rolled a cigarette and lay on the bed to wait for Anna Rashid.

Thirty-six

Claude Kellner, London director of International Aid to Asylum Seekers, peered closely over half-moon spectacles at an enlarged photograph of Yvette, lately au pair to Diane and Marcus Tennant, recovered from their house by Justin and Jack Langton in the early hours of the morning. Portly and sandy-haired, with an open, ruddy face and full moustache, he laid the spectacles on the desk and looked at John Kerr. 'I remember her very well, actually,' he said, with a rueful smile, as he poured black coffee into red mugs inscribed with the IAAS logo. His desk was piled high with annual reports and box files of studies and migration statistics from every country in Europe stretching along the walls. 'As a matter of fact, when I took up my post in 2011 she had already been here for over a year.'

Kerr nodded, preoccupied. Kellner's office was housed in a mixed residential and business mansion block off Victoria Street, within easy walking distance from the Yard and convenient for the House of Fraser department store, where Kellner had already told Kerr he bought most of his suits. The block was built on a square and the director's L-shaped corner office looked onto the inner courtyard, a tranquil urban garden peppered with shrubs, struggling plants and cigarette butts. But Kerr's eyes were fixed through the window from the longer section of the L that faced the street, clocking every vehicle. On his arrival, as he had parked in Rochester Row, the rider of a yellow motor scooter had pulled up alongside him, stared through the driver's window, accelerated and pulled up again thirty metres away at the junction with Vincent Square. Face concealed by his crash helmet and tinted visor, revving the engine, he had looked back at Kerr, apparently enticing him to follow.

Kellner cleared his throat. 'When she worked for me she called herself Monique.'

Kerr's head jerked round. 'I'm sorry?'

'Monique. Not Yvette. Monique Thierry. But the deception doesn't surprise me in the least. Ms Thierry had skills far superior to those of a simple domestic servant. May I ask what is your interest in her?'

Within an hour of receiving the photograph Alan Fargo had researched IAAS, checked out Claude Kellner and arranged Kerr's appointment. With offices throughout the world, IAAS assisted oppressed migrants to progress their claims for asylum and, in the event of rejection, facilitate their return to their country of origin.

Kerr sipped the stale coffee and dodged the question. 'Have you heard of Judge Hugh Selwyn?'

'Of course,' said Kellner, stealing a glance at his watch. He had already told Kerr he had to leave for his club by four forty-five to meet friends for drinks; evidently he was a member of the National Liberal Club in Whitehall Place. 'His murder is a tragedy, but I must tell you honestly that this judge was a thorn in the side of IAAS.'

The response did not surprise Kerr. According to Fargo, Claude Kellner was fifty-four, a wealthy Swiss attorney with a fabulous home on Lake Geneva. A migration specialist, he had forsaken the law to influence the migration policies of governments throughout Europe. He looked and sounded the antithesis of the European lawyer described in Fargo's research, one media profile praising him as 'that rare and treasured thing, an attorney with a conscience'.

Searching for an inch of clear space, Kerr balanced his mug on the window ledge behind him. 'Why do you say that?'

'To be perfectly honest with you, Mr Kerr, we regarded Judge Selwyn as little more than a reactionary agent of the British and US governments. At their request he devised ways to reject genuine applications on political grounds, with everything covered beneath the cloak of national security. A man with such dark skills makes many enemies.'

Kerr paused to check the street again. 'Would you say Monique Thierry's work here was satisfactory?'

'She was certainly very active.'

'So why did she go?'

Kellner immediately looked uncomfortable. 'I asked her to leave, as a matter of fact.'

'When?'

'In July last year. A Friday, actually. I remember it well because it was the day of the Olympics opening ceremony.' He checked his watch again as Kerr waited. 'Her work was . . . inappropriate.'

'That's a much overused word in the UK . . .'

'To cover a multitude of sins, yes?'

'And which did she commit?'

'It's more a case of who she was,' said Kellner, reaching for his coffee. 'Mr Kerr, IAAS is a welfare organisation, part charitable, with our budget partly paid for by the British government. Do you know anything of our objectives?'

Kerr nodded. 'They're admirable.'

'And entirely non-political.'

Kerr had memorised the various papers Fargo had emailed to him. Co-operating with non-governmental organisations, known as NGOs, caseworkers from IAAS in their distinctive T-shirts had become a common sight at airports throughout the developing world and were often highly imaginative. Fargo had unearthed a case from 2009 in which three prostitutes working illegally in the UK had been allowed to recover their earnings from the brothel-keeper before being deported.

'Over many years I have witnessed the agony of migrants forced to flee their homes, and the heartache and poverty that pursue them into their country of choice. So you will understand, Mr Kerr, why I cannot permit our work to be prejudiced by activities that are *clandestine*.'

'Dishonest, you mean?'

'No . . . Yes. I mean secret.' Kellner paused again, suddenly looking embarrassed. 'I learnt that Ms Monique Thierry was the secret operative of a foreign power. She was using IAAS as cover for recruiting failed asylum seekers to be secret agents on return to their countries of origin.'

'Talent-spotting, you mean,' said Kerr.

'Dress it in whatever euphemism you like, Mr Kerr. I prefer the word "betraying".' Another time check. By now, Kellner was looking desperate to get away. 'One of the girls, a Bulgarian, complained to me, said Monique asked her to spy in her home country. To be a honeycomb, I think.'

'Trap. Honey trap.'

'We are here to help these young women, Mr Kerr, not subject them to further abuse by allowing them to be used as informers.'

'Was she working alone?'

'Who can say with such people? Monique denied everything when I confronted her. She was very secretive, as you would expect.'

'Did you report her to the Home Office?'

Kellner shrugged. 'For all I know she was already working with your MI5. Collaborating.' He said the word deliberately, injecting the liberal's contempt for Kerr's secret world.

'Which country?' said Kerr. 'Was it the French? Come on, Claude, spit it out. Are we talking the DGSE?'

'She was using our organisation as cover. That is all I can say.' Kellner shifted in his seat and began locking his desk drawers. 'I can only guess at the environment you inhabit, Mr Kerr, but I find espionage distasteful. As you will have noticed, even the conversation we are having now is hard for me.'

'So how did you find out?'

'Through channels.'

'What the hell does that mean?'

Kellner got to his feet, conversation over. 'I am Swiss, Mr Kerr, working with NGOs from all nations to relieve the suffering of our disadvantaged brothers and sisters. Ms Monique Thierry served only the interests of her spy-masters.'

Thirty-seven

Kerr had driven to see Claude Kellner in one of Jack Langton's surveillance vehicles, an eight-year-old green Toyota Corolla abandoned with a puncture earlier that day near Victoria station. With the wheel replaced, Kerr had told Langton he would return it to the surveillance garage in Wandsworth after his meeting, taking the opportunity to speak with Langton and catch up with any of his operatives who happened to be in the office.

He saw the scooter again as he unlocked the door and this time the rider turned to take photographs of Kerr from the kerbside before disappearing at speed into Vincent Square. It appeared to be a Vespa LX 50, with the index partially obscured by an L plate. Kerr had several choices open to him. He could stay put, follow at a distance and call for back-up, or make a U-turn to the Yard and safety. He drummed his fingers on the steering-wheel. The revelation about Yvette was urging him to force the pace, and the scooter was low-powered, 125cc, capable of no more than forty on a clear run. It was a commuter's bright yellow toy, non-serious, and the rider was probably no more than a kid.

Kerr was intrigued. Ignoring his inner voice of caution, he rammed the manual gearbox into first, floored the accelerator and squealed into Vincent Square. On the central green dozens of teenage boys were kicking a football around. Kerr could hear their shouts and laughter through the open window and, above that, the engine of the Vespa buzzing at the opposite corner, an angry wasp luring him onwards. It led him left into Horseferry Road, then sharp right across the Thames at Lambeth Bridge, swerving easily through the traffic. The rush-hour was building, and as they drove along Lambeth Road the rider would slow down, but always kept at least three vehicles between them.

At the traffic lights by the Imperial War Museum he even stopped, idling in wait for Kerr at the kerb opposite the two massive fifteen-inch naval guns on the museum's forecourt. Then he took the green light into George Road heading south-east, always maintaining the same safety zone. Seeing, not touching distance.

Negotiating the giant roundabout at Elephant and Castle, the scooter turned south into the clearer stretch of Kennington Park Road towards the Oval. Just beyond Kennington Underground station, past Yusuf's Barber and Danesh Jewels, the rider threw a sharp left into a narrow street of Victorian terraced houses, almost colliding with an elderly Sikh on a mobility scooter leaving Ali Cash and Carry on the other side of the junction, stranding him in the middle of the road. A young Asian ran from his mobile-phone kiosk to help and Kerr had to brake hard to avoid them. The scooter accelerated sharply, racing over speed humps, turning left at the first junction, then right, the engine's whine echoing off the houses as it drew Kerr into a web of narrow, identical one-way streets with parked cars lining each side and no room to pass.

The rider threw another couple of turns before entering a long stretch heading east, so far as Kerr could tell, directly away from the main road. After about fifty metres the scooter braked without warning and Kerr's mirror was suddenly filled by a dark blue Volvo estate, as battered as the Toyota and trailing Kerr so close that the registration plate was hidden. Both sun visors were lowered but he could make out two figures, the passenger talking into a mobile or radio. Kerr had the Toyota's mainset on Channel Five, the protected frequency used by Langton's surveillance teams. 'Red One, urgent message, over.'

He felt a surge of relief as Langton bounced back to him, low and calm. 'Go ahead.'

'Where are you, Jack?'

Kerr could hear the roar of Langton's Suzuki GSX R1000. It meant he was on the move, which was good. 'Back to the garage, waiting for you.'

The scooter had speeded up again and the Volvo was still tailgating Kerr, almost touching now, pushing him onwards. Kerr had run out of side turnings and the road was dead straight, crammed with terraced houses and parked cars and devoid of passing places. He was out of escape routes, drawn down a rat run into a trap so obvious that a surveillance rookie on his first day would have spotted it.

'I'm in trouble. Dark blue Volvo estate right behind me, two white males. No visible index. Red Vespa 50 in front. They're squeezing me, Jack. I'm boxed in.'

Kerr knew that his deputy would soon be firing a barrage of questions at him. But for now, *in extremis*, Langton settled for just one word: 'Location?'

'One-way system east of Kennington Lane.' Kerr looked desperately for a school, church or business premises, anything to identify his whereabouts. He was being pushed along at about thirty-five, crashing over a speed hump every few seconds, and the Volvo had come so close that it was nudging the Toyota.

Kerr could hear Langton throttling the engine. 'Need a street name, John.'

He guessed Langton would already have pulled into the kerb, planning his response. 'I missed it.'

'Can you get out?'

'Negative. They've sucked me into a maze here.'

'Hang in there.' Kerr heard the Suzuki roar but Langton's bass Geordie voice never altered. 'I'm five, six minutes away. Keep talking to me.'

After nearly a mile Kerr could see houses at right angles to the street and hoped they were nearing a junction and potential escape point. Instead, the street curved sharp right. He passed a 'No Through Road' sign and found himself driving parallel with an overground railway embankment that he guessed was the main commuter line running out of Blackfriars. A train overtook him. It looked crowded as it rattled past, so Kerr calculated he must be driving away from the City. 'Just turned right. Dead end, no street name. Railway track alongside to the left, heading south.'

Imprisoned by parked cars lining the street to his right and a high red-brick wall bordering the railway to the left, with the Volvo stamping on his tail, Kerr knew he was running out of time.

Trapped with no visible means of escape, he realised the thugs in the car probably wanted him dead. The truth struck him like a hammer blow, but he wasted no energy on anger, panic and self-recrimination. Neither frozen by shock nor overheated by fear he stared ahead at the buzzing Vespa, clinically assessing the fight or flight options still open to him. He could screech to a halt and dial 999, lock himself in the car and wait for rescue, just like any other punter. Or leap out, identify himself and confront his aggressors on the pavement. There was surrender, a sprint for life, or an unequal battle to the finish. He changed down to second.

'Jack, I'm going to run him down.'

'I'm through Stockwell. I'll find you. Keep talking to me.'

They were nearing the end of the lifeless street, closing fast on the chained iron gates of what looked like a derelict factory.

Suddenly the embankment curved left, opening up a patch of wasteground between the wall and the street. The whole area was deserted and Kerr realised he had left it too late. As he began his chase the scooter veered left, lurching over the rubble and potholes, engine screaming, the rider bouncing off the saddle as he raced headlong for the embankment wall. A hail of grit struck the Toyota windscreen, like machine-gun fire, as Kerr floored the accelerator, scrabbling for the wiper switch to clear the mud from the day's rain. Then the scooter swerved violently left again as the rider revealed his escape route: a narrow cylindrical pedestrian tunnel sloping beneath the railway.

Kerr skidded to a halt as the scooter disappeared from view in a final hail of dirt and debris. He heard its engine screaming off the tunnel wall and roof, and then the Volvo rammed him hard, killing the Toyota's engine and spinning the car through a half-circle to bring Kerr face to face with his assailants. Before he could get a clear look the Volvo was on the move again, tyres screeching as it reversed for the next attack, skidding to a stop at ten metres. Kerr was still desperately turning the ignition as the Volvo charged, wheels spinning straight for him, kicking up a hailstorm of stones and dirt.

The impact was like a bomb going off. The Volvo propelled the Toyota a full car's length backwards, ramming it hard against the tunnel entrance as easily as a tractor shifting a bale of hay, crushing it so violently that the two cars interlocked.

Then the odds worsened as Kerr saw one of the rear doors open. There were three attackers, not two, their faces hidden by balaclavas, wielding baseball bats, the guy from the back seat head and shoulders above the other two but just as broad, shouting orders as he led the attack. They fanned out each side of the Toyota, smashing the lights and side windows as Kerr frantically tried to start the broken engine. The car filled with Langton's urgent voice and the strengthening smell of petrol. He yelled that he was police and ordered them to back off, raising his arms to protect himself from the showers of glass. The one Kerr had seen speaking on the radio was more athletic than the others and leapt on the bonnet to rain blows on the windscreen. The glass showed a different snowflake pattern with each strike, illuminated by the late-afternoon sun before disintegrating over Kerr's body.

Everything was futile and Kerr grabbed the microphone for the last time. 'Three men, repeat three, in the Volvo. Wasteground beside the railway.' Langton was saying something back but the commotion was too great and he had to shout to make himself heard. 'Near a factory. I'm stalled. Need you here, Jack.'

Then the tall guy pressed his masked face up against Kerr's window, taunting him before standing back and wielding the baseball bat like an axe. Kerr rammed his shoulder against the door but it was jammed, disfigured in the crash. The Toyota slumped as the attackers systematically stabbed the tyres, then the driver's window exploded against his cheek and the leader's face filled the opening again, crouching as he wrenched at the door, eyes wild with violence.

Kerr whipped his head away as the leader tried to punch him and glimpsed the driver taking a can from the back of the Volvo. The second punch through the open window found Kerr's right temple, stunning him. Kerr felt in the door pocket for the baton kept in every surveillance vehicle, hoping against hope that Langton's operative had not taken it with him when he abandoned the car. It was still there, clipped to the inside of the pocket, and he rapidly shook his head clear, closing his hand tightly on the grip.

Then he caught the flash of a cigarette lighter through the space where the windscreen had been as his crouching attacker leant in to grab his neck. Kerr twisted to bring his left arm within reach of the leader's head, grabbing a clump of hair trailing beneath the balaclava and wrenching him close, destroying his balance. Simultaneously Kerr jabbed the baton up hard into the man's face, stabbing him several times with all his force. There was a cracking sound. Nose and teeth, certainly, possibly cheekbone, too. Then the baton found the gap in the balaclava and sank neatly into the man's left eye socket, a perfect fit. There was a brief sucking noise as it destroyed his eyeball, then the man recoiled, screaming and clutching his face, eliminated from the fight.

Kerr smelt petrol again, even stronger now, and saw a curve of light as a flaming rag sailed through the offside rear window. He crashed his shoulder against the driver's door again as a second burning missile joined the first to set the Toyota alight. With Langton's voice in his ear and flames licking at his clothes, Kerr saw his attackers crouching by their leader. He felt a pulse of hope. Clambering across to the passenger seat he forced himself through the remnants of the windscreen onto the bonnet. He snatched a look around but there were no passers-by to come to his aid. He was trapped in an urban desert and saw the leader slumped against the Volvo now, angrily pushing his accomplices away to continue their assault. But Kerr had the high ground. Standing square on the bonnet, with flames pouring from the Toyota's windows, he landed the first blows as they came for him, crazily swiping and slicing and stabbing with the extended baton.

Flames were licking around the Volvo now. The Toyota's tank was full and Kerr guessed he had fifteen seconds tops before his car exploded. He leapt onto the roof, taunting his attackers. One of them threw his baseball bat at Kerr as the second tried to clamber after him, but Kerr stamped on the invader's hands and slashed his face.

With flames crackling around him and the Volvo alight Kerr used up three precious seconds to stare both men down. Then he dropped onto the boot, right above the petrol tank, slithered to the ground and sprinted to safety through the tunnel. In that instant the Toyota exploded in a deafening roar, magnified by the tunnel's echo. Then the shock wave was chasing him, scorching his back and neck as it lifted him off his feet, propelling him to safety.

The land on the other side of the railway line was a well-tended grassy park, accessible from the back gardens of the terraced houses beyond. Kerr slumped against the embankment wall as the Volvo exploded, shooting more debris through the tunnel. All around him dogs were barking but there was not a soul in sight, and no sign of the scooter. His blackened clothes reeked of petrol. Kerr took out his mobile and checked himself for injuries as he speed-dialled Jack Langton: blood on his face and a lump on his head, but probably nothing broken.

Langton picked up at the first ring. 'Where are you? You OK?'

Kerr craned his head up. Black smoke was billowing into the clear sky in acrid clouds as a commuter train slowed to a crawl.

'See anything unusual?' he said.

'Jesus.'

'I left you a bloody great smoke signal, Jack,' said Kerr. 'But I'm going to need a lift.'

Thirty-eight

Hurrying out of London Bridge Underground station, Kerr took three calls and a text as he scrambled down the steps from Tooley Street to the south side of the Thames, heading east. At ten thirty he was due outside City Hall to meet Stella Ward, star of the Mayor's Office for Policing and Crime and his saviour at the Ethics Committee, but by the time HMS *Belfast* came into view he was already seven minutes late.

The sky had cleared overnight and the morning was as bright as the previous day had been, but warmer and with no rain forecast. Kerr should have been enjoying the exercise but had seriously underestimated the damage from his near-death experience just over nineteen hours earlier. His legs worked stiffly as he tried the steps two at a time, his neck felt scorched as it rubbed against his collar, and he had done something bad to his right shoulder when crashing it against the door of the stricken Toyota. Every stitch of clothing was fresh, but the stench of burning rubber and petrol filled his nose and mouth. After two showers his skin still felt toxic, seeming to leak fumes from every pore. But everything was relative, as Langton had just reminded him in his second call that morning: John Kerr had escaped with his life.

After the explosions, still high on adrenaline but pushed back by the heat, Kerr had edged through the tunnel to find a couple of blazing cars but zero bodies. His attackers had evidently picked up their injured leader and run, leaving the area as deserted as when they had steamed in minutes before.

With the flames still high, Kerr had used them as a shield to check out the environment. He had detected no sign of life from the factory, though a clutch of five or six rubberneckers had materialised forty paces to the right, loitering beside the last house in the terrace. A couple of discordant sirens had been growing louder, one high and urgent, the other at half its tempo and pitch, heavy metal versus easy listening, and one of the voyeurs had been holding a mobile to his ear, presumably dialling an extra 999 in case of a competing emergency. Everyone looked disinterested, as if this was a common occurrence. Welcome to Torched Car Central.

He had heard the Suzuki's throaty roar well before Langton appeared, flashing across the dirt and skidding to a halt in a barrage of mud and grit. With the sirens seconds away, his deputy had done everything right. Dismounting, he had assessed the damage and leapt over the burning metal to hold Kerr's face in both hands, checking his eye movements as he insisted he was OK. 'Listen, John. How do you want me to play this?'

'No witnesses, so I'm not here. Can you do that?'

Langton had already been pushing Kerr out of sight down the tunnel as the police patrol car appeared, escorting the fire engine. 'No problem.'

By the time Langton had delivered Kerr home to Islington just after seven, the attempted murder of a senior Special Branch officer had been redefined as vehicle theft and arson, and near-assassination finessed to antisocial behaviour. With the destroyed cars hissing and spitting nearby, Langton had figured out his story while the fire-fighters were still unrolling their hoses. Flashing his ID, he had told the first PC on the scene that the Toyota was a surveillance vehicle stolen from Victoria that afternoon and tracked here. 'I'll get it taken away.

For us it's just an insurance write-off,' Langton had said. The radio on the PC's shoulder was vibrating with static and unintelligible chatter. 'I'll take care of the paperwork. No further action for you, if that's OK?'

Langton had seen the onlookers disappear as the officer turned, and caught the relief in his face. The PC had grinned and said that was fine by him: joy-riders were the least of his problems, though he would take another look at the Volvo once the metal and his radio had cooled down. Langton had given him his number, shaken his hand and eased the Suzuki through the tunnel to extract Kerr.

Kerr spotted Stella Ward as he passed Hay's Galleria. In black leather trousers, bright red lipstick, white blouse, pinstripe waistcoat and her trademark patent killer heels, she was perched on the wall in front of City Hall, between a newly mown stretch of grass and the Embankment path. She was studying a batch of official papers through giant sunglasses with gold-ornamented frames, but saw Kerr from twenty paces.

As he drew nearer she frowned and pushed the shades over her forehead. The eyes of the one-time gang member lasered on his face. 'Been fighting again?'

'Something like that,' said Kerr, dodging giant gold hoop earrings to kiss her on both cheeks. She smelt of flowers and her skin was as smooth as velvet. He sat beside her on the wall, to her right. Beyond him, the massive spans of Tower Bridge began to lift.

'So what do you want to know about the Ethics Committee?' The voice was authentic north London working class.

Kerr pretended to study the bridge. 'Anything you can tell me. Background, et cetera.' He had called Stella from the Fishbowl the previous morning, within minutes of Derek Finch charging out of Ajay's office. At that stormy meeting it had become clear that Finch and Julius had a joint interest in keeping Kerr away from Marcus Tennant. Their protection of the MP had only strengthened his resolve to get at the truth.

'Your interrogation, you mean?' said Stella. 'Come on, John, the whole thing was a total stitch-up. More like a trial than a case review. Disgusting. But we both know that.'

She pulled her shades over her eyes again and looked across the river to HMS *Belfast*. They sat in silence for a moment, enjoying the sunshine as a family of tourists wandered past, yellow windcheaters tied round their waists. A three-masted schooner sailed downstream under the bridge.

'Background I can do. "Et cetera" is no problem. But we're talking the lanky creep in the red socks, right? The guy I shut down?' The sunglasses slid up again as she looked Kerr in the eye. 'Don't be shy, John. You must always tell me exactly what you want.'

'Sorry?'

Stella laughed. 'Mr Gangly? The so-called lawyer? He's the one you're interested in, isn't he?'

She was right, except that Kerr's immediate priority had changed since their call. In his sights then had been an establishment cabal for frustrating his investigation; right now his target was the criminal gang that had tried to incinerate him. Overnight, Langton had worked with the local police to identify the Volvo, while Fargo had rung round local hospitals to trace a victim with a serious injury to his left eye. At this moment both trails remained cold. Kerr and the team were considering two possible motives. The first, revenge, placed Terry Bray firmly in the frame. If Bray had discovered Kerr's role in SO15, perhaps through a tip-off, then it was plausible he had ordered Kerr's murder in retaliation for infiltrating Melanie against him. Alan Fargo was also taking another look at the two men Kerr and Justin had interdicted in their chase down the Thames. They had to consider the possibility that

British criminals connected to them or Bray might have planned a revenge attempt on Kerr's life.

Kerr nodded. 'The Home Office guy, yeah.'

'Bullshit,' said Stella. 'He's a spook. MI6.'

'What?'

'John, don't insult me.'

'I mean, are you sure?'

'Stop pretending I'm revealing something you don't already know.'

'What I really need is the person who got him onto the attendance list.'

'None of us,' said Stella.

'Derek Finch?'

'Who organises the committee from your side?' she said, waving her hand and snapping her fingers. 'The anti-corruption people?'

'Professional Standards Unit.'

'Them,' she said, tapping Kerr on the shoulder. 'Finch got into your professional-standards crowd. The Bull on the rampage again.' She nodded at City Hall. 'I know because the secretary told me. The whole thing was a pantomime. Anyway, who the hell is the bloody Secret Service to lecture us about ethics? It's complete bollocks but no one's got the bottle to stop it.'

Deterrence was the second motive being considered. Alan Fargo had floated this possibility, sitting with Kerr in the 1830 reading room the previous evening after failing to persuade him to get himself checked out at St Thomas's. On Fargo's analysis, the set-up could have been a final warning to keep clear of Marcus Tennant that had spiralled into an attempt on Kerr's life. This trail had led Fargo inexorably to MI6. Kerr had shaken his head in disbelief but Fargo had simply shrugged. 'Depends how badly government needs to cover up for their man,' he had told him. It was a drastic but logical outcome, the dark side to which these particular dots had taken him. For Kerr, who had worked alongside many good and brave friends in MI6, it had been unconscionable, as remote as the possibility that MI6 had organised the gold heist.

Stella touched his temple gently. Her nails looked ferocious but her fingers were surprisingly soft and cool. A couple of middle-aged suits with shirt and tie combos suddenly appeared from their right, deep in conversation, and Kerr heard the words 'matrix', 'spreadsheet' and 'enforcer'. The man nearest the river acknowledged Stella as they hurried past, sneaking a glance at Kerr.

'Nosy,' said Kerr. 'Who's he?'

'Buses. Probably thinks we're at it.' Stella rested her palm on his brow and examined his face. 'Why is everyone so out to get you?'

'Not everyone.' Kerr jerked his thumb along the path to the right, past Tower Bridge towards Butler's Wharf. 'Come for coffee and I'll tell you all about it.'

Stella checked her watch, a complicated gold bracelet jangling around her wrist, and stood up. 'No time for coffee. But I'm free after one.'

Kerr winced. 'Sorry. Have to be somewhere else.'

'Some other day, then. Lunch would be very nice. We can take our time.' She flashed him her widest smile and touched his face again. 'Try not to get yourself killed first.'

Thirty-nine

'Somewhere else' was an Italian restaurant called San Giovese in the smartest part of Crouch End in north London. For this date Kerr arrived dead on time, driving home to park the Alfa and taking a taxi for the remaining three miles. He found Nancy Sergeyev already perched at the small bar to the left of the entrance. She was halfway through a glass of Prosecco and being chatted up by the barman, a good-looking boy in white shirt and red bow-tie with checked waistcoat.

Kerr had not seen her since the previous winter and thought she looked great in a simple white linen dress, low cut and decorated with big orange flowers. She wore a cobalt bead necklace, Skagen watch and white latticed shoes. Her tanned, bare legs were crossed right over left, the free shoe dangling from her toes. Reaching up for him, she reciprocated his kiss on both cheeks. She had silver stud earrings, and her dark, shoulder-length hair smelt of lemons. Kerr reluctantly dragged his eyes from her cleavage, smiled at the barman, signalled for two more drinks and looked around.

The restaurant was small, about fifteen paces square, with only four tables in the main dining area. Along both side walls there were three tables for two with banquette and chair, each separated by a smoked-glass partition. Kerr counted three other couples and a group of four businessmen in the middle. 'This place looks familiar.'

Nancy smiled. 'Registry party Christmas nineteen ninety-whatever.'

'So what was I doing here?'

'Coming on to me, mostly. Unsuccessfully.' She giggled. 'Your personal life was too complicated for me in those days. How's Gabi?'

'I'll tell you all about her. She was asking after you.' This was true, but not for the reason Kerr was implying. On Sunday evening Gabi had again tried to dissuade her father from accepting a date with another man's wife, and a friend at that. Kerr had kept it vague, then called Nancy to confirm.

As the drinks arrived Nancy frowned at his temple and reached out, exactly as Stella Ward had done earlier, her fingers just as soft and cool. It made him smile. 'I'll tell you about that, too.'

Kerr noticed Nancy was not wearing her wedding ring and held on to her hand for a second.

'You're wondering how long it is since Karl walked out on us?' she said, reading his thoughts. 'Over a year. I've stopped counting, to be honest.'

'And doing great, obviously.'

Nancy clinked his glass and flashed a perfect white smile. 'See for yourself.'

The waiter showed them to a table at the deepest part of the restaurant, one of two out of sight from the main dining area. It had a starched white cloth with fresh flowers, heavy cutlery, linen napkins, fresh warm bread in a basket with soft butter and an elderly waiter with a dodgy eye. 'I think they've given us the adulterers' table,' she whispered.

They both ordered salad to start followed by fennel risotto with ricotta and dried chilli for Nancy, *penne arrabbiata* for Kerr and a bottle of Sicilian red. They realised they had known each other since Nancy had joined Special Branch Registry straight from school, though their paths had rarely crossed again, mostly at the various squad summer and Christmas parties. They recalled cases they had worked on together, the Real IRA and the days of international terrorism pre-al-Qaeda, then talked about their families, Kerr's volatile on-off relationship with Robyn, Gabi's mother, Nancy's failed marriage and her newly discovered talent for painting. They chatted easily, incessantly. Twenty-one years of history fell away in two and a half hours, and an urgent mutual attraction pulsed into the space.

The waiter ordered them a cab for the short journey to Nancy's house, a neat Victorian three-bed semi in Hornsey Vale. Kerr had been there once before, at night, under quite different circumstances. The hall had been redecorated but Kerr could still make out the faint trace of a bullet hole above the front door. The living room was to the right but Nancy took him to the back of the house, where the hallway broadened beyond the staircase to accommodate an adjacent kitchen and dining room. Kerr found himself peering to check the french windows as Nancy pattered into the kitchen. The dining room was full. Children's clothes were draped from a dryer by the window and their toys and other clutter covered the polished wooden floor. Just inside the door Nancy had found space for the ironing-board and, within reach, a pile of clean washing spilt out of a green plastic basket on the single armchair. Two plastic laptops lay side by side on the oval dining-table. He wandered into the kitchen.

'I can offer you coffee,' she said, bending down to the fridge and brandishing a misty bottle of Prosecco. 'Or this?'

She had explained that her children, Amy and Tom, were staying with another mum. 'When do you have to collect the kids?' said Kerr.

Nancy grabbed a couple of glasses and led him back down the hall. 'I meant "staying" as in "sleepover". Peace!'

The living room was for grown-ups, warm and cosy, with a faded red three-piece suite against plain cream walls, an oak coffee table on a Turkish rug, original cast-iron fireplace and a small TV to the far side of the bay window. There were happy photographs of the children, some with Nancy on a windswept beach, others at school or with their friends. Kerr stood admiring a couple of Nancy's framed watercolours on the wall behind the sofa. One was of a vase of daffodils, the other a scene in her garden. In none of the downstairs rooms was there any sign that Karl even existed. 'I excommunicated my ex a long time ago,' Nancy had told him in the restaurant. Purged him, more like, thought Kerr now.

She let Kerr open the bottle and pour the drinks. As he lifted their glasses from the coffee-table he leant in to kiss her. They sat on the sofa for a few minutes, Kerr to her left, and she must have seen him wince as he lifted his right arm round her. 'Ouch.' He made a face. 'Sorry. Pathetic. Should have sat the other side.'

Nancy deftly reached inside his shirt to stroke his shoulder. Then he felt her lips brush from his cheek to his bruised forehead. She sat back so she could look him in the eye. 'Is your life less complicated now?'

Kerr smiled at her. 'Open book.'

She uncurled her legs from the sofa and kissed him again. 'Shall we go upstairs, then?'

Kerr took her offered hand and instinctively stroked his thumb against her ring finger. Gabi's words of warning drifted through his mind as he stood and drew her close. 'Why not?'

They stayed in bed for hours, loving, talking and dozing. 'You know my daughter told me I shouldn't see you,' he said finally.

'Why on earth not?'

He kissed her breast. 'I suppose she knew this would happen.'

'And?'

'She disapproves.'

'You need the say-so of your *daughter* before you go on the town?' Nancy gave him a playful punch. 'Does Gabi vet all your dates, or is it just me?'

'It's because you're still married to Karl.'

Nancy propped herself on an elbow. 'And you're feeling *guilty*?'

'She has a point, Nancy.'

'Really?' She threw her head back and laughed. 'John, neither of us needs to feel bad about this, believe me. Karl was unfaithful for most of our marriage. Everyone in the Branch probably knows that. If it had a pulse Karl would try to seduce it. Even that poor Diane Tennant.' She brought her fist down on the duvet. 'I mean, Jesus, my husband was having regular sex with his principal's wife.'

'Say again?' Kerr switched to red alert. With his good arm he pushed himself up on the pillows.

'You mean you didn't know?' This time Nancy sat up. 'Forget it, John. Sorry. I should have kept my mouth shut. It was just Karl being bloody Karl.'

'It's all right.' Kerr caressed her hair. 'But how did you find out? Who told you?'

Nancy checked his hand. Hurt clouded her face, as if she blamed her husband for the sudden change in Kerr. 'One of the secretaries in Tennant's private office rang me up out of spite.'

Kerr frowned. He knew from Karl that Marcus Tennant had two female secretaries. He lay down, gently pulling her beside him. 'Which one?'

Nancy gave a sigh. 'The ugly one, of course,' she said, turning to him. 'The only woman Karl has ever turned down.'

Forty

As the lovers slept, Melanie Fleming left the Old Star with Jez and the *Flag of Liberty* editors and wandered down Shoreditch High Street. Approaching the alleyway leading to the *Flag* offices, they did not even pause by the VW van.

'Where's my taxi, then?' said Jez. He was in his usual loud mood, fooling around, showing off to Melanie and making fun of Becky and Sacha. It was a warm, clear evening and he was carrying his denim jacket, circling it above his head a couple of times out of sheer exuberance. The editors dawdled behind, voices raised above the thinning traffic in a row that seemed to have been escalating all day.

Melanie gave a loud burp. 'I'm behind the white van,' she said, pointing to a Ford Transit parked twenty paces beyond the alleyway. They had bailed out from the *Flag* earlier than usual this evening, reaching the Star at just after seven. Sitting in their usual corner, Melanie had worked her way through three Cokes in the time it had taken half a dozen pints of lager to disappear down Jez's throat – they would be piling into her Renault again for the lift home to Stoke Newington.

Melanie had noticed changes in Jez since their brief kiss late on Monday. His body gave off the same earthy scent but he had evidently found a clean white T-shirt and trimmed his hair and beard. In the pub he had secretly brushed her face and she had pulled away, pretending to be annoyed. 'Ouch. Rough hands.'

'From the farm,' he had replied, switching to exaggerated West Country. 'What do you expect?'

She had tugged his shirt. 'Well, the rest of you looks like a nerd doing media studies.'

'Or editing the *Flag*,' he had said loudly, aiming a peanut at Sacha. As Jez had laughed and touched her again, Melanie had imagined another woman working on his appearance, then silently mocked herself for being so ridiculous.

When they were still five car lengths away she saw a woman exit the mouth of the alleyway, turn right and walk swiftly away from them. She had short dark hair with a bulky soft bag strapped over her left shoulder. There was something familiar about her. With Jez leaping around like a big kid and turning to yell something provocative, Melanie switched to full alert: the woman must have been visiting the *Flag* offices. Jez was still shouting at Becky or Sacha as the street-lights came on, suffocating the evening in a dirty orange blanket, but Melanie kept her eyes locked on the woman in front.

As she drew level with the alleyway she saw her walk up to the vehicle about four car lengths behind her Renault, with no other vehicle filling the space. She quickly unlocked the door, tossed her bag onto the passenger seat and climbed inside. Melanie increased her pace, covering herself by shouting at the others to get a move on if they wanted a lift. Craning forward, she saw that the other car was an old two-door Vauxhall Corsa. And then, as the side-lights came on and faded with each turn of the engine, Melanie remembered. It was the woman whose parking space she had taken on the evening of her first, gut-wrenching, visit to the *Flag of Liberty*.

The engine caught, revved loudly and died as the woman put it into first and tried to move off. It started again at the second turn, racing at full power, as if she had her foot hard on the accelerator. Then the Corsa surged forward and rammed the back of Melanie's Renault with a bang and a shattering of glass.

Jez was shouting something as Melanie heard the gears crunch into reverse and saw the car back away. She began to run but Jez overtook her, sprinting across the pavement as the Corsa lurched forward again with its right indicator flashing. Jez slammed his big hands on the bonnet, blocking its path, and it reversed again a couple of metres into its original parking place, as if he was actually pushing it backwards. 'Anna, what the fuck are you doing?' he yelled, then yanked the driver's door open and leant inside.

The actual collision had attracted little attention, but Jez was putting on quite a show. Passers-by were taking an interest and the proprietor of the nearby Selva Food and Vegetable Store paused midway in rolling down the shutter. A young overweight mother wearing a tank top and tracksuit bottoms stopped to light a cigarette and stare. She had a pushchair with a wonky wheel and two tired little boys sitting in it in tandem. The child in front rubbed his eyes with a grubby fist and made Melanie think of her own sons, tucked up in bed and fast asleep. Even a few drivers were slowing to catch the action, probably assuming the Renault belonged to Jez.

She stayed back as Jez and the woman traded insults, their exact words lost in the passing traffic, and Jez broke off for a second to raise his finger at a jeering man in a black Range Rover with tinted windows. He was making a scene about the damage to the Renault, but Melanie sensed an opportunity. She moved forward to check out the damage, calculating how to exploit the situation.

'How bad is it?' Suddenly Becky was by her side.

The impact had dented the bumper and smashed the offside rear light. 'See for yourself,' said Melanie, turning back to stare at the woman in the Corsa.

She was aware of Sacha scuffing fragments of the reflector into the side of the road, then Becky was trying to distract her again. 'But you can still drive it, yeah?'

'Do you get your ride home, you mean?' said Melanie, without turning away from the Corsa. She gave the Renault's bumper a kick in mock exasperation. 'What do you think?'

'Nasty bitch and drunken idiot,' said Becky, following Melanie's eyes. It could have been the middle of winter as she wrapped her arms around herself and blew out her cheeks. She nodded back up the street to the VW. 'Jez is well pissed. Will you take us in the van?'

Melanie shook her head, keeping her eyes on the Corsa as Jez crouched by the door, waving his arms and shouting. 'Have to sort this first.'

'Well, no way am I hanging around for her,' said Becky. Beyond the Corsa a 67 bus was held at a stop light. Becky tapped Sacha on the shoulder and pointed. 'I'm gonna bus it.' She made it sound like a trip through Devil's Gulch. Melanie walked off to speak with Jez as they hurried back towards the Star and the nearest bus stop.

The Vauxhall had hit Melanie's Renault square on, denting its bonnet but leaving the lights intact. The Corsa was still running but the impact must have damaged the radiator for water was dripping onto the road; the engine would soon overheat. The woman had stayed behind the wheel. Jez faced Melanie. 'I told her to get her bloody car fixed ages ago. Is yours driveable?'

Melanie grimaced. 'Better not.'

Jez reacted exactly as she had planned. 'No problem. Anna can take us.' He leant down again. 'Can't you? It's not far.'

The woman finally climbed out of the car and walked forward to inspect the damage. Melanie saw she was wearing combat pants and a mid-length woollen coat with Doc Martens. Every piece of clothing was black. She bent down briefly, then stood square to Melanie. 'It's one piddling light. You can drive with that. Get over it.' Her eyes held an ice-cold intensity that quickened Melanie's blood. The two women were roughly the same height and build, and for a second Melanie wondered if she was about to hit her. The threat gave her a sudden surge of strength after days of impotence, for there was something about Anna's naked aggression that drew her in. Melanie had been trained to spot what Special Branch called 'persons of interest', and on this muggy evening, when she had least expected it, her best prospect since the start of the operation had crashed right into her.

The two women stood face to face, raw intimidation versus cold, professional insight. Melanie blinked first – deliberately: she had the advantage, for she knew exactly how this part of the game would end. The goal was to spend quality time with Anna, and to score she had to break her number-one rule never to ask a question. 'You going to give me a ride?'

'Get the bus with the others.' Anna abruptly turned away and walked back to her car. Melanie unlocked the Renault and reached inside for a wrench she kept between the front seats. Slamming the door, she strode back to them, aimed the wrench at the windscreen and stared Anna down.

There was silence. Then Anna swung round and got back behind the wheel as Jez stared at Melanie open-mouthed. After a few seconds he held the door for her to climb into the back with the wrench and folded himself into the passenger seat.

Grabbing her bag from Jez, Anna lodged it between her right leg and the door, then took off up Kingsland Road towards Stoke Newington. Melanie had stayed on the near-side so she could get a better look at her new intelligence target and keep an eye on the temperature gauge, which was drifting closer to the red. Jez threw his head back, addressing the roof. 'We'll drop you first, Mel.' He clutched Anna's shoulder in his giant hand. 'This is Mel and she's all right.' Anna said nothing as she met Melanie's eyes in the mirror.

'It's no problem.' Melanie wanted more time with Anna. 'You first. You're in the front.'

'Doesn't matter,' said Jez. 'Which way?'

Melanie gave directions for the short drive to Dalston, taking them right into Laburnum Street, then left into Queensbridge Road. The anger from minutes earlier had evaporated into a torpid silence. No one mentioned the *Flag of Liberty*, which made Melanie ask herself why Anna had been there. On the street, in his comfort zone dissing Anna's rubbish car, Jez had been assertive. But here, as they lurched and bucketed east, her presence seemed to diminish him, as if he knew they operated on different planes.

The atmosphere convinced Melanie that Anna, Surname Unknown, 'SNU', occupied no part in the hierarchy of the *Flag* she had identified the previous week. She caught Anna's eyes again in the mirror, and they looked mean. Perhaps she was still angry with Melanie or annoyed with herself. Melanie looked away, certain the woman was motivated by something stronger than dead-end politics in a Shoreditch alley.

The journey took less than ten minutes. 'Here,' said Melanie, six houses away from her bedsit in Collis Street. Jez got out of the car and waited for her, but Anna stayed eyes front and silent as Melanie eased past her through the passenger door.

On the pavement Jez reached into his jacket and produced a half-bottle of whisky. 'Nightcap,' he said, brandishing it like a conjuror. 'Like we said the other night?'

Melanie's stomach lurched as her game plan veered off course. Her mind instinctively rattled through the operational security boxes of her false life: bed unmade, food in the fridge, drinkable milk, dirty washing, greasy dishes and cutlery on the draining-board, no telltale pile of unopened mail in the hallway. To Jez the silence around her mental checklist must have looked like indecision, which meant acceptance. He leant into the car and told Anna he would walk. She reached over to pull the door shut as the engine revved out of control, then let in the clutch and screeched away.

Melanie hid the wrench in her inside pocket and watched the car go, apprehension spiralling into fear. 'I'm just down there,' she said, as Jez threw an arm round her.

He felt the wrench inside her coat. 'Jesus, you were scary back there.'

In the hallway Melanie grabbed some post in her false name and caught a glare of genuine hostility from her upstairs neighbour. When she switched on the feeble ceiling light Jez seemed to absorb her tiny hiding place in a single sweep, which was all it merited. While Melanie nervously glanced about for anything that might betray her, Jez took a couple of chipped tumblers from the single cupboard above the sink, poured them a double shot of whisky, sat on the bed and tested the mattress. 'Very cosy.'

Melanie joined him because to sit anywhere else would look ridiculous; and she let him kiss her because he might identify her new subject of interest. She took a slug of whisky and risked another question, knowing that tonight she would be breaking all the rules. 'Is she always like that?'

Jez had his arm round her again. 'Complete fucking nutter.' He necked his drink, poured another for them both and stretched out. 'Never known anyone hate so much.'

Melanie pretended to sip her whisky: she knew she would have to drive that night. She leant over and kissed him. 'Why?'

'Too complicated,' he said, closing the conversation as he gently pulled her down beside him. Was that discretion or ignorance? Was it because Jez knew more than he could say, or nothing at all? She traced his hand reaching for her breast, but this time she held it there. 'So, are we going to do it, Mel?' he said.

Melanie sat up and pulled her shirt over her head. Abandoning her tumbler on the bare floor, she rolled over and drew in close, sliding her hand down his belly. 'Why not?'

She murmured the words to herself as much as him, caught in a dilemma. There were strict rules forbidding sex between undercover officers and their targets, written by chiefs who banged on about morality but had never worked in the field. Sex at the sharp end had become a hanging offence, so if Melanie went ahead and the Yard found out she would be sacked.

Dodge was always saying that success undercover was about the 'Four Cs': cover, cultivation, credibility and conscience. For Melanie, it meant identifying People's Resistance and disappearing without trace: that would be her mission accomplished, but everything depended upon a trouble-free exit strategy. And what the academics described as 'tranquil exfiltration' was going to be a whole lot more difficult with Jez sharing her bed.

Melanie watched as Jez pulled away to strip naked, then knelt over her. Her husband, sullen and resentful, had not slept with her for weeks. She was living without sex, rejected at home and a failure at work.

Why not?

She had to give herself to this man right now because he had information she needed. She slithered down the bed and pulled Jez onto her. That was the sole reason, and it was good enough. Necessity was her justification. It freed her from a tangle of mixed emotions and, if she kept saying it to herself, it might become true.

Afterwards, as Jez was drifting off to sleep, Melanie renewed her pitch, gently pulling his hair to keep him conscious. 'Have you ever done it with her?' She made herself sound insecure, exploiting jealousy to justify more questions.

'Who?'

'You know. Anna.'

'No chance.'

'As in you wouldn't want to, or she doesn't let you?'

He turned over, seconds away from unconsciousness. 'It's not like that.'

'She was a bitch to me,' said Melanie, massaging his shoulders. 'What is it she hates?'

'Anna's all right,' he groaned. 'At least she does stuff. Puts a firework up their arses.'

'She what?' Melanie resisted the urge to shake him.

'That's why the others can't stand her. Don't get her.'

As Jez snored, Melanie got up to empty her whisky down the sink and pour a glass of water. She sat in the only armchair, watching him. She was intrigued by what he had let slip, sure about her instincts in those seconds of aggression beside the Renault. There had been a weird aura around the woman, something far stronger than the gravitational pull of sexual guilt that Jez exerted over her. Jez's friend might simply be a repellent, antisocial misfit living on poison and bucketfuls of hate. But Melanie was in search of a hostility that was political and extreme, and the woman squaring up to her in the street that evening had seemed to occupy a force field all of her own.

She let Jez sleep for another half-hour, then kicked him out. 'Was I snoring?' he said, leaning against the door, half asleep and completely drunk. 'Did it get to you?'

She felt a sudden desperate need to rest in her own bed as she closed his hand round the half-empty whisky bottle. 'No, nothing like that.' She tidied his hair and kissed him on the cheek. 'It's never good to stay the whole night.'

Shortly before midnight she caught the 48 bus from Mare Street back to Shoreditch and drove the Renault home to Muswell Hill. Quietly exploring her house, she showered, kissed the children and slipped into bed beside Rob, who smelt as drunk as Jez.

She lay on her back and stared at a ray of moonlight on the ceiling. Tomorrow she would get her car repaired and tell John Kerr that 'Anna, SNU' merited an urgent, comprehensive enquiry. Suddenly she froze as Rob's arm stretched across her stomach and scrunched her nightdress above her waist. He cupped her breast before moving down between her legs. 'Not now, Rob. It's late.' He was murmuring something in his sleep and she felt his erection against her thigh as he hauled himself on top of her.

There was no kissing or stroking, nothing to remind her of how good they used to be together. 'Please, Rob. Not tonight.' He was saying something unintelligible as he positioned himself, some other woman's name, perhaps, and she tried to push him away. Then he was suddenly thrusting inside her, roughly, urgently, hurting her, burying his stubbled face against her neck as he mumbled the same thing over and over before coming in a long groan and collapsing on top of her.

Rob was much heavier now than at any time in their life together. Eventually Melanie managed to ease herself from beneath him and balance on the side of the bed. She stroked him and whispered into his ear, yet sensed he did not even know she was there. As he rolled away, the idea sparked in Melanie that Rob had mistaken her for someone else, that there was a new woman in his life. But who was Melanie to judge him? She had rejected the husband she loved only hours after taking a man she scarcely knew. 'Why not?' she had said. She could still hear herself as she turned away from the moonlight and curled into a ball. Moments earlier she had been racked with guilt about Jez, but that was nothing to the self-loathing she now felt beside Rob. Consumed with grief and loneliness, she clung to the side of the bed and silently wept.

Forty-one

On the evening of the third People's Resistance attack, Danny Brennan entered the Underground system at Bethnal Green using another of Anna Rashid's clean Oyster cards. It was a beautiful summer evening, warm in the street, hot in the station and stifling on the tube, yet Brennan stayed cool beneath two layers of clothing: dark combat pants over his chef's checked trousers and a lightweight zip hoodie concealing the white tunic. He carried a large brown canvas holdall concealing a blue cool box with a white lid. Inside the box lay a hat made from the same material as the chef's trousers and, beneath that, packed with bubble wrap to prevent them shifting during their final journey, the three dirty bombs Anna Rashid had given him, lined up in order from left to right.

Brennan took a crowded Central Line train to Holborn, standing with the bombs in the bag on the floor between his legs, then changed to the Piccadilly Line for the two stops to Leicester Square, where he left the system. He tugged the beanie low over his forehead as he loped past the station's CCTV cameras and surfaced on Charing Cross Road. Swinging right, he entered the pedestrian concourse of the square, heading west towards Piccadilly Circus.

The area was busy with tourists relaxing over wine outside the restaurants and milling around the shops and kiosks selling theatre tickets. Brennan appeared unremarkable, glancing neither left nor right, occasionally knocking his deadly load against people's legs and pushchairs as he forced a path through the centre of the thoroughfare.

In fact, Danny Brennan was distracted because he had set aside this particular evening for his first and only visit to the *Flag of Liberty* and had spent an hour sewing a special pouch into the black coat he would be wearing later. The timing was important because he knew Thursday was the evening the editors generally worked late, preparing the next edition of the journal. His personal mission had been disrupted less than three hours earlier, when he had heard Anna Rashid enter the kitchen. 'We're on, Danny,' was all she had said, the moment she reached the top of the ladder, pausing to catch her breath.

Lying on the bed in just his boxers, rereading the *Flag*'s diatribe against People's Resistance, Brennan had been startled. 'Tonight's not good,' he had said, watching her eyes on his body as she took off her coat.

'You going somewhere, then?' she had said, wiping her forehead. 'Hot date?' Swinging his legs off the bed Brennan had felt the sting of her sarcasm again as she had grabbed the remote, flicked off the TV and collected the chef's uniform tunic from the cupboard. 'The big cheese is going to be there.'

Brennan had noticed large circles of sweat radiating from Rashid's armpits. 'Is it that hot?'

'No car,' she had said, smoothing the tunic. 'Woman at the *Flag* crashed into it last night and it broke down.'

'Becky?'

'Doesn't matter,' Rashid had said quickly, reaching into her shoulder bag. 'They only gave me the address for the hit this morning. Security, probably.'

Brennan stretched. 'They don't trust us?'

'*Us?*' Rashid had given him a look as she produced three sheets of brightly coloured wrapping paper covered with

America's Stars and Stripes and dropped them on the work-top. 'The target is unbelievable, Danny. Spectacular.'

Brennan glanced at his watch: 19.02. He left the historic gardens fronting the Leicester Square Odeon to his left and hurried along Coventry Street towards Piccadilly Circus, concentrating on the mission but angry about the woman who had taken his lover's car out of circulation.

He was moving quickly because Rashid had ordered him to avoid using Green Park, the tube station nearest the target and therefore one of the places on which the cops would soon be focusing their attention. He had been walking for nearly twenty minutes before he saw the illuminated white bulbs of the Ritz hotel sign, the major landmark Rashid had told him to look for. Another time check: 19.16.

He crossed Piccadilly at the traffic lights outside the hotel, headed north up Berkeley Street and, as Berkeley Square revealed itself, entered a world that was completely alien to him. The area to his left was a famous rectangular oasis of tended grass and giant plane trees with wooden benches planted around the perimeter and bordering the central gravel path, many carrying messages from Americans grateful for their sojourn in London. Black iron railings separated the square from the encircling streets and it was the outside space of choice for office workers on their lunch break.

Berkeley Square was awash with money and heavy with risk because it was alive twenty-four/seven. A favoured location for hedge fund managers during the day, by night its streets danced to a quite different tune, an insistent hyper-track that throbbed till dawn. Every evening of the week, as the offices surrounding the square receded into darkness, a collection of expensive, gilded clubs burst into life. Red cordons of plaited rope stretched from each entrance, sepa-rating Joe Public from the *über*-privileged, guarded by heavy-duty doormen in bulging suits and clip-on black ties. From eight o'clock the banking masters of the universe were displaced by beautiful unknowns mingling with C-list celebs searching for paparazzi. Everyone was dressed to kill, geared up to drink, dance and snort the night away.

Some chose to conceal their wealth. Brennan carried his bombs past a luxury-car showroom, still brightly lit even outside business hours. Inside, like prince and pauper, a florid salesman in pinstripes and gaudy tie was earnestly pitching to an unshaven punter in jeans, sweatshirt and cheap canvas shoes. Separating them was a sky blue Bentley Continental GT, a Mayfair runabout with a price tag that would buy a northern house.

Near the top of the square he looked down a side-road towards Regent Street. Brennan picked out the target address on the south side, about seven car lengths away. As he crossed the road he paused only to snatch the briefest of glances, enough to see that a handful of guests had come outside. There were about a dozen of them, spilling onto the pavement with their champagne. Some of the men were in black tie and he could smell their cigar smoke; all the women were in cocktail dresses, garrulous and shrill, their raucous laughter washing down the street. The British contingent.

He continued about another thirty paces up the square before swinging right into the next parallel street, then another right into an ancient cobbled lane between a flashy Chinese restaurant and an Italian sandwich bar, making the third side of a square. Oak Lane was exactly as Rashid had described it, too narrow for a car, bordered on both sides by the towering brick walls of the adjacent buildings but clear of CCTV cameras. Three-quarters of the way down he came upon the industrial-sized black refuse bin on wheels that Rashid had told him to look for. It was as high as his chest and protected him from view by pedestrians in the bottom street. Here was Brennan's holding area. From this stinking back-street in one of London's brightest gems he would make his move.

Brennan swung the heavy lid open against the wall, scarcely noticing the stench of rotting food. Then he seemed to switch gear: from now until the action was accomplished, every movement would be rapid and decisive. He whipped off the beanie, hoodie and trousers, removed the cool box from its canvas bag and stuffed everything beneath a pile of flattened cardboard boxes. Crouching behind the bin, he pulled on a pair of thin latex gloves then opened the cool box and reached inside to check the three devices, each now dressed as a gift in Stars and Stripes. He exposed the three white switches in a row and activated them without any hesitation. Each moved with a satisfying click as it armed the bomb, followed by a vibration beneath the plastic casing as the detonating system pulsed into life. Brennan put on the chef's hat, closed the cool box and checked the time: 19.34. He had precisely thirty minutes to complete the mission before he was killed by his bombs. He calmly picked up the cool box with its deadly contents and made his way, past the point of no return, towards the light at the end of the lane.

Forty-two

His target was Charles Vine, Berkeley Square's most prestigious art gallery. Open plan and minimalist, with its doors to the right and a huge plate-glass window looking onto the street, it lay within a row of upmarket boutiques Rashid had dismissed as 'shops with fine art in the window but no punters inside'. At seven that evening the gallery had launched a public exhibition of American art entitled 'War Paint'. Sponsored by the US embassy in nearby Grosvenor Square, it featured American artists whose talent lay, according to the publicity blurb, in capturing the 'red heat of battle' in oils and watercolour, with a focus on Iraq and Afghanistan. It had been explicitly marketed to strengthen the 'special relationship' between Britain and the US, the world's two major wartime allies.

With the exception of Danny Brennan, it was strictly invitation only. 'The place will be full of Yanks and champagne,' Rashid had told him, 'expat movers and shakers with a few lower-grade showbiz.' They were expected to include the American ambassador and his wife.

The exhibition had become even livelier since Brennan's first walk past only a few minutes earlier. Party noise from the gallery assaulted him even before he reached the end of the lane and he could make out American accents. The air was rank with the talk and boisterous laughter of rich people having fun. It filled him with revulsion and loathing.

He rounded the lane quickly, swinging left to find he was only about twenty paces from the target, lying diagonally opposite him on the other side of the street. Brennan had a clear view through the tinted glass because the road outside had been kept clear of parked cars. A pair of shaven-headed suits each side of the giant double glass doors overshadowed the gallery's normal security.

He approached with the anxious, hurrying gait of a contractor delivering perishable goods and working against the clock, all of which was true. He walked past the gallery, crossed the road and disappeared into an alleyway one block further down the street, beside a shop selling Persian rugs. At the end of the alley he turned right again along the back of the shops until he reached the kitchen at the rear of the gallery. The voices heard through the open window were quite different from those at the front. He could hear Eastern European accents now, orders being shouted and received, the strains of men and women under pressure.

Brennan knocked on the kitchen door. It opened in a rush to reveal a young blonde woman in a white blouse with a black skirt, and the kitchen din rolled past her into the yard. A lock of hair had come loose over her forehead and she looked stressed, holding an empty tray by her side. Brennan mumbled something about a special culinary request but the girl was unquestioning, already moving back to replenish her tray with canapés, and Brennan had to stick his foot out to prevent the door swinging shut.

He stepped inside to find two men in tunics similar to his and four waitresses crammed into a space dedicated to the supply of canapés and champagne. Brennan was about to say something when a wooden swing door with a small reinforced window at face level crashed open and two more young blonde women with empty trays appeared. The place was a factory, with the men preparing food and pouring champagne, the girls circulating front of house, and demand outstripping supply.

The girl who had let him in backed through the swing door with her loaded tray. Stooping to remove the cool box lid and lean it against the wall, Brennan picked out the first of the three devices, on the left of the row, and followed her in. He reversed into the killing ground, bomb in one hand, cool box in the other, then turned around and came face to face with his victims. Everyone seemed to be laughing and shouting, putting up a barrage of noise that almost knocked him off balance. He heard mostly American accents, wealthy Yanks defeating the Brits at their own class-war game. Brennan took everything in, excising the party chaos from the neat lines of Rashid's diagram.

The main ground floor was about ten metres by twelve and given over entirely to paintings, apart from an unoccupied reception desk by the main entrance. A wooden shelf six inches deep ran around the perimeter at chest height and a wooden staircase in the centre led to a small wrap-around landing against the end wall. A handful of guests had migrated there to talk privately or flirt, but remained visible from the ground floor. The kitchen door was diagonally opposite the main entrance and a second door beneath the staircase led to the toilets.

Since Brennan's first glimpse through the window the numbers appeared to have diminished to a hard core of about fifty and he recognised the ambassador almost immediately from Rashid's photograph. He stood with his wife in the middle of the room just forward of the staircase, shortish and stocky with neatly trimmed grey hair swept back, crinkly eyes and a perpetual aw-shucks grin: no bodyguard alongside. No one sparing Brennan a glance.

He eased his way to the side of the gallery opposite the kitchen door and placed the first device halfway along the wooden shelf, immediately beneath a watercolour depicting a British foot patrol in Helmand province. A flush-faced

American took a look at the wrapping paper, smiled and gave Brennan a thumbs-up. He downed his champagne in one and stood the flute on the shelf. 'Is this for me, buddy?' he joked, lifting the bomb and shaking it, playing the game. Brennan managed a smile and looked down at his watch: 19.41. Twenty-three minutes until detonation.

He took out device number two and started to make his way across the room. His path was blocked by guests waiting to be introduced to the ambassador and his wife and he had to work his way behind the staircase. Another group made a horseshoe round the exact section of shelf where he had to place the next bomb. He used the bomb to nudge a blonde in a sparkly silver dress standing with her back to him. She spun around, flushed with champagne, with a smile that faded when she saw it was only a caterer. Brennan resisted the urge to tell the bitch she would soon be dead. Instead, he tried a 'Would you be so kind?' look, an expression he had never used in his life, waiting for her to take the bomb and put it on the shelf for him.

Brennan crossed the floor again to place the third and final device on the reception table by the main doors, then retreated to the kitchen, replaced the lid on the cool box, opened the door and escaped into the alley before anyone could speak to him. He crossed the road and retraced his steps to Oak Lane. He heaved open the lid of the wheelie bin, reached inside for his clothes, disguised himself again and hid the cool box in its canvas bag. Then he peeled off the gloves, stuffed them into his pocket, pulled the beanie low and circled round to his vantage-point, a gigantic plane tree in the square with a clear view of the gallery.

As before, Anna Rashid had ordered him to get clear of the scene as quickly as possible. Brennan disobeyed her again because he wanted to be certain the devices had worked and, as with his execution of the judge in Middle Temple Lane, to witness what effect his attack would have. He did not have long to wait.

The bombs exploded within seconds of each other at 20.03. Each detonated with a bright flash, like a giant firecracker, followed by complete silence. The third, probably the device nearest the reception desk, blew out the plate-glass window. It disintegrated into a million lethal shards, cutting down a trio of pedestrians on the other side of the street. Brennan saw a woman stagger through the open space. Her hair and sparkling dress were on fire and Brennan recognised her as the woman who had placed the second bomb for him. He watched her lurch blindly onto the pavement, surprised that she was not screaming. Then she fell into the road and lay perfectly still as the hair ignited her face and scalp. By the time other guests stumbled through the opening her whole body was ablaze and Brennan realised she must already be dead. He watched the security men fight their way inside, presumably to grab the ambassador, but there was no sign of him or his wife. Mesmerised, Brennan watched as more people fell out of the gallery. Some were on fire. All collapsed and lay still after a few paces.

The scene remained eerily quiet as Brennan picked up his cool box, rounded the top of the square and turned north up Davies Street. As the gallery burned and collapsed behind him there were still no screams, no shouts or sirens from the devastation he had caused. The only sound was the humming of luxury cars passing by with their high-end passengers, and he could almost smell the money. Brennan walked away to safety and his next, private, action.

Forty-three

Kerr was alone in his Islington apartment when he learned about the atrocity. Alan Fargo had been calling from 1830 but was unable to get through because Kerr had been on the phone to Nancy Sergeyev. Kerr's initial information had come from breaking news on Sky as he wandered through from the kitchen mixing scrambled eggs, phone locked in the crook of his neck.

He hit the road on the blue light within two minutes, made three calls for information during his sixteen-minute race to the Yard, then headed from the underground car park to Room 1830. He found the place empty except for the builders' stepladders and the gash in the ceiling, Monday's leak having proved more technically challenging than expected. He guessed Fargo's team would be on their way back to the office but, for now, the only signs of life came from the giant TV, switched as usual to Sky News, and Excalibur, with its dust sheet lifted to expose the keyboard.

Waiting for Fargo to appear, Kerr stood watching the live TV pictures from Mayfair and sensed immediately that this was no normal bomb scene. An extensive area around the site had been completely evacuated, with Grosvenor Square as well as Berkeley Square cordoned off, presumably because the first responders feared further attacks against the nearby US embassy. That was unusual but by no means unique. What gave him real concern was the glimpse of specialist fire-fighters wearing the protective suits he had seen only in exercises against a chemical, biological, radioactive or nuclear attack. Here something different was unfolding and, if his fears proved founded, terrorism in London had just taken on a terrible new dimension.

Expecting to see Derek Finch give an initial briefing from the scene, he stepped forward to turn up the volume. As he came within sight of the tiny reading room to his left the door swung open and Alan Fargo appeared. He was flushed and, behind him, Kerr could see Gemma Riley straightening her blouse. 'Shall I come back later?' said Kerr, turning back to the TV and the men in CBRN suits. Behind him he heard Fargo's futile attempt at formality, then Gemma murmured something about getting back to the comms room.

When Fargo was settled at his desk in the main office, Kerr took the chair beside him. 'Sorry about that,' said Fargo, fidgeting with embarrassment. His shirt was gaping open at the throat and a couple of dark patches of sweat had appeared on his chest, but for Alan Fargo such dishevelment could pass as normal.

'Awkwardness all round.' Kerr pointed to a spot on his own face and waited for Fargo to wipe his cheek.

He watched Fargo stare at the red smear on his handkerchief, as if Gemma's lipstick had found its way there by magic. 'She was updating me on something. Late turn comms.'

Kerr gave him a knowing look. 'Last time I checked, this room was a heavily restricted area and you were a stickler for security. And Gemma is not late turn because I saw her first thing this morning. So, what's going on, Al?' He nodded at the screen. 'Trying to get a quick one in before the meltdown?'

The electronic lock clicked behind them, breaking the tension, and they both swung round as Bill Ritchie appeared in the doorway.

Ritchie immediately homed in on Kerr's battered face and stood over him. 'What happened?'

'Domestic violence.'

'You don't have a home life.'

'Kitchen cupboard.'

Ritchie glared at the gaping ceiling, tossed his car keys onto the desk and nodded at the screen. He was wearing old maroon jumbo cords with suede slip-ons and a red checked shirt. Kerr knew he had spent the afternoon at the oncology clinic at St Thomas's and felt a sharp stab of concern. Each chemo session seemed to leave his boss thinner and more drained, and he made a mental note to call Lynn again in the morning. One of the 1830 callout officers appeared, so Fargo picked up Ritchie's keys and led them into the reading room, where Gemma's perfume lingered. He left the door open as Ritchie moved behind the desk and wrinkled his nose. 'How bad is it?'

Kerr sat opposite Ritchie as Fargo, with his back to the open doorway, briefed them without notes. 'Very. Gemma just brought the latest and we're getting updates the moment the info comes in.' He glanced at Kerr, seeming embarrassed again, and Ritchie stared at them both.

'Joe Drumm?' he said.

'The ambassador was killed, sir,' said Fargo.

'Oh, God.' Ritchie lowered his head in pain. 'The commander and I had dinner with him only last month.'

'No announcement yet. They'll be working something out with the embassy. At least seventeen others dead, many more likely to expire from burns and blast injuries, including the ambassador's wife.'

'They got Susan, too?' Ritchie glanced at Kerr. 'Where was the protection?'

'I checked on the drive in. Our protection guys were outside,' said Kerr. 'Personal orders of the ambassador, apparently. He wanted this to be informal. A relaxed evening among friends.'

'Jesus.'

'You know what he was like about security,' said Kerr. 'Our guys battled inside to reach them. They had respirators in the car but by the time they got them onto the pavement it was too late.'

Ritchie looked at Fargo. 'Respirators?'

'It's more complex than a conventional bomb scene,' said Fargo. 'Forensics will take a while, apparently.'

Ritchie raised an eyebrow. 'As in?'

'Hours. Late tonight.'

'Unofficially?'

'Off the record Finch's boffins are talking a chemical attack. Cyanide, possibly. But no one's saying anything yet.'

Ritchie fiddled with his car keys and looked across the table at Kerr. 'The whole of Mayfair glowing with CBRN suits and Derek Finch is saying nothing?'

Kerr shrugged. 'The public will have worked it out for themselves by the ten o'clock news.'

'And this is massively political,' said Ritchie. 'We need Ajay here now. I called him at home on the way in and got his son. Reckons Dad went out around seven.'

'Well, he's not in the building and hasn't rung in yet,' said Fargo. 'The embassy has already been asking for him.'

'We're talking London, not Libya. Their ambassador and his wife slaughtered in the world's oldest democracy. Grosvenor Square is the least of our problems. It's late afternoon in Washington and this will already be lasering straight into the White House from Number Ten. My guess is that the PM will invoke COBRA tonight.'

'Isn't that a bit soon?' said Kerr. 'He'll have nothing to work on yet.'

'He'll need to show the Americans that their best ally is doing something. Finch is going to be in the line of fire, closely followed by us. So keep ringing the commander's mobile. And when he picks up put him through to me.' He turned the keys again. 'Who do we think did this?'

'No claims yet.' Fargo glanced at Kerr. 'From what I've found out so far this is probably beyond the capability of a radical domestic extremist grouping.'

'Such as People's Resistance, right?' said Ritchie. His eyes flashed between the two of them, but his voice carried hope, not conviction.

Thursday, 8 August, 20.53; safe house, Bethnal Green

Brennan entered the safe house and acted with the same decisiveness that had been driving him since he had reached Oak Lane. He caught breaking news on Sky while he was dumping the chef's clothes in the drawer and reaching under the bed for his father's shotgun. This time he put on the black coat with the crude pouch he had stitched into the lining that morning, folded Rashid's communiqué into a pocket, took another Oyster card from the drawer and picked up a new pay-as-you-go phone. He loaded the shotgun, slid it inside the pouch, grabbed the box of ammunition and flicked off the TV.

He was back on the street within fifteen minutes, retracing his steps to Bethnal Green Underground station. The clutch of drinkers outside the Mason's Arms on the corner had scarcely moved, the red dots from their lit cigarettes puncturing the dark, their glasses still half empty.

Thursday, 8 August, 21.13; Room 1830

Bill Ritchie was squeezing every drop of information from Alan Fargo. Quite apart from the political implications arising from the murder of the US ambassador on British soil, Kerr could tell that the murder of Joe Drumm had hit Ritchie hard on a personal level. The two men had been roughly the same age; perhaps his death was reminding Ritchie of his own fragile hold on life. He was demanding a minute-by-minute update and waited impatiently while Fargo rang Gemma for the latest information from the scene.

Then Kerr's mobile rang and he saw Melanie's name on the screen. 'John, I'm in the car,' she said, as soon as he picked up. 'Just left the flat.'

'Everything all right? You got the light fixed?'

'First thing this morning. You looked at my intel?'

'It's brilliant, Mel,' he said, switching her to speaker. 'I'm with Alan now.'

'Look, I've been at the flat all evening and saw the news. I think I should go to the *Flag* right now to get their reaction.'

'Sounds good.'

Kerr looked at Ritchie, who was vigorously shaking his head and mouthing, 'No way.'

Fargo cut his own call to Gemma and leaned forward. 'Hi, Mel.'

'Tell you what,' said Kerr. 'We're obviously going to be here for a while. Stay where you are and I'll call you back.'

'What's to think about? This gives me an opportunity, John. Too good to miss.'

'I'm just thinking about your cover. I don't want you to compromise yourself by turning up so soon.'

'That's a chance I'm prepared to take. Listen, it's a no-brainer.' Melanie was speaking more rapidly than usual and her voice had risen a tone. 'I'm telling you, I know how to handle them.'

Kerr frowned. Impatience was the enemy of sound judgement, and when an undercover officer sounded impulsive, Kerr sensed danger. 'Where are you now?'

'Stuck in the gutter at Dalston. Look, I have to do something, John. It's my job. Isn't that right, Al?' Fargo leaned in to say something but Kerr saw Ritchie's restraining hand on his arm. 'So many people are dead and no one knows who did it. I can't just sit in that bloody bedsit watching TV,' she said.

'Mel, we've got a lot going on here,' said Kerr, as Ritchie shook his head again. He needed to cut the call before Ritchie intervened. 'Give me a couple of minutes.'

'I'm right in saying Melanie Fleming provided absolutely no pre-emptive intelligence on this attack?' said Ritchie, the moment Kerr cut the call. He looked irritated, playing with his car keys on the desk as he waited for Kerr's nod of confirmation. He turned to Fargo. 'What's the latest from comms?'

'Looks like we're talking devices, plural,' said Fargo, reading from his scribbled notes. 'At least two explosion sites, possibly more. Dirty bombs, each device with different constituent parts. The nature and severity of the injuries suggests a combination of incendiary, blast and poison.'

'And sophistication of this level equals international,' said Ritchie. 'Islamic. Has to be. Yes?' He looked from one to the other. 'You're reassuring me that this isn't domestic. Not People's Resistance.'

'But it *is* completely anti-American,' said Kerr. 'It fits their claims, so we really have to wait and see.'

'And while we're doing that I want Melanie Fleming to stay put.' He was twirling the tarnished car keys in his fingers. Ritchie had been driving the same ancient Merc for nearly two decades. 'You know I was dead against this operation from day one. Melanie should never have been deployed. You were stubbornly wrong to go down that path and Ajay made an error of judgement in supporting you.'

'Actually, Bill, that's not quite right—'

Ritchie banged his fist on the table. 'That's enough.'

There was silence, the only sound coming from the callout officers working the phones in the main office. Fargo spoke first. 'Boss, I think John was about to say things aren't that bad,' he said, with a look at Kerr. 'Melanie identified a woman of security interest last night. She's called Anna Rashid, a white British woman in her twenties who took her surname from her partner, Parvez.'

'And?' said Ritchie.

'Parvez was a Pakistani asylum seeker, studying at the London School of Economics. He was suspected of being a jihadi and arrested in Karachi on a return home to visit his family, held for a few weeks, then released. Shortly after he returned to London his asylum application was rejected, and a few months later he was dead. Suicide, according to the coroner. He left a note, apparently, full of allegations. Haven't managed to get my hands on it yet.'

'So what?'

'The secret tribunal that rejected Parvez Rashid's asylum appeal was advised by Judge Hugh Selwyn.'

'Anna Rashid has a powerful motive for murdering Selwyn in revenge for her partner's death,' said Kerr.

Ritchie frowned. 'Is there any suggestion she could be a link to this attack?'

'Who knows?' Kerr shrugged. 'Alan only just fleshed this out a couple of hours ago. But it's our strongest lead yet for the People's Resistance claims, Bill, and it came from Melanie.'

'How did Melanie get to her?'

'Through her car. Vauxhall Corsa. The uniforms picked it up mid-afternoon abandoned and broken down in Lower Clapton. Damage to the front end and false plates, which makes this whole thing even juicier. But Rashid had missed a cash till receipt under the driver's mat. Terrorist Finance made the ID and Alan did the rest.'

'Why didn't you tell me earlier?'

'Because you weren't here. Alan briefed Ajay.'

'OK.' Ritchie closed his hand over his keys and tried to stand, but the space was so tight that he had to shuffle along towards Fargo. 'Good work.'

'Melanie got to Anna Rashid by being around,' said Kerr. 'Doing just what she's asking to do now.'

'I have to try Ajay again.' Ritchie stood by the door and blew out his cheeks. He looked ashen as he gripped Fargo's arm. 'I'll be here all night, Alan, in the office. I want anything the moment you get it, understood?'

Forty-four

Sitting at the kerb in the Renault waiting for Kerr to call back was making Melanie anxious. The car was parked immediately beneath a streetlamp and every passer-by seemed to notice her. She felt vulnerable, trapped in a dirty goldfish bowl. A young man in a dark tracksuit swaggered by with a muzzled Alsatian on a leash and paused for the dog to defecate against the only healthy tree in the street. It left a wet pyramid, yellowish in the halogen glow, its steam curling around the trunk. The owner stared at Melanie, blank-faced, challenging her to say something. He walked off past a noisy gang of teenage kids in hoodies approaching from the opposite direction. They spotted Melanie observing them and the nearest banged his fist on the driver's window, crouching to leer at her.

Melanie glared at her mobile and drummed her fingers on the steering-wheel, suddenly feeling ridiculous for asking Kerr's permission to do her job. In the event it was her neighbour, not John Kerr, who made the decision for her. She saw him in her rear-view mirror, making his way home from the main street. He was drunk, lurching the full width of the pavement as he searched every pocket for his front-door key, limbs out of synch like a puppet with tangled strings. Just before swinging to the house he saw Melanie and changed course, as if he wanted to borrow her key. Pretending not to notice him Melanie started the engine and drove off. She would make her way to Shoreditch and speak to Kerr from there.

Twelve minutes later she was in Shoreditch High Street, reversing into the only free parking space within easy reach of the *Flag* office. There was no sign of the VW van and, because she had parked further away than normal, she failed to notice the young man in a beanie hurrying from the Underground station with his right arm stretched over his black coat as if keeping it closed against some non-existent wind.

Thursday, 8 August, 21.33; *Flag of Liberty*

Brennan walked steadily down the alleyway until he spotted the light in the *Flag*'s upstairs office. He checked behind him, paused to pull on a fresh pair of latex gloves, nestled the shot-gun closer against his chest and broke into a jog to cover the last twenty metres. The padlock on the heavy door was hanging loose on its hasp but he had to push hard with his shoulder to move it. It opened at the third attempt, scraping a neat curve on the concrete floor, but the deserted space beyond was in darkness and deserted. He stood by the door listening for signs of life, prepared to interrupt one of the heated editorial rows Rashid had described to him, but could hear no voices. The only sign of occupation came from the gentle creaking of floorboards as somebody moved around directly above him. He caught sight of the press in the corner to his left, a dark mass rising from the floor, like a slumbering giant, its acrid smell of oil and ink irritating his throat. He walked round it with a childlike curiosity, examining its complex mechanism, then dodged to the foot of the stairs and listened again. Silence.

He began to climb, pausing every few steps to check for movement. He was expecting to find Becky and Sacha, the editors Rashid had described to him so disparagingly, but when he reached the bookshop at the top of the stairs he saw only one figure sitting in the office cubicle at the far end. Drawing closer he realised that it was a woman and that she was watching TV with the volume low, breaking off every few seconds to tap something into her laptop. Becky. Medium height, slim and beatable. He felt another pulse of excitement.

He moved to the right, away from the stinking toilet, keeping out of Becky's line of sight, and watched the breaking news she was studying so intently. Shaky live pictures from a helicopter showed the ruins of the art gallery, with smoke still curling over Berkeley Square's giant plane trees, the dinner jackets and champagne of early evening displaced by space suits and body-bags. Brennan could see the exact point in the square from which he had observed the explosions and it gave him an exquisite rush of sheer pleasure.

Every few seconds he heard the clatter of the keyboard through the partition. Becky typed efficiently, in short, staccato bursts he guessed were machine-gun rounds of condemnation, like everything she had written about him. He leant against the wall to spy on her for a few moments longer, eyes flickering from the TV to the laptop, the street-fighter getting to know his antagonist.

Thursday, 8 August, 21.36; Bill Ritchie's office

Kerr had followed Ritchie round to his office from 1830. He stood by the door waiting for him to flick on the lights, unlock his safe and slump behind the desk.

'So, what do you think?'

Ritchie had left the computer until last, and seemed reluctant to press the button. He was old-school, the type Jack Langton described as 'walk, talk and telephone'.

'I think we're in the middle of a crisis and I need the commander here right now to help me manage it.'

'I mean about Melanie.'

'I've heard nothing tonight to change my opinion about her deployment. And I'm too busy to go into it right now.'

'So what do I say to her? Or are you going to leave her by the kerb all night?'

'You tell her to switch everything off and get an early night. If those bombs have the slightest connection to Anna Rashid and People's Resistance, then Melanie Fleming could be placing herself in danger. I want her nowhere near the *Flag of Liberty* tonight. We review tomorrow, when the situation is clearer.'

'And how will that happen when we have zilch intelligence? Melanie is our only intelligence lead.'

Ritchie gave a harsh laugh. 'And what does that tell you? Joe Drumm was a lovely guy and we failed him. And his wife.' He rolled the chair across to the safe to retrieve some papers. 'We need to up our game, and fast.'

'By going with Melanie right now.'

'No.' Ritchie pushed back in his chair. 'What if this connection to the judge through Rashid's boyfriend turns out to be no more than a coincidence?'

Kerr stared at him in disbelief. 'Do you really believe that?'

'It's happened before.' Ritchie flicked on the desk lamp, highlighting the shadows under his eyes. 'Don't you get it, John? You heard the stress in her voice back there. And why? She feels guilty because she hasn't produced a shred of useful intelligence and that makes her desperate to do something. Anything, including putting herself in harm's way. I've seen it before a hundred times.' He looked exhausted as he jabbed a finger at Kerr. 'Christ, the number of times I had to hold you back! It's classic and it's dangerous. And I haven't got time to argue with you right now.'

'Remember your golden rule in those days, Bill?' said Kerr, taking a step into the room. ' "Defer to the judgement of the officer on the ground." '

'That was then.' Ritchie checked a number in his diary, grabbed the phone and began dialling, conversation over. 'Tonight I'm ordering you to send Melanie home.'

Thursday, 8 August, 21.38; *Flag of Liberty*

Danny Brennan moved left towards the office door, but still Becky did not see him. The door opened silently and he stood for a little longer, observing her. 'Are you writing about us again, Rebecca?' He waited for her to spin round, enjoying her look of surprise, then nodded at the laptop. 'More disgusting cop-out middle-class shite slagging off People's Resistance? Anna told me it was you, so don't deny it.'

'Anna?' Becky slapped the laptop shut and glared up at him. She had never seen Brennan before and surprised him with her speed of recovery. She seemed fearless, which also made him feel good. 'This is you and her? You did this?' She was pointing at the screen. She stood up to face him and he could almost hear her mind rewinding the previous actions. 'Well, you're a disgusting fucking psycho. This is not why I became an anarchist. And, yeah, I am definitely going to write it up.'

With his free arm Brennan reached into his pocket for the phone and communiqué. 'You're going to claim it first,' he said, placing them on her desk and pushing her back into the chair.

She banged her hip against the desk, but she was still belligerent. 'You're crazy,' was all she said. Only when the shotgun appeared did her eyes signal fright, but she let out a satisfying scream when he held the gun by the barrels and smashed the stock down hard on her right hand. He stepped back, watching fear slide into terror as he seized her left hand and held it flat on the desk. She began shrieking hysterically but her arm felt weak, as if the fight had already drained from her.

Brennan used the barrels to maim her this time, jabbing them down repeatedly on her knuckles, hearing more bones crack with each thrust. Soon the screaming dropped to a whimper, as if she knew there was no one to hear her. She looked up at him with pleading in her eyes but left both hands on the desk, as if they no longer belonged to her or she was trading them for her life. Laying the shotgun on the desk, he took hold of them and made her shriek again as he manipulated the crushed bones. 'You're not going to be writing anything ever again.'

Thursday, 8 August, 21.41; Melanie's Renault, Shoreditch

Parked in the Renault waiting for Kerr's instructions, Melanie was feeling as vulnerable as she had outside her flat, constantly checking the mouth of the alleyway in her mirror. With a final 'missed calls' check, she stepped onto the pavement, locked the car and headed for the alleyway. She had just spotted the light in the upstairs office of the *Flag* when her mobile vibrated. Kerr's name was on the screen so she doubled back to the street before answering. 'What kept you?'

'It's chaos here.' Kerr's voice was businesslike. 'Where are you?'

'Almost at the *Flag*.'

'Turn round and go back to the flat.' He sounded irritable, too.

'John, I'm here now and there's someone in the office.'

'Too risky.'

'Why?'

'Orders from Bill Ritchie.'

'Is that what you think?'

'Mel, just do it.'

'That's crazy.' Somewhere in the night air, she thought she heard a woman scream.

'You still there?' said Kerr.

'What's going on? Do you know something you're not telling me? What's the big deal?'

'We need to meet tomorrow to talk about Rashid, so give me a call in the morning.'

'She might be in there right now,' said Melanie, with a glance back to the mouth of the alleyway. 'Anna Rashid is our best lead. Why won't you let me follow her?'

'Mel, I haven't got time for this now. Go home and let things settle.'

'That's the last thing I'm going to do. Stuff it.' Melanie cut the call and stood watching the traffic, undecided. 'Defer to the judgement of the officer on the ground' was the operating principle Kerr had taught her years ago. Melanie's natural inclination was to follow her professional instinct and take the consequences. A slap on the wrist from Bill Ritchie was nothing against the potential offered by Anna Rashid. Abruptly she swung round and headed back to the alleyway.

The upstairs office light was drawing her onwards again as another thought struck her. John Kerr had said a visit tonight was too risky, and she had never known him overstate a threat. Her mind raced through the possibilities. Perhaps Ritchie had additional intelligence about Anna Rashid they were holding back, or her intelligence had triggered another investigation from which they were excluding her.

'Too risky.' Did Kerr truly believe that, or was he simply being loyal to his boss? Perhaps she was just being paranoid, she admitted, as she turned round for the second time, or over-sensitive at the thought of being only one part of the picture, a small piece in a giant investigative jigsaw. In the end, her loyalty to John Kerr sent her back to the Renault.

She pressed herself against the car door as a bus raced past, searching for the car key. The street fell silent for a moment and she heard the distant scream again.

Thursday, 8 August, 21.44; *Flag of Liberty*

Ashen with shock and pain, Becky's shrieks had reduced to a child's low sobbing, hysteria melting into despair. Brennan took pleasure in the transformation as he took back Rashid's pay-as-you-go phone and called the Samaritans, using the same number he had dialled after murdering Diane Tennant. Levelling the shotgun at her head, he ordered Becky to read the communiqué.

' "This is People's Resistance. Tonight we attacked the US and British war machine, the giant military industrial complex that enriches the wealthy warmongers and murders innocent brothers and sisters throughout the world." ' She faltered and broke down in tears, so Brennan struck her head with the back of his hand. He could hear a woman's urgent voice at the other end of the line. ' "Let this be a lesson that the people are fighting back. These evil bastards have nowhere to hide. We are met by the cry, 'Dynamitists, assassins, fiends.' But we say it is absolutely necessary to act with violence against all that is bad: let us occupy ourselves with chemistry and let us manufacture promptly bombs, dynamite and other explosive matters." ' The cumbersome phrases made Becky stumble again and the Samaritans woman was interrupting her, insistent and controlling. Becky hesitated, so Brennan struck her again. ' "Much more efficacious than guns and barricades. That is all. Further actions will follow." '

Brennan immediately grabbed the phone, listened to the woman at the other end for a second, cut the call and replaced the phone in his pocket. Bending down close, he peered into Becky's eyes. 'Do our words offend you?' he said quietly. 'Do they make you feel dirty?' He screwed the communiqué into a ball and forced it into her mouth, then dragged her out of the office into the adjacent kitchen, squeezed between the office and the toilet. She felt almost weightless and disappointed him with her lack of resistance. 'So I'll wash them from your mouth.'

The giant butler sink was a metre wide and as deep as Brennan's forearm, stained and threaded with black hairline cracks. It was piled with dirty plates, mugs and cutlery that must have been there for weeks, half covered with brown, greasy water. Holding her upright against him he turned on the tap, releasing cold water in a torrent. It splashed onto a plate, missing Brennan but spurting water against Becky's chest and making her gasp. He filled the sink to the top, turned Becky to face him, lifted her off the floor and then crashed her down so violently that water gushed over the floor and her backside smashed the mugs on the top of the pile. He shoved her as deep as he could, scraping her spine against the tap right up to the nape of her neck. When it seemed she could sink no deeper he forced her even more, until her legs were pressed hard against her chest with the calves dangling over the edge, trapped and too weak to help herself as water slopped over Brennan's boots. He snatched a stained scrap of soap from the draining-board, lathered it and forced it between her lips. 'Soap and water to wash the mouth.'

Beside the sink he spotted a rusting toaster. On an impulse he flicked the lever down and watched the innards glow red. 'Electricity for the body,' he said, tossing it into the water. It erupted with a loud crack and an orange flash that made him start. He saw Becky's body turn rigid and shudder, eyes bulging from their sockets, before collapsing like a rag doll. He spent a few moments studying her, the teenage scientist observing his experiment again, before whipping the toaster plug from the wall. He leaned in to check her limp body, tentatively prodded her arm as if the current might still be passing through her, and smiled when he felt her faint breath on his cheek.

He pulled her from the sink, dragged her by the hair across the floor and threw her down the staircase. As he stepped over her inert body he heard a groan, and this pleased him, too. He grabbed her hair again and pulled her across the rough concrete to the press. He found the green button he had seen earlier and pressed it. The vast machine wheezed, coughed and filled the room with a loud hum, the telltale sound of faulty electrics. Brennan could smell burning, which might have come from the machine or Becky. Then, as if some giant invisible force had taken its foot off the brake, the press burst into life with a deafening, rhythmic commotion of clacking, thumping and sucking. The ancient machine sent Brennan recoiling from Becky's crumpled body as it channelled its energy through four cast-iron legs into the floor, making the whole room vibrate. For the second time in less than five minutes Brennan was transfixed, the power of the press invigorating him as much as Becky's frailty.

The contraption appeared to feed itself by sucking and collating sheets of paper from a large tray at the right end of the machine the size of a kitchen table. Brennan unhooked the protective cage, pulled Becky to her feet, stretched her onto the tray and fed her head first into the machine as casually as if he were shredding paper. He held her hips steady as the metal lever smashed down on her torso, then adjusted her body so that it landed on her head and neck. On the fifth strike he heard the cracking of bones again as it crushed her skull, before her body brought the whole machine shuddering to a halt.

Brennan scampered upstairs to collect his shotgun from the office and left the building without a backward glance at the corpse. Deeply satisfied, he scraped the door shut behind him and loped down the alleyway to the high street.

Forty-five

The Fishbowl looked like the storeroom it had once been, with three boxes of A4 paper piled in the left corner beyond the two chairs squeezed side by side in front of Kerr's desk and the floor crowded with bulging files stamped 'CR' followed by a four-digit number. These were the hard copies of criminal records files Justin had booked out from the Yard's main Registry and many reached back decades, with minutes attached to the left inside cover neatly written in fountain pen. The case-officer reports had been typed out on old-fashioned manual typewriters, some keys tapped so hard that they had made tiny holes in the paper.

Jack Langton and Justin Hine had spent most of the day investigating Tuesday's attack on Kerr and were working through the files while they waited for their boss to return from 1830. Like Kerr they had scrambled from home as soon as the news broke, and operatives were steadily drifting back to their desks in the main office outside, ready to stand by through the night in the hope of a breakthrough from the bomb scene. Langton had stood his helmet on top of the boxes and was sitting behind Kerr's desk; Justin had taken the chair nearest the door, with one file on the adjacent chair and another balanced on his lap.

Langton stood to vacate the desk when Kerr arrived, but Kerr told him to stay put, shifted the helmet onto the floor and perched on the boxes.

'Anything?' said Langton.

Kerr shook his head. 'Waiting for the forensics. And the Americans. Ritchie's bracing himself for the politics.'

'Is Ajay in?' asked Langton.

'Not yet.' He glanced at the files. 'What about this lot?'

'The Volvo they used to ram you is a blank. Stolen Vehicle Unit checked it out in the station yard this afternoon, or what's left of it. It's a ringer, John, cloned from two identical Volvo estates. False registration plates, obviously.'

'Unique vehicle number?'

'Destroyed. The engine block had been filed smooth.'

'And I've finished the call-round of A and Es in a ten-mile radius of Walworth,' said Justin. 'Plenty of people being bashed up in London, but no one presenting with the kind of facial fractures and burns that you dished out. The three men who almost wiped you out just disappeared into thin air. And you never heard them speak? No French accents? I mean, if we discover through Monique Thierry that DGSE have been working on Marcus Tennant, could they have organised the trap to get you out of the way?'

'It's possible. No one spoke a word. Balaclavas, no descriptions, apart from the leader's long hair. This was controlled violence. They were a team, knew exactly what to do.'

'They found out who you are and what you do, John, and this was a professional hit that went wrong,' said Langton. 'I'm still going with revenge for the Thames or Hope Farm, unless anyone else wants you dead and you're not telling us.'

Justin dumped his CR file on the floor with the rest. 'I've been through all friends of Terry Bray and his father going back three decades. Many are in prison or dead but I've isolated fourteen possibles who could have done that to you. I'm going to ask 1830 to help me identify any recent associations, if that's OK?'

'Sure, but we also need to approach this from the other end,' said Kerr. 'Run a check with prison liaison on Bray's outside calls. See if any of these names comes up.'

'I already did,' said Justin. 'They say they'll work on it over the weekend.'

'Tomorrow's Friday. Tell them I want it by close of play.'

The Fishbowl had only one fluorescent ceiling light and it had been playing up for the past couple of days, buzzing on and off, humming for seconds at a time before flickering to life again. It went off now, casting the office in a dirty grey shadow relieved only by the light from the main office, and Langton looked as if he wanted to wrench the whole unit off the ceiling. Kerr seemed scarcely to notice. 'There's a third possibility,' he said. 'What about revenge for refusing to back away from Marcus Tennant?'

'You're saying MI6 would go that far?' said Justin.

'Or surrogates acting on their instructions who, I dunno, overstepped the mark.'

'Ex special-forces types on contract,' said Langton, playing with the zip pull on his motorcycle jacket. 'It's a possibility.'

'I'm going with Julius and his friendly warning in the wine bar until we come up with something suspect,' said Kerr. 'MI6 are trying to suppress something here. Julius warns me off Marcus Tennant, you search his house and get into Diane's safe. Then he despatches his gang of ex-military psychos to have a pop at me.'

'Result? We get red-hot pics of Marcus Tennant shagging the au pair and they end up with scorched arses,' said Justin. 'Game to us.'

'And MI6 can't know about the photographs,' said Langton, 'or they would have got there first.'

'But poor Diane obviously did,' said Justin. 'And the other person who must have seen everything in that household is

Karl Sergeyev. Do you think it's worth having another chat with him, boss?'

The strip light began humming and flickering again before Kerr could answer, and Fargo's bulk blocked the light from the main office as he peered at Langton through the glass partition. Then the sticking door crashed open and he filled the frame, clearly agitated. It took him a second to locate Kerr on the wrong side of his desk. 'People's Resistance have claimed the art-gallery attack.'

Kerr did not move from the boxes. 'Genuine?'

'A call to the Samaritans again, but this time they managed to record it.'

Suddenly the scent of flowers drowned Fargo's fresh sweat as Gemma appeared at his shoulder and nudged him into the office. 'Different caller this time, guys,' she said. 'Female, youngish, as in mid to late twenties, calling from a mobile.' Gemma spoke clearly, without notes or hesitation, and got everyone's attention. 'But the Samaritans volunteer says she was reading the message and speaking under duress.'

'Can she be sure about that?' said Justin.

'We're talking the Samaritans here, Justin. She would know, wouldn't she?'

Justin reddened and held up his hands. 'Sorry.'

'The caller was reading from a script and kept tripping up. Someone was hitting her every time she stalled.'

'Finch's guys are getting a copy of the recording but Gemma's done me a draft,' said Fargo, holding up a sheet of paper. 'It includes extracts from the Anarchist Manifesto of 1895.'

'Which Alan recognised straight away,' said Gemma, admiringly.

'And stuff from the nineteenth century would obviously be even more difficult to read out if someone's holding a knife or whatever to your throat. That's all we have for now.'

'Have you told Bill Ritchie?' said Kerr.

'Yes, on the way here.'

'Ajay?'

'Commander's still a no-show.'

Langton was already zipping up his leathers and easing round the desk as Justin handed him his helmet. 'We'll get off, then, John. I've got a team on stand-by at Wandsworth.' He gave Fargo a conspiratorial wink as he squeezed past him and Gemma. 'Keep in touch, guys, and for God's sake send us a couple of targets.'

'Let's speak again in an hour,' Kerr called, as they disappeared, then looked quizzically at Fargo and Gemma, who were still lingering in the doorway. 'Just let me call Ritchie and I'll be round.'

'It's not that, actually, John.'

Kerr tapped the box beneath him. 'You waiting to steal some A4?'

Gemma stepped forward, pulled Justin's chair round for Fargo and leant against the desk, only an arm's length away from Kerr. She stayed silent, deferring to Fargo.

'John, about earlier,' said Fargo, clearing his throat. 'It wasn't what it seemed.' His awkward tone suggested it almost certainly was, and Kerr looked from one to the other, waiting.

Gemma rescued them both. She pulled her blouse straight again and crossed her ankles, left over right, stretching her tailored black trousers over a well-toned thigh. 'It's my fault, John,' she said, but her voice said it most definitely wasn't. 'I needed Alan's advice about the MI5 liaison chappie.'

Kerr frowned. 'Moxon?'

'Tim's taken to chatting me up whenever he's passing. Asked me out for a drink, the silly sod. Ridiculous, of course. I'm practically old enough to be his mother and he's definitely not my type,' she said, with a glance at Fargo. 'Anyway, I just played along, let him take me to some dive in Victoria to test him out. He was a real cheapskate, actually. Anyway, turns out there's more to our Tim than we thought.'

'Which is?'

'He's trying to recruit me, basically.'

'He's what?' MI5 had nominated Tim Moxon within days of Ajay's invitation to post a liaison officer within SO15's intelligence unit. Ex-Royal Navy, late twenties and blokeish, Moxon was exactly the type of armed-forces retread MI5 usually deployed to get alongside police.

'They already offered me a job in their comms at Thames House, remember? Which I turned down flat? So they have me on record. Tim wants me to get him on the inside track.'

Kerr was imagining Gemma Riley versus the boy from MI5. No contest. 'How?'

Gemma looked at Fargo, as if suddenly overcome by shyness.

'Access to 1830 is excluded under the protocol Ajay agreed with MI5, right?' said Fargo. 'I think he's been told to get in the loop through Gemma.'

'Why her?'

'You know what they're like, John. A written report to their line manager about every SO15 officer they meet. Keeping tabs, reporting gossip, weighing everyone up. Generally being obsessed. Moxon would have reported back that Gemma and I are, you know, on good terms.'

'Close friends,' said Gemma. She flashed Kerr a big smile and tapped Kerr on the shoulder. 'Just imagine the stuff they must have on *you*, John.'

'I think he's been told to exploit our friendship to get access to Room 1830,' said Fargo. 'Which would give them complete oversight of Ajay's command.'

Kerr shrugged. 'We've got nothing to hide, so why don't they just ask?' He stayed quiet for a moment as the strip light hummed and flickered, calculating whether Fargo was motivated by professional concern or jealousy. 'Doing it this way is certainly unethical. And an abuse of Ajay's goodwill, if it's true.'

'Of course it is,' said Fargo.

'Perhaps he just fancies you, Gemma, and he's playing the secret agent to impress. Have you considered that?'

Fargo was suddenly defensive. 'Are you saying Gemma would spin something as serious as this?'

'No.' Kerr looked up at Gemma. ' "The inside track," you said. His words or your take?'

Gemma calmly produced her iPhone from her hip pocket and held it out to him. 'Edited highlights,' she said quietly. 'You want to hear exactly how Short Arse weaves his magic?'

Forty-six

Kerr spent the night circulating between the Fishbowl, Room 1830 and Bill Ritchie's office, then drove home to Islington shortly after five to shower and change. Evidently Ajay had turned up around nine thirty, just as Kerr was about to send Melanie back to her cover address, and had gone straight to his office. Kerr's final call before leaving had been from Rich Malone, regional security officer at the US embassy in Grosvenor Square, the man responsible for the safety of the ambassador and all the embassy personnel. Malone was always telling Kerr he regarded him as his closest friend at the Yard because he could speak frankly about US security concerns without fear of kickback.

Kerr had breakfast on his terrace as the sun came up – three cups of coffee, cereal and a mushroom omelette – and arrived back at the Yard just after seven.

Malone wanted a meeting with Kerr at seven thirty and had invited him across the park because he needed their conversation to be off the record. It was a beautiful clear morning and Kerr decided to walk to the embassy as Grosvenor Square was still cordoned off and the whole area was already grid-locked. He took a call from Alan Fargo in St James's Park, halfway across the footbridge.

'John, you need to be aware of this before you see Rich Malone. Local police were called to the *Flag of Liberty* an hour ago. The address is tagged to 1830 so they gave me a call.'

Kerr stopped in his tracks and leant against the bridge handrail, looking over the lake towards Buckingham Palace but thinking of Melanie Fleming. 'What is it?'

'Female murdered in the print shop but it's nothing to do –'

'Jesus.'

'– nothing to do with Melanie. The guy who called them identified the body as Rebecca Heller. That's one of the names Melanie gave us, remember?'

A trio of brilliant white pelicans sailed beneath the bridge as Kerr swung round towards Downing Street and the Foreign Office at the other end of the lake. 'Leading light, one of the editors?'

'The informant was her boyfriend, worried because she hadn't come home.'

Kerr started walking again, rewinding Melanie's reports as he headed for the Mall. 'What are the circs?'

'Unbelievably gruesome. I'll tell you when you get back.'

'Heller wrote those pieces criticising People's Resistance, right? Any time of death yet?'

'The boyfriend found her around five and the pathologist says she hadn't been dead long. Six, maybe seven hours.'

'So, after the bombings. Hold on.' Kerr reached the Mall just as the lights changed by the Victoria Memorial and made a run for it. 'Do you think this could be some kind of revenge attack?' he said, as he reached the other side and entered Green Park.

'Whatever, keeping Melanie away from that place last night was a good call.'

'Does she know yet?'

'Not from me.'

'Have you told Ritchie?'

'He wants Melanie withdrawn immediately,' said Fargo. 'Says we can't justify the risk any longer. Weighing her deployment against the potential threats, blah, blah. And she hasn't produced much, apart from Anna Rashid. Ritchie's words, not mine, but he's got a point.'

'OK. I'll give Bill a call,' said Kerr, checking his watch and quickening his pace as he headed up the incline towards Piccadilly. 'Get hold of Melanie and fix a meet for us, will you, Al?'

'She's not going to like it.'

'So let's get it over with.'

'And I've heard back from Paris about Monique Thierry. Jean-Paul says she's not an agent of the DGSE. To the best of his knowledge. You know, "Such things can never be known with certainty." The usual cop-out.'

'Can't blame him. What about fingerprint and DNA results?'

'He's still waiting.'

'That's ridiculous.'

'It's Friday.'

The whole of Mayfair appeared to be a no-go area. To avoid the cordons Kerr had to approach Grosvenor Square from the west, skirting Chesterfield Hill and South Audley Street. He was familiar with the layout of the embassy. Since 9/11 it had been turned into a fortress, surrounded by concrete barriers against vehicle bombs and protected round the clock by police bearing Heckler & Koch semi-automatics. This morning the national flag hung limply at half mast. The police post had Kerr on their list of expected visitors, though he had to give his name twice, flash his ID and keep mentioning Malone's name before the guards would allow him into the sterile security zone between the street and inner doors. The complement of heavily armed US marines watching him dump his phone and pass through the security screen appeared to have doubled overnight, and all looked edgier than usual.

Rich Malone was waiting beside a pillar at the top of a short flight of stairs leading to the reception area, impeccably dressed in a dark suit with a Stars and Stripes pin on his lapel, tasselled shoes, white shirt and black tie. He gripped Kerr's forearm with his left hand as they shook. 'Thanks for taking the time, John. Appreciate it.' The marines stepped away as he led Kerr to his corner office on the first floor overlooking the front access and the private houses in Duke Street. He had a clear view of Roosevelt's statue in the square and, beyond that, the 9/11 memorial. The room was like the office of every other US bureaucrat that Kerr had known, with the US flag at one end of the light wood desk and the Union flag at the other. On the walls were photographs of a smiling Malone shaking hands at official functions in Washington and London and framed letters from figures in various US administrations, including a president and two VPs. On a side table a clutch of family photographs stood beside a British police officer's helmet.

There were two chairs on the other side of the desk, a conference table for six and a couple of black-leather sofas at right angles, but Malone headed for the desk, whipping off his jacket and hooking it on the back of the chair in one fluid movement. Four lights were flashing on one of the three phones; fresh coffee and chilled Coke waited on a table behind the desk, though Malone looked as if he had spent the whole night in a caffeine rush. He ignored the phone and Kerr declined the refreshment.

Malone raised the arm of his chair, then adjusted it down again. He was seriously worked up. 'John, can I give it to you straight?'

'Is there any other way?'

'The shit has well and truly hit the fan, with media outlets both sides of the Atlantic in a fucking frenzy. The political wires have been red hot all night, telegrams from State and the White House raining down on me like fucking confetti. Our secretary of state hollering at your foreign sec, plus Potus himself on the hotline to the PM. That's the president.'

'I know.' Kerr had guessed Rich Malone would not mince his words. The security chief had the mind of a trained lawyer but the language of the Boston street cop he had once been.

'I'm telling you, buddy, the pres is acting like a rabid hawk. The White House is already pissed about the Brits revealing our secret intel in terrorist extradition cases. Drumm's assassination is the icing on the cake. If your people don't get their act together fast this is going to screw the special relationship. That's the short version.'

'Sure.' This was regular Malone-speak and Kerr was unfazed. His friend could exchange diplomatic niceties with the best of them, but they were both short of time. Roughly the same age as John Kerr, the embassy's regional security officer was an intriguing mix of egghead and action man. A former director of the US State Department's Diplomatic Security programme, he had extensive operational experience in Pakistan, Vietnam and Yemen, consuming what he called the 'red meat' of the war on terror. Kerr knew Rich Malone had faced real-time global threats up close. He had helped disrupt many attacks on Americans abroad and bore a livid scar above his left eye from a joint raid to rescue kidnapped aid workers in Karachi. But Malone's anguished face told Kerr that all this paled into insignificance against the murder of his ambassador in the swankiest part of London. Both men knew the score: a catastrophe on this scale, within a stone's throw of the embassy, spelt humiliation and potential career meltdown.

'And in case you're not already aware, the fucking FBI are straining at the leash with their profilers and forensicators,' continued Malone. He picked up a pile of classified papers on his desk and dropped them again in frustration. 'Opportunistic bastards, probably already scrambling to Dulles International. The Bureau must have put a few calls in overnight because

Derek Finch just made a formal request for their assistance, probably dictated by private enemy number one.'

'Sorry?'

'The legal fucking attaché.'

'Right. Well, I hadn't heard anything yet.' Kerr drew another breath, but too late as Malone rolled onwards.

'This is going to make everyone's life hell. And the irony is that the stupid exhibition was not pro-war. No way. We sponsored it to highlight the *horrors* of battle. This was about the so-called "cost in blood and treasure", John, all that crap you Brits love to go on about. Hands across the ocean, the full works.'

'What was your security briefing to the ambassador?'

'You know what Drumm was like. Always insisting on openness to the public, expat as well as Brit, not just the champagne and cigars set. He was into his full-on liberal-man-of-the-people shit and I had to go along with it. Christ, he even made your protection boys wait outside by the limo.' Malone linked his fingers. He had a neat gold signet ring on his right hand, British fashion. 'Here's the deal, John. You take these three actions together, right? We have the American wife of a British cabinet minister brutalised, the slaying of an eminent judge, who knew the priorities of the US war on terror, and now the ambassador and Mrs Drumm. I've gotta tell you, the hawks inside the Washington Beltway are already dressing these up as a concerted attack on America. And do you want to know what they're saying? The Brits are either unable or unwilling to do anything about it.'

'Which is total crap.'

'Sure. But to fight them off I need to know what the fuck is going down here, John. Unofficially, before the sun comes up in Washington. Is that OK with you?'

'Of course.'

'Great.' Malone swung around to refill his coffee, poured some for Kerr in a giant red mug without asking and slid it across the desk.

Over the next five minutes Kerr talked him through the Bull's evidential investigation, acknowledging the lack of evidence or intelligence about People's Resistance, but keeping Melanie's deployment to himself.

Malone's expression was not encouraging. 'But this is beyond a bunch of British radicals acting alone, right?'

'Probably.'

Malone sipped his coffee and stared through the window across the empty square. 'And what about the guys who stole our gold? We briefed very few people about that consignment transiting London. I checked and we told only four officials on the British side. And hardly anyone knew it was stashed in that depository. Do you think there's a connection?'

'We're looking at every option.'

'Spoken like a diplomat. John, you're the guy who killed those hoodlums on the river, for Christ's sake. Don't you know?'

'Only the shooter. The other one drowned.'

'If you say so. Who's counting?' Malone gave a short laugh. 'The bullion robbery back in March was as political as the other attacks, and you know it, with everything directed against America. So, like I keep asking your guys, how the hell did it leak out? No one's getting back to me with anything I want to hear. Is anyone your side of the Pond seriously looking at the security breach? Be straight with me, John. You're the guys on the ground. What's the story here?'

'It's like I told you the day after it happened, Rich. We're checking every possibility.'

'Keeping stuff back, you mean.'

'Absolutely not,' said Kerr, as the photographs of Marcus Tennant having sex with Monique Thierry flashed into his mind.

'So tell me this.' Malone seemed to change up a gear, as if the fresh coffee had kicked in. He made another unnecessary adjustment to the armrest and immediately cancelled it. 'Why didn't you include the fact that Marcus Tennant was a fucking spy in Washington?'

Kerr drank his coffee and kept his voice neutral. 'Who told you that?' he said, as if it might be untrue.

'And sneaking back to the States as a director for Aircore? Don't bullshit me, John. Did you really believe I wouldn't have done my homework on this? What are the British hiding? Diane Tennant was an American citizen and we're supposed to be friends, on the same fucking side. Why are you holding out on me?'

'I'm not. And are you being completely up front with me, Rich? Giving me everything you have?' Kerr looked his friend in the eye, calculating whether Malone also knew about the hostile pitch to Tennant during his US posting.

'There'd better not be a spook connection here.' Malone sounded almost resigned, as if Kerr had just confirmed every-thing for him. 'I'm telling you straight, John. Another British espionage scandal damaging the US, and the special relation-ship goes down the toilet.'

'That's just press speculation,' said Kerr, with an attempt at levity. 'The usual mid-term wind-up.'

'You think what you want to think,' said Malone, eyeing Kerr levelly. 'I'm telling you what the director of the fucking CIA is telling me.'

Forty-seven

Obeying Kerr's order, Melanie had spent the night at her cover address. She had bought a Chinese takeaway, then bundled her sheets and pillowcases into a carrier bag and walked round the corner to Clean Dream, her local launderette, to wash away all traces of Jez. With the sheets and duvet airing over the armchair and table she had lounged on the bed's uneven, stained mattress glued to the breaking news about the massacre in Berkeley Square. Exhausted and distressed, still fully clothed, she had drifted into a fitful doze around four o'clock until the building's ancient plumbing gurgled and flushed into life again just before seven.

She washed her face, cleaned her teeth, made the bed and hurried downstairs, desperate to escape to her own home. Alan Fargo's call reached her as she was slamming the main door and she told him to hold until she reached the privacy of the Renault. A school bus swept past as he broke the news about the claim from People's Resistance and she hoped she had misheard. She made him tell her three times, and each repetition was like a punch in the stomach, winding her and crushing her voice.

'You all right, Mel?'

'Yeah.'

'I'll have more later.'

Melanie sat quite still, stunned with guilt for the people who had died. It was possible that Anna Rashid had brought her to the brink of People's Resistance two nights earlier, and Melanie was already convincing herself she could somehow have prevented this massacre. The tears flowed as she started the engine and pulled away to the junction with the high street, forcing her way into the busy stream of traffic. Melanie felt grief for the murdered but also an acute sense of loss from having let Rashid out of her sight. She had never suffered a close bereavement but imagined it must be like this. Outside Clean Dream she inadvertently cut up a courier van and had to pull in to collect herself. The driver braked alongside her to yell abuse but raced away as soon as he saw her tears. Melanie sat slumped behind the wheel, weeping and unable to function as Radio 4 confirmed what Alan Fargo had just told her.

After a few moments she seemed to find some inner reserve of strength. Switching off the radio she locked the car and ran into the newsagent next to the launderette to buy chocolate for the children and two Snickers bars, one each for her and Rob. As she queued to pay, every headline screamed at her about the bombings, mocking her and compounding her sense of failure. With this tiny impulse buy, Melanie realised she was trying to protect the only certainty left in her life.

The journey home to Muswell Hill was quicker than usual because she ignored the speed cameras, raced up a bus lane and ran a couple of red lights. Within fifty minutes she had secured the Renault in the lock-up and was hurrying home through the park. As she turned into her street one of the neighbours, Shelley, spotted her and jangled her keys as she tucked herself into a bright red coupé. Shelley worked for a property developer in Hampstead and was glamorous in her designer suit, white blouse and charm bracelet, with long, glossy hair, proper makeup and expensive shoes. Jealousy and embarrassment pulsed through Melanie, still in the clothes she had worn for the past twenty hours. She wanted to be invisible until she was safely inside her own home. Rob had always said Shelley was a stuck-up bitch, but now Melanie would have given anything to change places with her.

The house was silent again but the kettle was still warm, so she guessed Rob must be collecting the boys from his mother's. She refilled it, flicked the switch, wandered through the downstairs rooms, then made herself a coffee and took it upstairs to the bedroom. Lying open on the bed was their largest suitcase, the one they used for their annual summer holiday. Puzzled, Melanie methodically worked through her rehabilitation routine from undercover officer to working mum: underwear into the laundry basket, clothes into the bin liner, personal items into the canvas bag, everything to the back of the wardrobe; Aerosmith CD, bubble bath, soak, revive.

She heard the key in the front door as she was applying her makeup. It opened rapidly and slammed shut. 'That you, darling?' She padded downstairs to find Rob standing in the kitchen with his back to her. He was in jeans and a white T-shirt, supporting himself against the sink and staring through the window, apparently distracted by a pair of finches on the bird feeder just beyond the terrace. She crept up to him and wrapped her arms around his shoulders. 'Gotcha.'

Melanie thought she had surprised him but he seemed to have known she was there all along. Perhaps he had checked the kettle, too. Rob was surprisingly agile as he pushed himself back from the sink and swung round to her, making her step back in alarm. His body seemed to expand as he straightened and his face was like thunder, wiping the bright smile from hers as completely as a rain cloud blocking out the sun. 'What's happened to the kids?' she said at once, mistaking his anger for anxiety. 'Rob, what's wrong?'

Rob moved so fast that she did not even have time to flinch. Fixed on his face, she never saw his right hand swing out and make contact with the side of her head. He used the palm of his hand, not his fist, but she saw stars and stumbled into the kitchen table so violently that Brenda's little vase of fresh flowers crashed to the floor.

'Now look what you've bloody done,' he yelled.

Stooping to pick up the broken glass, Melanie only just managed to stop herself apologising. Suddenly she felt dizzy and hauled herself to the nearest chair, leaving the shards of glass on the table. 'Rob, what is it?'

He looked awkward for a second before resorting to pure anger again. 'I want you to tell me who you've been screwing.'

'Are you insane?'

He took a step forward and slapped her again, hard. 'My dick tells me you've been bringing your work home.'

'What the hell are you talking about?'

'I've woken with my crotch on fire, Melanie.'

'It's probably sweat. Heat rash.'

'I'm going with STD. You've given me a sexually transmitted disease, you filthy whore.'

'Don't be ridiculous.'

'And now you're going to tell me who you've been with.' Rob loomed over her, T-shirt untucked, belly drooping over his Levi's, a gross, angry shadow of the man he had been before she shot him. 'Is it him, that bloody John Kerr? Have you been fucking the boss?'

'No one. Just you.'

'Not good enough,' he shouted. 'Try again.'

For the second time that morning Melanie broke down in tears. She swept the broken glass back onto the floor and banged her forehead onto the table, sobbing uncontrollably. 'I'm sorry,' was all she could whisper.

'You what?'

She flinched, fearing he would hit her again, then cushioned her head on her forearms. 'I just love you. I had to do it,

Rob.' She sensed his face close to hers as he strained to hear. 'It was impossible. No choice. I had to, to keep cover.'

Then his laugh raided her right ear, harsh as sandpaper. 'To get some, you mean. The sex you haven't been getting from me. Don't give me that just-doing-what-I-have-to-do bollocks.'

'It's one man, Rob,' she whispered. 'One time.'

'Of course it is. And he means nothing to you, right? Who is he?'

'It doesn't matter.'

The laugh again. 'You don't even know, do you?'

Melanie sat bolt upright, so rapidly that this time it was Rob who recoiled. 'Don't you watch the bloody news?' she screamed back. 'Do you really have no idea at all of the things I have to do?'

He bent down and yelled into her face, 'So now's your chance to tell me.'

'Christ, you're in the job. People are still dying from those bombs last night. Poisoned to death.'

'And what's that got to do with you?'

'Can't you see how vicious their campaign's become? He's in the group. Or knows someone. He's going to lead me to them. I can crack this, Rob. I can destroy it, stop these terrible murders.'

'And you're going to keep fucking him until he talks. What a sacrifice.'

'It was one time and I'm so, so sorry. I had to do it to survive out there. To save lives.'

'Like last night, you mean. What's the body count so far? Very impressive.'

She peered up at him through her tears. 'You bastard.'

Rob stepped back and leant against the sink again. 'And what about our lives? Me and the children?' He crossed his arms, suddenly cool and businesslike, his voice calm and measured. The lightning change of demeanour terrified

Melanie even more than his rage: it showed he had everything worked out. 'What is it with you, Melanie? You already fucked up my leg and my career. Did you have to destroy our marriage as well?'

'Rob, it's not like that.' Sobbing again, Melanie stood up and walked to him. 'I'm so sorry.' She held out her arms to him but he pushed her away and wove round her to the kitchen door, grabbing his keys from the hook. 'I'm leaving now to get myself checked out.'

'You're not going to our doctor?'

'Don't worry, I won't embarrass you as well. Walk-in clinic off the Internet. Then I'm going to the range. This afternoon I'm seeing a solicitor.'

Melanie thought of the suitcase upstairs. 'Rob, please don't leave us.'

'*Me?*' He laughed again, loudly this time. 'Lose all this? I'm not going anywhere. I left the case out for *you*. I want you gone by the time I get back.'

'You can't do that,' she shouted frantically, as he turned into the hall. 'What about the children?'

'Mum will look after them, like she always has,' he called over his shoulder.

She hurried after him. 'When can I come and see them?'

At the front door he swung round to face her. 'You don't get it, do you? This is the end. I don't want you in my house again.'

Forty-eight

It took Melanie less than ten minutes to empty the bin liner
and change back into her work clothes. Within another twenty
she had packed the rest of her life into the suitcase and
bumped it downstairs into the hall. She opened the front
door and then, on an impulse, went into the dining room to
take her favourite photograph from the sideboard. It showed
the boys in their swimming trunks on a beach in Devon,
laughing with their arms around each other as they squinted
into the sun. She slipped it into the zipped compartment of
the suitcase and left home, setting the alarm and double-
locking the front door behind her. As she wheeled the case
down the street towards the park she bumped into the old
lady from two doors up on her way back from the supermarket, pulling her squeaking shopping basket. The old lady
beamed as Melanie wiped her eyes and put on a brave face.
'Going somewhere nice, dear?' she called, as Melanie found
her smile.

One of the plastic wheels snapped on the rutted path as
Melanie trundled the case through the street behind Cherry
Tree Wood and she had to carry it for the last stretch to the
lock-up, about twenty houses away. Breathless, she used
more force than usual on the metal up-and-over door and a
couple of dogs started barking as it screeched open. Heaving

the case into the boot of the Renault, she reversed out and headed into London for her meeting with John Kerr at eleven thirty.

An important part of Dodge's work as head of the source unit was to identify safe premises for debriefing undercover officers and agents away from the Yard or other official offices. Over a couple of years he had cultivated five trusted hoteliers willing to make rooms available to the team at short notice. The quality of the hotel depended on the value of the asset, and meetings with Melanie Fleming always rated the top end of the scale. The boutique hotel in Marble Arch which Kerr had chosen for that morning's meeting was called the Pelican, tucked away behind the Odeon cinema near Seymour Street between a classy curry restaurant and a private house converted into solicitors' offices.

Because Melanie had time on her hands, she swung into Park Lane and threw a left into a maze of side-streets towards Berkeley Square. Diverted traffic was very heavy so she parked on a meter off Hill Street and wandered as close as she could to the police cordon, tears rolling down her cheeks as she watched the emergency responders calmly going about their recovery work.

She was five minutes early for the meeting as she drove through a narrow arch into the Pelican's small car park. The hotel had only twenty rooms and the manager generally made available Suite 202, a corner unit on the first floor looking onto the car park, with a king-size bed, two-seater sofa, armchair and writing desk. A 'Do Not Disturb' sign hung crookedly on the handle and the dead bolt had been extended to hold the door ajar. Anticipating a routine one-to-one catch-up with Kerr, Melanie was surprised to find Alan Fargo sitting behind the ornate cherrywood desk with an A4 pad and pen at the ready while Kerr lounged on the dark brown sofa, his navy linen jacket lying crumpled on the bed.

Her immediate thought was that Kerr had brought Fargo along to brief her on the bombings, perhaps even to feed her leads from the identification of Anna Rashid. Coffee was on the table in front of the sofa and the two men had already helped themselves. They were sitting in silence, which was unusual, and their serious expressions immediately put Melanie on alert. Fargo had not seen her since the start of her operation and stood to kiss her warmly on both cheeks. 'We're missing you in 1830.'

'Tell them the feeling's not mutual,' was all she could manage as she gave him a hug. 'What's the latest?'

'You're tired,' said Kerr. 'Did you stay at the flat or go home?'

'Spent the night in Dalston watching TV, when you know I should have been at the *Flag*.'

Kerr had stayed on the sofa and gave Melanie the impression he was watching her more closely than usual. They had obviously left the armchair for her, so she spoiled their plan by perching on the edge of the bed. 'Is there anything more on the claim?'

'Welfare first.' He gestured to the coffee. 'Help yourself. How are things at home?'

'Fine.'

'Rob?'

'Busy doing his physio.' Melanie shrugged. 'His mum's helping out with the kids, which is great. Nothing to say, really. Everything hunky-dory.'

Kerr stayed silent, looking at her, so she bounced off the bed and poured a cup of coffee to break the tension and avoid eye contact. She caught sight of herself in the mirror over the writing desk and saw that Kerr was right. She looked shattered, eyes red-rimmed, cheeks deathly white, misery etched in her face. She held up the cafetière, offering them a refill.

'Anything you want to raise with me?' said Kerr, declining the coffee. This was standard procedure when Melanie was working undercover but today his tone was different, more formal than the usual jokey to and fro about her home life. The bruise on his forehead made him look battle weary, and an image flashed into her head of Rob yelling terrible accusations down the phone at him.

'Nothing.' Melanie topped up Fargo's coffee and went back to the bed, carefully balancing her cup and saucer clear of the white duvet. 'Mayfair is in meltdown but everything in the Fleming household is perfect. Absolutely bloody brilliant. So what does Alan have for me?'

With a nod from Kerr, Fargo ran through the intelligence about Anna Rashid, the failed asylum appeal of her lover, Parvez, and the role of Judge Hugh Selwyn in the rejection of his asylum appeal. 'Which gives Anna Rashid a powerful motive,' said Fargo. 'I just want to say we think this woman is gold dust. Great work, Mel.'

'And that's just for starters,' said Melanie, even more mystified by Fargo's presence now, since he was merely repeating the same information they had already discussed on the phone. 'I'm going to get you a whole lot more.' She tried to smile at him, but he was suddenly concentrating hard on his notes.

Kerr cleared his throat and drained his coffee. 'Have you heard about Rebecca Heller?'

'Becky?' Melanie looked from one to the other. 'I'll be getting the full lowdown tonight,' she said ambiguously, keeping her voice casual.

'She's been murdered, Mel. Tortured, beaten, electrocuted, then crushed to death.'

'Before or after the bombings?' said Melanie, her mind racing.

'Probably between ten and midnight.'

'So People's Resistance will have done her, too. She was always slagging them off. I'm right on top of it.' She slid forward on the bed, as if she was about to run from the room and find the killers within the hour. 'This is our opportunity, John.'

'It's not going to happen.' Kerr was shaking his head. 'You won't be going back to the *Flag*, Mel. Not tonight, not again.'

'Is that why you called me here?' Melanie was already on edge and Kerr's words struck her like an electric shock. 'All that crap about my home life and you're withdrawing me anyway? If you had any bottle I could have gone to the *Flag* last night and prevented this.'

'Or got yourself killed. This has become way too dangerous, Mel. I tasked you to gather intelligence on People's Resistance as a domestic group. To take a look and report back. That's what we agreed, remember? That's the deal Ajay signed up to.'

'Which is exactly what I've done. What I *am* doing.'

'The art gallery has changed everything. Highly sophisticated devices freaking everyone out on both sides of the Atlantic.'

'And you want to take your only asset out of the equation.' She glared at them both. 'I can't believe I'm hearing this. It's pathetic.'

'The scale of this campaign goes far beyond domestic extremism. Anyone can see that.'

'Whatever. But the claims are from People's Resistance, and I'm almost on them. You can't withdraw me now. This is insane. I can get to them through Anna Rashid, believe me. I'm almost there.'

'No. You've done brilliantly but the undercover operation is no longer viable,' said Kerr. 'That's the bottom line. I'm not prepared to risk your life against these odds.'

'That's why you brought Alan along, is it? So he could give

me a gold star before you sack me?' She turned to Fargo. 'Is that it, Al? Is this the cue for you to offer me my old job back?'

'No,' said Kerr calmly. 'It's the point where I tell you it's just too dangerous to leave you in the field. My priorities are you, your husband and children. I'm not prepared to place you in even greater jeopardy, Melanie. End of.'

'And I'm telling you it's mad to pull the plug just when I'm getting somewhere.' Melanie knew she sounded desperate but she could not help herself. 'For God's sake, you have to let me do this. You have nothing else.'

They fell silent. Outside a chambermaid was making her way down the corridor, tapping quietly on the door of the adjacent room. 'Housekeeping.' The voice and knock sounded small and meek, and made Melanie realise how strident she must sound. A stroppy bitch, getting what she deserved. Kerr was looking away, so she turned to Fargo again. 'That's right, Al, isn't it?'

'We're looking at other options to get to Anna Rashid,' said Kerr, before Fargo could speak.

'Which means you've got the square root of bugger-all.'

'Stop wasting your breath,' said Kerr. 'This was Bill Ritchie's decision at seven o'clock this morning, and I think he's right.'

'After a sleepless night?' Melanie bounced to her feet again, changing the dynamic to try another tack. 'Look, I can imagine the pressure back at the Yard. But that doesn't mean you have to act without thinking this through.' She saw the hollow left by her body in the soft duvet and plumped it up, just as she would have done at home. It was another distraction to avoid confrontation and gave her time to bring her voice under control. 'Just leave me in place for a few more days, John,' she said, as calmly as if she were asking for annual leave. 'I can soft-pedal, no problem. I'll crack this for you. I promise.'

Kerr looked her in the eye, and she could tell he was

unmoved. 'Start clearing your cover address today,' he said. 'I want everything done and dusted by Monday morning.'

'That's such a rubbish decision and I thought you were my biggest supporter.'

'I'm your boss,' said Kerr, in a harsh tone he rarely used, which upset her even more. 'Take some leave with the family or start back in the office next week, whichever you prefer. But I'm calling the operation right now. Understood?'

'No,' said Melanie, the tears welling up again. 'You have no idea, do you?'

'What?'

'The sacrifice I've made to get you this far.' Her voice finally cracked as she dumped her cup and saucer on the table. She stood over them, hands on hips, glaring from one to the other. 'How much it's cost me. Do you seriously think I'm going to give up now?'

Kerr started to wriggle up from the sofa, ready to say something, but Melanie was already storming from the room.

Forty-nine

The sun grew stronger as the day progressed, turning the cloudless sky a deeper blue. By mid-afternoon it had become one of the hottest days in August, making life even more difficult for the rescue workers in their protective clothing as they recovered the final bodies from the art gallery.

In Essex, thirty miles to the north-east of Mayfair, the temperature was even higher for Anna Rashid and Danny Brennan until they reached the shelter of Epping Forest. Rashid led the way from a tiny pull-in obscured by trees and bushes on the north side of Earl's Path, nearly a mile from the main Epping New Road. They walked steadily into the forest for twenty minutes. As they penetrated deeper, their pace was slowed by undergrowth, overgrown bushes and brambles, until the forest's canopy obliterated the sun. Fallen leaves from many autumns past provided a spongy carpet that deadened their footsteps in the still air and, like some vast soundproofed room, the forest seemed to absorb every other noise apart from birdsong and the cracking of deadwood beneath their feet.

In preparation for the fourth People's Resistance action, Brennan was carrying plastic bags containing watermelons and, hidden beneath his coat, a folded, specially adapted Barnett Ghost CRT crossbow, lightweight, powerful and accurate, with a refined scope and fifteen twenty-inch arrows.

Neither of them spoke a word, for Rashid was still seething with fury at him, letting branches spring back in his face as she negotiated their path.

Eventually she brought them into a clearing and paused, listening for signs of life. Shards of late-afternoon sun pierced the trees in this peaceful place, relieving the gloom and bringing colour to the foliage. Caught in the angled sunlight, a sapling three metres high had taken root close to an ancient oak. Three branches diverged at chest height from the younger tree, forming an inverted tripod, and the oak's enormous trunk provided a perfect backstop. 'This will do,' she said, as Brennan dropped the bags beside it. She took the largest watermelon, lodged it in the branches and walked back forty paces, which brought her to the very edge of the clearing. She shifted to left and right until she found a direct line of sight through the undergrowth. 'That's his head. See what you can do.'

She stood aside as Brennan unfolded the Ghost and loaded it with one of the arrows. He had never used a crossbow before but seemed completely at ease with his new weapon of destruction. His first shot missed and she heard the arrow thud into the oak tree, setting the forest's canopy alive with the squawking and flapping of birds taking flight. Rashid walked back to check the accuracy. 'Three inches high. Again,' she said, her voice echoing, then immediately falling away as she stepped aside to study his accuracy and stay alert for dog walkers. Brennan's next arrow came without warning and buried itself in the oak tree slightly to the left, but the third, less than half a minute later, hit the fruit dead centre, spattering red flesh and seeds all around. She took out another melon and had scarcely stepped away before the fourth arrow thwacked into the tree slightly to the right of the target, missing her chest by less than a metre. 'Wait for my signal,' she called to him, irritated.

The previous evening Rashid had routinely reported via the electronic dead-letterbox that Brennan had deployed to Berkeley Square. A single, urgent direction had been awaiting her: on no account was she to approach the broken-down Vauxhall Corsa she had abandoned in the street. Early that morning, as news of the art-gallery bombings flooded the airwaves, she had taken the tube to pick up her replacement vehicle. The twelve-year-old silver Fiat Punto had been parked exactly where they had said it would be, in the far corner of an open-air car park behind the Grove in Stratford, outside Morrison's supermarket, with the ignition key balanced on the rear nearside tyre and watermelons hidden in the boot with the crossbow.

She had driven straight to the safe house, arriving before eight with the crossbow in its canvas bag to find Brennan sprawled on the bed, glued to breaking news on Sky. He had shaved his head again during the night and seemed pumped up, like a fitness fanatic on steroids. He had flicked off the TV the moment she reached the top of the ladder, which she had thought odd, and pestered her for sex before she had even sat down. Only afterwards, when she had turned the TV back on, seen the news about Becky's murder and noticed a missed call from Jez on her mobile, had the truth fallen into place.

Testing the crossbow mechanism by the workbench, Brennan had admitted everything straight away, describing his attack in detail as Rashid slumped back on the pillows in disbelief, her mind flooded by the implications.

'Yeah, well, they won't be slagging us off any more. Or using that rubbish printing press again.' He had laughed, his eyes alight. 'Not after it's eaten her for breakfast.'

'You don't get it, do you?' she had shouted at him.

'Get what? What's it to you? All the time you've been moaning how Becky and the *Flag* were such a pain in the arse,' he had yelled back at her. 'So now I've sorted it. What else is there to get?'

'Only that the cops are going to be all over the *Flag* from now on. Which means they'll be looking for me, 'cos I'm one of the people that hangs out there and Sacha will have given them my name. And Jez's, and everyone else's who visits the place,' she had said, suddenly understanding the reason for the summons to the urgent meeting. 'And if the cops get to me the mission is over.'

Brennan had been unrepentant. 'Join the club.'

'Except I can't hide away,' she had said, climbing off the bed to get dressed. 'Do you really think they'll let you get away with this? Or me?'

'The cops are stupid.'

'You don't understand.' She had taken his face in her hands. 'Danny, I'm not talking about the cops.'

Brennan's next four shots hit the targets dead centre. Rashid led him back to the car in silence and dropped him at Woodford Underground station on the Central Line, seven stops from Bethnal Green. 'So who am I going to kill this time?' he said, as she waited for him to open the door.

'No idea.'

'Or you're just not telling me. Where, then?'

'You've screwed everything up, Danny.' Rashid looked sideways at him, fear coursing through her. 'Now we both have to watch our backs.'

Fifty

Anticipating that his meeting with Karl Sergeyev was going to be difficult, Kerr arranged to meet him away from the Yard. He told himself this was to protect Sergeyev, but Kerr also needed privacy to cover his own tracks and ease his conscience. He had told no one that Sergeyev had been sleeping with Diane Tennant because sex with a principal's wife was career dynamite and Kerr would have to disclose how he knew. And in a way he could not define, neutral territory made him feel easier about having spent Wednesday night in bed with Sergeyev's wife.

That morning Sergeyev had returned with Marcus Tennant from his constituency in Cheshire and was still at the Ministry of Defence, due to escort Tennant home to Hadley that evening. At Kerr's suggestion they met outside a coffee bar behind the ancient walls of the Jewel Tower, on the opposite side of Abingdon Street from the Palace of Westminster. It was a private, sunken oasis of calm beside the ruins of a medieval moat and quay a few metres from the main road, between Westminster Abbey and, just visible to the right, the grassed area where TV journalists camped out to interview politicians before the lunchtime news deadline.

They arrived at the same time, Sergeyev cool and relaxed, immaculate in a sharp two-piece navy suit with the jacket buttoned, Kerr in needle cords and open-necked shirt, jacket hooked over his shoulder. Kerr was battered and bruised after a sleepless night and two very difficult meetings, and had been brooding about Melanie all day.

The area was tourist free, so they sat on a bench in the late-afternoon sunshine with sealed paper cups of Americano coffee. Sergeyev had not bothered with the corrugated insulating strip.

'So how is he?' said Kerr.

'Terrible. The ambassador was a good friend, and not just on the embassy circuit. The wives, too. Diane used to meet Susan Drumm privately for lunch. I often escorted her to and from the restaurant. This has hit the boss very badly, John, really magnified his grief.'

Calculating that Sergeyev would be expecting an update on the murder investigation, Kerr dived straight for the bottom line. His objective was to induce Sergeyev to admit his affair with Diane, but he started with an easier question from the information Nancy had given him. 'How long have you been sleeping with Tennant's diary secretary?'

Sergeyev sat back in surprise. 'Who says so?' Kerr waited for the rebuttal, the throwing up of hands, but Sergeyev recovered quickly, calmly sipping his coffee and sliding Kerr a sideways look. 'John, who told you that?'

In Kerr's long experience, confrontation about a lesser offence sometimes elicited an admission of something more serious, provided there was an atmosphere of trust. He could almost hear Sergeyev's brain whirring as he tried to work out Kerr's source. With denial crossed off the list, Sergeyev could have opted for admission, regret, justification or meek acceptance of Kerr's rebuke. In the end he reverted to bravado plus mitigation. 'Is that the only reason you wanted to see me? For a lesson in morals? That woman was chasing *me*, for God's sake.'

'Anything else you want to tell me?'

'No. I'm not seeing her any more. What are you talking about?'

'Don't act the innocent, Karl. Do you really think that's all I know?'

Sergeyev was watching Kerr all the time but his expression had suddenly darkened and there were shadows behind his eyes.

'Karl, how many years have we been friends?'

'Are you saying too many?' he said quietly.

'I'm trying to protect you.'

Sergeyev gave a nervous laugh. 'And I haven't got a clue—'

'Yes, you have. And I want to hear it from your lips, not a secretary with a grudge because you dumped her.'

'And if she does? You going to report me?'

'No. I want to look out for you. But first you have to be straight with me.'

Sergeyev stayed silent as Kerr's BlackBerry vibrated. Kerr had been hoping for a return call from Melanie but it was a routine text from Jack Langton. He tapped a quick reply and stood to leave. 'I'm talking about saving your career, Karl.' He took a last sip of coffee and ditched the cup. 'Give me a call if you need my help, any time.'

'This is about Diane, right?' Kerr had already reached the perimeter of the moat, three metres away. The confidence had evaporated from Sergeyev's voice and, as Kerr turned, his body seemed to sag on the bench. Kerr sat down again and looked him in the eye. 'Like I said, you tell me.'

Sergeyev leant forward, away from Kerr's gaze, rotating the coffee cup as he spoke. 'All right. Diane and I became good friends, more than we should have been.'

Kerr grabbed his upper arm. 'Let's cut the crap. You were sleeping with her. Enjoying a fully fledged adulterous relationship with your principal's wife. Right?'

Sergeyev sighed. His voice was almost plaintive, as he said, 'It happened just before Christmas after I brought Diane home from a lunch with Susan Drumm. I wasn't expecting it and neither was she. She had a friend in Knightsbridge who let us use her flat. We never used the house after that first time.'

'When did you last have sex with her?'

'I think the Tuesday, a couple of days before she died.'

'Oh, brilliant.'

'It's not what you think, John.'

Kerr seized Sergeyev's cup and took a swig of coffee. 'Really?'

'Diane was deeply unhappy. Whatever the boss might say in public or private about his wonderful home life, he was very cruel to her. He had always been unfaithful, even before their marriage. Didn't even care when Diane found out he was shagging their au pair.'

Kerr locked eyes with Sergeyev. 'But Yvette was much more than a domestic, wasn't she?'

'Who told you that?' he said again.

'Who told *you*?' said Kerr, passing Sergeyev's coffee back. 'Right now I'm holding your career in the palm of my hand, Karl, so don't piss me about.'

Sergeyev gave a sigh. 'Diane told me Yvette had infiltrated her house to target Marcus. She believed he had been caught in a honey trap.'

'Her word or yours?'

'Diane's. She said someone had sent Marcus some incriminating photographs. Dozens of them. She found them and secretly kept a few back before Marcus could destroy them. For insurance in case they got divorced, I suppose.'

'Did she show them to you?'

'No, of course not. She only told me about them on our last afternoon together.'

'Where are they now?'

Sergeyev shook his head. 'I hoped Justin might find them during the house search, if they even exist.'

'Assuming they do, who do you think was controlling Yvette?'

'No idea.'

They sat quietly for a moment as a young woman in a business suit approached them, heading for the coffee shop. Kerr watched her eyes flicker past him and alight for a second longer than necessary on Sergeyev. 'When did Diane find out about the photographs?'

'Not sure,' said Sergeyev. 'Two, three months ago. And, like I said, she never let Marcus know she had kept some hidden.'

'Who did she say was blackmailing Marcus?'

'She didn't, otherwise I'd have told you, wouldn't I?' he said, looking Kerr in the eye. 'All she said was that Marcus had begun behaving strangely after the photographs arrived. Mysterious calls at home on his personal line, disappearing for secret meetings without telling the protection team.'

'Any specifics? Names, places?'

'All Diane ever said was if he could be so unfaithful to her all her married life he could betray anyone or anything.' He shrugged. 'That's as far as it went. She was very uptight that day. Making the whole thing up, for all I know.'

Kerr immediately thought back to his conversation with Rich Malone that morning. *Another British espionage scandal damaging the US, and the special relationship goes down the toilet.* 'Did she do that a lot when she was with you? Invent things?'

'Look, Diane wanted to destroy Marcus, leave the marriage and start again with me. She wanted us to move to the States, marry, have children, all that stuff. She was drinking too much vodka and going a bit crazy. She would have said anything to damage him.'

'Do you know if she told anyone else about this?'

'She used to talk a lot to her dad. He's a big-shot corporate chief and she may have said something to him. She told me he despised Marcus as a British upper-class prick.'

Shadows were slanting across the little square now and they sat in silence for a moment, looking out beyond the ruined walls to the Houses of Parliament opposite. 'And why didn't you report this up the chain, Karl?'

Sergeyev bounced straight back and Kerr guessed he had been anticipating the question. 'Report what? Complaints from an embittered wife I've been screwing for the past nine months? That I think the defence secretary is being blackmailed? For what? Secrets? Money? That he's a traitor?' Sergeyev swirled his remaining coffee, then tossed the cup in a perfect arc to the bin on the other side of the terrace, three metres away. It was a risky shot, but he got away with it. 'There was nothing specific, John. I'm no admirer of Marcus Tennant, but no way was I going to use pillow talk to sabotage his career.'

'Or your own, of course. But there was no need to admit the affair. You could have said Diane confided in you because you have high security clearance.'

'Not possible. That secretary in the private office would have grassed on me,' said Sergeyev, shaking his head. 'She's one hell of a jealous woman. Anyway, I had no way to test what Diane was saying. And can you imagine the political firestorm this would ignite, especially across the Atlantic? Is it really worth starting all that for the sake of a rumour?'

'You could have come to me.'

'I did try to point you in the right direction. That's why I told you about Tennant and Yvette, helped you get inside the house. If there was anything in what Diane had told me I knew you'd get to the truth. Alan Fargo would join the dots, like he always does.' Sergeyev paused and leant forward again, elbows on his knees, big hands clasped beneath his chin. 'It's like this,

John. Diane Tennant was a beautiful woman, but lonely and drinking too much. Kind spirits can have ulterior motives, can't they? What could be more dangerous? I grieve for her, truly. But I believe she was using me to destroy her husband. That's what I felt. Still do.'

'Did you love her?'

'Diane said her dad would give me a job in his company. But it was never going to happen. Things might be finished between Nancy and me, but no way will I leave my kids.'

'What would Nancy do if she found out?'

'Kill me,' he said, as his BlackBerry vibrated and he checked the screen, then his watch. 'Change of plan. The boss has to be at Downing Street for five. I should get back.'

Just before they reached the main road Sergeyev touched Kerr's arm. 'John, do you think I should ask for a transfer from protection?'

'No. I want you to assume the very worst about Marcus Tennant, watch him like a hawk and give me everything you find out. This stays between you and me. No more secrets between friends, understood?'

'I owe you,' he said, holding out his hand. Kerr smiled but Sergeyev was deadly serious. 'How did you find out?'

Images of Nancy Sergeyev flashed into Kerr's mind. He saw her in her dress at the bar in the restaurant, naked in bed as he made love to her, leaning on the pillow as they talked quietly into the night. 'I heard it from you, Karl,' he said, holding out his hand. 'Just now, when you decided to do the right thing.'

Fifty-one

For the meeting with her controller Anna Rashid had been summoned to Day Break, the fancy coffee shop near Highgate Cemetery codenamed Jade. The shop was due to close at six and Anna saw only four other customers. By the window a mid-sixties couple in tennis whites sat with coffee and cupcakes, laughing with each other like models for a retirement ad. Further inside, opposite the counter, a mother and daughter were sharing a fruit smoothie. The child was no more than five or six, cheeks flushed from a party, and a red helium-filled balloon tethered to her chair floated near the ceiling.

Only after returning the French proprietor's nod of welcome did Rashid spot the elderly gentleman in the far corner and realise that, for the first time, her controller had breached his own rule by arriving first. Peter was wearing his navy double-breasted suit and drinking a yellow smoothie identical to the little girl's. A chocolate chip cookie lay on a pale blue ceramic plate beside his trilby. Evidently he had also bought a CD from the pile for sale on the counter, a recording of guitar music by the owner's son, which drifted through the café. It sat in the ridge of his hat, still in its cellophane wrapper.

Peter took another sip as Rashid sat in the chair he had pulled round to give them both a view of the entrance, and beamed at the owner. 'Philippe's wife makes them to her own special recipe, apparently. Want one?'

Rashid shook her head. Brennan's recklessness in murdering Becky had left her uncharacteristically nervous, though if her controller was angry he was choosing not to show it. He dipped his head to use the paper napkin and Rashid noticed a dent across his forehead left by the hat. 'Car all right?'

'Fine, thanks.'

Peter took an unsealed white envelope from his breast pocket and slid it across the table. 'Some more photos,' he said. The little girl nearby was growing fractious, red-faced; she was evidently overexcited after the party, but Peter seemed to welcome the distraction. He checked Rashid's arm as she slid the envelope into her coat. 'No need to be furtive. Take a look now.'

Rashid took out four colour photographs of a man in his late fifties, one a head-and-shoulders shot, the other full length to indicate his height and build. In the first two he was standing by a river, fly fishing. In blue jeans and a white T-shirt, with his greying hair neatly trimmed, she could see that her next target was in good shape, tanned and fit. The other shots showed him in a dark, well-tailored suit, the height of middle-aged cool, with a second man in the background, also in his fifties but dark and heavy-set. 'The bodyguard,' said Peter.

In a fit of temper the little girl released the string on the balloon, screaming as it floated out of reach to the ceiling. 'The target's name is Mike Geraghty, a close friend of the vice president,' said Peter. He sat silently, observing the mother pacifying the child and trying to retrieve the balloon. 'And CEO of a large corporation dealing in weapons of mass destruction for use by the American and British governments.'

'I've read about him,' said Rashid, returning the photographs to the envelope and slipping it into her coat. 'He's a bastard.'

'And our highest value target,' said Peter, taking a bite of his cookie. They watched the owner come from behind the counter, stand on a chair and stretch for the end of the string. 'He arrives in Farnborough on Sunday morning in his company jet from Philadelphia, then goes to the Dorchester Hotel in Park Lane, usual suite. Is our boy ready?'

'Considering he'd never even picked up one of those contraptions before, he's good. But he needs more practice.' Rashid watched the owner refasten the string to the back of the girl's chair, wiping his hands on his apron and milking the mother's thanks as Peter nudged her with a second envelope.

'Logistics. Times, location, every detail. When you return to your car you will find a holdall in the boot containing other equipment. You have tomorrow to recce and prepare.'

'That's not possible,' said Rashid, drawn to a fragment of cookie on Peter's lower lip. 'We need another session in the forest and he's still too slow preparing the weapon.'

Peter shook his head, dislodging the crumb. 'Things have changed over the past twenty-four hours, leaving us with a reduced window. On Monday morning he has arranged to speak with people who have the power to damage us, so we cannot allow that meeting to take place. Sunday is our only opportunity. As soon as he reaches the hotel he will change and go for a run in Hyde Park.'

Rashid allowed herself a little laugh. 'How the hell can you know that?'

'Because he is a creature of habit and does this every time he flies to London. Two circuits, pausing at a specific tree for stretching exercises, which is where the boy will take him out. The shooting point is a tree within sprinting distance of the pedestrian tunnel beneath the road, his escape route. Everything is clearly marked.'

Rashid watched the child, sitting calmly now with her drink

while the proprietor uttered soothing noises and chatted up the mother. 'What about the bodyguard?'

'Out of condition. This man is not built for speed and the circuits will have tired him. Will he run after our boy, even if he sees him, or try to save the life of the man he should have protected? Who knows? What would you do?'

'What if he chases?' said Rashid.

'The boy must run faster.'

'I need more time to – to prepare and study the site.'

'There is another reason,' said Peter, without hesitation, then made her wait as he drank his smoothie. Rashid braced herself for his castigation about Brennan's insane attack at the *Flag* the night before, but what followed was far worse. 'You have allowed yourself to be compromised.'

'What?'

'They have sent an agent to get you. A woman they call Mel. Mean anything to you?'

Shock pinned Rashid to her chair as images lit her brain in a fast-forward video. She saw the crash and Jez's face yelling at her through the driver's window before the woman, Mel, filled the picture. She saw the pale, taut face, the body the same height as hers and just as strong. 'I think she helps turn the journal out.' Rashid spoke carefully, thinking hard, keeping her voice under control. 'Screwing one of the guys at the *Flag*.'

'She's a detective sergeant,' said Peter, levelly, 'and she's been sent to trap you.'

The images kept coming. Now Rashid saw the woman up close, staring her down, wielding the wrench and getting the better of her, forcing a lift in the stupid bloody car that Brennan had promised to fix. 'She doesn't know a thing about me,' she said, trying to suppress her rising panic.

'But you were kind enough to drop her home.'

'She lives in Dalston,' said Rashid, scarcely hearing him. 'I can find out exactly where.'

Over by the window there was a sudden flurry of racquets and white sweaters as the tennis couple got ready to leave. They were still laughing and loved up, as if dashing home for a quickie before collecting the grandkids, and Rashid felt an overwhelming urge to run into the street after them. 'What do you want me to do?' was all she could say.

Peter nodded at the envelope. 'Take out Mr Geraghty,' he said quietly, 'as ordered. On Sunday, while you still have time.'

'But what happens then?' Rashid could hear panic in her voice. 'About this cop?'

'You and your young friend will deal with her,' said Peter, 'as soon as your work for me is done.' He smiled, popped the last of the cookie into his mouth, slid the smoothie across the table to her and reached for his hat.

Rashid checked his arm. 'Don't go yet. Please.' She knew she sounded desperate and pathetic, but did not care. She knew nothing about the old man who sat beside her yet felt she belonged to him. Her plea was little more than a whisper. 'Promise you'll protect me. Please. Don't abandon me now.'

Peter sat back in the chair. 'That young man's private escapade last night and your carelessness have put our long-term hopes at risk.' His voice was as soft as Rashid's but the eyes were like granite and the hat mark on his forehead had turned a deep red. The little girl was crying again, as if she, too, could see the menace in his face. 'Double jeopardy, compound disappointment.'

Here, at last, was the condemnation she had been expecting and it left her feeling powerless and humiliated. 'I can't keep watch on him every minute,' she said lamely.

'You assured me he was controllable.'

'Sometimes he acts like he's bloody mad. He frightens me.'

'Is that why you still jump into his bed?' He sighed. 'The boy was always going to be expendable, but for you we held such high hopes.'

'I'm sorry,' was all Rashid could say, as close to tears as the little girl.

Peter patted her hand and stood to leave. 'I know you won't let me down again.'

Was it the offer of a second chance, or a simple threat? As she watched him weave through the tables, waving his CD in thanks to the owner, Rashid felt utterly abandoned. As her eyes welled with tears she saw the child watching but could not help herself. The old man had given her a renewed sense of purpose, and the dread of being cut adrift ripped into her as savagely as the fear of life in prison. She drank the smoothie and wept, her nerves shot, terrified by her own vulnerability.

Fifty-two

Alan Fargo was feeling tired as he crossed Victoria Street and followed his quarry up Strutton Ground to Cash and Grab, an open-all-hours mini-market aimed at New Scotland Yard workers tiring of the casserole and chips in the fourth-floor canteen. He had spent the whole of Thursday night in the office briefing Ajay, Ritchie and Kerr on the recovery operation at Berkeley Square and dissecting every word of the People's Resistance communiqué.

Fargo always said that the fallout occupied him even more than the bomb itself. Derek Finch's investigators would recover the bodies from the scene, extract every fragment of forensic evidence and unravel the crime, however long it took. In the meantime, as head of Room 1830, the heart and soul of SO15's intelligence unit, Fargo knew that the diplomatic and political pressure in the aftermath would be as intense as the investigation on the ground. From the fog of every terrorist attack snaked myriad lines of enquiry, with false trails criss-crossing each other and obscuring the true path. But Fargo saw his job with crystal clarity: to gather every shred of information and make sense of it for Ajay, Bill Ritchie and John Kerr.

This evening he should have been taking his sister, Pauline, to the theatre to see *Mamma Mia!*, her favourite musical, for the third time. Instead, because Ajay had called a meeting for eight o'clock and Fargo needed to follow up a lead of his own, Gemma had taken his place and would see Pauline safely home to Caledonian Road.

The mini-market was cramped, with three aisles extending from the open double doors and what Justin called 'shoplifting music' washing into the street. Fargo spotted MI5 liaison officer Tim Moxon disappearing into the most accessible section to the left, headed 'Simply Snacks'. He grabbed a basket, tossed in a couple of bags of crisps and wandered in pursuit. Moxon was slim, shorter than Fargo and boyish, with floppy blond hair and down-at-heel shoes that Fargo thought odd for an ex-serviceman. Fargo caught up with him frowning at a cheese and pickle baguette. He shuffled alongside, paused for Moxon to notice him but gave up after ten seconds. 'How's it going?'

Moxon acted casual. 'Heard your stomach rumbling from the street,' he said, squeezing the baguette and dumping it back on the shelf. He laughed and extended his hand, but Fargo caught a spark of anxiety in his eyes.

Claiming to have served as a lieutenant on frigates in the Gulf, Moxon was extrovert, friendly and enthusiastic. All things to all men, ecumenical in his drink and prejudices, Fargo knew he was MI5's number-one choice for cultivating coppers. Today he was wearing a dark blue tie with a complicated red and gold logo that Fargo did not recognise, probably a gift from one of Finch's investigation units.

'There's something I'd like your advice on, actually,' said Fargo, dropping the nearest sandwich into his basket.

'But not here, right?'

'Can you call by 1830?'

'Absolutely.' Moxon's enthusiasm was almost palpable. 'If you're sure it's OK with your management?'

'Sorry?'

'My terms of access?'

'I'm working on that,' said Fargo, with a dismissive wave. 'Say around seven?'

Moxon's eyes lit up. 'Ask away,' he said, with a big smile, and Fargo sensed him already mentally drafting his file note to Thames House.

Moxon knocked on the door of 1830 three minutes early and Fargo took him straight into the reading room. Knowing he would be punctual, Fargo had already poured two mugs of black coffee and brought out a large bag of cheese and onion crisps. He placed Moxon with his back to the window, away from the door. The MI5 man slung his jacket over the back of the chair and stood rolling up his sleeves, ready for action. As he produced a checked handkerchief Fargo saw that the seams of his trouser pockets were threadbare, the linings stained and discoloured. 'So, how can we help?' said Moxon, drumming his hands on the table.

Fargo needed an early admission. He tore open the bag of crisps and slid it to the centre of the desk. 'Do you remember the Parvez Rashid case a couple of years back?'

Moxon crossed his legs, hooking his right ankle behind his left calf. He popped a single crisp into his mouth and sat chewing. 'Asylum seeker detained in Pakistan who topped himself?'

Fargo grabbed a large handful and nodded. 'July 2011.'

'Vaguely.'

'But you were G Branch before coming here, right? Didn't you tell one of our guys you'd worked on him?'

'Only peripherally,' said Moxon, his face suddenly clouding. 'Rashid and a lot of others, actually.'

'Peripherally?' repeated Fargo, sending a volley of crisp fragments across the desk. 'Come on, Tim, running around the inside track, more like.'

Moxon put on a frown, as if struggling to remember. 'Sorry, I thought you wanted advice with current stuff.' He drank some coffee and surreptitiously wiped his cheek with the back of his hand. 'Parvez Rashid is ancient history.'

'Not any more,' said Fargo, eating again. 'Just some impressions will do, Tim. I mean, he was high-profile, wasn't he? Loads of media, even a piece on *Newsnight*. I've got all that, plus the sensitive material on Excalibur. It's recollections from a case officer I need right now. You know, something to bring our Mr Rashid back to life.'

'For instance?'

'Context,' said Fargo, flatly. 'We have a clutch of suspected British jihadis subjected to rendition, extradition, interrogation, torture and detention without trial. My question: how far up the scale of abuses do you slot Parvez Rashid?'

Moxon's young features creased again, but he wasn't smiling any more. 'Alan, what has this got to do with current ops?'

'Everything, because of his connection to Judge Hugh Selwyn.'

'Well, I can't help. This is a hellishly sensitive area. You know that as well as I do. Anything to do with rendition or enhanced interrogation is a policy matter for the Service. Highly classified.' He was looking less like a partner now and sounding right on message.

'I'll try again,' said Fargo, calmly, grabbing more crisps. 'Everyone knows Parvez Rashid was an innocent law student arrested and questioned as a terrorist. Then his asylum appeal was rejected because the mud from his detention in Karachi had stuck. That was a second blow, wasn't it?'

Moxon was looking a lot less boyish. 'What the hell are you implying?'

'Do you believe Rashid committed suicide directly as a result? Because if you do, a lot of people at Thames House must be feeling pretty sick. Forget your authorisations and bloody protocols, Tim. This is between you and me, and all I'm asking for is the back story on Parvez Rashid.'

Leaking anger at being ambushed, Moxon drained his mug, uncrossed his legs and shuffled in the chair as if he was getting ready to leave. 'Thanks for the coffee. And dinner,' he added, in a vain attempt at levity, as he spotted the recorder in Fargo's hand. He froze, evidently rewinding the conversation, then gave a mocking laugh as he found nothing to incriminate him. 'Don't you think that's bloody bad form, mate, eavesdropping on your liaison officer?' He began wriggling into his jacket. 'Clumsy. Come on, serious breach and all that.'

'Not recording. Playback time.' Fargo placed the machine on the empty crisps packet as Moxon's cultured voice filled the room, followed by Gemma's. Her performance sounded even posher than usual above the bar noise, easily outdoing Moxon as she made him spell out his offer. Moxon froze, his left arm trapped halfway into the sleeve of his jacket. 'Enough?' said Fargo, after a few seconds.

Moxon's face had turned pink. 'It was a chat-up line in a bar.'

'It was a pitch. You were asking Gemma Riley to work for you.'

'To join our comms at Thames House.'

'No. For you, personally. To be your mole inside the Yard.'

'Utter bollocks.'

'Have it your way.' Fargo slid the tiny machine back onto the desk. '*Now* I'm recording, and this is the story. Our commander invited you here as MI5 liaison officer and you attempted to suborn a member of our staff to report back to you on the work of Room 1830. Correct? One partner spying on the other, undermining our joint effort and confidence in each other. *That*'s the "serious breach".'

Moxon said nothing but his eyes were pleading with Fargo to switch off the machine. 'What do you want?'

'I already told you,' said Fargo, taking the recorder back. 'Have a think while I get us some more coffee.'

'No. Let's do this now,' said Moxon, collecting his thoughts before Fargo could move. 'Parvez Rashid was a really difficult case for us. '

'Because an innocent man killed himself?'

'And for me personally because the officer who witnessed his interrogation in Karachi was a colleague. Is. A close friend, in fact.'

'Witnessed or participated?'

'Alex took no part at all. His job is on the line simply because he was there and I'm anxious for him, obviously. Wrong place and all that. A lot of reporters have said some pretty tough things, you know, MI5 out there being tantamount to condoning torture.'

'How did Rashid drop into the frame?'

'He was travelling home to Karachi for personal reasons. Family reunion, I think. We shared his travel details with the Americans and they asked the Pakistanis to detain him on arrival.'

'When did the Yanks ever make a request of anyone?'

'OK, a directive. The Americans demanded his arrest and interrogation.'

'Did they take part in the interrogation?'

'Alex says the CIA were also there.'

'That's not the question.'

'All right, and took an active part. This is sensitive, Alan. Very bumpy territory.'

'So is killing yourself. Parvez Rashid was a law student at the LSE, turning up and studying every day. What was the intelligence that turned him into a terrorist?'

'I don't know.' Moxon shrugged. 'He must have popped up on the Americans' radar. Alex says he was suspected of attending a training camp in Pakistan, but it was never proved to us.'

'So he was a victim of mistaken identity.'

'Unless the Americans have more and they're holding out on us. Anyway, he was kicked out without being charged, came back to the UK.'

'Where the immigration panel rejected his asylum appeal. No leave to remain. And that was on the advice of Hugh Selwyn?'

'He was the conduit between my Service and the adjudicators on the panel.'

'But he was only handing over what MI5 gave him, presumably. Flawed US intelligence nailing Rashid as a terrorist.'

'I don't know.' Moxon was showing signs of recovery. 'But you'd better not be trying to point the finger at us, Alan.'

'Shortly afterwards Rashid managed to hang himself from a tree. The inquest verdict was suicide, which is curious because all his friends at LSE said he had shown no sign at all of being depressed. On the contrary, as everyone knows, he was a strong voice in the media, exposing other miscarriages of justice against asylum seekers. So why would such a motivated man kill himself? Did MI5 advise the coroner, too?'

'That's absurd,' said Moxon, making a second attempt on his jacket.

'But it has consequences for the people responsible for this cock-up. Our team believes vengeance against Parvez Rashid's unjust treatment may be a motive for Hugh Selwyn's murder. Reasonable?'

'How the hell would I know?' said Moxon, trying to stand in the narrow space, his thighs trapped against the top of the desk. 'I think we're done here.'

Fargo held up the recorder again. 'By the way, Gemma doesn't want to work for you.'

Moxon was shuffling sideways towards Fargo. 'Jesus, can't you people take a joke?'

When Moxon reached the end of the desk he stood and swept back his hair. He was slimmer and a different generation from Fargo, and his young face was clear again. Escorting him from the main office, Fargo felt a stab of jealousy. He bit his lip but could not contain himself any longer. 'And she says she doesn't want to go for a drink with you, either,' he called, as Moxon escaped down the corridor.

Fifty-three

Kerr arrived at the outer office a few minutes late for the briefing with Ajay to find his door closed and Donna still sitting at her desk. Three large carrier bags from Regent Street stores sagged on the floor beside her and she was examining a pair of brown leather boots. She stood up as soon as she saw him and moved to Ajay's door. 'Very nice,' said Kerr. 'And what are you doing still here?'

'It's been non-stop and I'm fielding his calls,' said Donna, as Kerr waited for her to move aside. She suddenly looked embarrassed. 'Actually I was also hanging on to catch you, John.'

Donna was a top PA, efficient, unflappable and discreet, which immediately put Kerr on alert. 'What's up?'

'I need a private word when you've got a mo.'

'Soon as I'm done.'

Ajay was speaking with Fargo at the conference table and flashed Kerr a smile of welcome. Kerr noticed that he had rotated his desk slightly, though the squash racquet was still visible, and the ugly grey security cabinet had been replaced by a neat black electronic job that looked tough enough to withstand a nuclear bomb. He was immediately struck by how energetic Ajay seemed after a gruelling day and the prospect of a second long night ahead. Tieless, in a fresh white shirt, he might just have emerged from the shower. With a nod of apology Kerr took the chair opposite Fargo, facing the window with a beautiful late evening view of St James's Park and a reddening sky over Highgate to the north-west.

'I know Alan is ahead of us all but this is the official COBRA version,' said Ajay, scrolling through his tablet. 'Just to be sure we're on the same page, OK? In essence, three devices presenting a potassium cyanide base compounded with incendiary materials and other chemical elements, as yet undetected. Fatalities have risen to twenty-four, including the ambassador and his wife, with others expected. Cause of death in most cases is poison rather than blast injuries, which were nevertheless severe. Mr Finch has little other evidence to go on until his troops recover all the CCTV footage from around Berkeley Square. A handful of survivors report seeing a chef in the public area shortly before the blasts but people are still too traumatised to give detailed descriptions.'

Kerr counted fifteen bullet points on the tablet, though Ajay barely glanced at the screen, speaking fluently from memory and making Kerr reflect once again what a class act they had as their commander.

'The politics are also pretty toxic,' continued Ajay. 'Media and politicians on both sides of the Atlantic in full assault mode with a single headline: America is under attack in the land of its greatest ally and the Brits aren't capable of resolving it. Diplomatic dynamite.' He glanced at Kerr. 'As I know Rich Malone has already made clear to you, John?'

Kerr nodded. 'The whole series of attacks, plus the theft of America's gold in London, constitutes a real and present danger to the special relationship, period. That's Washington's view in a nutshell and my ears are still aching.'

'So the pressure is on Mr Finch for now,' said Ajay. 'But he'll be deflecting whatever he can in our direction. Failure of intelligence, the usual garbage. By Sunday, unless the Bull has a miraculous forensic breakthrough, all eyes will be on me.

Us,' he said, cool as a cucumber. 'So it's over to you, guys. Let's have your ideas. Solve this for us and get everybody off my back.'

Ajay stroked his moustache and smiled at Kerr. Kerr looked at Fargo, who had reams of notes on a yellow pad identical to Bill Ritchie's.

'The sophistication of these three bombs proves beyond doubt that this is not domestic terrorism,' said Fargo. 'That's what the forensics guys downstairs are saying. Even if delivered by home-grown extremists, their technical design has to be external. We're talking state-sponsored, not some nutty terrorist cell, which means People's Resistance is a smokescreen. To find the real enemy we have to look behind it.'

'But can you take us there?' said Ajay.

'Here's what we have,' said Fargo, 'starting with the lovely Yvette. We strongly believe Marcus Tennant's French au pair is an intelligence operative, real name Monique Thierry. We can't tie her to any French agency yet, though I'm reserving judgement until we get the DNA and fingerprint results from Paris. Point is, the motivation for French DGSE activity abroad has been commercial espionage. It's plausible they would entrap Tennant to obtain defence secrets, or even arrange the murder of his wife in revenge for refusal to succumb. But dirty bombs are not their style, meaning we need to look at other possibilities while we keep the French on hold. John and I are trying to figure out which other countries would be so determined to torpedo our alliance with America. And so barbaric.'

Kerr looked at Ajay. 'The Russians?'

Ajay was already shaking his head. 'Moscow would have no interest in seeing that particular tree wither. On the contrary, it suits them to see it flourish. The UK and the US are both still major espionage targets. If a spying operation in either country brings the same reward, why would they slash the opportunity in half?' Ajay doodled on his tablet for a moment, then looked at Fargo. 'I believe the Chinese have used cyanide against state enemies in the past. Let's check that out.'

Kerr took a deep breath. 'I think we've also got to take a look at our own agencies,' he said.

Ajay was startled. 'You're not suggesting MI6 had a hand in any of this violence, surely?'

'Of course not,' said Kerr. 'But if we stand back while others lie, cheat and conspire, terrible things can happen.' He waited for Ajay to say something, but the room stayed silent. 'Why has MI6 been so active around Marcus Tennant, sending Julius to warn me off?'

'Tell me,' said Ajay.

'To protect a patriot or cover up for traitor,' said Kerr.

'And we're going with the second,' said Fargo.

Ajay frowned.

'Just accept for a moment that Marcus Tennant has been compromised through this honey trap,' said Kerr. 'What are the implications for MI6 if Marcus Tennant, one of their own, turns out to be a traitor?'

'Catastrophic,' murmured Ajay.

'Complete meltdown of the CIA relationship. The end of sharing. Invitations to Langley? Forget it. Overnights in Washington, dinner in Georgetown and schmoozing in the White House? No chance. And if Tennant has also betrayed US secrets, which is likely, the relationship will never recover.' Rich Malone's voice was yelling inside Kerr's head again, urging, cajoling, threatening. *Another British espionage scandal damaging the US, and the special relationship is down the toilet.*

'Unthinkable,' said Ajay. 'Unimaginable.'

'If our suspicions about Marcus Tennant are even partly true, the reverberations will echo across the Atlantic for decades. This is Philby, Burgess and Maclean all over again, plus the other bastards who never got found out. We're saying

MI6 will do *anything* to dodge the risk of the CIA switching off the US intelligence tap.'

'The Americans are already suspicious,' said Fargo. 'They're linking all these anti-American attacks to the day their gold was nicked, which they're seriously pissed off about. And Tennant was one of the handful of people to know about the transit through London.'

'OK, let's go for now with cover-up for a traitor,' said Ajay. 'How do we take this forward?'

'We have to identify the agents who have been targeting Marcus Tennant through the au pair,' said Kerr. 'Tennant is our way in but we can't get there because MI6 is acting as a roadblock. When they cover up for Tennant they also shield the enemy. Everything has consequences.'

'Starting with Diane Tennant's murder,' said Fargo.

'We believe it's possible Diane was eliminated because she was about to blow the whistle on her husband,' said Kerr.

'For what?'

'She said he had started behaving oddly after the photographs arrived, apparently.'

' "Oddly"? That doesn't really do it for me, I'm afraid.'

'She talked about his betrayal.'

Ajay held out his palms. 'John, she was being cheated on.'

'I think it was more than that.'

'But as we can't test the lady herself, how can we ever know?'

Kerr shifted in his seat. 'Diane confided in someone.'

'Someone?'

'A close friend. Just before she died.' He saw Ajay frown, dissatisfied, already framing his follow-up question as the door opened.

'Sorry to interrupt.' Donna had evidently been trying on her new boots, for the left one was still unzipped. 'Commissioner's been on. He's in the car but wants you to join him and Mr Finch in a conference call. Shall I dial you in?'

'Sure,' said Ajay, checking the time. 'OK, chaps. Let's circle back in, say, fifteen?'

Fifty-four

Kerr took Donna into Bill Ritchie's office next door while Fargo returned to 1830. He switched on the lights, closed the door and sat her at Ritchie's chipped coffee-table. Through the partition wall they could hear Ajay's voice puncturing the silence as he joined the call. Kerr spoke quietly. 'What's up?'

'It's about Ajay,' said Donna, looking awkward. 'I think he's having an affair.'

'And?' said Kerr, tilting his head to watch as she zipped up her boot.

'If he gets found out he'll probably get the sack. Then all the good things he's done will be wasted.'

'Why do you suspect he's over the side?'

'You know how he loves his squash?' She waited for Kerr's nod. 'Sometimes when he sneaks away he's not been there. To the court.'

'Are you sure of that?'

'He hides his sports bag under the desk – you must have seen it. Well, I checked his kit one day when he got back and it was clean and dry.' Donna looked embarrassed as Kerr stared at her. 'I had to make sure before I said anything.'

'Perhaps it's a spare set.' Kerr exhaled. 'He leaves the other stuff in the car?'

'I don't think so. He's making a lot of secret phone calls as well. Telling me he doesn't want to be disturbed, then locking the door. That's what made me look in his bag.'

'He is the boss, Donna, dealing with a lot of sensitive things.'

'He's calling his girlfriend. Ajay promised me right from the start there wouldn't be any secrets between us. He's always trusted me to cover for him.'

'Ajay has masses of things happening right now.'

'And the cheating is getting to him,' said Donna, as if she had not heard. 'He makes out he's all relaxed and laid-back to you, but it's an act. He's very stressed and I'm worried about him, especially with these bombings. It's making me feel very awkward.'

'Have you talked to Bill?'

Donna shook her head. 'Ajay sent him home to rest. Mr Ritchie's got quite enough on his plate with his cancer.' On the other side of the wall they could hear Ajay signing off. 'I'd better get back or he'll be wondering. Ajay is such a decent person and he likes you, John. You can talk to him. Tell him he mustn't throw everything away. Please, John. He's starting to make us feel like we're in Special Branch again. Tell him we don't want to lose him.'

'OK. I'll handle it,' said Kerr, as his BlackBerry began vibrating across the table. He saw Karl Sergeyev's name, pressed accept and smiled at Donna. 'Thanks.'

'Where were we?' said Ajay, when they had reassembled. He scrolled down his tablet. 'You were about to tell me why Diane Tennant distrusted her husband.'

'Things have hardened against him,' said Kerr, evading the question for the second time and glancing at Fargo. 'Marcus Tennant has just resigned from the cabinet citing personal reasons. Number Ten are holding the announcement back to keep it out of the Sundays.'

'He has just lost his wife,' said Ajay. 'In the most terrible circumstances.'

'Except it will be another lie. The PM dragged him in for a conversation without coffee and sacked him. Why do that to a loyal minister when he's just been bereaved?'

'Because MI6 were involved,' said Fargo.

Ajay frowned. 'You're saying they got at the prime minister?'

'Yes. They neutralise Tennant by cutting off his access to defence secrets when we should be arresting him,' said Kerr. 'They know their man is a spy and want the problem to go away. Tennant gets a free pass to the back benches when he should be banged up in Paddington Green.'

Ajay was slowly circling his thumbs. 'And is that your proposal?'

'I believe we should launch a full investigation tonight, in secret, to blow this thing apart,' said Kerr.

'Starting with a deep dive against Tennant, presumably?' said Ajay. 'You're asking me to authorise a clandestine operation against the defence secretary?'

'Why not? He's about to become a backbencher and they get nicked all the time. And we go all out to trace Monique Thierry and Anna Rashid.'

'We should bring in the MI6 bloke, too,' said Fargo. 'By covering for Tennant Julius has obstructed the course of justice and should go on the sheet.'

Kerr touched the bruise on his forehead. 'I'll be asking him about this, too.'

Ajay steepled his fingers, and Kerr recognised he was in data-crunching mode. After studying his tablet he took a deep breath. When he looked up, he was wearing an expression Kerr had not seen before. 'This is nudging the boundaries quite a long way, chaps,' he said. 'I'm supportive in principle, naturally. But I need to think about this over the weekend.'

He sounded different, too, and Kerr reflected that this was his first big test since he had taken office. Was their boss suddenly nervous at the prospect of making waves, despite his confidence and everything he had achieved so far? 'Understood,' said Kerr, with a glance at Fargo. 'It's just that every hour we delay leaves the public at risk of another attack.'

'I have to develop your idea with Mr Ritchie first. And MI5, of course, as we're talking counter-espionage.' His eyes settled on Kerr again, curious and intuitive, as if finally confirming something about Kerr's maverick character. Perhaps Bill Ritchie had already warned him and his misgivings had been right all along. Kerr saw dark shadows of anxiety behind them, too – signs of the stress Donna had spotted before any of them – and suddenly felt protective.

Fargo cleared his throat. 'I think it might not be a good idea to involve MI5 just yet, boss. I've been looking at the inquest report into Parvez Rashid. A dog-walker found him hanged in Epping Forest, but there was no tangible evidence of any intention to commit suicide. In fact, Rashid had been extremely vocal in the media. He started a campaign to expose everything about his arrest and interrogation in Karachi by the Pakistanis and the Americans. He described in detail how they subjected him to sleep deprivation, beatings and starvation, and claimed he was hooded and forced to stand in the stress position. We know that an MI5 officer witnessed his interrogation and says there wasn't a shred of evidence against him. Basically, Rashid's asylum application was rejected on the basis of inaccurate, single-source intelligence from the Americans. And MI5 passed it to the adjudication panel through Hugh Selwyn without any investigation, corroboration or rebuttal. MI5 accept the whole case was flawed.'

'How do you know that?'

'Tim Moxon volunteered it. Very up-front, actually. This was a miscarriage of justice against an innocent law student. That's the bottom line. But the point is that Rashid was fighting it. He was fired up, the last person to kill himself, and that raises a lot of unanswered questions.'

'For instance?'

Fargo shrugged. 'That he was silenced to stifle his allegations about the Americans and Brits being complicit in torture.'

'Is that your analysis, John?'

'In protecting Marcus Tennant, MI6 created cover for the enemy to operate behind him. And by *failing* to protect Parvez Rashid, MI5 motivated his partner to deliver the enemy's bombs.'

'Cover-up versus cock-up,' said Fargo.

'And there's something else,' said Kerr. 'Claude Kellner told me he'd heard about Monique Thierry's espionage activities "through channels". If that means MI5, then it's possible they knew about Thierry's honey trap against Marcus Tennant. Which means we can't trust them with the investigation we're proposing now. Ajay, we have to go alone.'

'All right.' Ajay laid his hands flat on the table, flexing his slim, manicured fingers. 'Give me the night to think about it and we'll scrum down first thing.' He turned to Kerr. 'Anna Rashid, our present from Melanie Fleming. What's the latest?'

'Melanie's fine,' lied Kerr, blanking Fargo's warning frown.

'Still producing?' he asked, as Kerr realised he had not heard about Ritchie's order to withdraw her.

'The *Flag*'s still a murder scene so she's lying low for a couple of days,' he said truthfully. In fact, since their confrontation at the Pelican ten hours earlier Melanie had sunk without trace, returning none of his calls. When Kerr had finally got through to her home landline Rob had picked up, curt and aggressive, blanking all Kerr's questions. 'Melanie doesn't live with us any more,' was all he could get Rob to say before he slammed the phone down.

With his anxiety over Melanie deepening, his discovery of their separation had come as a bitter blow: it left his best undercover officer without any anchor to her true life. After so many years' working together, Kerr had practically come to regard Melanie as a second daughter and now he was as troubled as if Gabi herself had disappeared.

'Whatever happens from now, I believe Melanie is the only person to emerge from this terrible campaign with any credit,' he said, containing his emotion.

'Though we don't know for certain that Anna Rashid belongs to People's Resistance,' said Ajay.

'But she's the only lead we have, and she didn't come to us from 1830 or Excalibur or the Bull or any of our so-called partners. So here's the thing, Ajay. Melanie Fleming has done better than anyone. We owe her.'

Fifty-five

The holdall left for Anna Rashid in the boot of her Fiat Punto contained a park ranger's uniform of dark green waterproof jacket and trousers with matching baseball cap and latex gloves. The clothes fitted Brennan perfectly as he pretended to collect debris in a black plastic bag, strengthened on the inside by a cotton sack. The bag was easy to carry, for the adapted Barnett Ghost crossbow hidden inside weighed a little over seven pounds and took up no more space than a small branch. He was loitering on the eastern edge of Hyde Park, little more than a couple of bus lengths from the mouth of Park Lane's pedestrian underpass and obscured from full view by a weeping willow. Into the left zipped pocket of the jacket he had stuffed his black beanie, in the other an Oyster card, a pay-as-you-go mobile and the next People's Resistance communiqué.

Friday's blue sky had disappeared, pushed aside by a pewter-grey blanket of cloud dropping a few spots of rain, and a cool front had advanced overnight from the east. The weather was good for running and perfect for hiding, because it shrank the number of potential witnesses. During his fifteen-minute wait Brennan tracked only two families with children, three middle-aged American couples and a couple of irritated suits probably having to work over the weekend. All were passing through, headed for Green Park or Buckingham Palace, an office in Knightsbridge or one of Park Lane's hotels, watching for rain and incurious about the groundsman with his head down collecting twigs.

The target appeared exactly where Rashid had said he would, emerging from the underpass near a gushing ornate bronze fountain called *Joy of Life* that sent water lapping over the edge of the pool in little waves. Mike Geraghty was immediately identifiable from the photographs, energetic in dark blue tracksuit bottoms and running shoes with a T-shirt, seemingly unaffected by his transatlantic flight. The shirt was stark white, a clear target on a gloomy day and, when drenched in blood, would prove Brennan had made his mark.

Dozens of footpaths criss-crossing the park offered joggers countless opportunities, though Rashid had promised that Geraghty would run exactly as he was supposed to, turning left to hug the perimeter as far as Hyde Park Corner before swinging clockwise to trace the Serpentine's northern perimeter. Brennan observed the bodyguard following in kit that left no room for any weapon: black vest with PREDATOR logo, red shorts and black trainers with white socks. Balding, with a neat moustache, pot belly and drooping shoulders, he was already breathless. Brennan studied the two men as Geraghty found his stride. The bodyguard was lagging behind by ten paces, a distance Brennan knew would lengthen as the running took its toll.

From the lake, Rashid had told him, they would continue as far as Speaker's Corner at the northern edge, then return to the starting point, where they would pause to stretch and rest before beginning another circuit. 'The bastard has a system, Danny,' she had told him in bed, after returning from her recce. 'Same place, same exercises. The life of a disciplined warmonger.' It was a strenuous run, about five miles, and Brennan's order was to take him out at the end of the second circuit, the point of greatest fatigue.

Brennan picked up his bag and walked to the point from which he would make his strike. It was a disfigured horse-chestnut on slightly elevated ground with a trunk split at chest level, easily thick enough to conceal a man yet leaving an aperture wide enough for Brennan to settle and take aim. It was open from the front but protected behind by laurel bushes and *leylandii*, leaving Brennan all but invisible in his green camouflage.

He put the bag on the grass and looked through the opening across the fountain to the spot where Geraghty would exercise. It was an old lime tree rising vertically between two stretches of thick bushes, high enough to shield passers-by from the traffic in Park Lane to Brennan's right and from walkers to his left. As he opened the bag he began counting in his head. By the time he reached fourteen he had unfolded the crossbow, tested the trigger mechanism, checked the scope and loaded a twenty-inch arrow. This satisfied him as much as Geraghty's white T-shirt, for it matched his best practice in Epping Forest and the night before at the safe house.

Brennan allowed them fifteen minutes to complete the route, but twenty-three had elapsed before Geraghty came into view again, jogging alone from Speaker's Corner on the final leg, leaving his exhausted bodyguard a long way further down the path. The time lapse was too great, so in that moment he decided to take Geraghty out there and then, in case he abandoned the second circuit to save the bodyguard. Brennan took his eyes off both men, lifted the crossbow into the fork, braced himself in the firing position and set the focus on the lime tree, waiting for his target to come to him.

Geraghty took ten seconds to appear in the line of sight. He was thirty metres away from Brennan but the illuminated scope seemed to bring him within a couple of steps, almost close enough to reach out and touch. Brennan could see every detail of his glistening face and upper body, from a small scar on his right temple to a tiny mole on the nape of his neck and even an inoculation mark on his arm. The silver hair was still swept back in place as he flexed his legs alternately against the tree while stretching his arms forward to touch each trainer and dipping his head as low as it would go. The T-shirt highlighted the rise and fall of his chest, rhythmically darting in and out of sight.

The fountain stood between Brennan and the target and slightly to the right, its bronze figures dancing above the water and rising from the pool, as lively as Geraghty. Then the bodyguard advanced along the path, the only ugly figure in the landscape. He was puffing and panting, leaning against another tree as if he was about to throw up, and for a second Brennan wanted to take him out, too.

As Geraghty's head dipped again to meet his thigh a third object drifted into the scope's left hemisphere. Brennan registered only the image of a blurred red cornet shape at least a hundred metres beyond his target. He caught a smaller figure moving around the lower rim before Geraghty's torso reappeared in perfect focus and changed the choreography. Standing straight with legs apart and hands clasped behind his neck he twisted his torso right to left, the white triangle offering a perfect target.

Brennan held his breath and fired. There was the 'thwack' of the release and the whoosh of the speeding arrow, then silence. Geraghty's body continued to function, still motivated and full of life, but in the distance the cornet toppled like a skittle. Brennan blinked hard and saw that the shape was a woman wearing a bright red plastic poncho, and the scurrying around her that of a child. Crows took flight from the trees above her but their cawing was scarcely audible from such a distance.

Brennan started counting again as he reached for another arrow. By the time Geraghty had completed four more twists Brennan was braced again, his focus ice cold, the collateral damage eliminated from his mind. He fired again as Geraghty stood motionless, hands on hips, head thrown back to suck in lungfuls of fresh air. He was aiming for the patch of white but the arrow entered Geraghty's gaping mouth, exited from the base of his skull and continued its flight. There was a spurt of blood as the victim seemed to reach for a final stretch, then totter backwards from the tree and crumple to the grass, both arms distorted beneath his body like a puppet's, head twisted to confuse the direction of fire.

Rapidly folding the crossbow into the bag, Brennan fixed his eyes on the bodyguard. Head down with his hands on his knees, immersed in his own recovery, the man was slow to react. By the time he saw Geraghty on the ground, Brennan was already on the move, escaping to the safety of the underpass. The bodyguard was in a state of panic, kneeling beside the man he had let down, crazily pressing his hands over Geraghty's mouth as if he might bring him back. And when, eventually, he looked for the assassin he was searching in the wrong direction, distracted by a child's screams and a man's frantic yelling far behind him.

Brennan raced down the tunnel steps but sauntered past a rough sleeper with a dog on a string and changed out of sight on the opposite staircase. In less than two minutes he had surfaced on the other side of Park Lane heading for the crowds of Piccadilly, just another young man in beanie, T-shirt and jeans, all black, with a nondescript bag slung over his shoulder. His free hand closed over the communiqué: his orders were to deliver the latest People's Resistance message from Piccadilly Circus before making his way back to the safe house.

The attack gave Danny Brennan another spark of elation, but this time he did not linger to enjoy the reaction. He kept his pace slow and unremarkable, though his thoughts were already racing ahead from Mike Geraghty to the coming night and his own personal mission.

Fifty-six

With the TV blaring in the corner of the room, Melanie
Fleming stirred mince, onions and tomatoes in the frying pan
while bending a fistful of spaghetti into boiling water. The Sky
News report about Geraghty's murder in Hyde Park had
come through late afternoon so she was keeping an eye on the
breaking news, hoping that Kerr would change his mind and
keep her in the field a while longer.

The Bolognese would easily provide for two, even three at
a pinch. It was certainly too much for one, but Melanie had
spent the last few hours at her cover address eating to excess.
As a child she had always been told not to waste good food, so
she had been gorging on remnants in the fridge for most of
the day: breakfast had been an omelette of four eggs with five
rashers of bacon, and for lunch mid-afternoon she had made
herself a double round of cheese and ham sandwiches.

A full tumbler of cheap Rioja, Melanie's house-cooling
present to herself, stood near the stove. The bottle, beside it,
was three-quarters empty. Earlier, catching her image in the
tiny bathroom mirror, Melanie had imagined she was balloon-
ing and promised to join a gym if the semblance of normal life
ever returned. But this would be her last night in the bedsit.
Right now she needed to eat and drink because she was desolate and there was no one left to comfort her.

The consummate professional, Melanie had left out enough belongings to make the place look lived in to the very end: well-thumbed political paperbacks, a couple of unwashed mugs, back copies of *Flag of Liberty* on a shelf beside the TV, newspapers on the chair and crockery in the sink. Her few other belongings she had tossed into a battered wheelie case lying open in the middle of the floor.

Tomorrow morning, Monday, she would disappear. After breakfast she would make herself homeless, banned from the cover address she detested and thrown out of the true home she loved. The boss she worked for so loyally and the husband she loved without condition had both turned on her. She tipped the spaghetti into a large bowl, poured the mince on top, overdid the Tabasco and carried it to the table. The first taste sent her choking for a glass of water, but the tears flowing into the sink came from the heart, not her mouth. Two men and a double life had cast her adrift, but she knew the blame lay with her.

Over the weekend Melanie had lost count of the number of times she had tried to phone Rob, but he had ignored her mobile calls and disconnected the answering machine on the landline, letting it ring out. And she had behaved no better, refusing Kerr's calls while she decided what to do next.

Melanie was angry with Kerr because she had worked so hard to get this far and keep her cover intact. In return, he had tried to sweeten her dismissal with compliments from Alan Fargo. A single weekend had left Melanie no time to close her life down and devise an exit strategy; and her disappearance from the *Flag*, so sudden and unexplained, ran the serious risk of blowing her cover. She could have fabricated a change of heart within a week, simply by pretending Becky's murder was freaking her out, so her annoyance with Kerr sprang from professional pride far more than injured feelings.

She grated more cheese onto the meat, swallowed some wine and forked more spaghetti as regrets swirled inside her head. Of these, the greatest was that she could no longer pursue Anna Rashid, the woman she was convinced could unlock People's Resistance, or at least leave a trail to the key. Lying awake on Friday night she had even considered ignoring Kerr's order and staying with her mission, but that idea had faded as the weekend progressed. Kerr must be concerned about her silence. If Melanie did not bail out first thing in the morning, she had no doubt he would send Dodge for her.

Tomorrow, after she had closed the case, pulled the door shut and ended her double life, she would have to find somewhere permanent to live, probably another bedsit masquerading as a 'studio apartment' like this, exchanging one pit of misery for another. After Rob's outburst she needed to get herself checked out at the clinic, too, even though she was experiencing no symptoms. Weeping again, she drank more wine to neutralise the Tabasco and dumped her plate on the draining-board. Sooner or later, probably before the week was out, she would face the humiliation of telling Kerr she was responsible for destroying her marriage. And if Kerr pressed him, Rob would probably blurt out the true reason simply to drive down the hurt, knowing he could ruin her life by screwing her job.

She drew the curtains and slumped in the armchair watching Sky, but reports on the latest People's Resistance attack made her feel even more of a failure. She gave up after twenty minutes and undressed to take a shower, bracing herself for a final sleepless night in the lumpy bed as she climbed unsteadily into the bath. The shower head was connected to the bath taps by a length of hose and the flow was lukewarm and intermittent, reducing to a dribble if water was turned on lower down in the house.

The two knocks on the door came when Melanie was drying herself on a threadbare red bath towel, followed by four more in quick succession as she pattered barefoot into the main room. There was no spy hole so Melanie wrapped herself in the towel and called through the door. 'Yeah?'

'It's me.'

'Hold on.' Melanie closed the lid of the case, kicked it over to the bed and opened the door ajar. 'What's up?'

The door scraped her bare right foot as Jez lurched in, seriously drunk, and Melanie pulled the towel higher up her chest. He focused on her for a moment, leaning back against the draining-board. 'Cops are crawling all over my place 'cos of Becky.'

'What do you want?'

'I need to keep clear, you know, lie low. That all right?' He watched her as she closed the door and walked to him. 'No problem, yeah?'

'Jez, it's nearly eleven o'clock.'

His eyes drifted across to the bed and found the case. 'You going somewhere?'

'Same as you,' she said, seizing the opening he had given her. 'Getting out for a few days. Sacha will be telling them about both of us. They'll be looking for anyone who lived around the *Flag*. It's only a matter of time.'

His eyes were all over her. 'You said it.'

'Are you hungry?' Melanie reached round him and grabbed the remains of the Bolognese. 'Do you want this?'

Jez reached his forefinger down into her cleavage and gave the towel a playful tug. 'Or this?'

She slapped his hand and pushed the bowl back on the draining-board. 'Jez, fuck off.'

Another half-bottle of whisky appeared as Jez shook himself out of his coat and heeled off his boots, nodding at the TV without taking his eyes off her. 'Cops will be too busy in the park to worry about us tonight.'

He emptied the Rioja into Melanie's tumbler and waited until she took it from him, then unscrewed the whisky bottle.

Melanie watched him take a long slug, his Adam's apple rising and falling five times. Then he clinked her tumbler and moved in to kiss her, his right arm strong behind her back as he danced her over to the bed.

'No, Jez. I don't want to,' she said, as red wine sloshed over her hand.

'So why did you come to the door naked?' he whispered, and she felt splashes of whisky against her cheek. 'Of course you do.'

He was holding her hard against him now as the back of her calves came up against the edge of the mattress. 'Jez, no,' she said, trying to push him away, the force almost toppling her backwards. 'I want you to go. It's my period.'

He released her and took a step back. 'No problem.' He grinned, undeterred. He held the whisky bottle out to her and she took it in her free hand. Then he reached forward, swiftly pulled the towel from her and spread it on the bed. 'You'll be OK on that,' he said, stripping off his clothes. While Melanie stood naked and rooted to the spot he took back the whisky and the tumbler of wine and put them on the floor. Then he stepped forward to kiss her again, his body pressing against hers until her legs gave way and they both collapsed onto the bed.

Jez must have been drinking for hours before setting his sights on her. The sex was rough, basic and lasted less than five minutes, but Melanie knew her guilt would cling for ever as the questions coursed through her brain. Why hadn't she got dressed before unlocking the door to him? Why had she not sent him away or pushed him off or screamed or run across the landing to her neighbour? She had not wanted sex with him and could have resisted more. Here was the man who had destroyed her marriage, but it was her fault for breaking the rules.

Melanie knew the law, too. This was rape, yet she had encouraged him before and drunk whisky with him afterwards.

It was assault, but Melanie had stayed in his arms, holding him between her legs and then beside her. And when Jez had fallen asleep, snoring heavily, she had felt powerless, too, tucked between his large, warm body and the cold, damp wall, eyes fixed on a stain on the ceiling when she could have been dressed and running out into the street.

Fifty-seven

Danny Brennan took Anna Rashid's call on his pay-as-you-go mobile just as he was entering Bethnal Green Underground station. She told him she was lying low but would come to the safe house at midnight because she needed to warn him about something. She sounded anxious but Brennan shrugged with indifference, knowing he would be elsewhere by that time and she would be too late to stop him.

The success of the afternoon's attack on Geraghty was beginning to cloak him with a sense of invincibility. As soon as he had reached the safe house he had taken a shower, raided the fridge and sprawled on the bed, flicking between BBC and Sky for news rolling out of Hyde Park, then gearing up for his second deadline. Buoyed up by the breaking news, he prepared for his private mission with military precision. In a neat line on the worktop he laid his father's overalls, carefully folded, beside the orange hi-vis jacket with its Transport for London logo. Unexpectedly, he had found a blue woollen hat in the pocket, which still carried his dad's smell and a few stray hairs caught in the wool; he put this on top of the technical diagram prepared for the inquiry into his father's death.

Two Jiffy-bags lay side by side, each containing one of Brennan's home-made incendiaries. Next to them he had placed a torch attached to an elasticated band, and an improvised miner's lamp that he would strap around his head when he reached his destination. At the very end, leaning upright against the wall, was the sawn-off shotgun his dad had hidden in the Dagenham attic. He had already loaded both barrels, ready to blast anyone who tried to stop him.

Taking the holdall from the cupboard beneath the worktop he carefully packed his bombs inside, followed by the TfL jacket, woollen hat and torch, then slipped the diagram into a side pocket. He dressed in the overalls, pulled the black beanie over his head, shrugged into his coat and hid the shotgun in the pouch he had sewn there on the morning of the art-gallery attack.

Brennan had kept his personal mission secret from Rashid but that did not stop him using another of her clean Oyster cards. From Bethnal Green he took the Central Line to Tottenham Court Road, then changed to the Northern Line heading for Camden Town, five stops away, arriving at twenty-eight minutes past eleven. He hurried through the maze of pedestrian tunnels to the southbound branch, arriving with a minute to spare. As anticipated, the platform was busy with travellers waiting for the last train, scheduled at thirty-three minutes past eleven.

He located the platform supervisor beside the exit, announcing that the oncoming train would be the last of the night. He could already hear the train rumbling down the tunnel, brushing warm air against his cheek as he assessed the scene. A couple of metres to his right there was a group of young men, drunk, boisterous and unsteady, their voices bouncing off the tunnel walls, and a scattering of new lovers getting properly acquainted. Seeking sanctuary at the end of the platform to his left, a cluster of middle-aged couples were returning from the theatre or a concert, programmes in hand. But most travellers were alone, like Brennan, and no one paid him the slightest attention.

He waited, hidden among the crowd in the middle of the platform, close to the access and exit points. The train entered the platform with a *whoosh*, drowning the supervisor's amplified voice for a few seconds, and came to a halt with a screech of brakes. There was a pause as the driver pulled down his window and looked back along the platform, then a lazy wheezing as the elderly doors shuddered open with automated messages about minding the gap and terminating at Morden.

The supervisor was a large woman with big hair and designer glasses, still smart in the TfL blue uniform even at the end of her shift. Everyone boarded as she rolled out her last train announcement, which she infused with the urgency of a dire warning. As she turned away to the rear of the train, Brennan ducked into the exit passageway, unzipped the holdall and slid the shotgun inside, replacing his coat and beanie with the TfL jacket and blue woollen hat as the train doors ground shut.

He reappeared on the platform as the supervisor raised her 'All Clear' wand to the driver. Exchanging a nod with her, he walked slowly with his holdall to the southern end of the platform nearest the front of the train. He was just another maintenance man about to start his night shift, nothing unusual. By the time the last carriage had lurched past, Brennan had reached the mouth of the tunnel. There was an information sign for drivers, 'HOT SPOT', and then, enclosed in a red circle, the letters 'SPAD', which Brennan knew stood for 'Signal Passed at Danger'. He shifted beneath the CCTV camera to put himself out of its range and carefully placed the holdall on the floor, catching sight of a couple of tatty mice scurrying between the rails into the tunnel. He took the technical diagram from the front pocket and pretended to study it, as if waiting for the rest of the maintenance gang to join him.

He had chosen this spot for his revenge attack not just because his father had been killed in the darkness nearby. As the SPAD warning made clear, the network of lines radiating

from Camden Town was notoriously congested and complicated. Its regulation demanded a signalling system and back-
up of such complexity that any failure seriously disrupted one
of the tube's most geriatric lines. For business types with tight
deadlines or a saboteur with evil intent, the importance of this
gateway to the heart of London was massive.

The platform supervisor was preparing to leave, her work
done for the night, and the only sound in the station came
from the escalator. With one eye on the diagram, Brennan
waited for her to look at him, gave a brief wave, then watched
her enter the passage leading to the opposite, northbound,
section. He could hear the echoing radio traffic of other TfL
staff, then the supervisor's laugh as she joined them. Soon
their voices faded as everyone returned to the surface.

Brennan moved quickly. Strapping the torch around his
head he dropped the holdall into the well beneath the rails and
eased himself over the platform edge, the diagram still in his
hand. He moved with great care: one mistake would be fatal.
There were no second chances on the railway, his father had
always told him. As a boy travelling on the tube, Brennan had
often selected a particular man near the platform edge and
imagined his body jolting across the track, flesh frying, hair
alight. In his teens his father had plugged some of the gaps in
his knowledge, describing the massive charge passing through
the live rails and its catastrophic effect on anyone who failed
to show respect: 'One foot wrong and you're dead,' he had
regularly told his mesmerised son.

Brennan stood squarely on both feet between the nearest
two rails, only inches from being electrocuted, grabbed the
bag and disappeared into the tunnel's blackness. Only when
out of sight of the platform did he pause to switch on the
torch, its jerky light throwing eerie shadows against the curved
walls. He had a particular interest in the clumps of thick black
cables snaking along the tunnel walls at eye level but for now

directed all his concentration to the tunnel floor as he continued south, careful to stay clear of the live rail just a step from
his left foot. He could hear his father's voice in his head, telling him to be careful, and remembered that he would have
walked alongside this very track on the last day of his life.

Brennan paused again to shine his torch on the technical
diagram, leaning against the tunnel wall with one foot on the
dead rail for support. It was a scale map of the tunnel layout
around the Camden Town intersection and included the exact
position of every signal, power junction, set of points and
potential hazard. The diagram had been prepared to assist the
internal inquiry into his father's electrocution and Brennan
was looking for a particular signal terminal, circled in red ink
on the diagram, marking the precise spot where he had met
his death.

He found it four minutes later as the tunnel curved to the
right, and checked the time: 23.43. He studied the diagram
again to be absolutely certain, but the distance from Camden
Town and the tunnel's curvature left no doubt. Moving his
head to illuminate the scene, he imagined his father meeting
his end in this dark, lonely place and recalled every word of
the internal report as he looked around him. There was the
signal junction box that had electrocuted him, and the wall
opposite where he had smashed his skull as the charge hurled
him across the track. Then he stared at the live rail, the lethal
stretch of steel that had incinerated any lingering shred of life.
He could hear the panic, the shouting and screaming as everyone realised their mistake, and hatred rose like bile in his
throat.

Brennan reached into the holdall for the Jiffy-bag holding
the first incendiary, armed it by slotting the battery into place,
sealed the flap and gently squeezed the bag between the cables
and the tunnel wall. Advancing five paces, one for each decade
of his father's life, he armed the second device and planted it

as he had the first. For Brennan these cables were the arteries of the system and he intended to destroy them. His previous experiments had been above ground so he had no idea how effective his devices would be in the tunnel: he hoped the confined space would magnify their intensity, but could not be certain. His mission was to avenge his father by igniting the cables and creating a powerful fire. In his imagination he had seen a burning train and suffocating black smoke roiling through the packed carriages, but knew this might remain just a dream. It was the recklessness, the unknowable consequences, that gave him the greatest pleasure.

Brennan had no intention of returning the way he had come. Instead, he kept walking steadily south until he came to the deserted platform at Mornington Crescent station. Knowing this would be closed, he removed the torch, pulled his dad's woollen hat lower, kept his head down and walked on. If the station cameras were still recording they would see a solitary, unidentifiable orange figure passing through, his chest the height of the platform edge, before disappearing again into the darkness. Brennan was heading for the next escape point, the major rail and bus terminus at Euston that remained open all night.

After walking steadily for forty-five minutes he saw a faint glow from the tunnel mouth. He stuffed the torch into the holdall and rubbed his neck, which ached from bending forward to light his path between the rails. From the cover of darkness he checked that the platform was empty and located as many CCTV cameras as possible. Gripping the holdall open in his left hand he kept the other over the shotgun as he emerged into the open. He placed the holdall on the platform edge, climbed after it and lingered for a moment, head down, pretending to make notes on his diagram. Then he sauntered to the exit, walked up the stationary escalator and escaped into the street, darting into the nearest dark place to change again.

The N253 night bus for Bethnal Green stopped at Euston but Brennan was cautious and walked back to the previous stop at Mornington Crescent, taking far less time to cover the distance above ground. The bus came within twenty minutes and, as it pulled in at Euston, he watched from the back seat on the top deck for signs of unusual activity or cop cars. When he saw that the station was dead quiet he relaxed, pulled the beanie over his eyes, crossed his arms over the shotgun and dozed.

At 01.47 he opened the kitchen door of the safe house, feeling avenged and inviolable, as if nothing could stop him.

Fifty-eight

In room twenty-nine at the Duchy, a boutique hotel just behind Park Lane, Jack Langton sat in an armchair and watched Mike Geraghty's bodyguard demolish the minibar. More than ten hours had passed since the fateful run in Hyde Park but Frank Noble's troubled face still glowed bright red, as if he had just emerged from a hot shower. It was already warm in the room but his agitation had raised the temperature another couple of notches so the top half of Langton's motorcycle leathers now lay on the expensive red-and-cream-striped fabric.

Langton was paying his call on Frank Noble in the small hours out of friendship as much as duty, and his visit had nothing to do with surveillance. They had met two years earlier at a counter-terrorism conference in Istanbul, and regularly kept in touch. Noble had a sister married to a Brit in south London and liked soccer; Langton, a former sports teacher and Newcastle United fanatic, could talk about the new rising stars. And both could go on for ever about security and the state of their nations. Whenever Noble was passing through London he would call Langton in advance to catch up over a few beers at the Red Cow, a proper English pub midway between his sister's home in Clapham and Langton's surveillance base.

Frank Noble was a fifty-three-year-old career Philadelphia cop who had jumped ship for the private security industry seven years earlier and, since May, had settled as close personal protection officer to Mike Geraghty. Three hours ago the detectives investigating his boss's murder had finally allowed him to check out of the Dorchester because he said he needed to escape the press frenzy, and this discreet hotel, hidden behind Hill Street, was the obvious alternative. But the reason for his drinking, he told Langton, was to shut out the endless bullshit calls from Belling in Philadelphia with their dumb statements of the frigging obvious.

Noble sat opposite Langton on the navy sofa, his jacket crumpled beside him with two dog-eared company letter-heads poking from the inside pocket. On the polished walnut coffee-table between them lay three empty Jack Daniel's miniatures. Noble had perfected the art of breaking the seal and unscrewing the metal top with one hand, a trick he performed now while welcoming Langton. The last thing he needed at this moment in time, he said, tipping the miniature and offering Langton a vodka and tonic, were calls from some Belling vice president expressing doubts about his fitness as runner and bodyguard, neither of which were words he used to describe himself, anyway. Langton, who needed to ask a few questions of his own, counted the alcohol units and waited.

He had spent the evening with Kerr and Alan Fargo in the 1830 reading room, helping to piece together a sequence of disturbing facts about the latest victim. According to Fargo's urgent open source research, since 2005 Mike Geraghty had been CEO of Belling Defence Systems, one of America's largest producers of military hardware, and was widely reported to be close to America's vice president. Before his appointment he had spent almost two decades rising through the ranks of Aircore Inc. This was the company that had employed Marcus Tennant, and the two men had worked together during the nineties. Geraghty was also the father of Diane, whom Marcus had met while employed at Aircore and still married to his first wife.

Geraghty had made regular visits to Belling's London office, always using the company private jet and transiting through Farnborough. He had been a man of regular habit, staying in the same hotel suite at the Dorchester and taking a run in Hyde Park as soon as he arrived. It transpired that Langton was not the only contact to have been left in the dark: Fargo had managed to raise the director of Belling's Mayfair base, who confirmed that no one at Belling London had known in advance about this particular visit, and there were no meetings in the calendar.

Frank Noble carried two mobiles, one for work and the other for people he liked. For Langton, he picked up on the third ring, telling him it was the only friendly call he had taken all night and, yes, it would be great to see him. Almost before Langton had parked his helmet and sat down, Noble was telling him how he had studied every scrap of information coming out of London about People's Resistance since the murder of his boss's daughter seventeen days earlier. Beneath the bravado he looked distraught, his nerves shot. Right now drinking was a higher priority than unpacking and his luggage lay unopened on the king-size bed, exactly where he had thrown it.

Langton waited for him to neck his fourth double shot of Jack Daniel's before showing him Alan Fargo's transcript of the latest communiqué. It had been phoned to the Ministry of Defence switchboard, and the recording left no doubt that the caller was the same man who had made earlier claims to the Samaritans: 'This is People's Resistance. Today we executed the boss of a global death machine that trades in weapons of mass destruction, a man who enriched himself travelling the world to peddle death and destruction. America boasts about freedom and democracy. Yet that country's warmonger made destruction possible through guns. Its ambassador glorified war through art. We treated them with the same contempt they have shown for thousands of others. We executed the architect of warplanes and missiles with a crossbow. We did this to prove that no one can escape the justice of the people. That is all.'

Langton had listened to the recording twice in 1830 before leaving for Noble's hotel. He had heard the young switchboard operator's voice rise from Sunday-afternoon boredom through incredulity and uncertainty to panic as he remembered the earlier attacks and struggled to take down the words. There was the same irritation from the caller at any hesitation or request to repeat things, and the sense that he had been timing himself as he made his claim.

Noble sat forward while he studied the communiqué, then scratched his bald pate. He shrugged. 'It's all in my statement, Jack. I'm telling you, this is a nightmare.' He tossed the empty miniature onto the table with the rest. 'You know me, I don't drink like this. It's disgusting. But this whole *thing* is disgusting. I mean, you should have seen him lying there, this master of the frigging universe suddenly snuffed out, just like that, and they hit the woman right in front of her kid. I mean, tell me, Jack, this is what I want to know. What is it with this town?'

'What was he like, Frank?'

'To be honest with you, I hadn't known Mike long, only got the assignment three months ago. But I can tell you this. Mike Geraghty changed just before his daughter got hit. Suddenly he was, like, not all there. Different. To me and everyone.'

'Perhaps he had some problems at home.'

'No, nothing like that. There was no domestic shit. He and Mrs G were happy. This was something more. And don't forget I got to know him better than anybody 'cos it was just him and me in the car early in the morning and last thing at night, know what I mean? He was kind of *distracted*. Not himself. Yeah, definitely distracted. Grief-stricken when Diane got murdered, of course. But the change came before that. Ouch.' Noble set his glass on the table and vigorously rubbed the cramp in his calf.

'Why did he come to London this weekend?' said Langton. 'No one at Belling knew about it. Had anyone been making threats against him?'

'No, nothing like that.'

'Was he checking on Diane's murder investigation? Some secret business deal that I'm not supposed to ask you about?'

'Maybe, maybe. But I've gotta be careful here, Jack, you understand?' Noble stood up, gingerly tested his leg and limped to the minibar again to find the supply of Jack Daniel's exhausted. Ignoring the other alcohol on offer he unzipped the case, produced an unopened bottle of Jameson Irish whiskey and splashed a triple shot. 'Duty free,' he said, raising his glass and lowering his voice. 'Look, Mike had a meeting planned for tomorrow but he set it up himself and didn't want anyone to know about it. Absent friends. Cheers,' he said, his face creasing in pain again.

'You need a massage?' asked Langton.

Noble took another swallow of the Jameson. 'I need a piss,' he said, limping to the bathroom.

Langton broke into action the second his friend found the light, snatching the papers protruding from Noble's jacket. The first sheet, prepared by Geraghty's secretary, was addressed to Noble as the personal protection officer showing pick-up times from Geraghty's home address, flight details (including the names of the flight crew and cabin attendant), and Noble's reservation at the Dorchester.

Langton glanced towards the bathroom. Noble had left the door ajar and was still peeing at full stream. The second, marked PERSONAL AND CONFIDENTIAL, set out Geraghty's programme in London, copied to Noble. It showed his arrival time at the Dorchester, a one-hour window for exercise in

Hyde Park followed by a rest period in his suite, dinner reservation at Langham's for 19.30 and final check-in call with his US office at 23.00 GMT (18.00 EST).

Monday showed the hotel check-out at 09.30 and return to Farnborough at 14.30 for the flight back to Pennsylvania, but it was the commitment in between, the sole purpose of his secret visit, that grabbed Langton's attention: '10.00 Briefing at VX.'

The flow reduced to sporadic, then Langton heard the flush as he slipped the papers back into Noble's jacket.

'So you're going to hold out on me, Frank?'

Noble slumped in his chair and rubbed his leg again, embarrassed. Langton could tell he had been thinking, probably weighing friendship against discretion. 'It's like this, Jack. You're my pal and I'd trust you with my life but a secret is, you know, a secret. Mike didn't even tell me what it was about.'

Langton smiled and zipped up his jacket. 'I'm only kidding.' He reached for his helmet. 'Try to get some rest. You still flying back tomorrow?'

'If your cops let me.'

'Call if you need anything at all. You've got our condolences, Frank. The whole team's.'

'Sure,' said Noble, but he stayed in his chair and Langton could tell he wanted to say something more, their friendship still pulling at him. 'It was like someone pulled a switch.'

'What?'

'The way Mike changed just before Diane got killed. It was like she told him something.'

'How do you know that?'

'It's just what I think.'

Langton put his helmet down. 'What's on your mind, Frank?'

'From the moment Diane died he hated that Marcus Tennant. He told me he cursed the day he'd brought them together. Blamed himself. Can you believe that? I'm telling you, it's true. And then he started acting like he blamed *Marcus* for her murder.' Noble shook his head and Langton could see he was close to tears. 'Unbelievable. I'm telling you, Jack. He talked like his own son-in-law wielded the frigging knife.'

Fifty-nine

Melanie had been dozing fitfully all night, her mind racing ahead to the following day. In a deep sleep beside her, Jez snored and sweated, one arm draped over her chest, his hips pressing her against the wall. At home in Muswell Hill she often slept lightly, but that was because she was listening for her children, or waiting for Rob to get back from an all-night surveillance operation, when he would sneak upstairs and slip into bed to warm his body against hers. But in this lonely place the sounds came from thoughtless neighbours or her corner of the roof, which seemed to have a life of its own, creaking and groaning with every puff of wind.

This noise was different and made her start. Someone was climbing the stairs. She distinctly heard the crack on the fifth step from the top, the one she had found on her first day. Then it went again. Two people. There was whispering on the landing and a man's low voice, angry and insistent as someone turned the door knob.

Immediately wide awake, Melanie thrashed around to get free of the bed, desperately punching Jez to make him roll over and give her room. She was too late. Just as Jez groaned and stirred, the door crashed in with such violence that a section of the frame flew as far as the window. A young man Melanie had never seen before stood in the doorway wielding a double-barrelled shotgun. He covered the room with the gun as he felt for the light switch and she could see that it was a sawn-off. Her immediate thought was that Terry Bray had sent one of his gang to finish her, but then the light came on and she saw that the invader was dressed in black from head to toe, his head covered with a beanie. Melanie had never met him but saw the madness in his face and immediately put Terry Bray from her mind. In that second, as he levelled the shotgun at the bed, she knew that People's Resistance had found her. The prey had tracked down his hunter, the nightmare reversal of fortune for every undercover operative.

A woman Melanie recognised appeared at his shoulder, confirming everything. Also in black, Anna Rashid was in the same clothes she had been wearing on the night their paths had crossed. Melanie lay perfectly still, trapped behind Jez, waiting for the gunshot. The man walked across the room and kicked Jez hard in the leg, then turned to Rashid. 'Is this her?'

Rashid nodded as Jez rolled from the bed, knocking over the empty whisky bottle and groaning with pain.

As the gunman aimed the weapon at her, Melanie sat up to face him, pulling the duvet over her chest. She felt resigned and helpless. Her chance of rushing all three and making it to the Renault was less than zero. Nothing flashed before her eyes because there was little about her recent life worth remembering. Perhaps this was what she deserved, how her life was supposed to end. Held at bay, braced for the blast, she coolly stared death in the face.

Jez had begun stumbling around the bed, pulling on his pants and jeans. The gunman looked hard at Anna Rashid. 'Who's this?'

Then Melanie saw fear in Rashid's eyes and guessed he had been threatening her, too. 'She must have used him to get to us,' said Rashid. Melanie heard a quaver in her voice. 'This is not my fault. It's all down to him.'

Jez was struggling with his belt, wide awake now as he recognised Rashid and seemed apparently unfazed by the shotgun. Still half drunk, he uncurled to face the gunman. 'And who the fuck might you be?'

'Danny Brennan,' said the gunman, without hesitation, as he brought the shotgun round and shot Jez in the face with both barrels. The double blast catapulted him onto the bed and his head exploded against Melanie, spattering his brains against her face like an out-of-control food mixer.

Melanie had frozen but the naked violence brought out a scream in Rashid, banishing her fear. 'Not him, Danny. Not here,' she shouted, making a grab for the gun. 'You'll bring everyone down on us.'

Brennan held the weapon clear, punched Rashid in the face with his free hand and shoved her away. 'That's what you get for screwing with the enemy.'

Rashid fell against the armchair clutching her cheek. When she looked up she was wearing a murderous look, too, but right now it was directed at Brennan. 'You just screwed the whole campaign, you crazy psycho bastard. None of this was his fault.'

Brennan took a step across the room, held the barrels and raised the shotgun above his head, like a trapper about to club a seal. 'Why don't you shut the fuck up?'

Melanie could taste Jez's blood and the blast had sent a sliver of his tissue flying into her mouth. It roamed around the back of her throat, making her gag. His torso lay hard against her, crushing her in death as in life. The pulverised mess of bone, flesh and hair spilt down her chest and stomach as his blood radiated through the duvet. A scream was forming deep in Melanie's chest as she shoved his corpse away to create space for herself, desperately recalibrating her chances. With one enemy down, two fighting each other and an empty weapon, she felt a tiny spark of hope. But then the balance shifted again as Brennan took two more cartridges from his coat pocket and reloaded like a pro.

He picked up Melanie's clothes from the armchair, threw them over to the bed and ordered her to get dressed. She tried to cover her nakedness with the bloodied duvet as she clambered over Jez, but Brennan pulled it away and held out his free hand. 'Car key.' Melanie reached into her coat pocket and tossed him the Renault key, then dressed quickly while Rashid watched and Brennan wrenched the splintered door aside to check the landing. Melanie spotted her neighbour's ashen face peering through a crack in the door and tried to shake her head to warn him. He darted back inside but Brennan went after him before he could close his door, grabbed his tousled hair and smashed the shotgun stock into his face.

Without another word Brennan waved Melanie downstairs. She went first, Brennan pressing the shotgun hard between her shoulder blades, then Rashid. There was no sound in the house as she opened the front door: if the other occupants had heard anything, they were lying low.

It was getting light in the street and a layering of overnight cloud had cooled the air. Brennan unlocked the Renault, then seemed to change his mind. He opened the driver's door and waved the shotgun at Melanie again. 'Get in.' Rashid climbed in beside her and Brennan took the back seat, behind Melanie. He reached over to hand her the ignition key. 'Drive.'

'Where?'

'To the end and turn left.'

Melanie moved slowly away from the kerb as Rashid suddenly slapped her face and twisted to face Brennan. 'It's her you should be doing. I crashed into her car, all right? That's how she got to us. Because the fucking accelerator was knackered or whatever. And how many times did I tell you to fix it? This is down to you, Danny. You brought her on yourself,' she said, her voice rising with every sentence. She took another swipe at

Melanie, the fist this time, and glared back at him. 'I should have left you at the prison gate when I had the chance.'

Melanie turned into Queensbridge Road, then Brennan ordered her left again and they entered a one-way system along deserted streets that were unfamiliar to her. In the mirror her face looked shocking, covered with red splashes and smeared where she had tried to wipe herself with the duvet. There were a couple of cuts on her forehead, probably from bone fragments, and brain tissue was caught in her hair, darkly glistening and sticking to her scalp.

'Where the hell are you taking us?' demanded Rashid, but she was yelling at Brennan, not Melanie.

'I already warned you,' said Brennan. In the past few seconds he had become more agitated, waving the shotgun and looking all around him.

Melanie rubbed her injured left cheek and drove slowly, calculating whether she could exploit their hostility to save her own life. Her one and only chance was to add fuel to the fire, knowing she risked being caught in the conflagration. 'If anyone betrayed you it was her,' she said, catching his eye in the mirror and jerking her thumb at Rashid.

'You what?' The shotgun rammed into the back of the seat against Melanie's lower spine but she breathed deeply and carried on, speaking so quietly that they both had to strain to hear over the engine. 'She made it easy for me. Boasting about People's Resistance at the *Flag*.' She had reached the junction with Bethnal Green Road. 'Which way?'

'Right,' said Brennan.

'No, Danny, you mustn't take her to the house. Go left,' she screamed, making a grab for the wheel.

'Do it,' said Brennan.

Melanie shoved Rashid away and threw a right. 'Always winding Becky up,' she said. 'She even talked about you. Called you a know-nothing wanker.'

'That's a lie,' screamed Rashid. 'Danny, it's all lies. Don't you see what she's trying to do?' She was squirming in her seat now, trying to swing round to confront Brennan. Then the shotgun appeared again above the seat and Melanie saw it was pointing at Rashid, not her. 'Is it true, Anna?'

'And it wasn't just me she was speaking to,' continued Melanie, scarcely audible now. 'She betrayed you, Danny Brennan, and there's a lot more I can tell you.'

'I bet there is.'

'You bitch.' Frantic, Rashid lashed wildly at Melanie again. 'Danny, this is insane.' She was hysterical now, twisting from Melanie to focus all her attention on Brennan. 'You're believing her over me? I always knew you were fucking crazy.'

'Take the next right,' said Brennan. 'By the pub.'

'No. You can't take her there. It'll spoil everything.' Rashid was kneeling on the seat now facing Brennan, her arms flailing as Brennan sat back out of reach. 'Give me the gun. Please, Danny. Let me do her.'

A night bus was approaching from the opposite direction, so Melanie indicated right and waited. She was looking for a street name but her only bearing was the pub, the Mason's Arms. When the bus swept past Rashid was practically climbing into the back of the car as she tried to grab the shotgun. 'Stop here, on the corner,' yelled Brennan, above Rashid's screeching, as Melanie made the turn. But Rashid's hysteria, Brennan's seeds of doubt and the hard energy flowing back and forth gave Melanie a pulse of calm. It was a now-or-never moment that carried only one certainty: if they forced her out of the car she would be killed.

Outside the pub she slammed the accelerator to the floor. The engine screamed as she reached forty, swerved right and left then braked hard for the fight. As the Renault yawed to a halt there was an explosion at the back of her head and the car seemed to expand as Rashid's pulverised upper body flew through the windscreen onto the bonnet, spattering Melanie with more flesh and blood.

Shattered glass spilt from Melanie's lap as she found neutral, yanked at the handbrake and swung round to attack Brennan in one fluid sequence, but the moment had already passed. Brennan was stretched back, feet braced against each of the front seats, pointing the shotgun at her. 'Only one barrel,' he said, shaking his head, dead cool.

He ordered her to switch off the engine and pass him the keys. 'And don't turn around.' But when he reloaded she heard him insert two cartridges, not one, and cursed herself for letting her last chance slip away. She handed back the key, her only lifeline.

She heard the door open behind her. 'Get out of the car.' Brennan was already in the road as she climbed out, covering her with the shotgun. He directed her round the front of the Renault, past Rashid's corpse. They had skewed to a halt in the middle of the street with both offside doors open, blocking any other traffic. The sun was rising through the cloud now, though it was still gloomy enough for the street-light to cover Rashid's body in a yellowish shroud. She lay sprawled across the bonnet, with the blood draining from her chest into the road. Brennan paused to stare at her and Melanie desperately looked around, trying to get her bearings. She managed to take in the maisonettes and the industrial premises on each side of the street and snatch a glimpse of the parkland behind them before Brennan prodded her in the back. A Royal Mail van flashed past the end of the street by the pub, but otherwise the whole area seemed asleep.

Then she found herself facing a Victorian terrace and caught a couple of young brown faces watching them from the upper floor of the third house along, their heads silhouetted by the landing light. Far away she could hear another siren, but Brennan seemed unconcerned. He directed her to the dilapidated end house at the left of the terrace, pushing her with the shotgun along the weed-strewn path down the side.

'What is it you want from me?' said Melanie, as she drifted out of sight and left the world behind.

He was silent until he had unlocked the wooden gate. 'You're going to be my final action,' he said, blocking her against the kitchen door.

Sixty

A few miles away in Islington Kerr lay dozing in bed, listening through the open window to the first stirrings of the new day around the market. After waiting in the Fishbowl for Jack Langton to return from the Duchy, then squeezing out every detail of his conversation with Frank Noble, he had arrived home shortly after three-thirty.

While his key was still in the front door Justin Hine had called with the result of a specialist computer search Kerr had ordered late on Friday night. The implications of their check were truly shocking. Later that morning, if a double check by Justin personally produced the same result, Kerr would be faced with one of the most difficult dilemmas in his professional career.

He had sat on the balcony before turning in, watching the deserted street and taking a few minutes to collect his thoughts about Langton's information. Details of the meeting he had stolen from Frank Noble were highly significant. 'VX', Vauxhall Cross, was the green glass ziggurat housing MI6. Showy yet austere, it dominated the south end of Vauxhall Bridge, a cross between a fortress and a casino, Whitehall dressed up as Las Vegas overlooking MI5's more conventional headquarters across the river. Ajay had joked that it was like Flashman sneering at Tom Brown.

Woven with Karl Sergeyev's confession about his affair with Diane Tennant, the intelligence Jack Langton had stolen from Noble left two rational conclusions: that Diane suspected her husband was being blackmailed to betray his country and had confided in her father; and that Mike Geraghty, vengeful against the man he blamed for the daughter's death, had come to London explicitly to expose him. In less than six hours, had he lived, Mike Geraghty would have been dishing the dirt about his son-in-law to the spooks.

Kerr had been reflecting on Marcus Tennant's hostility towards him and the attempt by MI6's Julius to deter him. Scrolling back through Friday night's meeting in Ajay's office, Kerr's thoughts boiled down to one simple question. *Was MI6 protecting a patriot or covering for a traitor?* If it was the latter, as Kerr believed, then Mike Geraghty would simply have been telling MI6 what they already knew.

By the time he drifted to sleep a single conclusion had settled in Kerr's mind. Mike Geraghty had been murdered for the same reason as his daughter: to prevent him blowing the whistle on the man who was about to become Britain's ex-secretary of state for defence.

His BlackBerry vibrated on the bedside table eight minutes later but Kerr was sleeping so lightly that he recognised Gemma's voice before she could get her apology out. 'What's up?' he said, shaking himself awake and pushing up against the pillows.

'John, a Marker Two just popped up on the screen here. Personal for you.' This was a coded warning that someone had made a police national computer search on one of the unit's nondescript vehicles or addresses. Such routine checks were commonplace against speeding surveillance vehicles, illegally parked covert vans used by Justin's engineers and the flats used to house agents, but Kerr was already leaping out of bed and padding to the bathroom. Only one registration number and one address were red-flagged direct for the personal attention of DCI John Kerr, any time of day or night, and he had been worrying about Melanie all weekend.

'Vehicle or address?'

'Both, actually,' said Gemma, calmly, as Kerr splashed water over his face and hair. Gemma was not cleared to know about Melanie's undercover operation and Kerr detected no anxiety as she read out the registration number with Melanie's cover name and address in Dalston.

'What's the info?' said Kerr, pulling on a pair of old jeans and a white T-shirt.

'A bit weird, John, as a matter of fact. The story is still coming in but Alan's helping and here's what we have so far. Shots fired inside the Collis Street address.'

Kerr froze, jeans at half-mast. 'When?'

'Not long. Suspects seen to decamp in the Renault.'

'Driven by? Gemma, who was at the wheel?'

'Conflicting reports.' He could hear Fargo's soft Cornish tones on a phone close by. There were other voices in the background, too, urgent and anxious, but Gemma was perfectly cool and controlled, as if she was the only person in the room. 'It's all a bit manic but we're trying to make sense of it. We got another report from Danby Street in Bethnal Green a few minutes later. That's just up the road.'

'Saying?'

'More shots fired.'

'What's the address?'

'No, I mean in the street, John. In a car. I'm afraid it's the Renault again.'

Kerr's heart was in his mouth. 'Any victims?'

'Apparently it's abandoned across the street, doors open,' said Gemma. 'Windscreen shattered.'

'I said who's the victim?'

There was a pause, which made Kerr think she must know about Melanie's deployment, and when Gemma found her voice again there was a catch in it. 'Thing is, John, I'm afraid there's the body of a woman on the bonnet.'

Kerr was ice cold as he slipped on his shoes, grabbed his keys and headed for the door, BlackBerry clamped to his ear. 'Gemma, listen. I'm going there now but I need you to keep the info coming.'

'Well, be careful,' said Gemma. 'Two of the neighbours say there's a weapon.'

'What kind?' said Kerr, taking the stairs two at a time for the underground garage.

'It's a sawn-off shotgun. Two people got out of the Renault and went inside the address.'

'Men or women?' said Kerr, as he flashed keys at the sliding garage door and the Alfa. 'Gemma?' Silence again. The signal was poor down here but in that instant he knew that Fargo must have told her.

'Is it Melanie, you mean?' said Gemma, her voice breaking again as Kerr started the engine. 'I'm so sorry, John. I'll keep on at them. I'll get you more, do everything. Commander's on his way in.'

Kerr was already screeching up the ramp on the blue light. 'I'm leaving for the scene now but I want you to keep it coming, Gemma. Every detail. I'll keep the BlackBerry open till I get there. And call the others, will you?'

'Alan's speaking to them.'

At the end of the street by the market, his mind racing, Kerr swung into the kerb, cut the blue light and switched off the engine. He wound down the window and breathed deeply, knowing there was something else he had to do, probably the most important obligation of all. The situation had no up-side. He would drive with hope and determination for a good outcome while steeling himself against tragedy. Within the confusion and fog there was the awful possibility that Melanie had been killed, abandoned inside her address or on the bonnet of her car. The best worst option was that she had been taken hostage.

Right now it was Kerr's duty to share his fears with Rob Fleming. As next of kin and a police officer, Melanie's husband had an absolute right to know and Kerr bore a duty to tell him. Kerr scrolled through his contacts. Whatever became known about his wife in the hours ahead, Rob would learn it from him, not the *Today* programme.

'Rob, it's John Kerr.'

'What's happened?' He sounded wide awake and Kerr wondered if he had even been to bed.

'It looks bad.' Kerr explained the situation exactly as Gemma had conveyed it to him, without embellishment, false optimism or the kind of management bullshit cops can smell from a mile off.

'So what are you trying to tell me?' said Rob, ice cold, when he had taken in every word. 'Is my wife dead or a hostage?' He sounded as if he was moving around, definitely not in bed.

'I'm just giving it to you as straight as I can, Rob. You know what these things are like. I'll give you another buzz when I get there.'

There were other noises in the background. A cupboard opened and closed and Rob mumbled something unintelligible. 'Where are you?' said Kerr, winding the window up as he strained to hear. 'Say again?'

This time the voice was crystal clear, leaving no room for doubt. 'I said if Melanie's the one lying dead on that car I'll be coming for you.' Click.

Kerr started up, flicked the main-set to Channel Eighteen and raced through Angel, swinging left down City Road towards Old Street, accelerating to eighty. The roads were clear but traffic on the radio was already jammed with call signs responding to a siege in Bethnal Green.

Sixty-one

The safe house that had protected Danny Brennan since his release from prison had become a stronghold. He grabbed a six-inch kitchen knife and ordered Melanie over to the workbench. She leant against the stool, legs tensed, shoes squarely on the floor ready to exploit any opportunity while Brennan covered her from the bed, shotgun in one hand, knife in the other.

A few minutes earlier, trapped against the kitchen door, Melanie had been convinced Brennan was going to shoot her there and then. A couple of sirens had been growing in the distance, converging with the dawn and pulsing hope, but Brennan had never taken his eyes from her. When he stepped beyond her reach and raised the shotgun she had felt her heart sink.

Then he had thrown a bunch of keys at her. They had struck her in the chest, making her breathe again. Brennan had made her do all the work, leaving a step between them as she struggled with the Banham deadlock and the heavy-duty padlock. Inside the damp and musty wreck of a house he had sent her in front and ordered her up the dangerous, unprotected staircase, prodding her in the back with the shotgun as she hesitated in the half-light. In her anxiety Melanie had lost her balance at one of the missing stairs near the top, reaching for the non-existent banister and almost lurching sideways into thin air. On the landing Brennan had stayed back and directed her to the secret button inside the cupboard, making her pull the ladder down and climb up first.

The high specification of the safe house would normally have impressed her, but this was the morning she accepted would be her last, so the aesthetics passed her by. It smelt stale, as if Brennan had been there for a long time, but sweet from cannabis, too, and she could see a plate by the bed with the remains of a couple of joints. The hideout's sophistication also told her that the madman holding her had serious professional backing.

She knew the drill for responding to armed sieges. Any moment now the cops would be taking cover in the street below and containing the area, cutting off any escape routes. Their priority would be to identify the people inside the stronghold and initiate some sort of contact. In the meantime, to have any chance of survival, Melanie knew she had to get Brennan talking, to seize the initiative by establishing some kind of connection with him. Without taking his eyes off her he darted back a couple of steps and pushed the bed aside. 'They won't let you go, Danny,' said Melanie. 'Let me speak to them. It's over.'

'No,' he said quietly, and she saw that he was smiling. 'I'm not finished yet. Not by a long way.'

'What are you going to do?'

'Shut up. You move from there and I'll kill you.' Brennan dragged a chair to the space where the bed had been. He stood on it and Melanie saw that this brought him level with the blacked-out skylight, perhaps visible to a Trojan sniper. She scanned the room, searching for potential weapons. The place was in a mess, as if he had left it in a hurry, and the unmade bed showed two dips in the pillows, which told her Brennan had just killed his lover. His clothes were scattered around the floor and she wondered why he would need overalls and an orange hi-vis jacket.

On the workbench to her right was a folded crossbow and, pinned to the wall above it like a trophy, a photograph she recognised from TV as Mike Geraghty. At the other end there was a box of shotgun cartridges and a marmalade jar containing clear liquid with thick dust on the cap. But the only knife rested in Brennan's left hand. Then she glanced at the orange coat again and spotted the TfL logo. It struck her like an electrical charge, jolting aside her own fear of death. 'Danny, what have you done?'

Before he could say anything an over-amplified male voice burst into the space, the words a jumble as they bounced around the street before finding the skylight. Melanie guessed this was to be the opening round in the police negotiation before they got the professionals out of bed. It seemed to drive Brennan crazy. He smashed the blackened glass with the shotgun and fired through the window, the explosion filling the room. Melanie checked, preparing to rush him, calculating time and distance. Only one barrel this time, saving the other for her. This was her last chance. Brennan was three paces away, two if she kicked away hard. Three seconds. If she was too slow he would blow her away; too weak and he would use the gun to smash her to death.

She could hear shouting from the street, orders deploying people over the place, then the scything of a helicopter. Brennan was screaming at the cops below but the helicopter drowned his words and flooded the aperture with its searchlight.

Brennan jerked his eyes away but he was perfectly balanced on the chair as he covered Melanie, holding the knife between his arm and upper body as he reached into his pocket for another cartridge. Melanie weighed the odds: unstable fighting position, hands occupied, vision impaired, disoriented. She watched him break the shotgun to reload. Click. Go now! As the cartridge went in she grabbed the jar, smashed the neck and felt a surge of strength as the liquid immediately burnt her wrist. Brennan's mouth fell open as he looked down at her. With her other hand covering the top of the jar Melanie leapt from the stool and rushed him, releasing the scream that had been building for so long. She heard the gun snap shut but all she saw was the look of astonishment as she splashed the acid into his face and body-charged him from the chair.

They both ended up by the external wall and Brennan was screaming as loudly as Melanie, dropping the knife as he clutched his eyes. She snatched away the shotgun, kicked him in the crotch as he tried to stand and smashed the stock down on his head, just as he had done to her neighbour. She kept clubbing him until his voice diminished to a moan, then seized the knife, grabbed the orange jacket and searched its pockets. On the floor beneath it she saw a sheet of A4 paper, torn and dog-eared, and risked a glance as Brennan came to. Flickering between the diagram and Brennan she made out the locations of tunnels and signals and terminals, and markings in red ink. It was only a snapshot, but enough to give her another stab of fear.

She dragged his semi-conscious body to the entrance hatch and threw him down the ladder. Holding the shotgun in her left hand and the knife in the other, adrenaline dousing the burns on her hands, she stood at the aperture and waited for him to move. He was lying in a heap at the bottom of the ladder, testing his limbs for breaks, but the look in his eyes as he glared up at her was of hatred, not defeat. She called down to him, 'If you move I'll kill you.' She stuffed a handful of cartridges from the worktop into her pocket, slid the knife into her belt and followed him down, using her right hand to support herself.

She could hear voices from the street, calling up to them and to each other, but they sounded disorganised. Brennan had raised the stakes when he blasted the skylight and she knew the cops would be planning for a full-on armed siege. 'Shots fired' was a whole new ball game, ramping the crisis from negotiation to deadly force. Heckler & Koch guns trumped loudhailers the moment any gunman started blasting away into the street. Melanie knew the drill, and it made her feel protected.

She gave Brennan another hard kick, dragged him to his feet and ordered him downstairs. This time she was sure-footed and confident, taking out the knife again and jabbing the barrels between his shoulders. She felt no pain, only a mixture of exhilaration at overturning the odds and dread at what he might already have done.

At the foot of the stairs Brennan turned left for the kitchen, but Melanie bashed him on the side of the head with the shotgun and swung him the other way, towards the front door. The hallway smelt as damp and greasy as the kitchen, made dark and almost inaccessible by a mass of junk and old timber piled high as far as the front door.

She walked him as far as they could go, then spun him round and held up the diagram, taking in the acid blotches spread over his lower face. 'What have you done on the tube?'

'Go screw yourself.'

'What do the red circles mean? Have you put bombs down there?'

'You'll find out soon enough.'

She gave him another shove with her boot, sending him crashing into the rubble.

'Clear it. We're going through the front door.'

Watching Brennan get to work, she thought of John Kerr and his words that sunny Thursday not far from the Yard. *Look out, listen in, report back.* She had done all that, and a lot more, just as he sacked her. She had destroyed People's Resistance single-handed and Danny Brennan would be her final action. She would deliver him. While the cops were getting their act together, she would prove to John Kerr that she had been right all along.

Sixty-two

Tearing along Bethnal Green Road from Shoreditch, less than a mile from the stronghold, Kerr had slowed to sixty as an old BMW Five Series coming from Hackney jumped the lights and T-boned him on the passenger side. Kerr instinctively steered right to avoid flipping over but the force flung him against the driver's window so violently that the glass shattered, lacerating his face.

The Alfa came to rest facing the opposite way on the wrong side of the road, its engine stalled, and Kerr sat for a moment in the deathly stillness carefully rotating his neck, blood dripping onto his T-shirt as he checked himself for injuries. His face looked rough in the mirror and his right upper arm felt sore, but all moving parts still seemed to be working.

Ten metres of rubber separated him from the BMW. He saw the doors open simultaneously, then three men got out and started walking back to the Alfa. Shaven-headed and tough, probably still coked up from the night's partying, no one was limping or showing any sign of injury. Kerr caught the look of aggression as they walked straight for him and was in no mood for negotiating. Reaching for his ID, he realised he had left it behind in the apartment in his rush to get to the scene. They started shouting and gesticulating as Kerr leapt from the car, making it easier for him to make his scumbag selection. Setting a collision course with the most belligerent, he kicked him in the crotch and felled him with a single punch. The other two recoiled in surprise as Kerr stood square in the middle of the road, hands loose by his sides, then they silently picked up their leader and retreated to the BMW.

Kerr made a rapid check of the Alfa. There was oil on the road, the nearside was completely crumpled and a panel had punctured the rear tyre. He tried to force the bodywork away from the wheel then retrieved the jack from the boot and kept bashing the metal until it was clear. Then he got back behind the wheel, turned the key and heard the engine fire. On three good tyres he rammed his foot to the floor.

Monday, 12 August, 06.32; stronghold, Bethnal Green

In the darkness of the hallway, braced against an old washing-machine, Melanie guarded Brennan as he cleared the rubble and timber. The burning in his face seemed to have made him even crazier and he worked fast, desperate for something to relieve the pain. Outside she could hear the crackle of radios, and the helicopter seemed to be hovering right above them.

The cop on the loudhailer was ordering them out, and he sounded a lot less friendly since Brennan had shot into the street. With the rubbish cleared, slivers of light found their way between the rotten door and its frame, giving Melanie comfort.

Monday, 12 August, 06.41; police cordon

Kerr swerved left by the Mason's Arms, which was as far as he could go because the Alfa, its engine overheating and rear tyre shredded, was about to give up the ghost. Local police had taped off the street and an ambulance was already parked at the kerb, standing by to treat any victims. At the fag end of the night shift a couple of PCs were loitering by their Astra, one

on his mobile, the other chewing gum and chatting with the
paramedics, until the Alfa livened things up for them. As they
stared at the wreck Kerr leapt out, ducked beneath the tape
and hurried alongside a row of maisonettes on the right side
of the street, desperately looking for the officer in command
as the PCs ordered him back.

Across the road from SeeJay Autos Kerr paused to take in
the scene. The focal point appeared to be an end-of-terrace
house beside a print shop. The stronghold. It had an unsightly
porch extending as far as the neighbour's wall, open to the
front with broken windows each side and large enough to
accommodate a couple of motor scooters. In front of the
house, abandoned at an angle in the middle of the street, was
Melanie's Renault, with both offside doors open. Blood glistened dark on the road into the gutter. He could just make out
a body on the bonnet but it was impossible from this distance
to tell whether it was Melanie's. The situation was exactly as
Gemma had warned him, and he felt sick with anxiety.

He had to get closer, to find out the worst. On his side,
opposite the house, there was a large open area of parkland,
bordered from the street by a low brick wall. At the other end
of the street he could see two BMW X5 armed-response vehicles and an unmarked black Range Rover, a sign that local
police had called in the Trojans, tactical officers from the élite
CO19 Specialist Firearms Command. The front yards of the
maisonettes beyond the park space were bordered by waist-
high brick walls, which provided cover for three armed officers and he spotted four more kneeling behind trees in the
park. Kerr guessed officers would also be deploying to the
rear of the house as they set up for a prolonged armed siege
and control passed from local police to the Trojans. Directly
above him, scarcely higher than the trees, was the helicopter,
the chop-chop of its rotors and glare from its mega-powerful
searchlight dominating the scene.

As Kerr edged closer to Melanie's Renault along the row of maisonettes towards the park, the front line of danger, everyone suddenly noticed the guy in jeans and stained T-shirt with blood leaking down his face. Cops began yelling at him to get down and get away but he kept walking, mesmerised by the car, and felt a surge of relief as the body came into view and he saw that it was not Melanie's. Twenty paces away at the far end of the park entrance, beyond the stronghold where the row of maisonettes resumed, Kerr finally spotted the cop with the loudhailer, a middle-aged inspector still wearing his cap. He was probably the local night-duty officer and had set up shop inside a chest-high brick rectangle, containing six wheelie bins at an oblique angle to the stronghold. He joined in the general shouting at Kerr just as the stronghold erupted again, this time with a crashing sound and the splintering of wood. In that instant Kerr was forgotten as the inspector swung back to bellow orders at the house, and even the helicopter sounded noisier.

Suddenly someone inside the stronghold yanked the front door open. 'Armed police! Stand still! Stand still!' The inspector was trying his best. He was probably untrained, pressed into tactical command of armed officers he had never met before, forced to resolve a situation that was clear as mud.

Then two figures appeared in the doorway and Kerr saw Melanie restraining a man, her right arm around his neck holding a knife at his throat. The man's shaved head and face were blotchy and disfigured, and then Melanie rotated him slightly to her left. Kerr felt a stab of ice. 'Jesus, she's got the gun.' He saw her pressing a sawn-off shotgun into the man's spine, arching him back so that their faces were almost touching.

Then everything changed up another gear. The street was supposed to be a sterile area, clear of trespassers like Kerr, but an extra charge crackled through the air as every officer switched from stand-off to fire-fight mode. There had been no time for the Trojans to devise an assault plan so orders came from every point of cover. In that split second Kerr saw his prime undercover officer morph into the hostage-taker, the perpetrator, the bad guy, with everyone screaming at her to put the gun down. He could see Melanie's mouth working frantically as she tried to shout something back at them, but she was no match for them plus the helicopter.

Then the atmosphere tightened again as he sensed weapons being cocked, like in a firing squad, and saw the dark metal of other guns he had missed, poking from behind parked vehicles and walls and trees, every barrel trained on the same porch across the street. And Kerr was on the run, hollering at everyone to hold off, racing for the Renault in the middle of the street, distracting, disrupting, weaving through the helicopter's down-draught to break the lines of fire as Melanie released the man's neck and stood back a pace, lowering the shotgun and screaming back at the cops.

Kerr reached the left of the Renault, the stronghold side, then swerved right, locked onto the loudhailer, waving his arms to take their attention from Melanie and screaming at everyone to hold their fire.

A Trojan was crouched beside the inspector by the wheelie bins, probably in the act of taking over command, and Kerr grabbed the barrel of his Heckler & Koch, forcing it upwards. 'Don't shoot! Tell them to hold fire!' he kept shouting, but the helicopter drowned everything and the Trojan treated him as a hostile, whipping his gun across Kerr's face as the inspector came to his aid and tried to hold Kerr still and they all slipped on a mess of putrefied food. 'That's our officer with the gun!' he kept yelling, but they were slow to comprehend, probably because Kerr looked and sounded like a madman out of control.

And just as realisation flickered into their faces, from somewhere behind them out of sight in the park, a shot rang out.

Kerr saw the round hit Melanie, spinning her around and crashing her against the frame of the door, half hidden inside the porch. The man dived for the knife and raised it to stab her as Melanie braced herself against the door-frame and fired at her attacker. Kerr saw the man thrown against the wall of the porch then disappear from view as Melanie dropped the gun and slumped in the doorway, clutching her chest.

As Kerr shouted her name and wrenched himself free he saw the man crawling towards her, his hip drenched in blood, protected by the porch from the cops' line of fire. Then Kerr was on the run again, spoiling their aim, sprinting to rescue the woman everyone thought was the hostage-taker.

He had reached the Renault when another figure emerged from his left, beside a white van marked Sonny's Print and Reprographic Studio. He was wearing a police-issue baseball cap, with jeans, running shoes and a dark blue shirt, also police issue, and had his left hand down by his side. He scissored his legs over the wall and held out his right palm at Kerr. 'John, stand still.'

Melanie was lying motionless as her injured attacker reached her, edging along on his right side and raising the knife as Rob Fleming took up position a pace away from the porch and fired a pair of shots into the man's chest. Kerr saw the knife immediately fall, then rise again, as Rob fired a third round to the man's head, then tossed the gun into the front yard and trampled over the body to reach his wife. By the time Kerr reached them, Rob was crouching at Melanie's side, speaking urgently as he tore at her clothes to staunch the bleeding.

All around was bedlam as the cops broke cover and stampeded for the house, but the only people Kerr wanted to see were the paramedics. While Rob worked on Melanie he stood outside the porch yelling for them to come forward.

Kerr stepped outside as a team of Trojans streamed through the front door to secure the stronghold, followed by the paramedics. Across the street he spotted Justin Hine and Jack Langton speaking to the inspector and pointing to himself. As the inspector turned away to speak into his radio, both men hurried over to Kerr. Langton was carrying the spare helmet and spoke urgently: 'John, get on the bike. We need to get you out of here right now.'

'Not yet,' said Kerr, still on fire. 'We have to identify the bodies. Exploit the chaos. Find everything we can about this place before Finch shuts us out. It's our only chance.'

Then Rob was calling for him, cradling Melanie's head and stroking her brow as the paramedics treated her. They already had a drip in her left arm and she was trying to tell Kerr something before she drifted into unconsciousness. As he knelt down she opened her right fist and a ball of paper rolled onto the ground. Kerr and Rob crouched beside her in the doorway, straining to hear. 'Tube,' she whispered. 'Tunnel. Rush-hour.'

As the paramedics gently lifted her onto a stretcher Kerr opened the paper and quickly studied it with Rob. 'I need to get there,' said Kerr.

A couple of cops had appeared beside Rob as he handed Kerr his keys. 'I saw your wreck,' said Rob. 'Black Fiesta parked outside the pub.'

Sixty-three

Kerr found Rob's car abandoned at an angle to the kerb in front of the Mason's Arms, less than three car lengths from the battered Alfa. As he ran up to it, he could hear the engine pinging as it cooled, and the inside felt red hot, with a smell of burning rubber from the brakes.

The diagram Melanie had been screwing so tightly in her fist was stained with blood. He straightened it against the steering wheel and spent ten seconds studying the detail, then flicked on the headlights and skidded right into Bethnal Green Road. Traffic was already building but he tore through the giant roundabout at Old Street and north-west into City Road without a single stop, swerving on both sides of the road, braking hard and accelerating through red traffic lights, leaning on the Ford's high-pitched horn at every tailback. His priority was simple and drastic: to get the whole Underground system closed down, to ruin Monday for the millions of people who relied on the tube to reach work. Even the IRA had failed to do that, but Kerr would still try, starting with Bill Ritchie and Ajay.

He cursed as he stretched back to find his pocket empty, realising he must have left his BlackBerry in the Alfa or dropped it during his dash to save Melanie. He knew the odds of shutting the network on the basis of a scrap of paper and

Melanie's muttered words were below zero, yet banged the wheel in frustration. Opening the window he shook his head to stay sharp, spun the wheels down Pentonville Road towards King's Cross, resolved to do it himself. He owed it to Melanie.

The journey from Bethnal Green to Camden Town was about five miles, and Kerr skidded to a stop in a bus lane outside the station in less than eight minutes. There was the smell of rubber again and Rob's Fiesta felt like it was about to catch fire. He leapt out almost before it had come to a halt, then went back and rifled through the glove compartment. As police officers, he had guessed Rob and Melanie would carry a torch and, sure enough, he found a silver Maglite behind the pens, packs of mints, screwdriver and RAC membership card.

He threw himself over the safety rail at the kerb, sprinted into the station and leapfrogged the ticket barrier, racing down the escalator to the southbound platform. The indicator showed the next train was due in three minutes. The platform was already filling and he looked in vain for the platform supervisor or anyone in uniform. He ran back through the access tunnel and found him on the northbound platform dealing with a rough sleeper taking a break from the street.

Kerr grabbed the supervisor and pulled him away to the exit. 'I'm a police officer. There's a bomb in the tunnel. Other side, southbound.' It was already hot down here and Kerr could hear himself panting. 'You have to suspend the system.'

The supervisor stared at him. He was in his late fifties, white and overweight, with thick, heavy-framed glasses and the pallor of a working life spent beneath the ground. Kerr managed to groan inwardly as he regained his breath. He would also be a veteran of crises that had come to nothing and had probably worked through the IRA campaign of hoax bomb threats. Kerr watched the man take in the injuries to his face, his jeans and bloodied T-shirt, his eyes magnified by the glasses. 'ID?' was all he said eventually, disbelievingly, and Kerr wanted to hit him.

'Tell your control they have to shut down the system *now*,' he shouted.

Other people on the platform were starting to show interest and staring at Kerr's dishevelled appearance, probably veering towards mental illness rather than serious threat.

The supervisor was bullish as well as sceptical. 'You're telling me you're a police officer?' Adjusting his glasses he nodded at the drunk. 'More like him, I'd say.' Kerr could take belligerence, but then the veteran revealed his jobsworth side. He lowered his voice, glaring at Kerr as if he had just gatecrashed his party. 'And we don't disrupt our customers without a proper risk assessment. If you were a copper you'd know that. So get your arse out of my station.'

Kerr held up his hands, turned and ran through the underpass just as the southbound train rattled into the platform. Passengers were entering in a continuous stream and he knew the whole station would soon be packed.

He walked to the mouth of the tunnel and waited impatiently for the train to accelerate past him down to Mornington Crescent. He took in the drivers' 'Hot Spot' warning notice with its 'Signal Passed at Danger' message and felt more certain than ever that Melanie had been right. As the train's red tail-lights disappeared, Kerr glanced back to check the empty platform and studied the track, lasering on the live rails. Then he took the Maglite from his pocket, hopped over the platform edge and trotted after the train into the blackness.

Monday, 12 August, 07.18;
southbound tunnel, Camden Town

As soon as Kerr was out of sight he leant against the wall, as far from the live rail as possible, lit the torch and looked at the diagram again, studying the focal point: a thick red circle drawn around a particular signal terminal. Dirty warm air washed against his cheek from the approach of another train into the station, reminding him that he had just walked into a desperate situation. At this time of the morning he knew trains would be arriving every three or four minutes and the tunnel left insufficient space to squeeze between the wall and a passing tube. He had travelled only thirty or forty paces and still had time to retrace his steps to the station before the train left the platform. Instead he looked the other way, towards danger, shining the torch deeper into the tunnel in search of a recess where he could take refuge and avoid being crushed. He could see for about fifteen metres but the walls seemed perfectly curved, with not a single break.

He moved off again, treading as quickly as he could with the live rail only inches from his left leg. The uneven surface was of rough concrete interspersed with stones, but he almost broke into a run as he chased the torch's beam. The warm air strengthened, pursuing him down the tunnel as he tripped violently on an abandoned length of rail and ended up on his stomach, his left arm a hair's breadth away from being electrocuted. He reached across the live rail to recover the torch, hauled himself up again, gulped a lungful of stale air and staggered deeper, searching the walls for a place to save himself.

Kerr estimated he had covered about fifty metres when he reached the first signal at the end of a gentle curve to the right, the sure sign that this was the location circled on the diagram. Shining the torch all around, he spotted something pressed between the right wall and the horizontal clump of thick black cables. He moved close and saw it was a Jiffy-bag, clean and new, recently placed. Behind him there was a *whoosh* as the train rattled into the platform, then the air grew calm. He heard the screech of the wheels and the rush from the air brakes, followed by the doors opening, like a sharp intake of breath. In less than two minutes the train would be on him.

Without another thought Kerr pulled out the envelope and ripped it open. He shone the torch inside and saw wires, a battery, a crumbly oblong shape the size of a firelighter and white powder in clear plastic bags. Behind him he heard the train's warning beep as the doors closed. Holding the torch between his teeth Kerr carefully reached inside to pull the battery from its housing and separate as many components as possible.

He heard the train whirring away from the platform and suddenly the cushion of air was chasing him again. Kerr dumped the Jiffy-bag by the side of the tunnel and jogged deeper, hunting for a refuge in the wall. As the train gathered speed, the air pushed him onwards. He had no way out, no place to hide, and shone the torch downwards, chasing the beam faster and faster as he tried to outrun the train. Stealing a glance over his shoulder, he caught the swaying beam from the train's tungsten headlight. The air grew staler and stronger, driving him faster and deeper into the tunnel, his fear of the live rail overpowered by the terror of being run down.

07.23

Just as the train emerged round the curve behind him there was a sharp crack, followed by a blinding flash as Brennan's second device detonated. The train was almost on Kerr now, easily outrunning him, its energy reaching him through the rails like an electrical charge, and he broke into a final sprint for his life.

Then the sound changed again, the motor replaced by a violent rush of air as the emergency brakes came on. The train might have been blasted by the bomb or the driver had spotted Kerr but he kept running because everything was happening too late. The train was still slowing when it hit Kerr squarely on his pumping shoulders, hurling him into the air. He banged his head on something and came to rest collapsed by the right of the track, his body caught in the headlight as he stared up at the driver's cab and the massive wheels just inches from his legs.

He smelt burning and saw smoke flooding the tunnel alongside the train. He got to his feet, squeezed alongside the driver's compartment and pressed the button to clamber aboard. The driver, ashen-faced, was already shouting into his radio. He looked terrified as the train became enveloped in thick smoke from outside and Kerr realised the bomb must have set the black cables alight.

The driver stared at Kerr, close to panic, and Kerr understood. Was this suicide or terrorism? A 'one under' or a bomb-maker? 'What the bloody hell are you doing down here?'

Kerr was pressing his shoulders carefully against the side of the cab, testing himself for injuries. He saw blood drip from his face to the floor. 'I'm a police officer. Drive on, now.'

The driver began gabbling into his radio again so Kerr grabbed his arm. 'Tell them someone planted incendiaries in the tunnel. I found one but there may be more, and they'll be in this sector. So take us to the next station. Please. It'll be safe, I promise you.'

Sixty-four

'So you're absolutely sure, John?' said Ajay, holding onto Kerr's hand. He was wearing a pink shirt with tan needlecords and Kerr knew he had been in the office since before six. Ajay's grip was firm and dry and there was real concern in his eyes. 'Come and sit down.'

Kerr marvelled at the commander's coolness in the middle of the crisis that was unravelling every minute. 'I'll be fine,' he said, tapping his head and sliding into the chair at Ajay's conference table, but Ajay and Bill Ritchie both seemed unconvinced. 'Honestly. Nothing broken. I'll get myself checked out later.'

Kerr had just splashed water over his face in Ajay's bathroom and knew he looked as rough as he felt, with his forehead bruised and his face scratched, battered and pockmarked from glass fragments. He had changed out of his blood-spattered T-shirt into a long-sleeved checked shirt from Alan Fargo's bottom drawer and it felt about three sizes too large.

Ritchie was sitting with his back to the window, wearing a new maroon tie, his cuffs rolled back, doodling on his yellow pad and looking fitter than Kerr had seen him for a long time. He took a closer look at Kerr's face as he sat down opposite. 'Jesus, what the hell ...' He was leaning forward, stern yet benevolent, and for a second Kerr remembered his dad chastising him after some boyhood escapade after school. 'How bad is it?'

'Let's say no one's getting home by tube tonight,' said Kerr, as Ajay padded into the outer office to make them tea, leaving the door open so he could hear what Kerr had to say.

Kerr gave an abbreviated version of the morning's events. Since returning to the Yard on Langton's pillion a few minutes after eight a multitude of things had been cascading through his mind and time was short. In the few minutes it had taken to rumble into Mornington Crescent, Kerr had heard the line controller ordering all trains to remain in the nearest station. The driver's mobile had worked underground, so Kerr had borrowed it to call Jack Langton. On the other side of the door the screams and yells had been replaced by coughing and choking as acrid smoke leaked in through the windows, exacerbated by the driver's shouted orders for calm.

Mornington Crescent had already been closed by the time they pulled into the platform. Kerr had anticipated that the bomb he had missed, and possibly others, would precipitate a catastrophic signal failure and bring Monday morning to a juddering halt. Before the driver could say anything Kerr had shaken his hand and escaped onto the platform.

On his sprint for the exit Kerr had seen black smoke, toxic and life-threatening, drifting out of the tunnel mouth, probably sucked along by the train. A mass of fists and feet had been banging against the windows as he passed and some passengers had actually smashed the glass. The bomb had exploded against the sixth carriage, its furthest section crumpled inwards by the blast, the red livery scorched black and every window blown in. As the doors opened and Kerr escaped, hysteria had flooded the platform like a swollen river.

He had run up the escalator past a yellow trio of descending British Transport Police and, as he stood with his head back sucking in lungfuls of fresh air, the streets had been filling with sirens. A patrol car and a fire engine had pulled up outside the station as he had run to the safety of Eversholt Street. Camden Town would soon be transformed into a car park for emergency vehicles.

Langton had growled up in less than five minutes with Kerr's BlackBerry. He had planned to rush Kerr to St Thomas's, but Kerr had refused point-blank. Monday might have been cancelled in north London but the only subject on Kerr's mind had been Melanie.

'Jack tells me the round passed right through her upper body,' said Kerr, as Ajay served the tea in cups and saucers on a tray and took his seat. 'Penetrated a lung but probably missed her vitals. That's what the paramedics are saying. I'll give it half an hour and ring St Tommy's.'

'What about Rob Fleming?' said Ritchie.

'They've probably towed his Fiesta by now.'

'Are you being funny?'

'That's what Rob's saying.'

'Where did he get the gun?'

'He's on bail, and I've not asked.'

'But I bet you've got a shrewd idea, right?'

Ajay was beckoning and Kerr turned to see Alan Fargo's head poking round the door. Kerr had asked that he join them because he had crucial information from the siege in Bethnal Green. Notes under his arm, Fargo was carrying a large red mug with 'A Good Day To Bury Bad News', in white lettering, and looked shattered. He nodded at Ritchie, checked out his shirt on Kerr and took the chair beside him.

'Perfect timing, Alan,' said Ajay. 'John tells me you have something from Jack Langton.'

Fargo took a slurp of coffee and sorted his notes. 'Basically it's chaos around the stronghold so the guys made themselves busy while the locals were getting their act together. The woman on the Renault is Anna Rashid. Jack found an electrical gizmo in her coat lining, which turns out to be some kind of transmitter.'

'What on earth for?' said Ajay.

Fargo shrugged. 'Definitely a bespoke job. Small, not much bigger than a key fob and certainly not the kind of thing you'd buy in Currys.'

'I mean, what would an anarchist want with a transmitter?'

'Good question,' said Kerr.

'Where is it now?' said Ajay.

'Jack borrowed it before it disappeared into one of Finch's exhibit bags,' said Fargo.

'I'd like to see it.' Ajay gave a little smile. 'Good work by Mr Langton.'

'And Justin concentrated on the hostage-taker, managed to grab some prints and flashed them over. They're rough, smudged and partial because he couldn't do a proper job but the system threw up an immediate hit.' Fargo looked down at his notes. 'The name is Danny Brennan. A London rioter from 2011 released from the Scrubs on the twenty-fourth of July. The Border Agency has been trawling through flight manifests. Traced a Danny Brennan departing Heathrow for Bangkok on the night of his release, no date of return. Any questions yet? Shall I go on?' Fargo looked at Ajay and waited for his nod.

'In the past thirty minutes Jack has traced Brennan's cellmate. Guy called

Ivan Dolgoff and he was released the same day as Brennan.'

'What was he in for?' said Ritchie.

'We're still checking, but in the meantime Excalibur has thrown up a trace of Dolgoff. His real name is Vladimir Durchenko and he's shown as a middle-ranking officer in the SVR.' Fargo looked around again but Ritchie was making copious notes. 'That's the Russian foreign spy service.'

'Go on,' said Ajay.

'In July 2010 Durchenko was expelled from the US for his part in managing the Russian spy ring in New York state. He's an expert in running anti-American operations.'

'I've sent Justin to the prison,' said Kerr, 'and Jack's going to join him. They're going to find out exactly how the Russians managed to infiltrate their agent alongside Danny Brennan.'

Ritchie held up his hand for a pause as he finished his note. 'So you're saying this whole campaign is Russian-based?' He glanced at Ajay, then back at Kerr. 'Is that what you're telling us?'

Fargo slipped a sheet from his notes and held it up. 'Fingerprint and DNA results from Monique Thierry. The French promised them on Friday. We thought they were delaying, but turns out someone high up the food chain slapped an embargo.'

'Why?' said Ritchie.

'We'd love to know,' said Fargo, with a glance at Kerr. 'My contact Jean-Paul sent these under the radar when I told him our officer was in danger. If this gets out, J-P is sacked.'

Kerr looked at Ajay. 'This is Monique Thierry, alias Yvette.'

'Intelligence agent alias au pair,' said Fargo, studying the document. 'And it's in French because it wasn't supposed to leave their office. But I think I've got the gist, and Jean-Paul went through it on the phone. OK, here goes. Born in Toulouse and attended Moscow University. Erm. Suspected of being an agent in Russian sexual blackmail operations against subjects in Europe and the US.' He passed it to Kerr.

'So here's our initial readout,' said Kerr, jerking the long sleeves on Fargo's shirt clear of his hands and counting on his fingers. 'One. All the attacks were planned and facilitated by the Russian SVR, not the French DGSE. Paris has clean hands, unless anything else turns up down the road, like Thierry freelancing for both sides. Two. They concealed their hand beneath the smokescreen of British domestic extremism, using Anna Rashid and Danny Brennan to carry out the attacks in the name of People's Resistance.'

'The aim being to . . . what?' said Ritchie.

'Inflict fatal wounds on the UK's so-called special relationship with the United States. Durchenko talent-spotted and groomed Danny Brennan in the Scrubs and Anna Rashid took over on the outside.'

'So who controls Rashid?' said Ajay.

'The people who gave her the transmitter. We solve everything the moment we identify them. That's where we go next. But in the meantime let's all remember one thing,' said Kerr, looking at Ritchie. 'We could never have got this far without Melanie. I asked her to look at the *Flag of Liberty*. She did that and found Anna Rashid. Melanie led us to People's Resistance, Bill, and whatever else we discover in the next few hours is thanks to her.'

'I quite agree,' said Ajay. 'Brilliantly, too. But I have to ask this again, chaps. Why on earth would the SVR wish to poison the special alliance between the UK and the US? As I said before, the sharing of intelligence gives the Russians a double whammy, yes? One secret shared is an opportunity doubled. The jewels of two nations from a single traitor. Makes sense?'

'Which brings us to Marcus Tennant,' said Kerr, rubbing his head. 'The elimination of Brennan and Rashid changes nothing for the Russians. The terrorism part of the operation is over. Marcus Tennant is their weapon now and the final blow won't kill a single human being.'

'So who is the victim?'

'We are. As a nation. The moment they demonstrate that Marcus Tennant has been working for them.'

'What are you getting at?' said Ritchie.

'Straight after Diane's murder, Karl Sergeyev told me Marcus was about to be moved out of government, remember? The sacking dressed up as a resignation? Well, for the

Russians it was a complete game-changer. They probably learnt about this weeks ago, and from that moment Marcus Tennant became an asset of plummeting value.' Kerr turned to face Ajay. 'The value now is the damage the SVR can inflict from exposing Marcus Tennant as a traitor. The political capital from burning a spy politician at the heart of the British establishment far outweighs any value in protecting him. Can you imagine the fallout when Moscow reveals that Britain's former defence secretary has betrayed British and US military secrets and that MI6 knew about it and kept it quiet? Remember the Cambridge spies? A catastrophe, and the Americans still haven't forgiven us. And it's about to happen all over again.'

'Consider the irony,' said Fargo, with a short laugh. 'MI6 has gone to these great lengths to *conceal* Tennant's treachery and the Russians are gearing up to *expose* it. We have two spy enemies acting against the norm. By covering up Tennant's blackmail and recruitment, MI6 was playing right into the Russians' hands.'

Ajay raised his eyebrows at Ritchie. 'So what are you proposing, John?'

'We have to act first. Today. Arrest Tennant and mount a full investigation to expose the SVR plot. Disrupt them before they move to the final phase.'

Ajay sat looking through the window, slowly interlocking his fingers. 'But what actual evidence is there against him? The only potential witnesses to anything are his wife and father-in-law, and they're both dead.'

'But we know what they believed, and the grounds.'

'The photographs, you mean? The belief that Marcus was being blackmailed? Diane's apparent worry that he had started behaving secretively? I suppose everything could be explained as an extra-marital affair discovered by Diane. Did she ever make any specific allegations? I mean, do we . . . does anyone know why Mr Geraghty had arranged his secret meeting at Vauxhall Cross?'

'I believe it was to tell them about his daughter's suspicions.'

'Which does not exclude the possibility that her allegations were motivated by revenge. You know, the determination to wreck her husband's political career. I'm only playing devil's advocate again, of course. That's my job.' He looked over the park for a few more moments, then turned back and tapped on the table. 'Right. I think I need to reach out to MI5. But first you have to set out the intelligence case in full. Chapter and verse. I need you to roll the pitch for me, understand?'

'What about giving them a heads-up, Ajay?' said Ritchie.

'Soon, Bill, absolutely. But first I'm going home to shower and get dressed, reflect on everything we've discussed.' Ajay drained his tea and laid a hand on Kerr's arm. 'And I want you to get yourself checked out, John. We'll meet later this morning to drill down and map our course of action. That OK with everyone?'

Sixty-five

Kerr and Fargo hijacked Ritchie in his office two minutes after Ajay had taken the lift. His safe already opened, Ritchie was dialling the first of many calls arising from the night's events. He replaced the receiver as Kerr closed the door, walked over to the desk and handed Ritchie an exhibits bag containing a device the size of a match box.

Ritchie stared at them. 'What's going on?'

'That's the transmitter Jack recovered from Anna Rashid's clothing.'

'So why didn't you show it to Ajay?'

'Because he's already seen one.'

'What are you talking about?'

Kerr retrieved the bag and passed it to Fargo. 'He's got a device just like it, Bill. Probably gone off to use it now.' Fargo had eased himself into the low chair by the coffee-table to work the laptop while Kerr remained by the desk and Ritchie stared from one to the other, uncomprehending. 'I was lying when I said Jack Langton had gone back to the Scrubs with Justin for further enquiries.'

'So where are they?'

'Heading to north London.'

'Doing what?'

'Following my orders. Watching Ajay.'

Ritchie looked thunderstruck. 'What the hell . . . Call them back *now*.'

'Here's the short version, Bill. Ajay Khan is being controlled by the SVR, just like Anna Rashid. And has been ever since he joined the Met.'

Ritchie shot back in his chair. 'Have you gone completely insane, the pair of you? Do you have *any* idea what you're saying?'

'I'm coming to that. But you need to listen because any minute now you're going to have to make a big decision.' Kerr glanced down at Fargo. 'Alan's done the research. We believe Ajay was recruited many years ago, as a young man, before he joined the Met.'

Ritchie spread his hands. 'To do what, for God's sake?'

'Bottom line? They targeted him against us, Bill, however long it took. To penetrate our intelligence unit and betray every operation, steal every secret he could get his hands on. And just to make it personal for a moment, to show you what a bad bastard Ajay Khan really is, we're saying he gave Melanie to them. When they tried to murder her last night they were working from his information. That's the bottom line.'

Ritchie finally exploded. 'No way. That's crazy!' he shouted, banging the desk.

Ritchie was reacting just as Kerr had expected he would, and he kept his voice low. 'We're short of time, Bill, and there's a lot more.'

'Like evidence. How about some proof?'

'We had a scrum-down with Ajay. The whole team.'

'Where was I?'

'You couldn't make it. What date was it, Alan?'

'Monday the fifth,' said Fargo, immediately. 'Week ago today.'

'He got me to stay behind afterwards,' said Kerr. 'Asked me how Melanie was getting on. Said he wanted personal briefings on her progress.'

'I'd call that welfare, actually.' Ritchie was looking even angrier.

'More or less ordered me to go to him direct. Wanted to keep you out of the loop because of your cancer. Something about keeping you stress-free.'

'Welfare,' said Ritchie again, throwing a glare at Fargo. 'Ajay told me he was doing this and why, in case you're wondering.'

'And before that he was pouring cold water on the honey-trap thing around Yvette and Tennant. Urging us to be cautious.'

'Which is also perfectly reasonable.'

'Except he gave himself away. Tell him, Alan.'

Fargo checked his note. 'He said Yvette had "found her way from Toulouse to London". Exact words.'

Ritchie frowned. 'What of it?'

'We only just learnt about her origins in Toulouse from Jean-Paul,' said Kerr. 'So how did Ajay know a week before us?'

Ritchie sat quietly for a moment. The corridor was growing noisy as the fallout from the night's events spread through the unit. Ritchie looked weary and distracted by a wispy cloud in the shape of a fish skeleton drifting over the park. 'What do we know about Ajay's background?' he said eventually.

'All key roles,' said Fargo. 'It's taken years but he couldn't have planned it better. Spells in anti-money-laundering, international liaison and the National Crime Agency. Seconded to the Cabinet Office for two years, 2001 to 2003, right through nine/eleven. Fast-tracked all the way. And in 2005 he wangled a place on the FBI course at Quantico when someone else dropped out.'

'And we all know how much the commissioner loves him,' said Kerr. 'But here's the best part. Remember Ajay's stated mission the moment he came here about developing a closer partnership with MI5 and MI6? All that peace-and-harmony we're-all-in-this-together crap? So we get Tim Moxon foisted on us and Ajay achieves more intelligence-sharing and walks a lot closer to Whitehall. You've got to hand it to him, Bill. It took him two decades but he's done a bloody good job on us.'

'And what if you're wrong?' said Ritchie, quietly. 'What if you've completely misread this whole thing?' Ritchie was looking from one to the other, his face ashen and deeply troubled, as if Kerr's terrible indictment was about to overwhelm him. 'Ajay has done incredible things here. Worked non-stop to give this whole outfit a new lease of life.'

'Do you think this is easy for me, Bill?'

'And I've seen how he works. I know him a lot better than either of you.' Ritchie stared at the cloud again as it lost its shape. 'I mean, have you listened to yourselves? Do you realise how disloyal you sound?'

'We've got more,' said Kerr, wondering how much more Ritchie could take.

'No,' snapped Ritchie. 'Call those men back. John, get yourself to hospital now. We'll pretend this conversation never happened.'

'Do you want to hear what Donna told me? About his mysterious excursions from the office?'

'He plays squash.'

'I got Justin to check the GPS readout on his Audi for every away-day. Every single trip shows a detour through Kentish Town on the return journey.'

'So what?'

'He parks for several minutes in the same side-street before returning to the Yard.'

'So he stops at a newsagent,' says Ritchie.

'See for yourself.' With a nod from Kerr, Fargo opened the laptop on Ritchie's desk. His face clouding, Ritchie watched CCTV footage of their commander getting out of his car and pointing a transmitter through black metal railings.

'I guarantee he's using an identical device to Anna Rashid's,' said Kerr, producing the exhibits bag again. 'This video is from Friday, the twenty-sixth of July, a few hours after Hugh Selwyn was murdered. Justin collected this late last night and enhanced it in the early hours. Only the one for now because there's so much going on. But we'll get the rest, every single frame. And I guarantee it'll be the same pictures every time.'

'What's he pointing it at?'

'Justin took a quick recce. It's a piece of concrete inside the railings, almost certainly an electronic dead-letterbox.'

'Right.' Finally something seemed to click inside Ritchie, like a call to arms. 'Are we monitoring this to see who else turns up?'

'From this morning,' said Fargo.

The video evidence had made Ritchie's tired eyes shine brightly again. He looked charged up, as if the cancer had suddenly left him alone. 'When are you suggesting the SVR recruited him?'

'We think they made their pitch when he was a young man,' said Kerr. 'Possibly in India. He studied philosophy at the University of New Delhi but was also a student in the US, at UCLA. A lot of embarrassed people at the Yard and MI5 are going to be investigating that very soon. And checking out his father, too.'

Kerr took a call on his BlackBerry. It was badly scratched from its fall in the race to save Melanie. 'I'm on my way,' he said, cutting the call. 'That was Jack and we're in play. Same routine by Ajay and Justin's got it on film. He's back in the car and they're following. Decision time, Bill.'

Jumping to his feet, Ritchie grabbed his jacket and came round the desk. 'I'm coming with you.'

Kerr stood square to Ritchie and laid a hand on his forearm, just as Ajay had done to him. 'That's not a good idea. We need someone to lead us out of this hole.'

Ritchie looked ready for a fight. 'You've got it.'

Kerr nodded at the partition wall. 'There's a vacant office next door and nature abhors a vacuum. Remember how Finch tried to shaft Ajay. We need you to move in there right now, Bill. Before we leave the building.'

'You really think I'll let him pull that stunt again?'

'Donna will be here in a minute. Let her make you a cup of coffee while you think about it. Do you really want to risk the Bull installing one of his oiks and selling all our secrets to the press?'

Sixty-six

Ajay drove north for Kentish Town, heading up Tottenham Court Road towards Euston against the rush-hour traffic but then losing time in the diversions around Mornington Crescent and Camden Town Underground stations. Kentish Town was closed to traffic, too, so he had to abandon the Audi three streets away and hurry on foot to transmit one word, 'Zorba', the warning that he was ten minutes away and had checked for surveillance. From a shop doorway Justin watched every move.

The meeting place was further north, a large white semi in a quiet residential cul-de-sac directly opposite Parliament Hill Fields. It was convenient, less than a quarter of a mile from the Russian Trade Delegation on Highgate West Hill and within a twelve-minute walk of Day Break, the coffee shop codenamed Jade that Peter had used to meet Anna Rashid. Approached through heavy white posts and a five-bar gate permanently wedged open, the house was an expensive asset in the embassy estate, highly favoured by visiting Russian officials and their families. It was reserved for use as a comfortable temporary London home with bland décor, neutral furnishings and nothing to identify the tastes, nationalities or occupations of its residents. Apart from a small safe and a printer in the garage to capture stills from closed-circuit surveillance footage, it had none of the special security features that bristled from other properties bankrolled in Moscow and was often left empty, aired and cleaned by an embassy housekeeper.

Ajay drove up a slight slope to the end of the road, swung the Audi round in the turning circle and parked just up from the house. He made a final security check all around before leaving the car and hurrying up the path. At the end of the newly mown lawn he found the front door ajar and, in the hallway, Monique Thierry waiting for him, wearing jeans and a long-sleeved shirt. They embraced as lovers before she led him upstairs to the master bedroom they used to conduct their affair whenever Peter had made the house available. She had taken him to bed there for the first time more than two years ago, fourteen months before she had been targeted against Marcus Tennant.

As well as the king-size bed the room was large enough to accommodate a sofa, armchair and side-table, but Ajay had to walk round two wheelie cases parked by the door. A large bow window overlooked the road and, against the right wall, a second high rectangular window gave an uninterrupted view through the white posts and across Highgate Road to the tennis courts at the edge of the fields. They found Peter standing there now, jacket buttoned up, hands behind his back, apparently observing a group of young women playing doubles. Either that, or remembering. During the Cold War Ajay's controller had served in London as a KGB officer, a player in Moscow's England Department working out of the Trade Delegation a stone's throw away up the hill. He knew this because Thierry had confided in him while they were lying together in this very room.

Peter turned to shake hands and directed him to the armchair. He stayed by the window as Thierry perched on the sofa.

Ajay poured himself a glass of water and took less than three minutes calmly to recapitulate the night's events.

'And what is the predicament that is causing you such concern?' said Peter, when he had finished.

'You have to move against Marcus Tennant today or lose the advantage. The pressure on me to act has risen significantly over the weekend,' said Ajay, simply. 'I don't think I can hold it back beyond this morning.'

'We expected you to derail, not delay,' said Peter, turning from the window to face him.

Ajay shook his head in irritation. 'No longer an option. John Kerr is a tenacious officer with an equally determined team. He is driving me hard.'

Peter gave a short laugh. 'And we believed you were the man in charge.'

'I am. Which is why I have to act as they would expect. I warned you about Kerr. Gave you the chance to deal with him decisively. This is not my failure.'

'No one has said that,' said Peter, glancing at Thierry. 'Do not distress yourself. We are where we are.'

'I'll deal with it.'

'And how will MI5 react? Nail their colours to your mast or dive for cover and try to take you down with them? How are they, these days?'

'Quiescent,' said Ajay. 'Enjoying their time on the PM's sofa.'

'MI6?'

'Busy covering up and protecting their own. Making our mission easier.' He jerked a thumb at the suitcases and looked at Thierry. 'Are you leaving me?'

'I have been recalled but will still respond to you,' said Peter. 'It is temporary. London is very warm at the moment and, with Rashid gone, I have no need to be here.'

Ajay looked at Thierry again. 'You too?'

'Monique must go where I go, naturally,' said Peter. 'And there will be awkward questions around Tennant, one way or the other. I have to protect her, of course.'

'Durchenko?'

'Vladimir travelled to Washington yesterday. Ready to move when Moscow gives the word. With Tennant demoted, we wish to move quickly. We must stay in control, Ajay, you understand? Far better for the world to see Moscow burning a Russian agent than Scotland Yard arresting another politician.'

'London may still smother the whole thing.'

'Then Moscow will reveal how the British choose to cover up for a spy rather than expose a traitor. A double prize. We are in your hands, Ajay, as the man on the ground. You can see how much trust is invested in you. We rely as completely as ever on your judgement.' Peter walked over and sat on the sofa beside Thierry. 'And you should be as proud of yourself as we are.'

Ajay smiled. 'This is going to hit the Americans bloody hard, Peter. Neither country will ever recover.'

'Let us hope not.'

Ajay started. 'Did you hear something?'

10.24

Using the first SO15 car he found in the Yard's underground car park, Kerr had joined Langton and Justin in the parallel street. They identified the house backing onto the target house, clambered over the side gate and sprinted across the lawn. From there they scrambled over the rear fence and raced for the back door. It was protected by a standard mortice lock and Yale, both of which Justin defeated within ninety seconds. They checked the ground floor, then Kerr led the way upstairs, pausing at the top and following the sound of voices.

They had anticipated heavy opposition but, when Kerr opened the door, he found three people sitting at the end of a large bed, an old man, a woman and Commander Ajay Khan. He caught the stunned look on Ajay's face but the woman was the first to move, jumping from the sofa and reeling round at them. She found Langton first and attacked him with her fists, pushing him back several paces to the door until he recovered and forced her onto the bed. Kerr made for the sofa as Ajay stood up and started to say something but he only managed a single word, 'John,' before Kerr head-butted him and held him upright by the back of his neck. 'That's for Melanie,' was all he said, before punching him to the floor.

The old man was standing now but Kerr easily shoved him aside. He wanted Justin to arrest Ajay, as the junior man, so beckoned him forward and stepped back to guard the door. Plastic cuffs at the ready, Justin searched Ajay's pockets for the transmitter and tossed it to Kerr. No one heard Justin use the caution as he swung his commander round to cuff his hands behind his back, but he definitely told Ajay he was going to jail. Even the old man heard that.

'John, take a look,' said Langton, pulling up the woman's sleeves to reveal dressings on both forearms.

'Tear them off,' said Kerr. She screamed as Langton tore at the bandages to reveal plasters covering burn wounds as far as her elbows. Then Kerr stood over her and looked deep into her eyes and had a flashback to the murderous attack in Camberwell. Suddenly he was there again, trapped in the Toyota as she stood on the bonnet, eyes wild through the slit of the balaclava as she wielded the baseball bat against his windscreen.

Kerr turned to Ajay. 'Did you set her on me?' Then he walked up to the old man by the window. 'Did *you*?'

The old man had stayed calm and unruffled from the moment the door had burst open, and his first words were defiant. 'You are trespassing on diplomatic property,' he said, looking Kerr in the eye.

'And you're under arrest,' said Kerr, swinging round. 'All of you.'

The old man stood upright by the window, the sun lighting his wispy grey hair. Hands behind his back, he began to demand that Kerr call the Russian embassy in Kensington Palace Gardens. Kerr calmly waited for the words 'diplomatic immunity', then grabbed the two suitcases from the doorway and scattered their contents all over the floor.

Justin had another set of cuffs ready and tossed them to Kerr. 'You can forget your holiday, you murdering old bastard,' said Kerr, swinging him round and crashing him against the wall. 'How would you like a long vacation in jail?'

Epilogue

In the afternoon Kerr went to see Melanie in St Thomas's before getting himself checked out in A and E. She had her own room and lay propped up in bed, her left upper chest and hands heavily dressed, with three intravenous drips and a steady heartbeat. Rob was with her, holding her hand and speaking gently, so Kerr stayed behind the glass, not wishing to disturb them. Rob had his back to Kerr but seemed to sense he was there and twisted in his chair. He looked at Kerr, then stood up, and Kerr wished he had not come.

Rob opened the door and stood silently, taking in Kerr's oversized shirt and battered face. 'I guess I rescued your undercover officer.'

'No,' said Kerr. 'You saved your wife's life.'

Rob slowly extended his hand. 'Sorry about what I said.'

Kerr gripped hard. 'Rob, I'm sorry, about everything.'

Later, after a dash home to shower and change out of Fargo's oversized shirt, Kerr was standing in a potholed street in Rotherhithe, outside the small terraced house of his murdered agent, Seagull. Dark clouds rolling in from the west reflected his mood. He had just spent fifteen minutes with Halgan, Seagull's widow, to find her still desolate from the loss of the man she had loved. Her two young daughters had stayed hanging about her knees, and all three had been shy with Kerr. He had tried to express her husband's bravery and explain the arrest of the people responsible for their terrible loss. But

Halgan's English was poor and the meeting had been unsatisfactory.

Back in the street Kerr realised that his visit had given the family scant comfort. Somehow this troubled him more than anything else. He rang Bill Ritchie, but Donna said her new boss was still with the commissioner. On an impulse, tapping Halgan's wrought-iron gate, he dialled Karl Sergeyev. 'Where can I find Marcus Tennant today?'

'At home.' Sergeyev seemed to have caught the edge in Kerr's voice. 'John, why are you asking?'

The rain started as Kerr turned to look at Seagull's house once more. Halgan was standing at the front-room window watching him, still tearful, the children's heads just visible above the window ledge. She managed a little smile and Kerr returned her wave.

'Because I'm coming for him now,' he said.